PRAISE FOR Em
The Mathema

"If you're in a book club torn between lo   ern fiction, *The Mathematics of Love* may be just the thing to square the circle. The bilingual dexterity of this novel is one of its several triumphs. . . . Anna and Fairhurst, living in the same space though separated by time and unimaginable social changes, are equally haunting characters, the parallels between their lives tantalizing and evocative. . . . [Darwin] portrays fifteen-year-old Anna with a remarkable fidelity to the odd mix of maturity and naïveté that marks modern adolescence. . . . The two stories that Darwin tells here add up to something hauntingly beautiful."

—*Washington Post Book World*

"This is that rare thing, a book that works on every conceivable level. Plot, pace, language, and tone combine to produce an uncommonly good read, a piece of quietly confident writing that is remarkable in a first novel. . . . A real achievement."

—*The Times* (London)

"[A] strong debut. . . . Similar to Ian McEwan's *Atonement* in its compelling, literary blend of war history and romantic relationships. . . . Darwin will be an author to watch."

—*Library Journal*

"A convincing and involving read. A book to lose yourself in this summer."

—*Daily Mail* (London)

"Impressive. . . . [An] ambitious, alluring tale."

—*People*

"Colorfully embellished with nineteenth-century language, [*The Mathematics of Love*] seems a worthy and reflective accomplishment by the great-great-granddaughter of British naturalist Charles Darwin."

—*Adelaide Advertiser*

"Highly entertaining. . . . Fans of Anita Shreve's *Fortune's Rocks* and A. S. Byatt's . . . *Possession* will probably gobble it down in one sitting. B+"

—*Christian Science Monitor*

"A daring debut novel that forces the reader to confront both the horrors of history and the destructiveness of misplaced passion. . . . Emma Darwin's prose is golden and convincing. The book is an addictive, engaging foray into historical fiction that leaves the reader believing in the art of perspective and the redemptive power of love."   —*Express* (London)

"[A] time-leaping novel of love and youth."   —*Entertainment Weekly*

"An ambitious beginning, as much a ghost story as a romance."
                                              —*The Observer* (London)

"A sweeping tale of love and loss."   —*USA Today*

"A novel rapturous with the joys of history. . . . Anna's story is told in a wonderfully convincing, brittle, adolescent voice. . . . [Darwin] gives her treatment of history in this novel a poetic force and philosophical gloss with an ongoing and absorbing meditation on photographic processes."
                                                       —*The Australian*

"Historical romance, Gothic tale, and bildungsroman, Darwin's novel ponders its own processes, mesmerized by the 'strips of time' that layer one another in a place. . . . The narrative of photography is electrifying. Darwin creates an imaginative language capable of suggesting the quality of the uncanny present in the humblest snapshot."   —*The Independent* (London)

"Anna is a marvelous creation, a sort of every girl, with no particular virtues or faults, but always compelling and believable. Her emotional credibility is evident no matter how trivial-seeming her subject in the voice Darwin has found for her. . . . The characters who surround her are also so wonderfully rendered that the reader can smell and feel them . . . most of all, the pathetic little waif Cecil, so beautifully rendered he almost seems Dickensian."
                                                    —*Los Angeles Times*

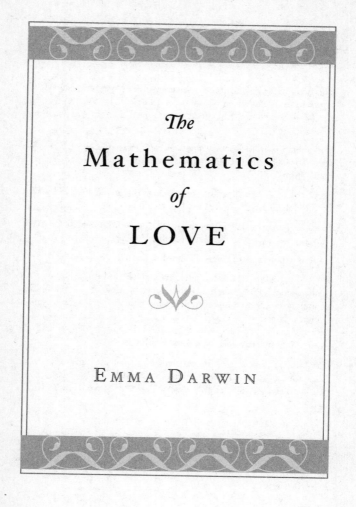

The
Mathematics
of
LOVE

Emma Darwin

HARPER  PERENNIAL

NEW YORK ● LONDON ● TORONTO ● SYDNEY

HARPER ● PERENNIAL

The quotation from Robert Capa's memoir, *Slightly Out of Focus*, has been reprinted with the kind permission of the International Center of Photography.

This book was originally published in Great Britain in 2006 by Headline Book Publishing, a division of Hodder Headline.

First U.S. hardcover edition of this book was published in 2006 by William Morrow, an imprint of HarperCollins Publishers.

P.S.™ is a trademark of HarperCollins Publishers.

FIRST HARPER PERENNIAL edition PUBLISHED 2008.

Designed by Betty Lew

The Library of Congress has catalogued the hardcover edition as follows:

Darwin, Emma.
   The mathematics of love/Emma Darwin.—1st ed.
      p.   cm.
ISBN: 978-0-06-114026-6
ISBN-10: 0-06-114026-0
   1. Young women—Fiction.   I. Title.

PR6104.A835M38   2007
823'.92—dc22   2006048132

ISBN: 978-0-06-114027-3 (pbk.)

08   09   10   11   12   DIX/RRD   10   9   8   7   6   5   4   3   2   1

For

Hugh

and

Lucie

But must not all these new prodigies efface themselves before the most amazing, the most troubling of all: that which at last appears to give man the power to create in his turn, to make solid the unreachable ghost which fades as soon as seen, without leaving a shadow in the looking-glass, a shiver in the water of the pool?

NADAR, *Quand j'étais photographe,* 1899

PART ONE

Perception becomes a language.... The far greater part of what is supposed to be perception is only the body of ideas which a perception has awakened.

THOMAS WEDGWOOD, "Essay on Vision"

LANCASHIRE, 1819

HAD I NOT BEEN THERE, NO ACCOUNT, NO PRINT, NO EVIdence of witnesses could have made me believe what I saw that day.

I had arrived at the Durwards' home only the evening before, and on the morrow there was enough uneasiness reported for Mr. Durward to feel obliged to go early to his printworks. His elder daughter, Miss Durward, was absent, and as the morning wore on, his younger daughter, Mrs. Greenshaw, could no longer disguise her anxiety for her sister. She set ever more stitches awry, and even wondered aloud if she ought to send for her son, Tom, to be fetched home from his favorite playground in the woods. In such a case I would always have offered my services to find and escort Miss Durward home. But I should mention that Mrs. Greenshaw was the young widow whose affections, though we all cloaked the fact in other words, I had come into Lancashire to engage.

My offer was greeted with relief and gratitude, and I received my orders: I must seek Miss Durward in the town, at the house of her old nurse Mrs. Heelis, which was in Dickinson Street, hard by St. Peter's Field, where the meeting which was the cause of so much unease was to take place. It was rumored that the magistrates were even now mustering the militia to disband the meeting. In the town, every shop that I could see was boarded up, every window shuttered, and while we were yet some distance away, my hack was brought to a halt by the absolute solidity of the crowd all about us. I paid it off and made my way on foot through the hot streets, assisted by the movement of the mass, which was almost as steady as I was accustomed to observe in the Peninsula, though rather more motley, and very much more good-tempered. As we arrived on open ground not far from Dickinson Street the crowd became still more tightly packed. I abandoned any notion of making directly for my goal, and began to work my way round the edges of the throng. Shirtsleeves and leather aprons and petticoats and Sunday-best pinafores may not easily be counted by company or regiment, but trumpets and drums there were aplenty, and flags, or rather banners, borne aloft in the heat-hazed air with every bit as much pride as that of a color-sergeant of the Guards. I was astounded too to see blood-red, tin caps of liberty bobbing on poles above my head. True, these ironworkers and cotton-spinners were perhaps not bred of the same stock as my slow-spoken, country people at Kersey, but I could scarcely credit that any Englishman would willingly bear so infamous a sign of revolution and foreign tyranny.

The distance I had already walked, and my slow progress in the crowd, had inevitably made my leg ache, and despite my stick, I stumbled in trying to get between human bodies and iron railings. The roar of cheers and cries and the crash of music in my ears was solid and unwavering, like the haze of sweat and sooty dust through which we all moved. Over the caps and hats and beavers I could just make out a little group—ladies as well as men—standing on what seemed to be two hay carts lashed together to form a platform. One man appeared to be making a speech, though only a few could possibly have made out his meaning, and the rest began to push and mutter in their impatience.

And then from my left—the southwest—I heard cavalry, charging. On they came, all order lost before ever they reached the open ground, their sabers out, cutting at whatever man, woman, or child was within range. Some of the people tried to flee; others stood their ground. I saw a special constable go down to a cavalryman who, through the dust, took his truncheon to be a cudgel. At my elbow a lad fell, blood all over his face, and I caught at the bridle of the militia-man that did it.

"For shame, sir!" I cried. "Won't you give them time to get away? Don't you see them down?"

He looked at me, but I was not in uniform, no longer commis-sioned, and he wrenched his horse's head out of my grasp.

"It's Billy Kirby!" cried a girl's voice. "Billy, it's us! You'll not hurt ye marrahs!" But the rider could not or would not rein in, and the girl went down beneath his hoofs.

I started forward, but was knocked aside by a huge man clad as a blacksmith and intent on wrenching the iron railings behind me from the ground. Even after several years I am not as nimble as a man with two legs of his own. I fell heavily, and in the time it took me to right myself the yeoman cavalry had hacked and slashed their way across the field under a hail of stones, bricks, and iron bars. At my feet lay a woman, her hands pressed to her breast from where blood oozed be-tween her fingers, her moans feeble from the extremity of her suffer-ing. Even as I looked round to seek help for her in the hurrying, scrambling crowd, her moans ceased. I knelt down beside her as quickly as I might, but she was as dead as any of my men in the breach at Badajoz.

The crowd was slackening a little. On the far side of the field I could make out a company of the Fifteenth Hussars picking their way among the fallen and using the flat of their sabers to hasten the re-mains of the great gathering back to the courts and mills and villages whence they had come. The people went, stumbling with fear, or with the dull, hunched walk of prisoners of war, dragging their wounded with them. Only a few foolhardy lads turned to fling a final, defiant stone.

The woman at my feet was beyond all aid, and I looked about me. I was almost level with Dickinson Street; as I tried to recall which of the little houses it was that I sought, one of the front doors opened and a lady ran out and down the steps, crying, "Tom? Tom!"

"Miss Durward?"

She stopped.

"Forgive me. I am Major Fairhurst. I arrived last night. Your mother asked me to come to escort you home."

"Oh—yes—I've lost Tom."

"You've lost him? Tom Greenshaw? He was *here*, then?"

"Yes"—she spoke pantingly—"he followed me here, this morning. It seemed safer to keep him with us, but I had no means of sending to tell Hetty, Mrs. Greenshaw. When he saw those accurst soldiers he ran out. I didn't know! He's lost!"

"We shall find him," I said. "He will not have got far, with so tight-packed a crowd."

Without a word she set off across the field. Most who could move themselves or had friends to carry them away were gone. I saw abandoned clogs, bonnets, a trampled cap of liberty, a scarlet spinning top. A still form—too big to be that of a lost child—lay beneath a banner carefully spread; stitched in red wool were the words LET US DIE LIKE MEN AND NOT BE SOLD LIKE SLAVES.

Behind us, a lieutenant of the Eighty-eighth Infantry called, "There's the Riot Act again, for all to hear! Now, men!" even as I saw the Hussars dragging up two six-pounders. I shouted to warn Miss Durward that she must take cover but could not reach her in time. But she barely flinched as the guns were fired, then continued treading methodically to and fro across the plain, calling the boy's name. She reached the hustings, and there she found him, lying all but under one of the wheels.

She knelt with a cry. The child lay awkwardly, one arm twisted beneath him and his jacket thick with dirt and dust, but I could see no obvious wounds, barring a bruise on his pale cheek.

"He breathes," she said, and tried to gather him to her. "Oh, how will I tell Hetty?" I tried to prevent her moving him, but she pushed my hand away. "Nonsense! He's not too heavy for me. I'm strong enough."

"Perhaps," I said. "But I think he's been trampled. We must keep him as still as possible." I wrenched a plank from the hustings and laid it on the ground. "We must get him indoors, and I'll fetch a doctor."

And so a lame man and a lady carried this broken child through the hot, dust-laden wind that threw lost handkerchiefs and crumpled handbills across his insensate face.

By the time I returned with the news that the only doctor I could find would not promise more than to be with us by nightfall, one of the Durward grooms had arrived. In fact it was he who let me into the house again. "You'd be Major Fairhurst, might I make so bold as to ask? I was told off by Mrs. Greenshaw to bring word of Master Tom's running away in case he was here," he said. "She said as you might be here, and to seek you out. But I had my horse taken by some scum of an agitator trying to get away. Miss Durward is writing a note now." I nodded, relieved that at least he had not had to tell me that the worst had happened, and climbed upstairs as fast as I might to tap on the best bedchamber door.

Tom still lay insensate, limp and straight under nothing but a thin sheet, for the room was hard beneath the roof and baked under the August sun. He had his mother's dark hair, thick with dust, but his face had the absolute pallor of deep stupor. The nurse, Mrs. Heelis, her eyes red with weeping but her wrinkled hands quick and quiet, was bathing his brow. Miss Durward was sitting in the window, writing hastily on a sheet of paper that appeared to have been torn from the sketchbook that lay before her. I told them about the doctor. "He is not known here—his practice is in Shrewsbury—so he is not so busy. But he appears to be a very experienced man—he was well known to a couple of gentlemen that I ran across."

"Thank you," said Miss Durward. "Nurse is doing what she can— there is so little when we do not know the nature of his injuries. We have decided not to use salts or burnt feathers to rouse him, in case he should sneeze or cough."

"Have you finished your letter?" I asked. "The streets seem quiet enough; it should be safe, if your man doesn't delay."

"Yes," she said, dropping wax onto the paper with a steady hand and pressing a seal into it as neatly as any clerk.

"Or I could take it back, if you think Mrs. Greenshaw—and your parents—would be reassured by my doing so."

"No," said Nurse, straightening up and wiping her hands on her apron. "That James can go. Do you take Miss Durward downstairs, if you wouldn't mind, sir, and see she drinks some tea." Miss Durward rose, walked a pace, then stayed, standing helplessly by the foot of the bed. "Go on, Miss Lucy, dear. You've written to Miss Hetty— Mrs. Jack, I should say—and that's what I couldn't do, not as you can. The blest lamb'll be none the better for your hanging about. I'll call if I need you."

I followed Miss Durward downstairs into a neat little parlor. On entering the room, she sat down very suddenly on the nearest chair and started to weep, so that it was I who went in search of the maid-of-all-work, and asked for tea in Miss Durward's name. When I returned she was already calmer, as if such tears did not overwhelm her habitually, or for long. As the tea tray came into view, she sat up and wiped her eyes but made no effort to smooth her disordered and dusty hair, and still appeared so far from well that I poured out her cup of tea and took it to her where she sat by the door.

"Thank you," she said, in a low tone. "I'm sorry. Tom is the apple of Hetty's eye, and my parents' too. Since Jack's death and the loss of her—her indisposition—she has only him, and if . . ." She looked up. "It's silly, but I can't forget that it is his birthday next week. Hetty has planned all sorts of treats. If he should . . . Oh, if only she could be here!"

"Mrs. Greenshaw would not be able to come, of course. But Mrs. Durward?"

"My mother would come if she could. How safe would you judge it to be, out there?"

"I can't say." I got up and looked out of the window. There were no bodies now lying on the trampled earth, although the field was still strewn with fallen placards, bricks, bars, walking sticks, and blood-smeared kerchiefs. Faintly I could hear small outbreaks of fighting and musket fire. On the far side of the field a group of burghers and gentlemen in dark coats were hurrying away towards Dean's Gate, surrounded by a force of what I took to be special constables, twice theirs in number. "It may be perfectly safe, though I would not advise a lady to travel. But——" I shook my head and drank my tea in one gulp, wishing it were brandy or even cold water. Miss Durward continued to look at me. "In ten years of soldiering, I have never known anything like this. For soldiers—men such as my own—to charge peaceful civilians, their own countrymen . . ."

"But you said it was the militia, not the regulars."

"Yes, for the most part. They cannot have been properly commanded. But even so . . ."

She did not answer me directly. "The people could not get away. Even when they tried. I was sitting in the window upstairs, the better to see. There are so few ways out of St. Peter's Field. Women—boys—children . . . Oh! It makes me so angry to see such things. . . . But they cannot be new to one of your profession."

"No, in point of blood spilt. But on campaign, if they were not the enemy, they were at least harboring him. We could——" My thought was ill-developed, and was in any case interrupted by a brisk *rat-tat-tat* at the front door, and the shuffle of the little maid along the passage to answer it. A man's voice requested her assurance, and received it, that this was the house to which Major Fairhurst had bidden the doctor. I hastened out. The doctor himself was being helped out of his carriage, while under the shifting of his considerable weight I saw that a few books tumbled out from where they were stacked by its open door.

Miss Durward greeted him as his footman assisted him up the steps, and led him upstairs as quickly as her good manners and his bulk would allow. I was left to contemplate the cooling teapot and the worn but spotless furniture, the wool-work proverbs and brightly colored tracts that hung on the walls, and a gaudy print of their Majesties and their royal offspring, made many years ago, it appeared, when it was still possible to show innocence and sobriety in the children, and sanity in their father. Among the pictures with which Mrs. Heelis had chosen to ornament her parlor, and more absorbing to the eye that had taken notice of them than any other, were a number of sketches. Peering at a charmingly drawn head of Mrs. Greenshaw, I saw writing at the foot: *Mrs. Jack, for dear Nurse,* and the initials L.D. Miss Durward had sketched her sister. In the softening light the silvery pencil lines seemed to conjure life itself from the rough, cream-colored paper on which they were laid, so that the rosy cheeks in the small portrait in oils of the same subject, which hung nearby, seemed merely colorful. Was it that Miss Durward was a more skillful draughts-woman than she was a painter? I pondered, seeking occupation for a mind troubled by events, but impotent. Was it the deliberate omission of so much descriptive power—in the omission of color—that demanded the onlooker engage his own sympathies with the subject, and thus breathe life into the image? In following the pencil sweeping over the paper—smudging a shadow here, touching in an eyelash there—one all but saw the hand that had drawn those lines. Very young and very pretty Mrs. Greenshaw's face was, as I had been promised. I had been promised too that her health, and her mourning for her dead husband, would mend soon enough, and that the improvement in her circumstances consequent on our engagement would itself speed her recovery. If that were so, then her only child, the broken little boy who lay upstairs, would become my child.

That the thought of having a child I could, after all, call mine nearly overwhelmed me, I ascribed to the events of the day, and the circumstances in which I found myself. I pulled myself together and looked at the drawing again. In following one sister's hand, one could see the other sister's face as immediately as she had. What is real life to us, I wondered, if it can be brought forth by such means? And what can such life have to say to the loss of it?

The door opened, and the doctor entered the room. My thoughts snapped to attention. "How is he?"

"He has regained his senses," said the doctor. His voice was very high pitched for so tall and broad a man, but he spoke with great calm and authority. "I never like to discuss things in such a child's hearing. Miss Durward will be down directly."

"I'll leave you, then," I said, but at that moment her step sounded on the stair, and as she came into view she said quickly, "Please don't go, Major Fairhurst. Doctor, what do you think?"

"Well, anything is possible. He's badly concussed, but the broken arm is only a greenstick fracture. And he's hurt internally. But I think you may entertain good hopes of his recovery. I can find no evidence that any of his organs . . ." He hesitated.

"Please go on," said Miss Durward.

"I should say, thanks to Major Fairhurst's good sense—and yours, ma'am—his internal wounds were prevented from being very seriously aggravated. As far as it's possible to tell, I should say that all the organs are intact. I congratulate you, Major."

"I have some experience of injury, sir."

"More than just musket-ball and saber-cut, I'll warrant."

"Battle injuries are the least of it," I said.

He nodded and turned again to Miss Durward. "So, we may hope for the best. It is unfortunate that your sister cannot come. All boys need their mother. . . . But you're quite right: from what you tell me of your sister's condition it would be most unwise, and I am sure he's content to have you. Now, I shall tell you what you must do, and I've every confidence that all will be well."

The partial relief afforded by his diagnosis seemed to allow Miss Durward to recover her composure. "Would you like some tea, Doctor? Tom is asleep, and Nurse is watching him."

The teapot was empty. Miss Durward rang the bell, but the maid did not appear, so I took it from her and went in search of the kitchen.

When I returned, she was saying, "My father and I are much interested in mechanical reproduction of the original too, though his interest is commercial rather than artistic."

The doctor settled deeper into his chair and accepted a large piece of Nurse's plum cake, although I observed that Miss Durward ate nothing herself. "The key seems to be the knowledge of which substances are affected by the action of light, and how they are thus affected. My brother-in-law Thomas Wedgwood was much taken up with the question. I think he knew more about it than any man." He stopped but went on again after a moment. "He died some years ago. But his paper—or, rather, my good friend Davy's paper on his work— was published by the Royal Institution, I recall. If your father doesn't have that volume of the *Journal*—I think it was in the year two—I could let him have a copy. And now I must go. I am putting up at the Crown, if you should need me again, but I don't at all anticipate it. If I'm absent—I've several more of those wretches to see—my man will know where I am."

"They were not wretches," I said.

"I speak of the magistrates and their minions. A damn— A dashed ill-managed business they made of it, it seems. But one of their number knew I was in town, rather than safely in Shrewsbury, and so I'm called to several bedsides. Besides, even those who oppose reform may bleed, and I'm bound to help all that I can."

"I shall pray for Tom's recovery," said Miss Durward, following him into the passage.

"Oh, yes, certainly. But carry out my instructions meanwhile." And with that he heaved himself into his carriage and was driven away. Faintly we could still hear military tramping, orders, cries of fear and defiance, and the crack of breaking glass.

"Is there much to do for the boy?" I asked as I shut the door.

"Only that we must give him a draught when he wakes, and not move him at all for some hours. There is nothing left to do but wait . . . I must send another note to Hetty."

"If you can write it now I may take it with me," I said as she started upstairs. What agonies of mind Mrs. Greenshaw must be suffering I could not imagine, and now that the immediate need for my aid here was past, my chief thought was that such good tidings as there were must reach her as soon as possible.

Miss Durward turned back. "Oh—are you leaving?"

"Yes. It's getting late."

"Could you not stay? Forgive me, but I'd so much rather you were here than a servant, should Tom—should we need help. I've no right to ask it of you, but . . ." She looked very like her sister, with the same dark hair and blue eyes, but taller and much slighter, with a tautness about her that might be bred of her present anxiety. In the dim light of the passage, and lacking Mrs. Greenshaw's sparkling color and plump cheeks, which I had so much admired in last night's candlelight, she also looked thin and ill.

"Willingly I shall stay, if it would be of any use," I said, "but I cannot think that your mother would agree."

"Nurse is here, and I am not a girl anymore. If Mama does not like it she will have to fetch me herself."

A clatter at the back of the house and a cry of fear from the maid made us whip round to see the cause. I gestured to Miss Durward to run upstairs while I made for the scullery, but she held her ground; and the intruder proved to be no rioter, but the Durwards' groom.

"For I'd have got back here earlier, only there's never a hack nor a horse to be had in the town, miss—Major, sir—and it's best part of five mile to walk home. Mistress said as I were to stop here, and carry back tidings when you could spare me."

Miss Durward was right: there was nothing to do but wait. She went upstairs to scribble another note to Mrs. Greenshaw telling of the doctor's visit, and I went back into the parlor. There was a small writing table in one corner furnished with ink and paper of sorts, and to steady myself, I sat down to write to my bailiff at Kersey of a few matters of no great urgency. Although I could not believe the doom-sayings that I had heard in the town, that the day's events spelled the beginning of a revolution, still less that if it did it would spread quickly in the prosperous and peaceful fields of Suffolk, I did close by suggesting that he make sure that no legitimate grievance among my tenants or servants went unaddressed, and no radical talk unchallenged.

I sealed the letter, and sat in the weary aftermath of action and anxiety, listening to the quiet outside. As uncounted minutes passed, my love came to me, so present that my hands all but reached out to grasp hers, my lips felt the shadow of hers, and my arms ached with her absence.

It was growing dark when Nurse insisted on sending in cold meat and bread and cheese. "I'm sorry there's nothing more, sir," she said, coming into the room in the wake of the girl, and keeping a sharp eye on the setting out of the dishes, "but we dined at midday, and there's not a bite to eat in the larder beyond this, with all the trouble."

"It is more than enough, Mrs. Heelis," I said, "and with all you have to do . . . Has Miss Durward eaten?"

"She'll be down. I'm going to sit with the blest lamb. She needs her food."

"Mrs. Heelis, are you sure that Mrs. Durward will be willing for me to stay here?"

She trimmed the oil lamp and replaced the chimney. "That's better. Don't worry, sir, Mrs. Durward knows I'm here, and things being as they are, I'm sure she'll not object. And what the rest of the world doesn't know can't hurt them, that's what I say. Miss Lucy always did do things her own way, even from a child, and never mind what the busybodies thought. If I called her down from halfway up the big oak in the garden once, I called her down a dozen times, and it made no difference. She'd say she was sorry, but it didn't stop her. She could see better up there, she said, even with all the leaves. Miss Hetty was a different kettle of fish. You'd not catch *her* tearing her best gown by climbing over a gate, you needn't worry about that, Major Fairhurst, sir. She'll do you proud, bless her. And Master Tom too, if he's spared. Now, if you'll excuse me, I'll go and fetch Miss Lucy to her supper."

Mrs. Heelis's frankness as to the reason for my coming into Lancashire was the cause of my slight embarrassment at Miss Durward's entrance, but she looked merely impatient when I rose to hand her to her seat, and although she did not eat a great deal, she fell on her food as briskly—although more elegantly—as any ensign given bread and cheese after three days of raw bullock meat and handfuls of flour. She looked up, and saw that I smiled.

"I was thinking of how many evenings we dreamt of a supper like this, on campaign," I explained, lest she mistake the cause of my amusement. "More often than not, it seemed, we outstripped our commissaries, or they simply lost us."

"How I envy you, having seen so much of Europe," she said, "although—did you have much time to admire the landscape?"

"Plenty, when we were encamped, and still more so on the move. Even the Light Division marches slowly enough to afford one a good view from horseback, unless the dust rises too high."

"Is it true that in battle one can see almost nothing for the gunsmoke?"

"Well, that depends."

"On what?" she said, cutting herself a scrap of cheese.

"On the wind, largely: how much there is, and in what quarter it sits. And on the weather, and the lie of the land, and the commander's dispositions. I have had a view of a battlefield that a general would envy, and I have been where I could not see my hand in front of my face, let alone my men, or the enemy."

She nodded. "I thought so."

"You thought so?"

"Yes. I'm working on a set of prints for my father—*Twelve Views of the Rise and Fall of French Tyranny*—you know the sort of thing."

"Indeed. But not that ladies concern themselves with their production."

"And I'm always seeking other subjects for such work. That's why I came here: to sketch the meeting. Didn't you know?"

"Your mother said only that you were visiting your old nurse."

"That also, of course." She laughed, and her mirth brought color to her cheeks. "She doesn't speak of it if she can help it, and nor does Hetty. Why, I don't know. Mama worked with her mother in the dairy and the stillroom, and Hetty cares as much for her needlework as I do for drawing. But for me to be involved in my father's business affairs is different, it seems. Or perhaps it is the times that have changed. I do try not to lose my temper when they speak of it as young-lady drawing."

"Which you also do," I said, gesturing to the walls behind her. "But better than most young ladies."

"Oh, yes," she said, without any blushing denials of the truth. "But there is a different interest in animating a whole scene, with hundreds of figures, and a crucial moment of history to explain. It must be pleasing to the eye, but be truthful as well. But I don't know if I shall have the heart to work these sketches up." She put down her napkin and got up. "I must go. I have wrung a promise from Nurse that she will go and rest as soon as I get upstairs." As I held the door for her she said, "May I call you, if I need help with him? He must have his next draught at midnight."

"Of course."

"Thank you." She went swiftly upstairs.

I returned to writing my letters. Outside, the curfew was rung, and slowly a hot silence fell over the town.

It wanted two minutes to midnight when I tapped on the bedchamber door. "I thought you might need help with his draught."

She nodded, and moved quietly back to the table, where stood a bottle and glass, next to an oil lamp burning very low. "Thank you. He must be turned as well, the doctor said."

Tom's splinted arm lay across his chest, rising and falling with each shallow breath. His shirt had been ripped to allow the setting of his arm. Beneath the linen were bruises as dark as ink, spilt to make a picture of the boots and stones that had struck his soft flesh. I raised his shoulders as gently as I might, careful of his arm, feeling him heavy with torpor though thin and childish. He would soon celebrate his sixth birthday, I knew. I wondered that the fate of so small a body, so insignificant a soul, could engage grown men and women.

Miss Durward sat on the other side of him, and held the glass to his lips. Tom blinked, but she slipped the medicine drop by drop into his mouth, and I saw his throat clench and swallow. When he had taken it all, she said, "I must put him on his side." She picked up some pillows from the heap that had been taken off the bed, and I gently rolled him over, away from me, his injured arm uppermost, while she walked round to my side of the bed and propped pillows against his back, and another under his arm. She smelled of paint and turpentine, sweat had stuck a curl to her cheek and dried it there, and her plain stuff gown was dusty, and smudged with whitewash on one arm.

She shivered. "It's getting chilly. I must cover him."

The flap of the coverlet in the still air blew a sheet of paper from the table onto the floor. I stooped to pick it up, and saw that it was a sketch of Tom, lying with closed eyes in the lamplight.

"I had to do something!" said Miss Durward. "And I thought it might—I thought Hetty might . . ." She was silent.

"He looks very peaceful," I said, laying it on the table.

"Nurse hinted that she had plenty of needlework, if I wanted occupation, but hemming kerchiefs doesn't occupy me."

"No, indeed," I said. "I have never understood how it can be the chief activity of so many of your sex, who have no lack of servants to do it for them."

"Oh, because our mothers tell us it is so. For myself, the only needle that can engage my interest is an etching needle," she said. "But for many, it truly is their delight. Hetty sews exquisitely, she worked the most beautiful linen for . . ." She did not finish, and I could not comment on such a matter, although I knew of the event for which the linen had been made, and had been told of Mrs. Greenshaw's grief at the loss of this hoped-for child, so soon after the death of her husband. After a moment she said, "Won't you sit down?"

"Thank you. Yes, I saw some of Mrs. Greenshaw's work last night, and admired it very much."

"She has excellent taste, and the skill to match it."

"Shall we disturb him?" I said as I set a chair for her.

"Not if we speak quietly. I wish you would tell me something of your travels." She picked up her paper and pencil as she spoke, and realizing that even drawing was not occupation enough for her anxious mind, I started to speak.

I told of elegant Lisbon where every *palacio* had its spies, flickering like shadows across the sunshine; I told of Madrid where the brilliant air streamed with Bourbon colors one day and Buonaparte's the next; of Moorish castles silhouetted against a Spanish sunset; and of the crags and ravines of the Pyrenees, scarfed in mist, and the icy streams that tumble like lace against gray and golden rocks. As if my earlier reverie had made these things too present, I faltered at this last recollection and fell silent. Miss Durward regarded me for a moment, her pencil stilled in her hand, before she looked back at her drawing, but said nothing.

After a moment she spoke. "I had hoped, if it were not too tedious for you, that you might advise me about my drawing of Waterloo. I am not sure that I have it right, though I've read all I could."

"Certainly I can do that," I said, and for a while we were silent, so that the only sounds in the room were Tom's little breaths and the whisper of Miss Durward's pencil. At my elbow the lamp burned steadily.

At four, we gave Tom another draught and turned him again onto his back. His eyes opened, and he seemed more aware of his surroundings. He even choked a little over the medicine, as if he did not like it. When I had lowered him again onto the pillow his eyes followed Miss Durward about the room. Then his brow suddenly creased. "I got lost," he said.

"Yes," she replied, "but we've found you now."

At her words his eyes closed again, and within a moment he was asleep.

As the clocks struck five, Nurse began to move about in the next room, and further away, the shouts of the knockers-up could be heard in the courts and backstreets of the town.

❧

LONDON, 2006

I DON'T NEED it in front of me to believe what happened—that I was there—any more than I need my photographs, convincingly young and clumsy though they are. Or even Stephen's letters. The letters tell the beginning—one of the beginnings—just as this tells some of the endings. But I don't need to keep it out on my desk. Besides, it's too fragile.

It's an early daguerreotype, more than 150 years old. That's a positive process, I usually explain, the plate exposed directly, so each is unique. If the glass got broken, it'd be gone forever. The case is worn leather, like a jewel box. The catch is a bit stiff with age, but the lid lifts easily. Inside, the glass plate lies tucked into its black velvet pillow. If you tilt it toward the light, the image gleams and shimmers, so exact, so bright and so dark, that the moment of its taking seems to live inside the glass. The sun touches the pillars and chimneys of Kersey Hall and flickers among the dark, late-summer trees. Its light lies on the lawn, strokes the curve of the steps, slips through the half-open door to where a figure in a long dress stands. It was then—that moment—that the shutter opened, and snatched a scatter of the light and dark, throwing it onto this piece of glass, fixing the sun and shadow of those few seconds forever. And the sun moved on and took the day with it, while the plate held those shadows and kept them, and carried them to other places and to other times before it was found again. One of those times was mine.

SUFFOLK, 1976

AT FIRST THE road through London was the same as the one all the times we went to Southend for our holiday. Summer after summer for years I hoped for Spain, like Mum promised, but we never went. And by the time we were through London and on the dual carriageway I was quite lost. The coach roared along, half empty, miles and hours of hot nothing-time, and when it pulled up in the coach station it was a moment before I could stand up and deal with the next bit. Uncle Ray was there when I got off. He was sweaty and his breath smelled a bit of drink, like it did when he came to the flat, and his clothes looked as if they'd once been expensive, but hadn't been washed and mended enough lately.

"Anna! You got here all right!"

"Wasn't difficult, just a coach."

"Of course. Let me take your luggage. Nancy—your mother—got off to Spain all right?"

"Yes." I wasn't going to talk about that, not to an uncle I'd only met twice, and the first time I didn't remember.

I could feel that he might have said something more, perhaps about how I must miss her, but he didn't: there was just one of those silences while we walked along with the heat beating up from the tarmac, till he said, "There we are."

It wasn't a car, it was a dusty old white minibus, like a van, completely empty, so I could see the vinyl seats were split, with the foam pushing out. It must have been baking in the sun for a long time because when I opened the passenger door I was hit in the face by the smell of hot rubber and petrol fumes and feet. Uncle Ray put my cases into the back along with a couple of shopping bags, and I climbed into the front.

The engine sounded rattly and wheezy—needed a tune and the exhaust mended, that boyfriend of Mum's would have said. For a while Uncle Ray was busy squeezing through the traffic and narrow streets and didn't say anything, which suited me. But I couldn't help wondering what it was going to be like, Kersey Hall School.

Mum'd tried to make me feel better about dumping me there. Not that I wanted to go to the Costa del Sol with her and Dave, and have them slobbering all over each other just to make me feel left out. And, like she said, with my coloring, I looked as if I'd had a fortnight in Fuengirola after a sunny weekend, so I didn't have to actually go there to get a tan. But I should have known that anything she planned I'd be the one losing out. The thing was, she wouldn't let me stay on in the flat.

"Anna, I can't afford the rent," she said, "and anyone else except Ray I'd have to pay them, more than for your keep," but it wasn't that either. She didn't *say* she didn't trust me, but she went on and on with other words to cover up what we both knew, what was really going on.

"It'll be great," she was babbling on. "Big house in the country, it sounds like. There might even be girls to be friends with. Ray said sometimes some stay on into the holidays. And some of the teachers, and a matron. And he'll be there. He lives in a flat at the top of the school. You remember Ray, he came that time, when you were— I don't know—five? Six? Uncle Ray Holman—I changed my name when I had you, you see. But Ray's all right, and . . . and she won't be there. He said she's never—she lives somewhere else. Miles away, the other side of England. She . . . I wouldn't send you if she was there. Your grandmother. I've met up with him a few times now, and it's time you knew him—he is your uncle. He's even younger than me. Only thirty," she'd said, but he didn't look it, kind of creased, and with that sort of blond hair that looks as if it's going sour instead of gray. "I've asked him for a drink tomorrow," Mum'd gone on in a hurry, and I could tell it was because she knew she hadn't found out about it all properly, just grabbed at the first place she could dump me without too much trouble. "I've booked your coach ticket—next Tuesday, straight after we go. You can have a nice holiday, and soon as Dave and I've found the right hotel to buy, one that'll really do well, I'll send you the money for your fare."

Ray was saying something about how the new bypass made it much quicker, and after a while the houses on each side of the road began to trickle away to nothing, and then we turned onto a fast dual carriageway, the kind made of slabs of concrete with tar squidging out between them in ribs, so you go *thud, thud, thud,* like an uncomfortable sort of heartbeat.

"One piece of news," said Uncle Ray suddenly, in sort of a gasp, as if he'd been trying to say it for a while. "One thing—not important, really—but your grandmother's here. She arrived yesterday."

"Oh," was all I could think of to say. My grandmother was the one thing Mum had never, ever said anything about. Except that one time. *She lives somewhere else. Miles away, the other side of England. She . . . I wouldn't send you if she was there. Your grandmother.* Never before then. I must have asked sometime mustn't I? But I didn't remember. It was like her not-saying was as solid as a brick wall that I couldn't hope to climb. I hadn't even tried to ask what her name was.

"She . . . It's unexpected. But I'm sure . . . She's much better. I'm sure you'll get on. I'm sure it'll be fine." Then he looked away from the road, away from me, and pointed into the middle of a great hedge of trees, and said, "There it is—Kersey Hall School," as if I should be impressed or something.

I just turned my head and said, "Sorry, I missed it."

"I've told her you're coming. She's looking forward to seeing you."

Perhaps it would be like something in a film, a kids' film like *The Railway Children*, when Roberta runs up the platform to her . . . No. It wasn't going to be like that. I wasn't going to hope that it might be. Nothing ever is.

We went on for a bit, and then turned off into little sunk lanes, and at last we turned up a drive among some more great big dark trees, and after a while there was the school. I mean house.

It was very big for a house but small for a school. It was a sort of dirty-looking stone, pale, with greenish patches running like beards down from the gutters, and rows of dark windows, which were too smeary to shine, and chimneys at each end and all along the roof, like a giant's doll's house dumped in an attic and all grubby because no one wants it anymore. The minibus stopped at the back, and when I got out it was totally quiet, except for the dual-carriageway noises on the other side of the house, behind the trees. The grass was sort of stringy-looking. I hadn't seen properly green grass for weeks, the way the weather was.

Uncle Ray took both my cases out of the boot. "It's this way," he said, and it was a moment before I saw where he was going, towards a little door I hadn't noticed among the dustbins and falling-down sheds and things. He looked over his shoulder and smiled as I caught up with him. "I'm afraid it may be a little confusing at first. This passage leads to the kitchen. It's quicker than the front door, to get to the hall and the stairs." The kitchen was big, a school kitchen all right, steel and machines, and there was another passage and a swing door with green-felt padding all torn, and then the hall.

But it wasn't a school hall for assembly and stuff, it was a hall like a house has, but huge, huge, huge. I stood at the bottom of the stairs and thought suddenly that I knew how you'd feel if you'd been pushed out of a plane before it crashed. Tiny, and lost, and all round you the sky and sea cold and gray, and the emptiness—everything you couldn't see—pressing against you.

Ray stopped in the middle of the black-and-white floor and turned to me, a bit awkwardly because of my cases, which he was carrying. "Welcome to Kersey Hall, Anna. It's very good to have you here at last."

"Where is everybody?" I said, because I wasn't going to let it show, how I felt. I wasn't going to look like I'd been hoping for anything different.

"They've gone home. The staff as well as the children. The school has closed."

"Already?"

"The bank . . . Well, I've closed down for good. I'm afraid I didn't have a chance to warn Nancy. It's been a bit complicated. And then I had to go down to Devon to collect your grandmother. But I'm sure it'll be fine. I—we really are very pleased to have you here. Come on, I'll show you to your room. I hope you like it."

We went up hundreds of noisy lino stairs and along corridors with numbers on the doors. My room was really a dormitory like something in a boarding school film, *Daddy Long Legs* or *Goodbye Mr. Chips*. Ten metal beds lined up in two rows and with naked stripy mattresses. Curtains on the windows, long and droopy and so faded you couldn't see if there'd been a pattern. On one bed there was a neat little pile of sheets and blankets and a bald-looking towel. The bottoms of all the windows were bubbly glass like a bathroom, so you couldn't see out.

"Here you are," said Uncle Ray. "Make yourself at home." Since home's always been some shitty council flat or other, it would have been kind of hard to do that. "I—we usually help ourselves to lunch at about one. There's always food in the kitchen. But if there's anything you particularly like to eat, do let me know. I can pick it up next time I go into town."

I'm not that bothered about what I eat, as long as there's enough of it, which there always has been, just about. "Thanks," I said.

"Well, I'll leave you to get unpacked. If you need anything, I'll be somewhere downstairs. Just give me a shout." He sounded as if he meant it, I couldn't help thinking. Then he gave me another smelly smile and went out.

I looked at my watch, which I hate, because Dave gave it me in one of his winning-Anna-round campaigns. An hour to food, and I don't do the not-eating thing.

I don't have a cuddly animal either or any of that stuff, so the only thing I wanted to unpack was my clock radio. I found an electric socket and plugged it in, and seeing it sitting there made me feel a bit more like I was at home. I turned the radio on, because with a radio station you know they're there at the same time you're here. It's real. But I couldn't get a London station, just hissing like space going on forever, and the clock said 00.00. The journey had wiped out the time.

I twisted the dial and did get a newsreader, going on about the hi-jackers at Entebbe, and Northern Ireland, and the drought. Then the traffic, but the names were just words; they didn't feel like a place I could go, a place that was real. It was like somewhere you were lost, and all the faces and the names were strange and you wouldn't find anyone to help you.

I chose my bed, the one in the corner with windows on two sides, and the sun coming in in squares all over it. When I looked away from the windows the—what had sarky old moron Moran called it in art? The afterimage—yes, the afterimage was bright black with white bars, fizzing away inside my eyes.

I started to unpack my big case. Then I heard footsteps on the lino. I turned round. It was a woman, not young but not really old either, just sort of teacherish. She came down the room. "Are you Anna?"

"Yes."

"I'm Belle," she said, as if it should mean something to me. "Your grandmother."

My grandmother. She didn't come and try to give me a hug or anything, thank goodness. She didn't look as if she was specially pleased to see me.

She was wearing a saggy tweed skirt and thick, mud-colored stockings even in the heat, and worn-away flat court shoes like boats. Her hair was mousy brown and straight, not gray a bit but greasy-looking, done up in a bun. Mum's would be the same, I thought, only I can never remember what color hers is because you can never see the roots long enough to be sure. I get mine and my black eyes from my dad, whoever he was, and the waviness too, Mum says when she's doing a let's-be-like-sisters, so that's another thing not to thank him for, because I wish it was dead straight and silky and blond. She never says more about him than that, but she'll hold my hair on top of my head and try out different styles or put clips or whatever in it. Sometimes I wish I could get it straightened, but she says it'd make me look like something in the Addams Family, and I'm about to argue when the doorbell goes and she gives me a great big messy kiss and grabs her bag and runs to the door, and I might not see her again that night.

"Welcome to Kersey Hall. Have you got everything you need?" my grandmother was saying.

"I think so," I said, and added, a bit late, "thank you," though I wasn't really sure what for: it wasn't like Ray had had to arrange a bed or a room specially for me, and it wasn't like she'd done anything at all.

She sat down on the bed I'd decided was mine. "Are you unpacking, then?"

"Yeah," I said, thinking, What does it look like I'm doing?

"Call me Belle," she said. I couldn't think of anything to say. She went on, "And how's . . . how's Nancy?"

"Mum? She's okay. She's gone to Spain."

"So Ray said." She looked round. She was very thin, sort of restless, even when she was sitting down. She smelled older than she looked, with some perfume over it. "Your mother . . . she would have been welcome here too, you know. Ray says he told her. To get you settled in."

Mum hadn't said anything about coming with me, or that Ray had suggested it. Did she not want to help me? If it meant coming here? "She hasn't had much time. They had things to arrange, passports and flights and money things."

"She always did rush about. Ray's the reliable one." I didn't know what to say, so I went on putting things in the drawers. It wasn't like I could say, "You're not supposed to be here." Besides, I couldn't see what was so bad about her, not really. Maybe Mum was just doing one of her usual over-the-top things, true love or broken heart, everyone's either wonderful or terrible. And it was all a long time ago. Maybe my grandma—Belle—maybe she was all right. She was family, after all.

She got off my bed and looked round sort of peeringly, like she was shortsighted. "Well, I must get on . . . ." I wondered what at. She started again. "I hope you have everything you need. Ray said he had everything the children needed. They couldn't fault him on that, at least." She started to walk away from me. Halfway down the room she stopped and turned round. She had to raise her voice, so it sounded a bit croaky. "Did Nancy . . ." She stopped. Then she went on. "Well, we're glad you're here now. If you're writing to her, do give her our best wishes," and turned round and went out.

That was my grandmother. *The bank*—Ray said. *I had to go down to Devon to collect your grandmother.* Where she'd been? Had it cost money he didn't have anymore?

Somehow, it felt like something I didn't really want to think about. But, even so, I knew the wondering would hang around underneath everything, wondering what was wrong, why the school closed, why Belle'd been . . . wherever.

I spread my stuff around, but it looked like it didn't belong, as if the room couldn't be bothered to listen or change its face for me. Not the red cases that Mum said would be easy to spot at the airport, not the scarves and beads I draped round the mirror. I found some Sellotape and put up some pictures, and they helped a bit: Tanya's card saying, *Good Luck in Your New Home,* and the ones I tore out of *Cosmo*—

Paul Newman and John Curry, and one of a polar bear in the Arctic, because he looked so cold and nice. Mum said she'd send a card from Spain, of course, but it would take a week, even ten days. I could put that up and then maybe the room would look as if it wanted me.

When I went downstairs Ray and Belle were sitting at a tiny table in one corner of the kitchen. There were plates and a few smears and bread crumbs on it, and she had a glass of water in front of her. The sun was coming in, and the room felt hot and dead with the big extractor fans in the windows not moving. There was a normal-size electric kettle and toaster kind of swimming around on one of the counters, but everything else was huge—stoves and mixing machines and fridges with handles like big bolts, all looking grubby and dead in the heat.

"Oh, Anna. Yes, of course. Lunch. There's the fridge. Help yourself."

I found some bread and some cheese and made a sandwich with some rather manky lettuce.

"I hope you have everything you need," Belle said, like before.

"Yeah, I think so." There wasn't anywhere to sit.

Ray saw me looking round and got up. "Have the table, Anna. I've finished." A fly landed on the crumbs. When Belle reached out to brush it away he flinched, but that was all she did, and after a moment he picked up both their plates, went over to one of the big sinks and turned on a tap. I sat down and took a bite of my sandwich.

"So, you've left school?" Belle said.

My mouthful was difficult to get rid of. At last I said, "Yeah."

"I didn't know you were sixteen."

"I'm not. It wasn't worth finding another school just for the extra bit."

"When's your birthday?"

Suddenly I thought, She should know that. Okay, she and Mum don't talk, but she is my grandmother. She should know. "December. The tenth."

"What GCEs did you take? Or did you only do CSEs?"

"I didn't do any. They don't do them till next year."

"Well, really!" Belle got up and filled her glass from the cold tap. Ray ducked and moved aside with a sort of stumble to make room for her. "Not that it's your fault. I suppose I might have guessed how it would be."

"I'll—excuse me, Belle, Anna—I've got things to do," said Ray and went out. Then he put his head back round the door. "Belle, were you going to give me a hand with those files?"

"In a moment, Ray," she said as his head disappeared. She looked back at me. "No, it's obviously not your fault. It's Nancy. She never could get anything right. Luckily Ray saw her mistakes, and learned from them."

Did she mean I was a mistake? If she did, it was only what Mum never really said, but I knew she thought it often enough, every time she couldn't go somewhere or do something because of me or because of what I cost to feed and clothe.

I finished my sandwich. The last bite didn't taste any nicer than the first. Belle was still standing at the sink, not drinking her water. After a bit she said, "There's coffee somewhere if you'd like some." I looked round. There were a lot of cupboards. "I don't know where, I'm afraid. I've only just moved here myself."

"Yes, Ray said," I said, and managed to sound not very interested. Though I couldn't help being curious, in a way.

"I've been . . . living in the West Country for the last few years. For my health. A—a nursing home. But with the school closed Ray couldn't . . . we could be together again. And, of course, it's not so far from where I brought him and your mother up. But maybe—maybe your mother told you that."

"No." My voice sounded not just uninterested but flat and rude, and I added, "Not really."

"And now you're here, which is good too."

"Yes," I said, and realized I even sort of meant it, at least while I had my back to her and was opening cupboards. Mostly they were empty, but in the third there was a big tub of coffee marked CATERING SIZE.

I was making myself one when this incredibly dirty little boy came wandering in from the garden. He was about the age they start school, I supposed, but he wore a mucky pair of shorts and nothing else. His body was patchy with dirt, and his hair would've been blond if anyone'd washed it, and both of his knees had those scabbing-over grazes. He didn't look at me, just sideways at Belle. She didn't even move, and after a moment he went to the fridge, and tugged it open, and took out a half-empty packet of ham. He pulled out all the slices at once, so the slimy stuff made the dust on his hands go dark like mud, and then he stuffed the ham into his mouth.

In the end I said, "Hello," but he just looked at me sideways.

"Answer her," said Belle, and he flinched. "She's your cousin."

He mumbled something, which sounded like "hello," and bits of chewed ham splatted onto the floor.

"Really!" she said. "Pick that up at once," but he just sort of shrank inside his skin as if he wanted to be invisible. Then he turned and slipped out of the garden door again.

"Wow! I didn't know I had a cousin," I said. "What's his name?"

"Cecil." And the way she said it made it sound even sillier, like "sissy." "Actually, he isn't your cousin, it's just that his mother was a friend of Ray's. Goodness knows who the father is. And I've always suspected she was quite unstable, or why would she not have him? Ray's too good-natured for his own good. She talked him into looking after the boy for a while, and then she just vanished. He treats Cecil as one of the family," she said, sort of scornfully. "But now you're here. Real family. I hope you have everything you need?" That was three times she'd said it.

"I think so. Only, where are the shops?"

"There's one in Kersey village. I don't know how long it would take to walk. I think your uncle drives into Hadleigh sometimes. You could ask him for a lift," She pushed herself away from the sink. "Well, I'd better go and help Ray. There's a lot of sorting out to do, he says. He needs my help."

Trouble was, what on earth was I going to do with myself? I hadn't even seen a telly. Time was when if you'd told me I'd have eight weeks with nothing I had to do beyond keeping a few T-shirts clean, I'd have felt that the universe had decided to give me a break for the first time ever. I suppose I might have guessed it wouldn't be like that in real life. For a start, I was a hundred miles from the nearest Woolies—even more, probably, from Boots and Our Price—and thousands of miles from Tanya and Holly.

I know what girls get up to, left to themselves, Mum was thinking, but if she thinks I'm going to turn out like her, she's wrong. It's not because anything bad's ever happened, just boyfriends. I don't know why she doesn't think I can be left on my own. It's not *me* that needs telling that men are only after one thing and they leave you once they've got it. *I* know that sex is just sex. Full stop. I've always known it, right from the first time. *I* know there's no point in letting yourself hope for anything else—you just have to enjoy it while he still really really wants you, because he won't for long. It's Mum who needs telling, every bloody time. Because it's not love she falls into, it's amnesia, and it's me that hears her crying all night through the wall every time some bastard man makes her memory come back by dumping her. At least her amnesia doesn't extend to contraception. Not after me, anyway, and I don't know what happened then, because, except about how I got my Mediterranean coloring, she never talks about him. So that's all right: I've never fancied having a little brother or sister. I don't do the children thing, like I don't do the falling-in-love thing. Living with Mum would put anyone off either. Sometimes I think she does it on purpose, makes a terrible fuss about how dreadful it all is, in case I end up like her.

But thinking like that doesn't help. Better go and find that shop, I thought. There was a map on the wall in the hall and I found a bit of paper and drew how to get to the village so I wouldn't get lost.

It was very, very hot, but we'd all got used to it by then that summer. And it was nice to get away from the Hall and know I wasn't going to bump into Ray or Belle and have to deal with . . . what? I didn't know really. But it was there, whatever it was.

For a while the road was shaded by the big trees, and I saw the little boy Cecil among them, digging in the pine needles. Then suddenly I could see much further and there were fields of crops bleached like crushed bones all around me and the sky hanging over them darker than the land. Shouldn't there be birds singing, if this was the country? The sun beat on my head and back and baked the road so that it burned up through the thin leather of my Indian sandals. It was like it could get you both ways.

Kersey village turned out to be about six incredibly old houses on each side of the only street, falling down the hill to a mucky-looking stream that wasn't even there because of the drought. And the shop was about the size of the sitting room in our smallest-ever flat, with just bread and tins and milk like a corner shop. My period had finished the week before, so I didn't have to worry about that yet. I couldn't see anything about buses. They probably made it as difficult as possible to get anywhere. They usually do.

It was stuffy in the shop but not as hot as outside, so I hung around until the man behind the counter started giving me funny looks and then I took a Coke off the shelf—though I didn't really want to spend the money—and paid for it. They didn't have a cold one, he said, not grumpy, but as if I'd asked for the moon and then a carrier bag to put it in.

The Coke was sticky and fizzy and didn't feel like it was quenching my thirst, though I supposed it was. I walked and walked, and when at last I stepped into the shade of the trees and leant against a propped-open gate it was like someone had dipped me into cool, dark water.

A voice behind me, on the other side of the gate, said, "Are you all right?" Oldish, posh-ish, a bit foreign, a woman's voice.

I jumped away. Of course I was. And I was right about her: the face went with the voice, kind of bony and bright and dark all at once. She came nearer. She had a curl of hair that had sprung out from the rest and stuck to her cheek. "It is hot, isn't it? Please go on resting if you would like to."

"No, it's fine. I haven't got much further to go."

"Do you stay with Ray up at Kersey Hall? I saw you coming out of the drive."

"He's my uncle."

"Oh, I understand. It is certainly better to be in the country in this heat. And now your grandmother is there."

"Yeah. I suppose. London's pretty horrible when it's like this . . . I must go," I said, though I didn't want to.

"I should introduce myself. We are your neighbors. We live over there, through the trees. It was once the stable block of the Hall, though now it is separate. My name is Eva Peres."

"I'm Anna. Anna Ware."

"Please drop in sometime if you would like to, Anna, and have coffee with us. Our house is just up this path, and we are always here. We would be delighted to see you, my partner and I."

I wondered if she meant it. "You've got a business?"

"No, no. That is, yes, we both work from home. But Theo and I live together."

"Oh, I see. Um—thank you."

"We shall look forward to it. Well, good-bye for now." She turned and went back into the woods, while I trudged on to the Hall.

There was a big school clock in the kitchen, the kind where the second hand moves in slow jerks and you stare and stare at it and can't believe that a stupid little minute can take sixty of those jerks, because it feels like it's an hour and geography is never, ever, ever going to end. It's almost as bad as looking at the alarm clock ticking beyond a boy's shoulder, and wondering when he's going to finish, so that you can breathe properly again, and mop up, and tell him no, really, it was great. Sometimes it is, otherwise you wouldn't do it, and anyway, you always hope.

It was three o'clock. I felt like I'd been walking for hours, all sweaty and grubby. So I thought I'd go and have a wash. Or even a bath—I had nothing else to do. In the hall, the door by the bottom of the stairs was open—it looked like an office or a study or something. Belle was in there: I saw her opening and shutting a filing cabinet, and again, and again, the same *scrunch*, *clunk*, like a child kicking a chair leg. For a minute I wished I could go in and just say hello. You should be able to do that. But perhaps she wouldn't be interested, not really.

The bathroom was weird—flimsy-looking cubicles with huge great baths all green round the plug hole and kind of scratchy inside, and the taps spotty and green too and scaly-looking round their mouths like monsters. The toilets were old-fashioned, like old public ones only not smelly, and with paper. The mirrors had gone spotty too. I saw that my makeup had smeared with the heat, making my face look all blurred, as if I wasn't quite there. And behind me the doors and walls looked sort of blurred too, wavery, as if they weren't solid either, as if whatever was behind them was pressing inwards all the time, until one day you'd be able to see it, if you just kept quiet enough.

The water came out of the taps in great pale steamy green dollops, and the bath was so deep it was like getting into a swimming pool. In the sun I'd thought I'd like a cold bath, but the hot was lovely, because it was right to be like that when it was water. I closed my eyes so the light was warm and pink from the high-up windows, and felt the water lapping up my knees, thighs, belly, breasts, collarbone, until only the back of my head was anchoring me to cold hardness, and all the rest of me—arms, legs, body—drifted to and fro.

The drops of hot water felt cold like pearls on my skin as I was lying on my bed, sleepy because the air was still so warm and quiet. Sleep was all round me like the water had been, only somewhere there was a child crying, a little child not a baby. All flats come with a baby just through the wall, but this wasn't a flat and it wasn't a baby. It was a child, a child who'd been given something to cry about, crying, crying, even when I sank towards sleep. Even in my dreams.

And the crying wasn't here but the dream was, I knew suddenly, the way you do in dreams, a chunk of certainty. It was an old dream, bringing the crying with it from somewhere else. Aeons, my mind said in its sleepiness, like it had words hidden away to use when mine weren't good enough. Aeons ago, but here.

The rats'll get you, Stephen, if you bawl, that's what Mother Malpas said to me. She says rats like eating dirty little boys who shit their breeches. She took my breeches and my boots and put me in here. It's cold. She shut the door.

She wants the rats to get me. I didn't mean to, I didn't, I'm sorry. The latch sticked and she was asleep. She be cross if I wake her. I tried to wait.

My ears hurt—she boxed them again. I'm a dirty little boy, she said, but she'll beat me till I'm good. I mustn't tell Vicar and Doctor not ever or they'll know I'm bad and throw me on the Parish where they give dirty little boys what they deserve.

I can hear the dark but I can't see. Will I hear the rats before they get me? If I don't bawl at all? I'll be very quiet. Then I might hear them before they get me.

Wat Bailey says there's secret ways the rats use, from when the witches sent their fetch to do spells on people. Making children lost, and falling-sick spells and plagues and curses. He says when they burned a witch she'd scream, but her fetch couldn't help. Wat Bailey says Mother Malpas is a witch.

It's cold. I'm cold. Smells like the cellar, cold things growing, rotten but growing. I mustn't go to sleep, the rats might come and I wouldn't know. They'll eat me away to nothing, eat the flesh off my bones, my belly and throat, eat my ears and eyes, and I won't know. I won't know at all, just wake up in hell.

I mustn't go to sleep. Please, God, don't let me go to sleep.

I COULD BY NO MEANS LAY CLAIM TO A BROKEN HEART CON-
sequent on my withdrawing my suit to Mrs. Greenshaw, but my return to Suffolk also returned me to the conditions that had prompted
me to contemplate matrimony in the first place. Darkness drew in
earlier each day, and behind it stalked true night.

It was some two weeks after Peterloo before we were certain
enough of Tom's being out of danger that I felt it proper to overcome
a natural reticence, and offer my hand and my acres to Mrs. Greenshaw. There had been no coquetry, no intended cruelty, in Mrs.
Greenshaw's scarlet-faced, stumbling request that I say no more. I
felt for her even as I expressed my regret, for she and I were fellow
creatures in embarrassment at our faded hopes. We stared out of the
morning-room window most determinedly, seeing the plum trees of
her father's garden heavy with fruit, and the great brick chimneys
soaring behind them.

"I—I'm sorry, Major," she said. "You see—I had not thought,
when the rector of Kersey wrote to Papa . . . And then you were so
good about Tom. But—that is—your—the war . . . And it would not
be right to—to subject you to Tom's naughtiness."

"Please, Mrs. Greenshaw, you must not feel obliged to explain.
You cannot be more conscious of my deficiencies as a suitor than I
am myself. If you have determined that we should not suit, then there
is no more to be said. But would you prefer to tell your father, or
would it spare you embarrassment if I were to do so?"

Having been absent from Kersey for some weeks at the height of the summer, on my return I found work enough awaiting me to keep any man from brooding, once I had dispatched the letter of thanks to Mrs. Durward that good manners demand. I was surprised, therefore, to receive a letter from Lancashire almost by return, and took the first opportunity of a heavy shower halting work to return to the Hall and reply.

My dear Miss Durward,

I was so very delighted to receive your letter, & very glad to know that Mstr. Tom continues to mend. Pray tell him that marching is the best possible work for the 1ˢᵗ Battalion of the Birthday Regiment, even when they have been carved by so indifferent a toymaker as myself, & that their fitness will be better ensured by military exercises on the coverlet than by any postings further afield.

Please be assured that the only feelings that I cherish towards Mrs. Greenshaw are those of the warmest admiration for her countenance, & gratitude for her honesty. Certainly a disability such as mine is not a negligible matter for a young lady seeking the guidance & protection of a husband; nor am I so convinced of the value of the rest of my circumstances as to consider that they outweigh my damaged person. If your mother regards this correspondence with complacence, then I trust that your sister will feel no embarrassment at it.

I should be delighted to set down those descriptions & anecdotes of the late wars that you were unable to hear because of your attendance on your nephew. I should not like you to think that I did not take great pleasure in the company of your sister and your parents, but there were many occasions during those days when I felt that my tales would have been better told for being drawn out by the incisiveness of your questions and the breadth of your knowledge. While I hesitate to make any claim

for the historical completeness or literary merit of my tales, if
the pen of an eyewitness can assist you in your work, or merely
amuse you or your family's leisure hours, then it will have served
its purpose. I shall look forward to hearing as soon as you have
leisure to set it down, of what you would like to know, & what
tales would best entertain your family. Ladies, I have found, do
not take kindly to long descriptions of military strategies &
troop movements. Knowing that in general the fair sex is more
interested in those small matters which yet make life happy or
miserable, it is not my intention to set down in these letters long
passages of military history, lest they prove of interest only in
serving your maidservant in lighting the fire or curling her hair.
When your work requires information of a more technical nature,
I propose to add it on a separate sheet, & hope that it will prove
worth the extra sixpences that the post office will demand of you.

You observed most justly that a great many of my anecdotes
concern food or the absence of it. I should think that not the least
of the military wisdom of our late opponent Buonaparte was
contained in his assertion that an army marches on its stomach,
although I might add that one of my fellows, Lieut. Barry, who
found in military history the recreation that I prefer to seek in
Virgil or Mr. Wordsworth, maintained that Buonaparte had
adopted this maxim from Frederick the Gt. If this is so, it is
merely proof that even the greatest commanders gain by
studying their predecessors.

We were generally in particular want of bread, since meat
can be found on the hoof at the cost of no more than a moment's
work with a knife, but corn only becomes bread by way of milling,
baking & sundry other processes. However, on occasion the
demands of strategy & the demands of the stomach coincide, as
when, just before the battle of Sabugal, we came upon the French
rear guard grinding corn in a windmill . . .

*. . . I must end here for the present, so that I may be certain of
these pages' safe dispatch towards their destination from the
hand of your obedient servant*

Stephen Fairhurst

From hay making to nut harvest there was not a soul in the county
who had time for anything but work and sleep. If I looked heaven-
ward it was to judge the chance of rain on the morrow; if I thought of
Spain it was only to bless the weakened, hazy slant of this Anglo-
Saxon sun. The harvest was said by my bailiff to be a poor one. It was
all the more important, therefore, to gather every grain. Steadily the
stiff stalks of wheat and barley fell to the advancing blades, and rose
again as a village of stooks, standing proud on the razed ground. The
great horses dozed in the sun, their ears flicking at the flies while they
waited to draw the sheaves of pale corn to the threshing floor and the
barn. The thatchers knelt at work high on the stacks, nimble figures
against the sky, and in the cottage gardens the last carrots and turnips
and potatoes were lifted and stored carefully away. Cabbages were
pickled, cheeses washed and turned, marjoram, pennyroyal, and
lemon balm cut and hung to dry. Small fingers were set to pick peas
and beans and store them away. The river gave up its reeds to the
scythe, and fish to the traps for salting. Old trees were culled; stacks
of logs and kindling grew at every door. Clutches of giggling girls in
the lanes caught hands and pinafores on the brambles, their mouths
and fingers stained with fruit, and little boys hunted through the orchard grass for the last stray-laid eggs, lest any escape embalming in a
jar of isinglass. Hogs rooted urgently among the wasps and the wind-
falls: perhaps they knew their end was near. And one after another
each raddled ewe received the mark of her reprieve.

Thus we cut and carted and stored away the first fruits of our efforts to rescue the land from the neglect and impoverishment into
which it had fallen in my cousin's later years. But as the golden days
cooled and shortened, such tasks as might work my body and mind

into a peaceful exhaustion grew fewer, and the consequences of Mrs. Greenshaw's most reasonable decision once more became apparent to me.

Not that I had the least desire for an unwilling wife, and I told myself so yet again, as I stood in the library at Kersey on All Hallows' Eve with a glass of brandy in my hand, watching the village lads tramping up one of the rides towards the kitchen door, and swinging their devil-faced turnip lanterns. It was a year since I had first come to Kersey, and now the Hall lay about me again, smoky and dim in the autumn quiet, for it was that hour when the light is dying but the lamps are not yet lit. A further thought came to me. Perhaps it was better that this air, so thick with all the memories that I had brought with me from Spain, would not be stirred by the rustle of a lady's petticoats in parlors that now were shrouded in holland covers, or by her clear, high voice speaking of servants and linen, or by her scented, dutiful presence in my bed.

Although this conviction released me from the necessity of taking action in the matter, it was nonetheless a most agreeable diversion, to be able to turn to the necessity of reading and answering Miss Durward's letters, which arrived with a celerity that argued a great press of business at her father's works.

My dear Miss Durward,

I trust you & your family will forgive me for the delay in replying to your last. Had I only my own wishes to consult I would have replied by return, but I had not. However, now that the harvest is in, & the evenings grow long, it is a pleasure to be able to write more fully than nature & agriculture have lately allowed.

You ask how I came to join the Army. Certainly, I have long thought it to be to a man's profit to follow some profession, but I am afraid that my choice was governed neither, as you suggest, by a boyhood passion such as that which animates your nephew, nor by a tradition such as that you speak of in relation to families of painters or musicians. In short, I had very little choice in the matter.

My father was the 3rd son of the 4th son of a landowner of whom I for years knew only that he had held extensive property in the county of Suffolk. My father inherited little more than a good name & a good education from my grandfather, & at the age of 20 married my mother, who was the only inheritrix of a Dorset farmer. Alas, within a year of my birth, both of my parents succumbed to an inflammation of the lungs, & my great-uncle was persuaded by the Vicar & the Doctor, who had long known my mother's family, to pay for me to be cared for by one Mistress Malpas, a widow of the parish there in Dorset, until I was old enough to leave her house for good, and go away to school. As I grew older, it was clear to all those who were concerned in my welfare, among whom I numbered myself, that I would need to follow some profession, & since I had too little taste or scholarship for the Church, still less for the law, & all too many inches to be comfortable in the Navy, the Army was agreed by all parties to be my fate.

You ask, à propos of my account of our progress through France after Toulouse, whether I am content to have beaten my sword into a ploughshare, & I can truly say that I am. With the harvest in, I feel that for the first time in my life I have been able to make more of what Fate has offered me: to bring good out of ill. There were times in Spain when it seemed that we had only to set our eyes on a gentle prospect or a fruitful scene for it to be instantly despoiled. A commander would seek out a viewpoint, & study & record the scene, not with the delight of an artist such as you, but for strategy. Your pretty bridge arching over a river was blown to rubble to hinder the French, your flower-strewn field scythed to yield so many c^{wt} of fodder. Even a stand of fine trees crowning a hill, or a picturesque ravine, meant only cover for my men, or concealment for our enemy, & soon would be some man's grave.

It is a great blessing that I need no longer look at the beauties of the world before me thus, & if the price for such a blessing is a certain country tedium then I should reflect that I have, all in all, seen more of the world hitherto than most men do in a lifetime, & be content.

As winter drew closer, those families whose coverts, counting houses, or cure of souls kept them away from paved and lamplit streets, looked about them for amusement. More than one provident matron invited me to dine, and consulted me as to the merits of Paris and Brussels as a source of good society, a term which was understood by all to signify more particularly a source of husbands. If such ladies' intention was to draw my own gaze to the unattached affections of Miss Jocelyn, Miss Euphemia Jocelyn, Miss Sophy Stamford, and the other maidens, their efforts were superfluous. I was quite as conscious of these young ladies' attractions as they were of my acres, and I enjoyed their company, for the length of an evening at least.

On one such occasion, Miss Jocelyn came rustling over with a cup of tea for me almost as soon as I had entered her mother's drawing room with the other gentlemen. She had heard—such chatterboxes country gentlemen were!—that a fine collection of portraits adorned the walls of the dining room and library at Kersey. "I do love pictures of real people. My governess used to make us study all those silly history paintings. Who cares about Andromache, or Actaeon, or those tedious Romans?"

"Not most young ladies, I know," I replied. "Of course, you would be most welcome to see them, if your parents would care for the invitation. Or perhaps your brother might escort you one day? Though I fear you will find that in the flesh the pictures are a sad disappointment."

Miss Jocelyn took a little sip of her tea, and for a moment my gaze was transfixed by the soft red of her lips as they pressed and then parted about the white and gilt of her mother's best china. She looked up again, and caught my eye. A little blush crept into the round of her cheek. "Oh, I'm sure I would not be disappointed. I know nothing about art, but I do know what I like! Provided that I may recognize a friend, I care nothing for perspective or shading."

"I fear that you will see few friends on my walls, for all the originals are long dead."

"Oh, Major! You speak as if the Hall were haunted! But surely you have bespoken a portrait of yourself?" She tilted her chin down and looked up at me through her long, pale lashes. "I should like to think that I shall be seeing one friend, at least. Tell me you have commissioned a portrait!"

The notion was absurd. I laughed. "No, no! I have no thought of it."

"Mama!" Mrs. Jocelyn looked up from her tea tray. "Mama, the major says he will not have his portrait taken, to hang in the library at Kersey. Tell him he must do so, to mark his possession of the Hall."

"You must not allow my naughty girl to tease you, Major," said her mother, smiling, before resuming a low-voiced conversation with Mrs. Stamford.

"Oh, do have one taken, Major!" Her blue eyes were bright, her breast rose and fell. She put her hand on my arm. "Do!"

I was silent. If in my eyes she read my capitulation to her expressed desire, she was not altogether mistaken, although it was rather my own desire and the thought of her capitulation that had suddenly gripped me. To pull her down with me onto the rich Turkey carpet, wrench off her bodice, and bury my face in her round, white breasts, thrust aside her petticoats and take possession of her plump, pink flesh . . .

I got control of myself, for I knew—none better—that such passing passions were of no account to one who has known what I had known.

"Major?" she said, after a moment. Perhaps something had shown in my eyes after all. Then she continued, with a little laugh, "Forgive me, I have been neglecting our other guests, and must ask you to excuse me."

She turned away, and her quick, nervous glance towards her mama was answered by that lady's nod, and a small, satisfied smile.

I had no particular desire to gaze upon my own likeness, but I could not deny that with the bringing in of the harvest I had come to feel that it would not be mere vanity to claim a place among my predecessors at the Hall, by virtue of my yet modest success in promoting the prosperity of the land and the families that had tended it for so many centuries. So it was that I did after all go in search of a portrait painter in Norwich, and took considerable trouble to find out a good one. Miss Jocelyn might avow a lack of interest in perspective and shading, but despite knowing that there was small possibility of her ever seeing it, not for the world would I commission a work that would disgrace my own judgment of such matters in Miss Durward's critical eyes.

I was not, I realized, immune to desiring these teasing young ladies, or to indulging their interest in me to the extent of an expensive commission. But I could not bring myself to offer them my lineage or my acres in return, and my desire must therefore go unsatisfied.

But why could I not bring myself to that point? It was a question that puzzled me a good deal. Such an exchange was a usual one among our society. And had I not, only a few weeks since, been prepared to journey into Lancashire to seek a companion for my days and guardian of my sleep in just such an exchange? Time and again, as I got into bed at night, I wondered if it was simply that I shrank from the knowledge that yet another of the fair sex might find that the regeneration of my estate—which was the talk of the county—could not reconcile her to the unregenerate, ill health of my damaged person. To be the object of such disgust as even so kind a lady as Mrs. Greenshaw could not overcome, and to suffer it not once, but every night until death . . . No, I would not willingly expose myself to that.

But as the darkness settled about me I knew that it was not really this unwillingness that held me back, but something much stronger: the perpetual, ardent sorrow and painful joy that lay at the heart of my existence. Such companionship as I might now seek, such bodily desire as I might satisfy, could only betray my heart, because there I held the untarnished memory of a happiness quite short, and a love quite perfect.

I propped my crutch nearby, before blowing out my candle. So real was the feeling in my missing limb as I slept, sometimes so vivid my dream of my old happiness, of walking and running with my body whole again, of Spain, that it was only my hand knocking against my crutch as I arose in the morning that had on occasions prevented me trying to stand and walk on thin air before I woke fully again to my loss. Other nights that I passed in my great feather bed, with flowers and fruits worked on Chinese silk drawn between me and the dark, were not as benignly dream-filled as this, or as they had been under the Spanish sky, which once lay above my head like velvet stitched with stars as big as mirrors. But what man of my years, I told myself, has not some part of his history that troubles him a little when his guard is asleep, and darkness covers the approach of his old enemy?

But of this I did not, of course, write to Miss Durward. I did not even tell her of the portrait, still less the origin of my decision to commission it. What she asked for, and what I wrote of, were details of uniforms, of troop dispositions and scenery, of Corunna, and of the form and significance of the lines of Torres Vedras. She sent me a sketch of the Ninety-fifth at Quatre Bras, for me to amend as I saw fit, and asked for incidents of military life too.

Much as I should like to spend half a day in answering
your last in full, in the matter of Corunna I must rather refer

you to some of the published accounts, for I was not there. My memories of the year '8 are of the horrors of the Light Division's ragged retreat to Vigo—dragging ourselves as bait to draw the French after us through ice & snow—& of our grief at hearing of the death at Corunna of the noble Sir John Moore, founding father & genius of our Regt. Such memories can never be erased . . . .

You must know that it was the justifiable boast of the 95th that we were invariably the first in the field & the last out of it, & so, also it seemed invariably, we outstript the sometimes lackadaisical efforts of our Commissary to keep us supplied with food & shelter. Our thus necessary skill at obtaining supplies by less orthodox means soon also became justifiably famous— & envied—among the rest of the Peninsular Army. The 2 young men that we encountered, one hungry evening in March of the year '12, were well dressed in the colourful fashion of the younger bravos of that country, and they were carrying two plump and protesting fowls. With apologies for my draughtsmanship, but in the confidence that yours will more than make up for my deficiency, I have sketched them on the back of this sheet.

I am sorry that the observations of her acquaintances have spoilt your mother's pleasure in your birthday gift to her. I should have thought that her fondness for Tom—& the pleasure that anyone knowing him must take in what must be a most delicate & loving portrait as nature made him—would take precedence over the views of those in whom the dictates of propriety overcome the impulses of human affection. But perhaps one should make allowances for a generation whose opinions were formed without the assistance of a rational, natural education.

With less work out of doors for me, and longer evenings, the hours I expended on estate business grew in length and frequency, and so did my correspondence with Miss Durward, to the point where I looked for the arrival of the letters each day with an eagerness that I had never known, neither at school, nor even in the Regiment.

One gray December day I rode into the village to call on the rector. Old Dora ambled along the rutted lane on a loose rein, and the view between her ears was dreary enough for me to have withdrawn my attention from my road. Suddenly she shied. Her quarters dropped sideways, and her silver-threaded mane twisted before me, flicking the reins from my hands. From under her very hoofs, it seemed, a child ran sobbing into a cottage. "Mama! Mama! I was lost."

"I do trust she's not hurt!" I called into the dark of the doorway as I dismounted.

"No, sir!" said the child's mother, emerging to bob a curtsy. "There, you bad girl! Giving Squire a fright, running out like that. You do it again, and Boney'll get you!"

I thought of the sometime emperor, whom I knew to be bored and unrepentant in his distant, tropical prison, appearing from the mists in our peaceful woods and fields, made flesh from the darkness that lies everywhere, latent, malign. When at last I remounted and looked back to wave farewell, the mother and child, holding to each other, appeared to me suddenly to have become one.

The cause of my meeting with the rector was some repairs to the church, which must be put in hand before the winter rains began in earnest. The sexton, Bonnet, shook his head and spoke of loose guttering and split downpipes, while the rector hauled himself—rheumatic but game—up a ladder to look sorrowfully at two ancient figures, St. Luke and St. John, standing in their niches at each side of the porch, and stained black and green by the rain that spilt over them. Their hands were cut off at the wrists, and their faces were blank and flat, as if waiting for some supernatural hand to coax their likeness again from under the water.

"Surely the water hasn't done all that damage?" I said.

"No, no," said old Bonnet. "That were done in the war, o' course, like so much hereabouts, with that siege o' Colchester an' all."

"The war? Oh, you mean the Great Rebellion."

"Aye. That were as bad as it was in France a few years back, so they say."

The rector sighed as he clambered down. "Alas, yes. To think that perhaps again . . . And they were peculiarly zealous here in East Anglia. Well, Bonnet, I think we have seen all we need. Will you let me know what the mason says?" Bonnet touched his forelock and began to fold up his ladder. "Now, Fairhurst, a drop of something back at the rectory, on this nasty cold day?"

I accepted, and as we walked through the wicket gate, he went on, "The Puritans had so little respect for the art of our forebears."

"Or for the saints themselves."

"I find it easier to forgive their hatred of graven images than their destruction of our common history. Besides, one might have thought that Puritans would care for the Evangelists, whatever they might do to what they would call the Popish trappings within. Oh, Mrs. Marsh, I've brought the major back for some wine."

"But I have seen in Spain the power that such images—even Papist images—can have over people's hearts," I said, putting down my stick and shrugging off my greatcoat. "And how they are missed in France. People seek solace from them as well as hope." I did not add how painfully I had been shown the strength of that solace, by those few days at Bera: such memories had too great a place in my own heart to need expression.

"Of course, for simple people, and the illiterate, that is understandable. I have had some correspondence with one of my colleagues near Bristol, about his twelfth-century tympanum; he's most knowledgeable, a veritable antiquary. But we should all seek hope and solace and everything else from the Lord, through Jesus Christ. Now, as one who has drunk it in its native land, tell me what you think of this sherry."

I was easily persuaded to stay for dinner, and Mrs. Marsh—my own Mrs. Prescott's sister-in-law—bustled to and fro with the dishes while the rector lit the lamps; we were nearing midwinter, and it was past four o'clock.

We spoke a good deal of local matters, for one of the banks had stopped payment in the last few months and it was certain that others would join it.

"And if the price of corn after so bad a harvest rises any higher we shall have trouble on our hands," said the rector. "It needs only a few men with ranting talk of reform to turn hunger into radicalism."

"I have seen it."

"Indeed . . . Which reminds me, my dear Fairhurst. I didn't like to enquire . . . in short, on the matter of which we spoke in the spring . . ."

I hastened to relieve his embarrassment, and said that Mrs. Greenshaw and I had agreed that we would not suit.

"But I hope that you are not giving up the notion altogether," he said, reaching for the decanter. "I've seen you following hounds— what woman could ask for more? Not necessarily some romantical girl, mark you, but a good-looking, sensible woman who wishes to establish herself comfortably."

I sighed, for I could not disagree. The rector was not to know that to one who has tasted nectar, the plain water that he offered me was bitter cold. He leaned forward to top up my glass of port and then his own. "I know, I know. Pink cheeks and bright eyes, eh? But seriously, are you being practical? You have had a year as a bachelor at the Hall. Companionship is important. I know we also spoke of the value of a natural outlet for your passions, to ease the pressure of the past on your mind. But that is something that so often comes with time, and fondness."

I was silent. His arguments were good and familiar ones. Perhaps it was the drab weather that made them seem more dreary than ever.

It was as well that my wise old Dora knew every stone and pothole of the road home, however dark the night, for the solace I had sought, even to the bottom of the rector's decanter, I had not found.

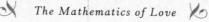

AFTER MY BATH I slept. I woke all curled up and shivering and it was almost comforting to see the dusty paint and straight lines of the walls and beds. There couldn't be anything here like in the dream, creeping along, cold and dank and growing in the dark. It was only in the dream that it was dark and the door was locked.

I rolled onto my back. The pearls of bathwater had dried on me, and it was incredibly quiet. It wasn't evening quite—I hadn't slept that long—but the patches of sunlight on the floor had stretched and yellowed like a favorite old T-shirt spread on the washing line, and the light was filling the air so that it was like opening your eyes under golden water. Then downstairs I heard a crash and a voice shouting, then another crash. I felt suddenly cold and bare, like when the last of the bathwater goes, making that scraping noise in its hurry to get away, and all that's left is the sides of the empty bath, just breathing the warm ghost of what's gone.

The numbers on the clock radio flipped. Six. I wondered if tea had a time it happened, since lunch obviously didn't, not really. And I wondered about the crash and the voice shouting. There was stuff going on. You can't live in as many different places as I have without knowing something about that kind of thing. I put the radio on loud while I got dressed in a clean T-shirt and jeans, because I needed at least to hear that other people were out there.

The old lino under my feet felt smooth, clean, cool but not cold. I never go barefoot at home—whichever home we're talking about—because our floors are always dirty. There's cigarette ash and spilt beer, and gravel from those oily puddles that never go from outside where the tarmac's broken, and washing powder because no one noticed the box was leaking when one of us took it from the kitchen to wash knickers in the bathroom because the kitchen sink's full of yesterday's supper and the new re-con washing machine wasn't re-, just a con, and it broke down again and the shop that whichever boyfriend got it from's gone bust. I wondered where the washing machine was here because with this weather you got through tons of clothes, unless you didn't mind everyone thinking you'd got BO.

And that made me think suddenly how really weird it was, being here. I'd lived in a lot of places but never anywhere nearly so big. It was less crappy too. No lifts stinking of piss, no one fucking round the back of the garages or dealing drugs in the hallways, no dog shit on the stairs, no Jimi Hendrix cracking the walls—I mean, Jimi Hendrix is cool, but not at three in the morning when I've only just got to sleep because Mum's been sobbing on my shoulder since she came in at midnight, telling me not to grow up because life's a bitch and then you die.

There wasn't any of that, but still the Hall was weird. Once, there must have been a rich family, and all those servants they had, working away in the basement and the attics and up and down the back stairs, scuttling and scrabbling just beyond where you could see them. Who had they been, all those vanished people? Now there was just space. It was like the places were waiting, like the space itself was standing in the rooms, breathing the air, walking up the stairs. The space that was the people who weren't quite here, but so nearly might be if you just listened, so nearly that only the thinnest dust had had time to settle.

I walked along the corridor barefoot and quiet. Belle was coming up the stairs towards me, very slowly, red in the face and pulling herself up the banisters.

She stopped at the top. "Oh," she said, puffing, "hello. You don't look like your mother."

Her breath smelled strong—gin, I thought. "No, I know." I meant to go on quite casual-sounding, only it came out too loud: "I look like my father."

"She wouldn't stay, you know. It wasn't that I told her to go. I'm her mother, I would have let her stay. I know what it's like to be . . . Of course I wouldn't do that. I'm not that kind of mother. Even if she'd told us she'd gone and got herself into trouble. Only of course she didn't. What's she said to you?"

"Nothing," I said, not quite wanting to go downstairs even though I didn't want her to be saying this sort of thing. It was true too: Mum hadn't said anything. Nothing about it, about my father, about what happened. His name wasn't even on my birth certificate. I saw that when Mum did the passport applications. Anna Jocelyn Ware— "Anna" I don't mind, but she never said what made her choose "Jocelyn." It's not even a proper girl's name, more like a surname. Father: unknown. Mother: Nancy Annabelle Ware, born Holman, unmarried. Not that I wanted to know. That kind of hope's just asking for grief. I've always known it's only in the movies that that kind of stuff comes out wonderful. I said again, "She hasn't told me anything."

"I expect not." She straightened up and peered at me. She was definitely a bit drunk. "It doesn't matter anyway, does it? Ray and I moved away from Bury St. Edmunds, and . . . and later he came back to Suffolk and bought the business here, and I went to . . . he made a fresh start, and now I can too. It's not over, just because the school's closed." The hand that wasn't holding on to the banister sort of half stretched out towards me. "Now we can . . . we can start afresh, with you too. We don't need Nancy to be here, do we? We can make a family on our own. Just us. You'd like that, wouldn't you?"

I wanted to be able to say yes so much that it hurt in my throat, even though she was old and a bit drunk and didn't know when my birthday was. I wanted to reach her, to find her; she was my grandmother. I wanted her to find me. My hand even let go of the banister rail.

But the ache was sour because I didn't see how you could be a family with someone you'd never known.

In the end I muttered, "I must go," and went down a couple of steps and, when she didn't say anything, on down the rest. I heard her stumping up the stairs that went up from my floor to where they lived.

The stairs were lino too, with those thick edges on the steps that are supposed to stop you slipping but actually just catch at your shoes. But I was safe and silent in my new bare feet. I could go anywhere.

There were still desks and chairs and beds and blackboards and a couple of big bins overflowing with crumpled paper and torn books. But they all looked like they didn't belong, like the rooms just let them be there, put up with them, like they did the grubby gray paint and the fire exits and the numbers on the doors. The children had gone, and it would all go soon enough, because things always do. Only the space stays, waiting for the next thing.

In the kitchen Uncle Ray was stirring ravioli in a saucepan. The little boy Cecil lay on his front, digging round the edges of a hole in the lino. Deep down in the hole was a scrap of wood with eyes and a mouth drawn on it.

Uncle Ray looked up as I came in. "Hello, Anna. All sorted out? Hang on a minute." He put the saucepan on the table above Cecil's head. "There you are, Ciss—mind, it's hot."

Cecil got up and peered into the pan. He had a pointy sort of face with a big, bumpy forehead and a scrape on one cheek. Then he took the wooden spoon and started to poke ravioli into his mouth with the tip, which was all that would fit. It made him look kind of reluctant to eat, but his jaws munched as if he was starving.

"That's him done," said Uncle Ray. "You all right to help yourself?" He waved a hand towards a door. "There's plenty in the larder."

There was plenty, if you like tinned new potatoes or custard powder or gallon bottles of vegetable oil. I don't, but after a bit of ferreting there and in the fridge I found a smallish tin of corned beef and some hard, sour tomatoes, which together looked sort of like supper once I'd got them sliced on a plate. I'm not much good at fancier cooking than that, because though Mum can do a mean roast dinner when she wants to, there's only one kind of when she wants to. Then she won't let me in the kitchen because I'm in her way, and anyway I'm supposed to be sitting prettily next to the new boyfriend and impressing him with my charm and my being about to leave home and not get in *his* way.

"Thinking about your staying here, I take it you're happy to be independent," said Uncle Ray. In between washing up Cecil's pan he was drinking whiskey but the empty bottle in the dustbin was gin, I saw when I threw away the corned beef tin. Cecil'd finished his food and gone back under the table. Now he was pushing the dust back into the hole, on top of the little wooden figure. "I—we love having you here. I wish I could show you a bit of the countryside, but there's so much to do here still. Maybe in a few weeks." He smiled, a little bit crookedly. "I—I'm afraid I've rather had to let things slide. Besides, you won't want to be hanging around with oldies like us. And Belle gets tired easily."

There wasn't a polite answer to that. "I can't sign on till my birthday," I said. The corned beef was cold and greasy. "But I can get a job."

"Not as easy round here as in London. And I don't know how you'd get there. Of course, I'm happy to give you a lift whenever I can. But we lost our railway to Beeching, and there's only one bus a week, on market day. I'm afraid you'll find you're in the back of beyond, really—no mains drainage or gas, and the electricity goes off sometimes too."

I wasn't going to get put off that easily. "Then I'll just have to walk."

"Well, why don't you have a break first? You've been doing exams, haven't you?"

"Didn't bother, mostly."

"Even so, I'm sure you deserve a rest. If you're short of cash I can let you have some." He reached into his back pocket and brought out a worn, expensive-looking wallet. "Here, have five pounds. That keep you going for a bit?"

It ought to have been nice. I wanted so much for it to be kind of him. I suppose it was, really. But it felt too like Mum giving me pennies for sweets to stop me crying when I was little, or Dave or one of the others giving me a pound to go to the flicks and get out of the way. Last time that happened, Tanya'd been there, and since we couldn't stay in my room painting each other's nails and listening to T. Rex and talking about sex, we'd put makeup on and gone and got drunk in a pub and tried to find something better than Abba on the jukebox and talked about sex. And narrowly missed having it too, with two boys who'd been chatting us up. But it's stupid to go for sex like that—I've done it often enough to learn that much. It's too easy for him to pull out and go without even pretending to check whether it was good for you too. Besides, if you're standing up they'll try and persuade you you can't get pregnant that way, really you can't, when you know it's just because they don't want to use a Durex. And Tanya won't do it in cars, even if those boys had had one. She says the only thing worse than *Playboy* under his bed is *Auto Express* under your bum.

Uncle Ray was still holding out the fiver, so I shut my mind up and took it. "Thanks, Uncle Ray. I'll pay you back as soon as I can."

He patted my shoulder. "No need. Call it pocket money. And how about dropping the 'Uncle'? Not so formal, eh?" He went towards the door. "Well, if you've got everything, I ought to go and check on Belle. She's a bit under the weather."

I said, "Yes, I could tell," without thinking.

He stopped, and then said slowly, "I know you weren't expecting her to be here. I—well, it was unexpected that she had to . . . . But she's so pleased to have you here. She hasn't had an easy life, you know. When she was evacuated—the war. The way—the way they were treated. And sometimes . . . But she's very pleased, you must believe that. As I am. Which reminds me. A van will be coming tomorrow to collect the school equipment, the desks and beds and so on. Not yours, of course. And if there's anything else you'd like, just say the word—a table or whatever. Do say the word." He smiled. His teeth were the same yellowy color as his hair. "I'm delighted to have you here, you know. I—we do want you to be happy, now that we've found you."

I just nodded because I suddenly thought I might start to cry, and he went out and I stuffed the fiver in my jeans pocket and then washed up my plate and glass. Then I went upstairs to get my sandals and went out into the hot twilight.

My dear Miss Durward,

I fear that the description of life in a peacetime army will provide you with few subjects to uplift, or edify, or even amuse your audience, unless they have a taste for strange tales of daring brass polishing & the exotic delights of reviewing fodder contracts. But I like to think of you reading my small tales aloud in the evening & still more to think of your pinning them above your desk as you describe, the better to transform my mere words into your pictures.

We who best knew the horrors & deprivations of War were yet in some sense dismayed on our return to England at the Peace that was concluded in April of the year '14, by the experience of their cessation. The 95th returned to England & was stationed at Dover. Furlough that I was granted I took at the homes of Peninsular friends, & if we bored their newly wedded wives with our talk of battles & strategies, we always took care, unless the evening were far advanced, to tell tales no less true (although no truer) but better suited to a lady's ears. Other tales, you may imagine, were reserved until after the ladies had retired, for an army is made of men, & men are but flesh & blood. Indeed, the risk to their own flesh which they daily endure makes soldiers perhaps still more conscious than civilians of their natural desires & gives a certain wild urgency to their fulfilment, particularly in the dull life of a garrison town such as Dover.

Otherwise, the time passed pleasantly, but the months in

England, after 7 yrs. in Spain, taught me 2 things. Firstly, that peace is a pearl without price, that men toss away at their peril, & secondly, that I could not endure it.

My constitution, like that of so many of my fellows & our men, is subject to bouts of Walcheren fever, contracted in the ill-fated campaign to that island of the year '9. The damp air & chilly summers of England made the sickness more insupportable than I had found it in Spain. Besides, when there were any number of us gathered together, we were always conscious of those who would have been with us, but that we had left them under the earth in Spain.

It was as if the English fogs had entered my mind. I could not clasp a friend's hand & rejoice at his good health without the knowledge that my joy had been the greater when both our healths had been in danger. I could not lie in a green English meadow, smelling the sun-warmed honeysuckle in the hedgerows, without recalling the dusty scrub of rosemary & oleander, the heat that blisters the skin, the mountains & rivers & snows of my other life. It was as if in Spain danger & the constant presence of death had sharpened my senses & my sensibilities, & in England I could no longer see or feel with the same urgency, the same passion & delight to which, though for grievous reasons, I had been long accustomed.

You may imagine, then, with what mixed emotions I received the news of Buonaparte's escape from the island of Elba. At Dover Barracks suddenly all was bustle & preparation. But the tale of the last act of the war against Buonaparte & my small part in it must await another day, since I shall be taking this letter into Bury St. Edmunds myself to catch the Mail, & to hurry over those cobbled lanes is to court disaster. As a rifleman I was trained never to expose myself or my men to unnecessary danger &, besides, there is nothing like the loss of one leg to make a man cherish the health of the other.

Christmas and New Year at Kersey were enlivened by what I had discovered were customary festivities—about which I had cross-questioned Stebbing in order to omit nothing that my tenants and neighbors expected—and only a little depressed by relentless rain. Spending more of my days indoors as I was forced to, I came to know my household better and they me, so that even the kitchen maid was not too dismayed by a friendly greeting to answer me with reasonable composure, unalloyed by either shyness or fear. Then there was a little lad whom I had sometimes seen in the hayloft, or even flitting like a shadow round a corner within the house on quiet afternoons when no one was about. I did not enquire as to his origins, lest Stebbing feel obliged to choose between lying to his master and betraying some poor girl's shame, and when I did not see the boy at the dinner I held for my tenants and household on St. Stephen's Day, I knew my reticence had been prudent. The other children made enough noise for twice their number, though frequently scolded for it by their parents with as much affection, I was interested to observe, as admonishment, but I never saw the lad in company.

It did not snow a great deal, but the weather continued cold and wet enough to make outdoor pursuits, barring shooting and hunting, far less appealing than they had been in the smoky frosts of November. But my coverts were in good order by now, and the local masters for the most part quite capable of making the best of our gentle, open country, so that it was with a clear conscience that I invited a couple of Peninsular friends down for some sport, a week or so before the end of January.

"So, none of those Spanish beauties lured you into matrimony when you went back to San Sebastian after the war?" said Welford, stirring the punch and sniffing it with an expert nose, before adding the brandy.

"Not a one." I squeezed the lemon that he handed me into the wine. "Somehow, they don't look so well without Soult snapping at our heels."

"Well, I don't blame you for loving and leaving them," said Buckley, from where he was stretched out on the sofa.

We had been out all day, tramping the woods to shoot over dogs, with just a couple of loaders. We had done no more on coming in than shed our muddied coats and boots before sitting down to a late dinner, and now were tired with the pleasant weariness of well-used muscles and a well-filled game bag. Two of the dogs and Titus, my spaniel, lay by the fire with much the same expression on their faces as Buckley's bore.

He went on. "I wouldn't marry, even if I could afford it. It's not as if you can't find a woman when you need one. Who wants to come back to a drawing room full of gossiping females when one can have an evening like this? Which reminds me, did you hear that Fraser's been caught? Her father insisted, so I heard—don't ask who told me—and threatened to go to his colonel. Rather him than me."

"Hear, hear," said Welford. "Though she's not a bad looker. Surely you agree, Fairhurst, about being caught, I mean?" He stirred the punch bowl gently again so that the wine lapped up the inside of the silver like a molten jewel. "Though I must say, I've never had you down as a lifelong bachelor. Besides, this is a big place for one man. Is that poker ready?"

"Yes, it's hot enough." I picked it up from where it had been heating for some time among the coals. The tip was almost white, the rest dull orange. I steadied the bowl with the other hand, and thrust in the poker. It hit the liquid with a crack, and went on crackling with the rush of heat that surged and trembled between my hands; the scent of wine, cloves, lemon, and cinnamon bark rolled up as strongly as if I had plunged my face into the red depths.

When it was over I saw my friends looking at me curiously.

This moment was the closest I had ever stood to telling anyone of my love, but even as the memories awoke, as new and sharp and sweet as the wine, my friends' tone debarred me from putting words to them. Were I to describe the facts, they would sound little different from a hundred other such tales over which we had all chaffed our fellows, and the pain and risk of conveying even a small part of the true nature of those days at Bera, and still later those months at San Sebastian, was more than I could possibly contemplate.

The punch was still steaming. I dipped in the ladle and filled each cup in turn. We drank to the king, and the regiment, and then to absent friends.

There was an accustomed silence, while all our memories were busy. Then Welford dipped us each yet another cupful and raised it first to the portrait that I had, with some reluctance, hung above the fire, and then to me. "And a toast to you, Fairhurst, now you've come into port at last. Good health, long life and happiness to the new squire of Kersey. I don't know a man who deserves it more."

I swallowed, clapped each of my friends on the shoulder, and after a moment was able to ask Buckley for the news from London.

On the morrow we were called early, as I had ordered, for the meet was at ten at Cavendish. We set out as the sun rose—it was the first day for weeks that there were no rain clouds to cover it—and we rode three abreast, with my grooms bringing up the rear on our spare mounts.

"You still have Dora, then?" said Buckley. "Surely she's too old to give you much of a ride."

Into my silence, Welford said, "Youth's no substitute for cleverness in a horse, I always say, nor strength for wisdom."

I patted Dora's neck. "I don't take her out if it promises to be a hard day. She'd be no use to me in the shires, but she does well enough for what we have hereabouts."

At the meet I introduced them to the members of the hunt, the few ladies that chose to brave the frost and the disapproval of their more straitlaced neighbors, and a couple of the local farmers. Before the horses had time to get cold the master gave the nod. The whippers-in positioned themselves, and we started down the lane at a jog-trot.

Hounds found quickly. The going was heavy, but the scent rose breast high on the gilt mist, and hounds and horses alike were so fresh and eager that in the first burst I kept back, for even phlegmatic old Dora was inclined to be carried away with the herd on such occasions. As Welford knew, I could not control even her so well as in the old days, with only one and a half legs to do it. We jumped and galloped and scrambled through hedges in our turn, Buckley ahead and Welford behind, our narrowed eyes and sweating bodies as alert as on the battlefield, oblivious to twigs, thorns, or mud. Once we had kept watch for sharpshooters or ambush; now our necks were in danger, perhaps greater danger, from an overhanging branch, a stone lurking in the grass, or a rabbit hole.

The fox had been sighted, and at the view halloo we started again over the rain-sodden ground, hounds and men full out, down a ditch and up, each horse's hindquarters pushing to get out.

Snap. I heard it go, and Dora fell even as I dragged my leg free of the stirrup and leapt clear. The back of the hunt thundered past, and we were fortunate not to be trampled. Dora rolled and lay still, then staggered to her feet, her off-hind crooked to the side. She tried a step, and fell again onto her fore, whimpering. When I had got to my feet and gone to her I could see the bloodied, jagged end of her thigh bone where it stuck out from the skin.

Welford had pulled up and turned back, but it hardly needed speech between us to agree that there was nothing to be done. We looked about, and caught sight of a farmhouse amid the trees.

"I'll go," said Welford, remounting.

"Gosling, I think their name is," I called after him, and he raised a hand in acknowledgment as he rode off.

I unbuckled Dora's girth and she heaved herself a little so that I could get it out from under her belly and put the saddle aside. Then I settled myself on the ground by her head, for she had stopped struggling and was now just looking at me, her dark eye blinking occasionally. I stroked her head, pulling her soft, tough ears through my hand as I used to on the horse lines in Spain or in her loose box at Kersey. It was an Austrian captain that I took prisoner at Vittoria who gave her to me; a horse is the only prize of war that an officer may legitimately keep, and he told me in bad French that she was Irish bred, a five-year-old, and that he loved her dearly. Sitting in the Suffolk mud, I remembered Dora plodding the dusty roads of Estremadura and slipping on hard-trampled snow at my shoulder as we gasped in the thin air of the Pyrenean passes. Sweetest of all was my memory of her standing guard outside the barn at Bera, blowing gently into the green grass like a blessing on our happiness. When I went to Brussels I sold her to a friend and, without a moment's hesitation, bought her back when I came to Kersey: she remembered me, as horses will, and neighed like a trumpeter when I took her bridle. She was a bay, paler than most, with a lustrous black mane arched like an Argive's crest. Now, her docked tail beat restlessly while her flank rose and fell, and the warm velvet of her muzzle was soft and anxious in my hand. If she were a man, I thought, it would have been possible to mend her leg or even replace it, as mine had been.

When Welford came back with an ancient flintlock I resolved to do it myself, for I was sure that she knew what we were about, and I did not wish her to leave this world alone. I loaded the gun and put the muzzle between her eyes, at which she looked tired—almost, I fancied, puzzled. I pulled the trigger, but it jammed, and I withdrew the gun, trying every rifleman's trick I knew as she started to shake her head and push up onto her forelegs again, so that Welford had to catch at her bridle and try to quiet her. Finally I got the wretched flint-lock free, but she would not hold her head still, and when I fired I made a mess of it. Still she squealed and shook, until I reloaded and shot again, and her body trembled all over and finally lay still.

MY DECISION WAS not hastily made: I told myself for many weeks that I could not abandon Kersey on a whim bred of the death of my old horse. I had lost more than one mount in action, and I could not allow a small though natural sorrow to endanger the well-being of my land and people. Still, my spirits were weighed down with a wintry melancholy that even the sight of the first aconites, breaking through sodden earth and long-dead leaves, could not dispel.

Time and again, as I sat shivering with fever by the fire, or gazed over barren fields or down muddy lanes, or saw the same dull, good-natured faces sitting about some dinner table, or ranked in church with their scrubbed and fidgeting children about them, my memories of Spain came before my mind. It was not the Spain of dusty olive groves that I saw, where bare mountains rear up in air that trembles with the weight of its own heat, nor the Spain of black monks and gold-encrusted toreadors and ladies tossing flowers. No, it was not Wellington's Spain at all. Rather I thought of the small, comfortable smells and noises of my life in San Sebastian after the war: the tarry, salty scent of ships and wharves, the chatter of the girls as they washed and dressed and compared the night's takings, the cry of a water carrier in the street, a hundred church bells tolling high and low for the mass, a whining beggar, the squawk of seagulls and the flap of clean, wet washing in the sea wind. But I would not go back to San Sebastian. That time was past, and besides, only the simplest of its recollected sounds and smells were innocent: the place as a whole carried for me all the pain that I would not allow my memories of Bera to bear.

No, I would not go back to Spain. But I could seek out those same comfortable things elsewhere: the faces of travelers; printshops, jewelers and coffeehouses; hawkers crying ribbons and ballads and hot pies; constables and lamplighters; the clatter of foreign tongues; the rattle of coaches on paved streets; the converse with men who knew the world and women who did not shrink from it. These things I longed for, I realized slowly, as spring crept over my acres, as a banished man longs for the food of his homeland, and even the welfare of that land, which I must now call home, could not weigh more heavily than my yearning for that former life.

When I wrote to Miss Durward, to apprise her of my intention, the memory of her quietly enquiring gaze prompted me to a fuller explanation of my decision than I had made to any other.

My dear Miss Durward,

    I was most grateful to receive your good wishes for my departure. Please also pass on my thanks to your family, for I know that I shall travel easily with such kind farewells to speed me. As you suggest, it has been no simple matter to leave my affairs here in such a way as to be certain that neither my tenants nor my land will suffer. Were it not for the trustworthiness of my bailiff & upper servants, & the goodwill of the rector & my neighbours, I would not feel able to leave at all. However, I am most fortunate in this respect, my determination is fixed, & I depart for Brussels on the 4th day of May.

    My choice of Brussels as a destination is founded neither on mere caprice nor, I can assure you, on the desire for the soi-disant good society that I recall discussing in a previous instalment of this correspondence. You write of how the riot which we both witnessed has rendered you less tolerant of the society in which you live. Perhaps you feel, as I do now, that such lives—though good lives by most reckoning, & not without advantage for the nation's wealth, nor philanthropy for its poor—are founded in some way on brutality and lies. I cannot deny that that day & its aftermath have some part in my decision to leave England. As for my destination, perhaps I can best explain it by setting down some of the circumstances of my last sojourn there. Besides, as an afterword to our discussion of the peacetime life of the military, I ought in any case to describe a few of my experiences of a civilian existence.

    When I had recovered sufficiently from the injuries I had sustained at Waterloo to travel back to England, I soon realized that if I had found the life of a serving officer in peacetime

*irksome, my situation now was insupportable. In wartime,
injuries such as mine, or worse, were commonplace, &
considered no bar to continuing to serve His Majesty. But the
army in peacetime had little need of our services, & paid us
correspondingly less, & so like others who had left much of their
health & strength on foreign soil, & received only half-pay in
return, I sold my commission, found good situations for my groom
and batman, & took lodgings in London. Many of my fellows
were in the same case & we would often gather to drink &
exchange tales. But such had been the slaughter at Waterloo
that the ranks of my friends were sensibly diminished.*

*The news that our Regt., in unique recognition of our part in
the Peninsular War & the battles of Quatre Bras & Waterloo,
was to be created a corps in its own right as the Rifle Brigade,
was glorious indeed. (The day happened also to be my birthday,
which is an occasion that I am wont to mark with some relish,
since I never knew it until, the Army clerks demanding to know
the date before I might be gazetted, I had occasion to write to the
incumbent of the parish of my baptism.) Our celebration was loud
& long. Nonetheless, I cannot attribute my feelings the next day
only to the after-effects of wine. I was now 27 y*rs*. of age, & given
proper care, my injuries were not such as to affect materially my
chances of reaching 3-score years & 10. I sat in a threadbare
civilian coat & pondered my future by the meagre fire which was
all that my landlady thought necessary for an ex-officer who had
lost his leg & gained the fever in preserving her liberties.*

*My melancholy did not long survive a change of lodging. My
new home was kept by a middle-aged Belgian émigrée, Mme. du
Boeuf, who well knew how to make an old soldier comfortable, &
shortly did more. Upon my describing how I had found that my
willingness to recount tales of war to a country house full of ladies
& gentlemen often resulted in other invitations elsewhere, she
exclaimed. Her brother-in-law, it seemed, was the proprietor of a*

prosperous coaching inn on the S. W. outskirts of Brussels, & was frequently asked by well-to-do travellers if he knew of someone who could escort them on a tour of the battlefield of Waterloo & further abroad to other important sites of that campaign. If I were interested in performing such a service for ces hommes gentils, Mme. was sure that an arrangement mutually agreeable could be made with her brother-in-law at his inn, L'Arc-en-ciel.

I was interested, & matters were speedily concluded. I found Mme. Planchon to be as hospitable as her sister, & Planchon to be an honest-dealing, business-like fellow who worked hard & expected others to do likewise. I was nothing loath, & was soon escorting ladies in sandals & delicate muslins over the ditches that had so lately been a charnel house of the dead & dying. I made a good story too of my own injury, as evidence that, although the British Army is without doubt the greatest in the world, it would be a mistake to attribute all casualties to heroism.

I was not the only retired officer to be seen escorting fashionable parties, but the excellence of the hospitality of L'Arc-en-ciel &, I flatter myself, my own diligence in combing the diaries & memoirs of the campaign that were then beginning to be issued, & turning such records into entertainment, rendered my efforts some of the best-liked & most recommended.

I should say that of course a good many of those who engaged my services had greater & more woeful reasons for walking the slaughterous ground where their loved ones' final hours had been spent. All who made such a pilgrimage took comfort, from the peace & prosperity all about them, in learning that their own bereavement had not been in vain. Then we would repair to the nearest inn at which I knew good food & lodging could be found. On one occasion I earned the gratitude of a fond mother thus: hearing her offspring's refusal to be taken to the barber's for a sorely needed haircut, I tossed him up onto my shoulder, and told him how C^{pl}. Hanley, on returning to camp with 27 captive

French dragoons, was fired on by his own comrades, as the
approach of so many horses <u>with long tails</u> could only mean an
attack by the French. Would he like to risk the same fate, or
rather be restored to proper Englishness?

It was the recommendation of this lady that took me to
Portugal & then into Spain at the behest of 2 scholarly
gentlemen. Then for a few years I made my home in San
Sebastian, a prosperous & ancient port that I knew to be a
frequent landfall for such travellers as might engage my services,
& it was while I was there that I received the news of my cousin's
death at Kersey & my inheritance.

I have indulged myself with a long epistle, knowing that,
despite the excellence of our modern mails across a pacified
Europe, it is likely that our exchange of letters will be somewhat
less immediate. It must be a great joy & relief to you all to have
Mrs. Greenshaw restored to full health & to have passed the
anniversary of her bereavement without any more distress than
may be considered natural. Please feel free to communicate my
good wishes to her in whatever terms you think suitable.

THE BIG DOUBLE front doors in the hall were open a crack. The back
of the house was where I'd gone in and out, where I'd arrived. That
felt like days ago, I thought suddenly, not just this morning. It was like
the quiet and the emptiness were so thick that even time went slower
in the country. I thought that even in the biggest, grayest housing estate I'd ever lived on it hadn't felt like this: there'd always been people
somewhere. There was Ray, but I'd heard him go upstairs with Belle.

I pulled at the double doors and they opened slowly towards me,
as if they were pressing against the emptiness of the house. Outside
was a porch with moth-eaten-looking pillars and flat round steps and
a drive curling round a circle of grass covered with weeds and making
for the trees. Beyond them I could just hear the cars flashing past on

the dual carriageway where it sliced across the old, grand entrance like something in another world. To the left the grass was marked out for a football pitch, nearly bare where the goals and the center were, with short fuzz and lots of straggly bits and naked earth in between, like the way blokes with curly hair go bald. On the far side were trees and a fence. By the light in the sky you would have said it was still daytime, but it was like the night was growing up from the ground already, and when I got to the trees the dew had already begun to creep among the long grass.

There was a gate in the fence, just a one-person gate with a bolt on the other side you could reach, only it was rusted too stiff to move, like the gate had been put there in case it was wanted one day, and never was. I started to climb it. My skin felt so clean and dry from the bath that even my tight jeans shifted a little up and down round my thighs. And the stretching felt good too when I swung over the top, like it never does when you get told to do it by some fascist PE teacher.

I jumped down on the far side. Beyond the fence there were bushes in heaps under the trees, so I couldn't see far and there wasn't really a path. By the time I'd found a way through I couldn't see where I'd come from. The trees and bushes tangled together all round me, and the quiet seemed to press down until I felt lost.

And then the trees stopped, like a clearing in the forest, and there was a house in a big space, only not a gingerbread house, and beyond it was a gap, and I could see fields stretching away to a greeny blue sky. The house had a pointed roof and twisty chimneys, and there were big double doors, like an old-fashioned garage only bigger, and little windows above and a smaller door on the side. It was the stables, I realized. I wasn't lost: this must be Eva's house.

I'd meant to wait till I was going to the village: this felt like sneaking in the back door, and it wasn't a time of day when you can be just passing. But it was too late. Something dark moved behind one of the downstairs windows, and then the small door opened.

"Hello!" It was a man, not a witch. "You must be Anna, from the Hall."

"Yes. But I didn't . . . Sorry, I got lost."

"Eva told me about you. Are you in a hurry? I was just going to make coffee. She's upstairs." His voice was a bit foreign-sounding too, and he said "Eva" like it was spelled "ever." He had silvery hair sticking up, the kind that would be prickly and springy under your hand, like moss, and his face was dark, like thin, tough leather. "It's this way."

He went up some narrow stairs straight ahead of the door and I followed him, only thinking too late that this was what people meant by talking to strangers. Except he must be old enough to be my father, for heaven's sake, not that I knew how old that was. And he had said Eva was upstairs.

It was a big room, low with little windows all round, and books and books and books all along one wall, more than I'd ever seen in a house, like a library, and a whole long shelf of records, LPs and 45s, and a cooker and sink and cupboards in a corner, and a big squashy sofa and armchairs covered with jazzy-looking tapestry stuff. There were more books on a coffee table, big thick ones, and one of those iron stoves like in a cowboy film, with logs piled up next to it. On a big table there was a box with lights inside like the ones they put X-rays on, only flat, and Eva was sitting at a messy-looking desk, the big headmasterish kind, writing things on a pile of typed sheets. She got up. "Anna! How good to see you. And you have met Theo."

"I saw her from the studio," said Theo. He went over to the kitchen and started to put together a sort of coffeepot thing. "How are you settling in at the Hall?"

"It's a bit weird. Being a school building, I mean. But it's okay."

He put the coffeepot on the cooker. "So, what brings you to stay with Ray?"

"He's my uncle. My mum's gone to Spain to start a business. She's going to buy a hotel. I'm going out to join her as soon as she's got it all sorted out." It always sounded better out loud than it did in my head.

"How exciting!" said Eva. "You are looking forward to it?"

"Sort of."

She opened a tin. "Do you like *Lebkuchen*?"

So even they wanted to trip me up. But people can't trip you up if you won't let yourself be tripped. "Sorry, I don't know what that is."

"Little biscuits—German—with icing."

"Sounds good."

She tipped lots onto a plate and put it on the coffee table. They were all shapes—fat stars and hearts and crescents, some covered with dark chocolate and some with thin white icing, which was sweet and crackly, and inside they were cakey and chewy and my mouth was full of gingeriness for ages. The coffee when it came was in tiny little cups, and there didn't seem to be any milk, but it was so strong it was like whiskey and it went up the back of my nose and turned into tears. Then Eva put a jar of sugar on the table and I took lots, which helped so much with the last bit of coffee that I almost liked it.

The room wasn't what you'd call tidy, but everything looked like it belonged, somehow, like it had always been like that. I thought maybe it was because what wasn't tidy wasn't like other people's mess. In most places it's chip papers and sweaters and old cups of tea. There was a sweater all right, but it was thick, thick wool, all puddles of bright colors you'd expect more in a painting. There was a long snake-skin pinned to the wall, such neat black-and-white-and-gray, and four silver candlesticks, quite short and rather tarnished, sitting on a piece of thick silky stuff, which was stained and fraying round the edges but embroidered all over with flowers and fruit. There was a small telly in the corner, but I didn't think they could watch it much because it had a pile of newspaper cuttings drooping down over it. And there were big pale stones like I'd seen in the fields but broken across so you could see the inside, dark and glossy like the night. On the coffee table there was a big piece of wood, a thick log without the bark, white as if it'd been lying in the sun for years, and black in the knots and cracks. I wanted to stroke it—the light from the window was telling my hand how smooth it would feel and how when I reached the split and broken ends they would press into my palm.

"Pick it up if you like," Theo said.

Eva went to the cooker. "It came from a fallen tree in the park. I think it had been struck by lightning many years before. More coffee, Anna?" The way she said my name, long and round, it sounded like singing.

"Yeah, please." I reached out to pick up the piece of wood. It lay warm across my hands just as I'd thought it would, and the light from the window stroked it.

"When I brought it in, Eva spent two days photographing it," Theo said.

"Is she a photographer?"

"We both are."

"Like in newspapers and things?"

"My work is like that, yes. I am a photojournalist. Eva is the fine-art photographer."

"My art teacher says photography can't be art."

He smiled and I wished I hadn't said it, but he didn't sound as if he thought I'd been rude. "That is like saying that painting isn't art. If the paint is on a house, possibly not. If it makes a picture that says something worth saying, then it is. And you can make a picture just as well with silver halides."

"With what?"

"The chemicals—the light-sensitive chemicals that are in the film and the paper."

"Oh."

Eva came over and filled up our cups. This time I put the sugar in straightaway and picked up the hot little cup in both hands, and the coffee slid strong and sour and heavenly down my throat.

I was still feeling shaky and extra awake from all the coffee when I left. They offered to see me home, but I said I'd be fine. It was warm and completely dark among the trees. I was the right side this time to unstick the bolt, and I opened the gate and walked through. There was moonlight spilling across the grass of the football pitch so that it looked like white hair, and more moonlight falling on the dark floors of the Hall and in through the big windows of my room. It was so empty, it was easy to think of it being a school, busy with people who had only just gone. Ray said it had been little ones here—a prep school—just a bit bigger than Cecil, no one my age, so Mum'd got that wrong too, and that was another thing I shouldn't have hoped for. But somehow the people in my mind were bigger, older, talking and fighting and screwing, like being jammed in together at school makes you do, big shadows of boys and men in the white spaces the moonlight made.

For ages I couldn't sleep, but I didn't want to wake up enough to get up and draw the curtains, and after a while the heat and the moonlight and the waking and the sleeping muddled themselves up in my mind and spread into my body.

When Baxter hits Pierce, the blood sprays round the walls, making the firelight flicker. One of the prefects uses his cane to push Pierce back into the ring chalked on the floor, and then takes another glass of wine. Pierce tries to keep his broken left arm out of reach and still hit Baxter. Baxter tries to hit back, but his mouth is already smashed against his teeth. Everyone is jumping on the tables and the benches, baying like hounds, stamping their feet and laying bets on who will stand the longest. There is nothing I can do, though I have tried, and still have the weal on my cheek to show for it. I go to sit on the windowsill, pretending to want a better view, so that I can look away. The first time, I went to tell the housemaster. He adjusted his spectacles, and said, "Duas tan-

tum res anxius optat, Panum et circenses. *From where does that come, Fairhurst? You don't know? You shall. Now cut along."* Through the crooked glass of King Edward VI, I can see carriages drawn up at the headmaster's door. Ladies and gentlemen are invited to dine.

Pierce has fallen; nothing will make him stand. Baxter is the victor and is carried round the hall on shoulders, while Pierce coughs up blood onto my coat. In the infirmary the surgeon bleeds him, and puts leeches where the bones of his arm broke through the skin, but it is not enough. It is the second death this year. Everyone else goes home for Christmas. For the first time, I was to have gone too, with Pierce to his people, and now I must stay here, in the empty school. I lie alone and shivering in the dormitory, and it is as if his blood has spread to my sheets and my nightshirt. I cannot see it in the dark, but it is there every night, I know. It can pour forever from Pierce, emptying him, leaving his body to the fever. The chaplain said, "We brought nothing into the world, and it is certain we can carry nothing out. The Lord gave, and the Lord hath taken away; blest be the Name of the Lord."

PART TWO

Parastasis: *the act or action of abstracting an image or representation from the continuous flow of time, where the original and its replicant, for an instant, coexist within the same temporal and spatial dimension.*

Oxford Latin Dictionary, 1856

I ARRIVED AT L'ARC-EN-CIEL CLOSE TO MIDNIGHT, AND
weary after four days' traveling, but Planchon insisted on bringing out
his best cognac to drink to my return, and even when I got to bed I
could not shrug off a residual anxiety that all might not be well at
Kersey, in spite of my efforts to make every arrangement for its proper
management and oversight. At last I slept, but a large coaching inn
that stands foursquare at the crossroads of Europe is only quiet for
the few hours of the deepest night. It was barely light when, below my
window, postboys began to be called for. Horses stamped and
snorted, from downstairs came the scent of coffee and new bread, the
clank of mop and bucket, and hoarse voices arguing over lost bags
and muddled waybills. Then there was a rumble and a clatter that
drowned all else as with a cry of *"Attention à vos têtes!"* the mail swept
out of the yard.

I lay and watched the dawn illuminate the handsome bedchamber
that Madame Planchon, under the double influence of our old association and my new prosperity, had seen fit to allot to me. I was not in
Spain, and though a little closer to it, I knew that proximity could not
strengthen my love, any more than time and distance could fade it,
for it was part of my being. But in some way that I could not fathom, a
way that was not concerned with ownership or birthplace or native
tongue, I felt that I had perhaps reached a place where I might reasonably hope that the present and the past could peacefully coexist.

When I awoke again—for my newfound contentment had overcome my soldier's habit of early rising—the sun was well up. I rang

for shaving water and coffee with one hand and pulled a clean shirt from the press with the other. It was freshly ironed, and the coffee arrived swiftly; I concluded that my decision to forgo the trouble and expense of bringing a man with me was not likely, at L'Arc-en-ciel at least, to lead to my demands or my belongings being neglected.

I dressed and breakfasted, declining Madame Planchon's suggestion of calling a hack, for it wanted but a week or so to the beginning of May, and the day was bright, and the breeze sweet with the scent of the great Forêt de Soignes just to the south. One source of the sweetness I soon discovered, for as I stepped beyond the bustle of the inn yard I heard a cry from the far end of the street: *"Muguets! Venez, M'selles, 'dames, 'sieurs! Les plus belles—les vraies fleurs du printemps! Venez acheter!"*

The owner of the voice read my intention almost before I knew of it myself and appeared at my elbow, as if made corporeal by the spring sunlight. She held out a small sheaf of lilies of the valley, wrapped in a twist of paper, their tiny white bell-heads trembling. As I dropped a coin into her cupped and grimy palm I heard a whimper and was startled, on looking down, to see that under her shawl she had bound a pale-haired child to her. She shifted her basket onto her other arm, then reached inside her shawl, pulled her bodice asunder, and lifted the baby's gaping, birdlike mouth to her breast.

"Beg pardon, M'sieur," she said, pulling her shawl across again to cover her child, "but I can't abide to let her cry. I've not offended you, have I, M'sieur?"

"It's nothing," I said.

"Only I left my last with a nurse, but he never thrived, and when the fever came I lost him. When I fell with this one I swore to the Holy Mother I'd never be parted from her."

"Truly, it's no matter." I put more coins into her hand. It was warm and faintly damp. *"Bonjour,* Madame."

"The blest saints keep you, M'sieur," she called after me, then took up her singsong again. *"Muguets! Venez, M'selles, 'dames, 'sieurs! Les plus belles—les vraies fleurs du printemps! Venez acheter!"*

I walked on towards the center of the city. After some minutes I found myself abreast, on the one hand, of a large coffeehouse that I remembered well, and on the other, of the Théâtre du Sablon. I had had little leisure, in preparing to leave Kersey, to alert those of my former acquaintance that might still be supposed to live in Brussels of my return, so that I had, thus far, no engagement for that or any other evening. I assessed my position and took action: I noted the time of that evening's performance, and then, entering the café, called for coffee, ink, pen, and paper.

> *My dear Miss Durward,*
>
> *Before I have written more than the assurance that you ask for, of my safe arrival in Brussels, I must apologise for having put you to the necessity of concealing from your family the letter of which you write. I do recall the offending words clearly, & blush for my thoughtlessness in risking your exposure to your father's censure & your mother's disgust. Indeed, I congratulate you on the quickness you report in reading aloud; I apprehend that you were able to overpaint the picture that I drew of the flesh & blood of military men, with the image of magnificent dolls that the world prefers to regard as its heroes. I honour you too for your own broad-mindedness. As you most generously imply, I truly had no intention of offending; my excuse, such as it is, can only be that so wide-ranging in tone, & so liberal of subject & opinion, has been our converse, that I have ceased long since to feel any constraint in setting down such tales & thoughts as occur to me. Should you have the slightest apprehension that my earlier carelessness has made our continuing correspondence ineligible, I shall of course return your letters forthwith, & receive mine from you in the same spirit. My great regret in so doing will be*

*tempered by knowing that you are—& can be—the only proper
judge of your own conduct.*

*Knowing too how you have no desire to appear to your
family as being engaged in a clandestine correspondence, I offer
the following incident as an example of life on campaign, which
should be acceptable to any taste.*

*Since it was impossible to be certain that the regimental
baggage wagons that carried such modest comforts as tea &
blankets were likely to be at hand at the end of a day's march
when they were most wanted, it was the custom of the officers,
as in many another regt., to employ the services of a Portuguese
boy, who was entrusted with these necessities. . . .*

Having sought only some amusement to fill my evening, I had not
paid much attention to the nature of the performance that I was to attend. I took a seat in the center of the pit under the glare of gaslights,
and looked about me. My fellows on the benches were a cheerful lot,
no sweeter-smelling than my troops, although instead of black powder, I smelled an admixture of many trades: butcher, innkeeper, gentleman of leisure in his cups, lady of the town, and tanner, among
others.

The orchestra stilled, the first actors stepped onto the stage and
began to speak, and I realized that though the play was billed as *Un
Conte d'hiver*, it was, unmistakably, *The Winter's Tale.*

My understanding of the French was no more indifferent than
some of the company's playing. King Leontes had the loud voice and
superfluous gestures of an unintelligent colonel, and King Polixenes
was drunk, while the shepherds' comedy disgraced the heirs of
Molière. In the pit my fellows peeled their oranges and chattered of
the day's doings, and in the boxes ladies and gentlemen came and
went as their other amusements dictated. The gas lamps in the audi-
torium were somewhat dimmed, which drew the eye more strongly
to the stage than in the oil- and candlelit theaters of my youth, but

what could be seen on stage, in the white, hissing brilliance of the new light, were darned hose, paint that failed to make dull eyes bright, and smiles that smeared in the heat.

I knew the tale, and its end. Queen Hermione was no more dead than the actress that played her, nor her daughter lost. And yet each step that Hermione took, heavy with the weight of her child and of her honesty, seemed to stab me to my bones as my newly halting steps once had on the stones of the city. Her baby was abandoned on the seashore, lost even while the child's father contemplated the ruin he had made of all his hope. When Perdita was found, grown and sweet, and stood—the lost child found—before the cold marble of her mother's image, no ignorant groundling in the days of Elizabeth could have watched with more wondering joy than I, as breath and blood stole from the child into her mother's still limbs, and brought Hermione to life.

So overwhelmed was I by this picture, which seemed to bring my own past to life and yet to embody a future I could not dream of, that I sat on for a moment as the clapping about me faded. Then I put my handkerchief away, fumbled for my stick, and rose hastily before the farce could begin. And yet, as I made my way through the emptying streets back to L'Arc-en-ciel, everything on which my gaze alighted seemed to have an import for me—a meaning—that was felt rather than understood. A glove, lying limp and lost in a pool of lamplight; a plaid ribbon tied to a railing by its finder, its colors dimmed by the yellow streetlamp; a child hesitating at a junction where five roads gaped; a man and woman pressing together in the dark of a doorway. It was as if the scrap of time in which each met my eye bore everything within it of past and future.

I blinked, and found that I had reached the inn. I felt as weary as if I had been traveling all day, and made my way straight through the entrance towards the stairs.

"*Un petit cognac pour m'sieur?*" said Madame Planchon as I nodded good night to her.

"No, I thank you," I said, my foot already on the first step.

"Oh, one moment, M'sieur, I have your mail," she said and bustled into the office to fetch it.

The letter was addressed in Miss Durward's hand. It must have crossed the letter that I had dispatched from the coffeehouse that morning: somewhere on the road from Ghent to the coast, I reflected, turning it over. It was thick enough to make me hope that it consisted of at least two sheets, and such indeed proved to be the case. After some preliminary and heartfelt hopes of my being safely arrived and comfortably settled, it bore the news that Mrs. Greenshaw was engaged to be married.

"Mr. Barraclough is a paper merchant and a long-standing business acquaintance of my father's," wrote Miss Durward. "He is somewhat older than Hetty, and lives in Liverpool; we tease Hetty that she should be putting her life into the hands of a Mersey man! He is a widower, and his sister, who has kept house for him, has lately also died. Nor has he any children, so he is well-disposed towards Tom. My parents agree that it is an excellent match, which promises well for all parties to it."

I read the letter to the end, taking note of her request for a sketch-map of Waterloo, and some information about Highland Regiment uniforms, then extinguished my candle and lay awake for some hours. Not for the first time I wondered that I could feel so much more pain in my absent limb than in the mere weariness of present flesh and blood. At last it receded enough to allow me to fall asleep, although I was a little troubled by dreams, which, though unpleasant for the mind that lived through them, faded as always before the light of day and the clatter of milk churns and vegetable carts.

On the morrow I told myself that my reluctance to reply to Miss Durward was due not to the news about her sister—for who could begrudge Mrs. Greenshaw her happiness?—but to my not yet having received Miss Durward's direct assurance that our correspondence might continue. I determined that I would wait for that assurance, but that in the meantime it would do no harm to visit a print shop I knew from my former life, for they might well have for sale a map of Waterloo to supplement my own efforts.

It was too early for a crowd to have gathered about the windows of the shop. I stood before it for some time, renewing my acquaintance with the United Netherlands' particular scandals of venality and nepotism. I might have been standing in Pall Mall, but that the clerical victims of the caricaturist's art wore cardinals' hats, and the politicians Paris fashions.

In the glass before me I could see the movement of men, women, and goods in the street behind me. My own reflection too was divided into sections by the panes. No woman would call me handsome, but none, I thought, would see much in my countenance to displease. I was tall—five panes at least, by the printmaker's measure—broad in the shoulder and neither corpulent nor puny. My face and eyes belied the sickliness hidden in my blood, and now that I could afford a good tailor, none would know until they saw me walk—perhaps not even then—that my cane betokened not some minor sporting hurt, hidden beneath the well-cut cloth of my pantaloons, but a dead stump seamed with scars, even the knee clothed in damaged flesh, where once my body had been whole. It was revulsion from this that had driven Mrs. Greenshaw away and into the arms of an elderly paper merchant who had buried one wife already. None would guess, I thought, gazing at the pane wherein my leg was reflected: no woman could tell. But that thought brought little comfort, for I knew that, in the end, desire or duty must carry such a woman to the point where she realizes the damage—the incapacity—of her patron and protector.

The houses behind me were blotted out by a hack that drew up, and a lady stepped down in a murmur of petticoats, then mounted the steps into the shop. Realizing that I had been standing before it for some time, I entered in her wake.

A shopman produced three maps for my inspection, and did his best to interest me in a print of the new monument to the Prussians at Plaçenoit, but I was not paying attention. The proprietor himself was attending to the lady, and her voice, though low and sweet, cut through the clank and clatter of the presses in the workshop behind so clearly that the conviction grew in me that I had met her before. I recalled my former friends in Brussels and could think of no wife or daughter that she might be, though she had the brown hair and eyes of Brabant, and too much the accents of a lady to suggest an altogether different association. Under cover of inspecting the map that the shopman had laid furthest away from me on the counter—it was published in Paris, I observed, which accounted for the many errors in size, disposition, and designation of the Coalition Army—I looked towards my fellow customer.

She was well and quietly dressed, and she was inspecting a theatrical print of a woman who held up her hands as a puppet might, in the accepted gesture of wonder and recognition. It was a representation, it stated at the foot of the sheet, of Mademoiselle Métisse as Hermione in *Un Conte d'hiver, par William Shakespeare*. That was where I had seen the lady before! I caught my breath, and she looked up.

"Do you like the picture, Monsieur?"

"I beg your pardon, Mademoiselle. I saw you performing last night."

"And now I have stepped down from the stage into daylight. Did you enjoy the play?"

"Very much, Mademoiselle."

"You are English, I think. What did you think of our attempt at Shakespeare?"

"It was very fine."

"Thank you." She took up another print from where it lay on the counter. It was the same image, but the lines of the engraving were filled out with sequins, scraps of lace, chips of emerald and ruby glass, gold and silver wire and mother-of-pearl, so that it appeared to shimmer and tremble like the carapace of some exotic creature in the dusty light from the window. Mademoiselle Métisse opened her gloved fingers so that it slipped back onto the counter.

The proprietor gathered up the prints with a bow. "It will sell very well, Mademoiselle, I have no doubt."

She nodded, and I observed how the satin strings of her bonnet brushed her cheek. "And the more sequins the better, I suppose."

"It is the public taste, Mademoiselle. But for the connoisseur—" He waved a hand, and the shopman scuttled into the back room.

Mademoiselle Métisse smiled at me. "I fear, Monsieur, that you think this an exercise in feminine vanity."

"Not at all," I said, although the vision of a handsome woman so coolly regarding her own image had turned my thoughts to considering what such a woman is thinking as she does so.

"Since such pictures will be made in any case, it seems wisest to have some say in the nature of their execution. Besides, we dare not let our audience forget us."

I was about to say "Surely none could forget you, Mademoiselle," when the shopman returned, bearing carefully a large print, which the proprietor took from him and set before the lady with a bow.

It was a fine engraving of Mademoiselle Métisse as Andromache, the lines so delicately forming the sheen and shadow of her classical gown as it slipped from her shoulder that one might have thought to hear in the next moment the soft rustle of silk falling to the ground. Her eyes looked towards a phantasmal image of Hector, and her mouth seemed to gasp with grief and ecstasy.

"Mademoiselle Métisse sat for Monsieur Terveuren last year, which he had long desired," said the proprietor, catching my eye, "and he did us the honor of commissioning us to make the engraving. It will sell on two grades of paper, one a little less dear than this, for we must always remember that educated taste may not be accompanied by wealth. But it is still a good paper, be assured, for it is a work that a connoisseur would wish to keep for many years, when a mere souvenir is long discarded."

"Perhaps," said Mademoiselle Métisse. "I must go. I have a rehearsal at ten o'clock." As I opened the shop door for her, she paused for a moment, looking at me, and then said, "We are playing *Le Mariage de Figaro* tonight. Do you know the play?"

"I know of it, Mademoiselle."

"If it would amuse you to see it, I will arrange it. Just call at the box office."

"That is most kind. I should enjoy that very much." A sharp spring wind had found its way through the open door, and in the window beside us the obese clerics and two-faced ministers flapped about among patriotic songs, gallant sailing ships, and images of love and mourning. She trod down the steps into the street, and I followed.

"You must come round afterwards," she said, over her shoulder, "and tell us what you think. I shall give orders at the stage door." Suddenly she turned back and held out her hand. "What name, Monsieur, should I give the box office?"

Her kid-gloved hand was firm and warm and slight in mine. I bowed very low. "Major Stephen Fairhurst, at your service, Mademoiselle Métisse."

"Katrijn Métisse . . . Major? Ah, I think we would say, Commandant Fairhurst."

The sound of my rank rendered in French rang strangely in my ears, for I was accustomed to hear it as the designation of a feared but defeated enemy. Such a worthy foe was no more, and the enemy, we were told, were mill workers and hungry children. Mademoiselle Métisse heard my silence and laughed in her warm voice. I pulled myself together and handed her up into the hack. As I closed the door, she said, "*À bientôt, Monsieur le commandant.*"

MY ACQUAINTANCE WITH Mademoiselle Métisse grew quickly, for my time was largely at my own disposal, and she was a lady who, when she had decided to do anything, from learning her part to establishing a friendship, did it with method and dispatch. I watched her play Hermione, Susanna, Andromache; she invited me to accompany her to supper with her friends, and I watched her as herself. The regard of men and women she accepted as willingly as she might the gaze of a portrait painter, and even returned it, but I was nonetheless surprised when, as I escorted her home after we had supped one evening among a group of her theater associates, she invited me up to her apartment in the rue de l'Écuyer.

The concierge admitted us, so sleepily that I had little fear that he might draw any unwanted conclusions.

"My cousin will be asleep," Mademoiselle Métisse said, as she led the way upstairs. "Late hours do not suit her. Poor Cousin Eloise. It was very good of her to agree to come and live with me when I moved to Brussels, and I am determined that the demands of my profession shall not make her change her mind." I tapped on the door of her apartment, and almost instantly it was opened by a middle-aged maidservant. "*Bonsoir*, Meike. Major Fairhurst and I will look after ourselves." The servant took her cloak and my hat and cane, cast a businesslike glance over a side table where was set out fruit, wine, and cheese, then whisked herself away. Mademoiselle Métisse sat down at one end of a small sofa by the fire. "Please help yourself, Major."

I took the stopper out of the decanter. "May I pour you some wine, Mademoiselle?"

"Please, call me Katrijn. Yes, just a little, if you please, and I hope you will take some as well."

It was good claret that swirled into the crystal glass. "You were not named Cathérine, in the French fashion?"

"My mother was Flemish, and I was named for her, so I am half bred, you might say."

When I brought her the glass, she invited me to sit beside her. Then she raised it to her lips and sipped, and my gaze was drawn to where a little ruffle curled about her wrist, and thence to where more lace and rosy silk spanned the soft shadow between her breasts. She lowered her glass again, and I glanced away and drank deeply from my own to cover my confusion.

When I raised my head, she looked me in the eye. "I am accustomed to be looked at by men, Stephen. If we are to be together, then you must not be embarrassed by yourself—or by others."

"Are we to be together?"

"If that is what you want."

I had wanted it since her eyes had rested on mine, and her lips had formed the words "Do you like the picture, Monsieur?" But I had not seriously considered that my desires might be fulfilled.

"I did not think——"

"Thinking is not necessary," said Katrijn, tilting her chin up towards me, so that candlelight broke about her cheek and spilled across her parted lips and small white teeth. "Perhaps you think too much about your wounds—your missing limb."

"I did not know that you——"

"Of course I know. I am trained to study how people move and determine why, as you are trained to decide how best to kill them."

"Only other soldiers." It was true, and yet I saw suddenly the woman who had died at my feet at Peterloo, although it was not I who had killed her.

Katrijn smiled and reached out her finger to touch me between my brows. "Yes. But, dear Stephen, that is in the past."

Thus it was that we took each other, equals in our eagerness and delight, so that when I entered her, her back arched with a cry of pleasure that was almost my undoing. But she was wise, and I need not have worried. Only when the dawn light of early summer was blooming across the ceiling did we sleep in each other's arms.

You ask how I spend my days, & my reply is, very pleasantly.
The latest news & modes are to be found in the shops &
coffeehouses, & the small size of the place suits my halting steps.
I have looked up old friends & made new ones, not least among

the artists associated with the Théâtre du Sablon, so that should I choose to do so, I may start an evening in an elegant salon sipping tea under the gaze of half a dozen Mesdames Une Telle (as they say, where we would say Mrs. So-&-so), & end it in a coffeehouse hung with paintings given to pay the reckoning & peopled by King Leontes, Andromache & the Count Almaviva.

I trust you will not be shocked by the company that I sometimes keep, nor by my frankness in alluding to it in a letter to a lady. I know that your liberal mind will acknowledge that true goodness of spirit, as well as intelligence & compassion, if not always the outer appearance of what society terms propriety, may as easily be found in the company of artists as elsewhere.

I am most anxious, if you can spare time from your labours over the wedding of your sister, to know more of the enquiry into Peterloo, for few details reach the Belgian news-sheets. I should not like to think that the authorities are eager to punish those responsible for throwing stones at the magistrates, unless they are also willing to punish those responsible for throwing half-trained, ill-disciplined, mounted troops at women & children. Here in Brussels I can see everywhere the mark of Spanish &, more recently Revolutionary, tyranny, & reflect that Peterloo has been well nicknamed. I live within a few miles of the field of Waterloo, where so much blood was spilt in the halting of the march of a more recent tyranny, & it angers me to read that in England the gold of self-interested cotton merchants & baronets paid for the blades that cut down unarmed Englishmen. & gold too has since bought the honour of great men, for I can see that Parliament has no idea of preventing another massacre by regulating the ordering of meetings, but only by repressing the ordinary man's natural right to meet at all.

The campaigns that I was privileged to witness were full of sorrow as much as happiness, but since that day at St. Peter's Field even those memories have been corroded, so that the images

of the past that I carry always with me are eaten away by the
bitterness of that day into the likeness of some cruel caricature.

I hope you are able to keep the preparations for your sister's
marriage from interfering with your work. I know that the world
not infrequently assumes that an unmarried lady living in her
parents' house in comfortable circumstances has infinite time to
expend on the needs & desires of others. Certainly your journey
to see Mr. Wedgwood's work promises to be of interest, & I look
forward to hearing more of it on your return.

Pray convey my heartiest congratulations to your sister on her
marriage, & my best wishes for her future happiness as Mrs.
Barraclough.

I had meant to apologise at the start of this letter for my delay
in answering your last, but your question about my days diverted
me. Please believe that I had no intention of appearing reluctant
to reply. In the first place, I felt bound to await your assurance
that you felt able to continue this correspondence (& now that I
have received it, I may admit how greatly I would have felt the
loss of it, had you not felt so able) & in the second place, I lacked
for some days the leisure to do your letter justice, as a consequence
of a little domestic disruption. Seeking more quiet than may be
easily found at L'Arc-en-ciel, hard by the Porte de Namur as it
is, I have taken lodgings in the rue de I'Écuyer, & append my
new direction at the end of this letter.

Pray forgive me for having reached the 3rd sheet before
fulfilling your request about the siege of Badajoz. You will find a
sketch of the town & our dispositions about it on the reverse of
this. In the event, the bare strategic fact of having taken Badajoz
by storm was all that we were able to celebrate. All 3 of the
breaches, that the artillery had laboured for weeks to make, were
effectively impassable, one from a deliberate inundation of water
engineered by the French & 2 from being packed by them with

live shells, beams studded with nails, & finally a forest of swords
so embedded as to spit each man as he advanced. . . .

. . . That the Spanish had originally surrendered the town,
with no attempt at resistance, to the French, who then defended
it to the last long after its fall was inevitable, was felt by all to be
counter to the unspoken rules of war, & our men sought their
revenge. Once in the town they gorged themselves, & their
officers, ourselves dreadfully reduced in numbers, were helpless to
stop them. Murder, torture, rapine & looting exceeded anything
one might see on the battlefield, while we did our best to escort
women to safety, & send those few soldiers still capable of
recognising their officers back to camp.

Ld. Wellington allowed the sack to continue for 3 days, then
sent in a division of English-officered Portuguese, who hanged a
few soldiers & drove the rest out of the town, to be stripped of
their loot & flogged & cursed into sobriety & obedience.

⁂

BEING HOT MAKES you dream. I woke up soaked, with sweat running down me as easily as blood. It was only when I opened my eyes I knew it was pale gray dawn, and the firelight and the boys shouting like dogs weren't there at all. Waking had closed the door against them.

The birds outside were making an incredible noise, every kind of cheep and trill and whistle all at once, a sort of stream of just being alive. They do it in the city too, but when I've heard the dawn chorus there it's only been about waking up sour in my mouth from not enough sleep, and being late for school.

I couldn't be bothered to run a whole bath and there wasn't a shower that I'd found, so I crouched in the tub with both taps on and sloshed myself clean and so cool that I shivered in the draught from the open window when I walked all wet back into my bedroom. The radio was chattering but I wasn't really listening: it was like what they were talking about was so far away there wasn't any point.

When I was dressed I went to the mirror. But was it worth putting on makeup when it all slid off in the heat? There wasn't anyone to see who mattered, I thought, staring into the mirror, really looking at my bare face for the first time in ages. What did people see, anyway, other people? No one would call me beautiful, or thin, but there wasn't too much wrong. Not that boys could see, anyway. Not on the outside.

I went downstairs. There was no one around. In the kitchen I found some sliced bread in a bin on the worktop and couldn't be bothered to put anything on it. I stood at the window eating it and watching a hugely fat pigeon wobbling on a bendy twig. Cecil pattered in. He was still naked except for a pair of Y-fronts with a tear in them, and no one had washed any of yesterday's dirt marks off him.

"Hello, Cecil," I said.

"Hello." He went towards the bread bin and stood on tiptoe to try to reach it, ten mucky little piggy toes splayed out on the floor.

"Do you want some?" I said.

He nodded, and I lifted the lid and dragged a couple of pieces out of the plastic bag and handed them to him. He stuffed one into his mouth, still watching me as if I was an animal that looked quiet enough but might be about to pounce.

"Is school finished?" I said in the end. "Do you go to school?"

He shook his head.

"How old are you, then? When's your birthday?"

He shrugged, then shook his head again. His cheeks were swollen with dry bread in his pointy Martian's face. I wondered if he'd always been so unlooked-after. But I know the social workers don't go after people like him and Ray. Even when they should.

I said, "Where's Ray?" Did he call him that?

"Dunno. Asleep." There was a *rat-tat-tat* at the back door and I jumped. Cecil suddenly wasn't there. After a moment I saw him, crouched in the shadow behind one of the big fridges. *Rat-tat-tat* again. It was only the postman.

"Morning," he said. "Hot enough for you? Registered letter for Mr. Holman."

It was too soon for a postcard from Mum, I remembered after a moment. I signed the book that the postman was holding out. Not that I minded, of course. It was nice to have some peace and quiet. And then among the others I found a letter from Holly.

When I went back into the kitchen Cecil was still hiding.

"Look, I've got a letter too," I said. The registered letter was typed and fat, and the others all looked like bills. I put them on the table. "Look, my friend Holly's stuck pictures out of magazines all over it."

Cecil came slowly out and peered at the envelope. "Why?"

"To make it look pretty. Look—here are some flowers," I said, pointing at a hash plant, "and that's the Eiffel Tower. It's in Paris."

"I see'd a tower once. It had people spiked in it. They were dead."

"Nasty," I said. "But they don't do that now."

"But they did that time."

"Only in history."

"What's history?"

I had to think about that. In the end I said, "Once upon a time. And far away, usually." Last night's shadows suddenly flickered in my mind. "Though I suppose here must have some history too. Look, here's a teddy with a heart on his tummy."

"I like teddies." He pulled the envelope towards him and looked at the address. "Why's it got curly writing?"

"Because my friend Holly thinks it looks pretty, like the pictures."

"Do you think it looks pretty?"

"Yeah. Specially because Holly did it for me."

"Is she your friend?"

"Yeah," I said again, and my throat went lumpy and sad.

"I've got a friend. I see him sometimes."

"Do you? That's nice. Listen, Cecil, is there a toilet down here?"

"Yes."

"Can you show it me? I need to go."

"Next to my room."

"Where's your room?"

"I'll show you." He walked out into the passage to the back door, and turned left through a different door that I'd thought was a cupboard or something. There was another passage, dark and concrete with no windows, but it felt thin like a shed, as if the outside could have crushed it any minute. There were three doors in a row at the end. One was a bathroom, smelly like the boys' toilets at school always are. "Thanks," I said, going in and trying not to breathe.

When I came out he was standing in the next doorway. "Is that your bedroom?" I said.

"No," he said. "It's Susan's."

"Who's Susan?"

"She does the washing."

"You mean clothes?"

"Yes. And the floor. And she plays with me. I get into bed with her when I have a bad dream."

"Where is she now?"

"She went home like the others, Uncle Ray said."

"Do you miss her?"

"Yes. I drawed a picture of her. Come and look."

Cecil went into the last room, and I followed. It was stuffy-smelling and had a dark, shut window with curtains half opened and dirty clothes on the concrete floor and gray-looking sheets on the bed. I'd been expecting pieces of paper stuck up on the walls—and there were some—but he'd been let paint straight onto the walls too.

He must've stretched up as high as he could reach and then he'd drawn a person with a big smiley face and long black hair and blue eyes, with lots of toes on blobs for feet, and sticking-out arms. Now he stood pointing at it for a moment, and then ran forward and pressed himself into her green dress so that her arms looked as if they might come round and hug him.

On the other wall he must've got hold of a fat paintbrush, because he'd splodged red, wet-looking dots everywhere, stabbing them into the wall as if they were spurting from his mind.

When I looked round he'd gone.

I saved up reading Holly's card until I got back upstairs. She'd written very small on a card with a rainbow on it, but the card wasn't very big, so she couldn't fit much in except she'd got a job in Tesco's for the summer and her mum was cross because she'd wanted her to go to Marrakech with her. "Only I'd rather spend the money on Mallorca maybe in September. Any chance of you coming? Mum says we can go if I've got the money, and Sky and Kurt are going too. I bumped into Eileen in Our Price and she said she's going out with David Carter, only Eileen's mum's giving her a hard time because David's dad's colored, and her mum won't let them meet at Eileen's at all, so old-fashioned, so my mum said they could come here, so I get back from work and all I want to do is get out of my uniform and get washed, and there they are, all over my bed, and I mean, *all over. . . .*"

I finished reading and put the card away. Even with the birds still singing in a lazy end-of-the-party sort of way and the air coming in smelling of grass and sun, just at that moment I'd've given a lot to be in smelly old London like Holly was, and even to have aching feet and hands stinking of coppers and be unbuttoning a Tesco's uniform while Eileen and David snogged on my bed. Only it was early morning, so it wouldn't be like that. The card couldn't tell me what Holly was really doing now. But yes, I'd have given a lot to be there, if I'd had anything to give.

I heard engines and looked out of the open bottom of my window. The white tops of two vans were lurching round the end of the house towards the old front door. They seemed quite close up under my window, and I could see the old, yellowy, scratched-looking plastic roofs. I'd been with a boy in the back of one once—it was his dad's, and it was cold, and smelled of other people's stuff, and the roof let the light in, like an old woman's eyes.

Boots on the stairs, knock at the door, a stink already of sweat. "Oh, Anna," said Ray. "Sorry to disturb you. These are the men who are taking away the surplus furniture."

I did wonder about offering to help. I knew all about moving house, after all. Done it hundreds of times. Each time a new boyfriend of Mum's came on the scene, and each time he left. Each time the rent got too high, or the estate too grim. Each time Mum got a new job, and each time she lost it. I knew just how to wedge the pot plants into the back of the van and wedge myself into the front seat next to her and whichever man it was. Sometimes a neighbor would wave good-bye, once or twice a schoolfriend. Often there was nobody: the places we lived weren't mostly the sort where anybody noticed. I wondered if Holly and Tanya would, the next time.

But this moving wasn't the same at all. Belle was sitting in the office and telling them to be careful while they dragged out filing cabinets that weren't even hers, and Ray was smiling and sweating. Every time she called out he hurried in to see what she was saying. Though actually it was him who knew what needed doing, even with all the stuff there was.

"Can I help?"

He straightened up from tipping rubbish into a bin-bag. "I don't think so, thanks, but it's good of you to ask." He glanced round. "No, I think it's all the big things now. Don't worry. It'll be better when it's all gone, and meanwhile, if I were you, I'd just go and enjoy yourself and leave it to me." One of the men picked up the empty bin and went out with it: I heard a clang as he stacked it with all the others. "But—while the men are here—is there anything you'd like in your room? I'll get them to move it in."

"A table'd be nice, and maybe a chair."

"Of course," he said, friendly, but a bit as if he was surprised, as if he hadn't really thought about what it was like in my room. I wondered if he'd thought at all about what I would do with myself. Of course, he'd thought there'd be some people around—teachers and so on. It had all happened suddenly, it sounded like, the school closing and everything. *The bank just pulled the plug,* I remembered Mum's boyfriend with the Jag said, when he came round one evening without it. He kept starting to say things and trailing off. Maybe Ray was a bit stunned still, the way Mum's boyfriend was. And Belle coming—having to come back. *She hasn't had an easy life, you know. When she was evacuated—the war. The way—the way they were treated. And sometimes . . . But she is very pleased, you must believe that,* Ray said.

They took all the beds and wardrobes except mine, and I did get my table and chair. All round the house they went, lugging out stacks of chairs, tables, lockers, cupboards, blackboards, some bits of gym equipment, the big kitchen machines and the two fridges, and dumping it all out on the grass. So I went outside, and when I looked back it was like the house had finally managed to sick up the school stuff.

It was incredibly hot. The thick gray cloud pressed down like a glaring sweaty quilt. You couldn't shade your eyes, because there wasn't a sun to shade them from. I was blinking and headachy before I'd reached the gate into the wood.

I was glad to be away from the Hall, but I wasn't meaning to go to Eva's because I'd have hated them to think I was hanging around. But she was coming through the trees towards me.

"Anna! Good morning! I was just coming to find you. Theo and I are driving into town and I wondered if you would like a lift?"

Would I? Would I ever.

They had a big old Volvo, the sort that looks like it was built out of iron boxes just after rationing ended and hasn't been washed since, and smells of exhaust and dried-up leather inside. On the backseat next to me a parcel was done up and ready to post, addressed to a company in Germany, and in the boot I could see cardboard boxes full of picture frames. Under my feet there was a tangle of jump leads and a tripod and old foreign newspapers.

"We have an exhibition," said Eva, over her shoulder. It was difficult to hear her above the roar of the engine. Theo was driving very fast with one hand while he held his cigarette out of the window with the other, but there didn't seem to be anyone in the lane, and it was nice to be belting along. "We shall be hanging all morning, so you will have plenty of time for shopping."

It seemed dim in the back of the car. The seat was all squashy with being so old, so you sank down into it with each lurch of the car, swaying along and kind of peaceful. Then we were roaring up a long, narrow street with tatty old houses close along each side and a bridge over a river with miles of cracked mud and a trickle of water down the middle and some rather fed-up ducks standing around. Theo stamped on the brake and stopped outside a big toffee-ice-cream-colored house standing flat on to a narrow pavement. The front door opened and an incredibly tall, thin man came out and waved at us, and as we were climbing out he propped the door open with a green glass ball, as big as a football. Somewhere a telephone rang, and he waved again and went through another door into an amazingly untidy office to answer it.

I helped Eva and Theo lift the pictures out and carry them through the open door, like we were feeding the house with them. Not that it was really a house: it was a museum. It was very old, and everything was slightly sloping, including the floor, and none of the windows were quite square. You'd have thought they'd do it up ye-olde-worlde, with fancy wallpaper and black beams and brass lamps, but they hadn't, although there were a couple of bits of old furniture, very clean and soft-looking and smelling of honey and lavender. But they hadn't done modern things either, like vinyl floors and covering up the paneled doors and the fancy banister rail. The floor was just floorboards, but glossy gold, not gray and dusty like when you pull up a carpet that's too disgusting to keep. And the walls were plain bright white, with spotlights pointing at them, as if the light was doing the colors instead of the paint, so that the furniture sort of glowed and the few old pictures they'd put with them seemed to come at you, hot and alive.

Eva and Theo's photographs didn't exactly come at you. Even though they were all black-and-white, it was more like someone'd taken a chisel to the walls, *tap-tap-tap*, and knocked small, square windows out onto the street one by one. They had a room each upstairs, with a big arch between them with double doors folded right back. You got to Theo's room first. In most of his pictures there was lots going on. There was one with some soldiers and Chinesey girls in a bar, and the label said SAIGON, 1968. I knew what the men's faces were about, but the girls' faces were quite blank, smooth, like their eyes and smiles had been painted on china, and I wondered if it was because they had tons of makeup on, which they did, or whether it was because inside they were thinking something quite different, and didn't want it to show. I knew about that too. And suddenly I saw how all the soldiers were sitting round the edges of the picture, you could say, and the girls were in the middle so they couldn't get out, but they were what you looked at, you and the soldiers. It wasn't news really, but I thought if you had it on your wall you would keep looking at it.

"Anna, do you have the spirit level?" Theo said, from across the room. I took it over to him. He rested it along the top of the picture he was holding against the wall and shifted it till it was straight, narrowing his eyes at the little shivering yellow bubble in the glass. "Please would you mark for me where the holes for the brackets should go?" he said. "The pencil is behind my ear."

I took the pencil—his hair was like warm, sharp wool where my fingertips touched it—and marked in the hole of one bracket where it stuck out from the frame, and dodged round behind him and marked the other one. When he put the picture down, and dug a bradawl into the pencil mark, I saw the muscles in his arm bunch and relax, and again on the other side. Then I held the picture up while he went round behind me, screwing it neatly and firmly against the wall.

We stood back and looked at it. For a moment, I thought it was someone sitting in a car with the window rolled down, throwing his head back and laughing. Only it wasn't, and my stomach sort of heaved. It was a car, but it was burned-out and the person was a body, not a skeleton but a body, burned whole, arching back, black and gray in cracked, overlapping scales, with only the teeth looking like a face, screaming.

"Anna?" said Eva, from the other room, for the second time.

"Yes. Sorry."

"I would love to have your opinion."

I went over to her. "Look," Eva said, "this is the place of the first image you see when you come through from Theo's. But you see it from a distance. Most people will then turn right, and work their way round, standing much nearer to those ones." She waved at the row of unwrapped pictures propped along the far wall. "So, which of these should be here when you enter?"

For a moment I couldn't think of anything to say, because the burned man was still making me feel sick, and because Eva's all looked so boring. There was one of a rather tatty petrol pump, the kind with a light-up shell on top, only the hose was lying limp and flat along the ground with the nozzle dry and lost at the end.

"What do you think?" Eva said. "How about this one—Berkeley Square?" I'd have expected nightingales or people in top hats and ball gowns or something, but it was just railings, I worked out, straight park railings, with their shadows falling across square gray paving stones, and a curb scooping round, and just the wheel of a motorbike scooping the other way with its spokes like a starburst.

"I like it," I said, walking backwards and colliding with Theo, who'd come over. "But it's kind of confusing from further away."

"Yes, she is right, Eva," said Theo.

"And who asked you, Todos Besnyö?"

I flinched, but they were both laughing. "Any fool could see it with half an eye," said Theo. "It's not the right image for that position."

"So, Anna," said Eva, "what should we hang instead?"

I looked along the line of propped-up pictures again, and this time I had some ideas at least. Something big and simple that you could see all at once.

There it was—one of the piece of wood I'd held at the stables. Eva'd made it look as warm and smooth as it'd felt, and when I picked up the picture I could see how the specks of the ink, or whatever it was, were part of what made it silvery—*halides*, Theo'd said, *silver halides*. I held it up against the wall. "This one?"

Eva stepped back to where Theo was standing, and they both stared at it.

"Yes," she said, "you're right. Isn't she, Theo?"

"Yes."

She came and took the picture from me. "Then help us to put them up, Theo, and I can have my turn to tell you what mistakes you have made."

We had just got the last of hers placed when there was a click of shoes on the stairs. It was the thin man.

"Theo—Eva—I am so sorry! So unwelcoming! How's it going? I got caught on the telephone—it was the chair of the trustees, and she won't be choked off, try as I may."

"Oh, Crispin," said Theo, "this is Anna Ware. Anna—Crispin Cordner. He's the director here."

"And telephonist, bottle washer, and soother of outraged local egos," said Crispin, shaking hands with me. "How do you do, Miss Ware?" He looked round. "My dears, it's *splendid*. And the contrast!"

"Not too much?" said Eva. "We've not shown together before."

"Not at all," said Crispin. "Shake the old dears up a bit." He nodded at Eva's pictures and then turned in the arch to look at Theo's, so we all did. I tried not to see the burned man.

"Theo!" said Eva. "I thought you decided not to show that one."

"I decided I could not omit it," said Theo.

"You never have been able to edit your work," said Eva. "To leave things out makes the others more powerful. And besides, this one . . . this one is too much."

I stared out of the window. There were dusty leaves on the trees, a sort of old dried green, but my mind's eye could still see the scales of black and gray that had been a person, speckled and split like the branch I had held.

"Crispin, what do you think?" said Eva.

He looked for a long time. At last he said, "It's pretty shattering. And there might be complaints."

Theo said, "Would that stop you?"

"Of course not," said Crispin. "Well, not at the moment. The trustees are pretty happy with us just now, after the Girtin show. But perhaps—"

"Surely *you* are not siding with Mrs. Disgusted of Ipswich, are you, Crispin?" said Theo.

"No, of course not. But—was it Tim Page who decorated his office in Vietnam with all the images Reuters said were too ghastly for them to accept?"

"No, it was Horst Faas," said Eva, "and Associated Press. But that's my point entirely, Theo. To us it is a wonderful, powerful image, beautifully shot. And printed almost as well as I would do it." Theo grinned. "But to most people, it will just give a bad shock. A sick shock, like a cheap horror movie. A fix. It panders to the voyeurs."

"Then we are all voyeurs," said Theo. "If that is what you are worried about, what about the brothel?" He pointed across the room.

I said, "But that's quite different." They all turned and looked at me, but I wasn't going to let that put me off. "That one makes you know you're like the soldiers. It's about you being part of what's happening as well as about Vietnam. This one's—well, it could be you just want it to hurt you. Like you like it. Being hurt, I mean."

"Bravo, Anna!" said Eva.

"But it's very beautiful," said Crispin. "Perhaps therein lies its salvation—and all of ours."

They were silent. I wondered how it could be beautiful, when even thinking about it made me feel sick and shaky. Then Theo said again, in a dead sort of voice, "We are all voyeurs. And I need a drink. Crispin, can you join us?"

"If only I could," Crispin said, shaking his head so that his hair flopped, "but I've got about a thousand things to do. I'm sorry."

"Ach! Next time, then," said Eva.

"Drink!" said Theo. "Crispin, we shall come back later and make sure there is nothing we wish to change."

"So, Anna—may I call you Anna?—do you live nearby?" said Crispin, waving to me to go before him down the stairs.

"Anna is staying with Ray Holman at Kersey Hall," said Eva.

"Are you now? We have what's left of the Fairhurst archive here."

"Fairhurst?" I said.

"The family that owned Kersey. They deposited a few deeds and letters and so on with the trust that owns this place when the Hall was requisitioned in 1939. I think it was filled with evacuees, so goodness knows what went on. Anyway, when the estate was split up and sold after the war, they asked us to keep them. Strange to survive Peterloo and the Corn Law riots and deaths and two world wars, and then be broken by income tax. . . ." For a moment he looked as sad as if it was a person he was talking about, not just a family who'd once owned a big house, and then couldn't afford it. "There isn't a lot of it, but if it would interest you I could get it out sometime."

"Thanks," I said as we went towards the front door, because it was nice of him and he did seem to mean it, even though it didn't sound very interesting. He probably wouldn't be bothered in the end.

"That portrait at the foot of the stairs is one of the owners," Crispin said. "Stephen Fairhurst. Early nineteenth century, I think. It's due to be cleaned next year. Come and have a look."

I turned back, mostly because his tone of voice seemed to expect it. The paint was old and dark, and it had a spider's web of cracks over it, like a veil. It was just a man, holding a half-unfolded letter. Eva called from the door, "Anna? Are you coming for a drink? It's the least we owe you, after all your help," so I sort of half smiled and followed her out.

Outside it was hotter and stuffier than ever, as if all the petrol fumes were lying between the houses like smelly mud in a gutter. We walked up a sort of steep market square, and into a pub. It was Eva who went to the bar. Theo and I went towards a table in the bay window, which had old greenish glass in small panes, making the people going past look wavery. I wondered what they saw of us.

"They see their own reflection, I think," said Theo, behind me. I heard the scrape of a match as he lit his cigarette. He sat down beside me in the curve of the window.

Eva called, "Anna, what would you like?"

"Half of lager, please."

The barman coughed. "And how old might the young lady be?"

I'd never been asked before. But I'd never gone into a pub in a T-shirt and shorts and no makeup before either.

Eva and Theo were both looking at me. If they hadn't been there I'd have lied straight out without a second thought, but they were. "Fifteen," I said.

"Can't serve you then, Miss, sorry," said the barman. "Only a soft drink."

"I'll have a Coke, please." I could feel my face all hot and red and my T-shirt sticking to my back.

Theo smiled at me. "That does not happen very often?" he said.

"Not often. Not ever."

He was still looking at me. "No, I would think not. You remind me a little of Eva, when I first met her in San Sebastian. The same coloring. You have no Spanish blood?"

"Not as far as I know," I said, sort of laughing.

Then Eva brought the drinks over—they both had pints of lager—and later she got the pub to make us some sandwiches. After we'd eaten we went back to the gallery and Eva asked me if I'd mind taking the parcel to the post office, if I was going shopping.

"No, of course not," I said. I really did want to help her, as well as say thank you for the lift. It wasn't a bit like Mum sending me to the shops because she wants to stay in bed with her boyfriend.

"It will need to be registered, and have a customs form," said Eva, handing me some money. "It is a lens going to be repaired. You had better say that the value is—oh, fifty pounds? The post office is up there beyond the church."

"Okay," I said, "I can cope with that," and only then was amazed that she was trusting me with something worth that much. But she just gave me the parcel and the money and I took it and went off up the market square to the post office. The town wasn't big enough to get lost in, so after that I went for a wander. I got cards in a stationer's for Holly and Tanya. There was a rack of kids' stuff and I suddenly thought Cecil would like something, because he didn't seem to have any toys or anything. So I bought a water-painting book, because I remembered how magic it seemed to me when I was little, and folded it tight into its paper bag so that he'd have something to unwrap. Mum always used to do it like that.

She'd put a hundred pounds for me in the building society to last till she sent me the fare to Spain, but of course she hadn't checked whether there'd be a branch here, and there wasn't. I'd have to find out where there was one. There weren't many clothes shops I'd be seen dead in, except one with a top I rather fancied, nylon with Indian patterns, but when I tried it on it didn't look good in the mirror, kind of cheap. Shop mirrors do that; you'd think they didn't want you to buy it. And it was too hot to be bothered with anything more, so I wandered back to the gallery.

Eva and Theo were standing on the pavement, talking hard, hands waving, and Crispin was in the doorway with one hand up on the frame and the other full of papers, watching them and joining in. They all looked so easy—arguing, laughing—with the old car squatting sleepily beside them in the road. Maybe it was because I was tired but I stood and watched them and it felt like the heat was filling the distance between us so thickly that I'd never find my way to them.

Then Eva saw me and waved, and I went towards them and it wasn't very far at all.

"Hello, Anna," Crispin said. "I was in the storeroom, and I found the letters I was thinking of. I'm afraid I can't let you have the originals—they ought to be microfilmed, really—but I've done you some photocopies."

Small, old-fashioned black writing leaping neatly across the shiny, flippy photocopier paper, and the shadows of creases. I peered but couldn't make out any words beyond "My dear Miss Someone."

"Thank you," I said.

"Mind you, photocopies are often easier to read than originals, because the ink's blacker. A nice long lot. They'll keep you going when Eva and Theo decide to disappear abroad again," said Crispin. "I had a quick look—I'd forgotten, they're from Stephen Fairhurst. The one in the portrait."

Then I did go back.

He had short brown hair and eyebrows that had a sort of twist at the corners, and a dark jacket, and one of those old-fashioned cloths round his collar instead of a tie. He looked at me. I wondered for a mad moment what he could see of my world, and what I would be able to see in his if I looked back at him hard enough through the time-darkened paint.

⁂

My dear Miss Durward,

Please do not read into my expressions of surprise any lack of enthusiasm for your sister's plan. Our fellow citizens' liberty to

travel abroad in safety—not least on a wedding journey—was
one of the freedoms for which the Army once fought. I shall
look forward very much to welcoming you to Brussels & I am
delighted that Mr. Barraclough sees no objection & Mrs.
Barraclough no embarrassment in such a visit. I hope that my
knowledge of the area will prove useful in making it a pleasant
one. It would give me great pleasure to escort you to those sites
that you & I have discussed at such length; I only trust that you
will not find the evidence of your own eyes too much at variance
with my account. I am sorry that Mstr. Tom is not to be of the
party, but no doubt you are right—it is not a matter of which I
have any experience—in thinking that his residing at his
grandparents' house will provide solace for them, in the absence
of both their daughters. & privacy is important too, for Mr. &
Mrs. Barraclough to forge that perfect sympathy of heart &
mind which ought to be the foundation of every matrimonial
union.

To answer your questions: the climate of the Low Countries is
not unlike our own, always excepting that in the summer months
it may become peculiarly sultry for some days at a time. But if, as
you say, you expect to arrive some time in June, you may look
forward to all the delights of an English summer, & in
comparison to Lancashire, rather less rain. The Brussels
apothecaries & drapers are well stocked with everything that
the traveller might require, & the domestic arrangements at the
better Inns are most efficient, so I can urge you to travel as lightly
as may keep you supplied for your journey. If you will be so good
as to send me word of the day on which you expect to arrive, I
shall engage rooms for you at L'Arc-en-ciel; & if there are any
other arrangements that Mrs. Barraclough desires, I trust you
will not hesitate to communicate them to me, that they may be
fulfilled by your obedient servant,

Stephen Fairhurst

I have drunk enough to make me brave, and I catch an admiring glance from Hanmere across the crowded room, for I have Jane already on my knee. I want to know what it is like, and this is the only way. Jane is not well washed, and her face is painted, but she smells of earth and warmth. She makes only a token squeal when I touch her round breasts. Then she says I must pay Mrs. Maggs first.

She lies on the bed, which smells of others, but she is laughing and holding her hand out to me. "First time is it, sir?" she asks, opening her legs as I stumble out of boots and breeches. "Don't worry, Jane'll look after you, soldier man." I have some idea of what I want to do and how to do it, and under my hands she is everything that I have been hot for on so many nights. But for all her earlier words and smiles she just lies there, waiting for it to be over, and try as I will, I cannot make it happen. To cover my shame I blame the wine and try by kissing her to engage her interest, her cooperation. The paint smears under my mouth as she turns her head away, and my disgust overwhelms me and I strike her face and call her a whore. "Well, soldier, what did you think I was?" she says, nursing her cheek without surprise. "A fucking lady?"

I pull on my clothes and leave. Behind every door I think I can hear whores and men, each doing what they must to get what they want, heaving, touching, kissing, pretending pleasure or pretending love. Someone has puked on the stairs, and further along is a man who has been robbed by one girl while he buggered another. My head begins to swim with wine and vomit and the smell of copulation, and all the other faces come towards me in the dark, diseased with fear and disgust and hatred of ourselves.

II

IT WAS SUNDAY, AND THE THEATERS WERE CLOSED, SO WHEN I had dispatched my letter to Miss Durward, I walked the few yards to Katrijn's apartment. Cousin Eloise, said Katrijn, was visiting a sick friend.

"Would it be impolite to your cousin, or flattering to you, to express my happiness at the news?" I said, pulling her towards me.

"I know," she said, returning my kiss with one of her own that promised much, then slipping from my grasp to pour the wine. "I forgive you, because you are so courteous to her when you meet. You must understand that my profession is a sore trial to her respectability, for I have all the appearance of a lady, and yet cannot be one among the *bourgeois*. Half bred again, you see. I believe it was not always thus: some of the older actors recall the days when society was not so squeamish. I cannot think actors are different in their birth or their behavior since the century turned. Perhaps it is the times that have changed, since the revolutions ended. Cousin Eloise tries to make up for my unrespectable profession, and of course she cannot, however much she chatters about the servants she has been accustomed to command. If I did not need her, I should send her back to where she would be more comfortable. She cannot make you more impatient than she does me, poor soul."

So we dined alone, sitting in the long windows of the salon, which were open to the courtyard, the pale muslin of Katrijn's gown billowing against the wrought iron of the little balcony, and the candles dipping in the warm air. Even when Meike had long removed the last of the dishes, we sat on while the well of the courtyard filled with dimness, until only the topmost chimneys still caught the last of the sunlight.

Katrijn reached to touch my hand where I held the stem of my wineglass. "What is it that you are thinking?"

"I don't know," I said, for I was, indeed, not certain what had suspended my being for those uncounted minutes. It was not the memory of the days at Bera; those I might hardly call memories, so much were they part of my existence, although I had never spoken of them to Katrijn. Rather it was a sense of recollected joy—so vivid as to be almost painful, and yet without recognizable sound or identifiable sight. It had been illuminated for me by the light above us, so that two visions lay within each other in the eye of my mind. I seemed to exist within both moments at once, and I could not tell whether my memory had arrested this moment, or the moment had conjured the past even to the quickening of my senses and suspending of my rational mind.

"Stephen?"

"I'm sorry. I was thinking of Spain."

"Good, or bad?" she said, taking my hand in hers and pressing her thumb gently into the pit of my palm.

"Oh—good." I grasped her hand. "I was recalling the sunsets we used to see in the Pyrenees." I spoke the truth, for with Katrijn's voice my power of reason was reanimated and I found that I knew what memory had been filling my senses. But I could not have described it to her in any way that would have made her understand, for her intelligence was directed at the habits and passions by which human creatures live on earth.

She was looking at me with the utter stillness that held the gaze across a table as irresistibly as it did across the footlights.

Then I did think of a form for my thought that she might understand. "When you play, say, Andromache, you are standing on a stage under gaslights, not living at the court of King Pyrrhus. But . . ." I tried to shape my still inchoate thoughts into words, and started again. "You are not the widow of Hector, nor the mother of Astyanax. . . ."

She started to laugh. "No, indeed I am not!" she said.

"So how is it that I can watch you, whom I know so well"—she smiled at me in the way that never failed to make the hairs rise on the back of my neck—"I watch you, and feel as moved with sorrow and anger as if I *were* watching Andromache in the grip of her dilemma. Those true feelings exist, when her seeming situation is but played by Mademoiselle Métisse among paper and shadows."

"If I acted grief or happiness you would sit in your comfortable box, and watch a puppet—a print—making gestures that indicate those feelings. But when I shape my thoughts into those of my character—Andromache, if you like, or perhaps Susanna—then . . . then her feelings arise as truly within me as mine do in my own life. And my voice and body move as her thoughts and feelings dictate. Her image is made on me." She smiled. "Even my name, Métisse, means 'half-breed,' did you know? I am half myself, and half another. . . . Is it true that in English you use our word *voyeur* for a particular meaning?"

"Yes."

"I thought so. . . . It is perhaps not so different. I suppose, if you are watching me on stage, my words and movements make your thoughts follow my thoughts, and my happiness or sorrow quickens yours. You see me, but you also feel your self." After a moment she sat back, and the twilight mixed with the candlelight glowing on her face. "And, of course, I must make sure that I am seen and heard, and do not trip over my gown, and remember that Monsieur Meunier has been too long in the wineshop again this afternoon, and may not give me my cues."

I leaned across and kissed her long on the mouth, as if I were drinking in the very light of which she was made. "And even when he doesn't, I see Andromache across time, and Katrijn across space, and myself—if you will have it so—in both of you."

I may perhaps surprise you by saying that the most extraordinary memory of all my years abroad is of the close of a quiet day, when I stood on the heights of the Pyrenees & looked into the plains & valleys of France. Certainly the country—all lonely crags & rushing torrents—was extremely fine, & the knowledge that we had all but won the prize of French submission was a cause of satisfaction. And yet, though I have witnessed Busaco, Vittoria & Waterloo, where the fortitude, even heroism, of our men & the brilliance of our commanders was such as to live long & proud in the memories of those who took part, my memory of that moment above the valley of Bera to this day transcends all others.

The air was clear, & the clouds piled high above the mountains were just beginning to be glossed with pink & gold rays from the early evening sun. And I knew suddenly that without taking a step or counting a second, I had yet reached some other world that co-existed with my own. I felt the infinite space about me, & knew that I & Dora & each tree & human being were carved from that infinity of time and space. The fading leaf & uncurling petal each held a place in the great design as important as the mountains & towering clouds, & all bore within them the seeds of a majesty beyond our horizons.

I cannot believe in the Heaven that I was taught to hope for, nor much fear the alternative, & yet the clockwork universe that natural philosophy forces us to contemplate cannot explain such matters either. At such a moment, even a weary soldier, with his mind full of orders & rations, surely contemplates something more than the activity of particles: something more, that nature shows to him as the Sublime.

But Mars does not allow his agents to contemplate such places for long, at least not until he dispatches them there for good, and some uncounted minutes later, the sound of skirmishing broke out in the valley below.

It does not surprise me that you find that many of the

*preparations for even a quiet ceremony, such as that which your
sister & Mr. Barraclough consider proper, have little to do with
the true spirit of matrimonial love. I must suppose that, the world
being what it is—& I trust that I shall not offend you in saying
it—the bustle & business of getting gowns & making settlements
may truly reflect the nature of the contract between a particular
husband & wife. Perhaps it is impossible that the laws of property
& an Established Church should take account of the infinite
variety of human lives.*

The mails to Lancashire are some of the swiftest that I have known,
for the merchants depend on intelligence from all quarters of the
globe quite as much as His Majesty's government does, and have
greater means to pay for it, so that even from Brussels, my correspondence with Miss Durward was in the nature of a conversation. But
this was the last letter that I could be confident would arrive before
she departed for Belgium. I was surprised to find that in the interven-
ing days time hung a little heavy on my hands, and very grateful that,
although Katrijn was busier than ever, she rarely denied me the comfort of her company or the exquisite oblivion of her body.

There were nights, however, when she had been rehearsing all day,
and then played a great role such as Iphigenia in the evening, when it
would have been a brute indeed who forced himself on her. It was my
habit to escort her home even when I had not been in the audience,
but on such nights I needed but one glance in the lights of the stage
door to see her wide-open red-rimmed eyes and quavering hands,
and hasten to summon a hack. On the first such occasion, as I climbed
in beside her and pulled the door shut against the still-cheering
crowds, I saw that she shrank slightly. "I shall see you home to Meike,"
I said. She nodded. In the cramped space I could feel that the elevated
mood and strained attention of performing was draining from her
and she was as bone weary as any soldier bivouacking on a hard-won
battlefield. The hack was no more spacious than any other of its kind:

after a few yards she sighed, and relaxed against me with her head on my shoulder; I looked down, to see that her eyes were closed. At her apartment I escorted her upstairs and gave her into the care of Meike, and then I walked the hundred yards to my lodgings, the ache of my love's absence and my dread of what the empty night before me might bring a little eased by the ghost of Katrijn's perfume that still lay on my cheek.

On the day before Miss Durward and the Barracloughs were due to arrive Katrijn had no rehearsal. We dined together, and then I sat in my usual box and watched her in the character of Susanna, seducing us all with every step, speech, and look as she fought to defend her honor from the lust of her master and the jealousy of her betrothed. Later that night, as we lay in the warm drowsiness that keeps us safe from the *tristesse* that the ancients declared inevitable, Katrijn said over her shoulder, "Will you have to see much of your friends when they arrive?"

I kissed the back of her neck, where her dark hair lay tousled on her cream-colored skin. "I have undertaken to show them Waterloo, and perhaps Quatre Bras. And no doubt they will seek my advice as to places of entertainment in Brussels."

"Will you bring them to the theater?"

"If they desire it. Miss Durward would enjoy it, I am sure. But I know nothing of Barraclough—his tastes, or indeed his views on the theater." Katrijn shifted suddenly, as if she found my weight on her uncomfortable, and I rolled off to lie beside her. "They are only here for a few weeks, as a wedding journey, with Miss Durward supporting her sister. It is not uncommon. I shall have to see something of them. But as it is, you and I do not meet every day, nor expect to do so."

"No . . ." She turned onto her side so that we were lying face-to-face, and reached out her hand. "So it need make no difference to us?"

"No, indeed, and I would not wish it to."

I slept so well that Katrijn was dressing by the time that I opened my eyes. She was standing at the foot of the bed, braced for Meike to draw up her stay-laces. I lay at my ease and watched her. My skin still felt her soft flesh so exactly that it was as if it were my hands and not the calico that closed about her, gripping her belly, waist, and back, ever tighter, hook by hook, inch by inch, until only her breasts could swell with each breath above the constriction of cloth and bone. Had Meike not been present, I would have taken her then. Katrijn watched me out of the corner of her eye as she went on dressing, slowly sliding her stockings up over the smooth skin inside her thighs, tying her garters tight with little bows, bending to button her stiff black boots close about her ankles, stretching to sweep her hair from about her shoulders. I was wishing that I did not have to leave so soon, when Meike was called for by Cousin Eloise, who never left her chamber in the morning until I had departed. I seized the moment and Katrijn, who had been watching me as she coiled her hair into the smooth bands that I loved to pull apart, proved as eager as I, so that my desire found all the fulfillment towards which her dressing had urged me.

After that, there was time for little more than coffee before Katrijn hurried off to her rehearsal, and I reached L'Arc-en-ciel only a little later than I had intended. I should have arrived earlier, but that I had chosen, in spite of a light drizzle that made the cobbles slippery, to walk from the rue de l'Écuyer. Even with my cane I walked slowly perforce, but I was not sorry to have an interval of cold air and physical exertion to calm myself. Planchon came out of his office to greet me, and then I established myself in the private parlor that I had bespoken for the Barracloughs at their request, with *Le Moniteur* to distract my thoughts from the slight embarrassment that I feared would attend my meeting with the new Mrs. Barraclough.

I was reading a report of the Princess of Wales's journey from Brunswick to claim her place in her husband's coronation—for the scandals of our royal family reach the Continental news-sheets when the scandals of political brutality and military incompetence do not—when an English voice, close before me, said, "Major Fairhurst?"

I leaped to my feet and grasped her hand. "Miss Durward! How do you do? How was your journey? I do trust that you are not too exhausted. Nor Mrs. Barraclough."

"Not at all. We have come only from Ghent this morning, and the roads were very good," she said, and though her pelisse was travel stained and her bonnet crooked, her expression confirmed the truth of her words. We had just ceased shaking hands when Mrs. Barraclough came in, putting up her veil as she did. We too shook hands, and with only a little consciousness I congratulated her, and asked after Tom, so that news of him took up the few minutes that elapsed before Barraclough entered. He proved to be much as I had imagined, although rather younger and much taller; he was plainly but not cheaply dressed, and had only a little more country burr to his voice to distinguish his from his new father-in-law's Lancashire accents.

The ladies disclaimed any desire for rest, and Mrs. Barraclough declared her intention of changing her gown, then commanding her husband's escort in walking out to see a little of the town.

"And yours too, Major, if you are at leisure? Your tales have quite whetted my appetite!" she said, from the doorway. "Pray excuse us, we shall not be long. Come, Lucy."

"What, Hetty?" Miss Durward had brought out a sketchbook and was standing by the window, drawing.

"Are you not coming to change?"

"Oh—yes, I suppose I should," she said, glancing down at her gown and then up again. "Bother this old glass! I can't see a thing. I'll be there in a minute." But it was several minutes before she had the ramrod figure of a postboy holding a horse set down to her satisfaction, and went to join her sister.

"No doubt they'll take their time," said Barraclough. "Shall we have a drink? The roads are good, but I've more dust in my throat after a week's traveling than there is in a desert."

I rang the bell, then asked about their journey. It was only when the waiter had brought beer for us and sherry against the ladies' reappearance that Barraclough settled further into his chair and said, "Hetty tells me that you know Brussels well. She was desirous in any case of going abroad for her wedding journey, but she felt it would be easier to go first where we might be sure of finding a friend."

I was uncertain what he knew of my acquaintance with his wife. "I was here a few years ago, yes. Before I came into my cousin's property at Kersey."

"You were at Waterloo?"

"Yes."

"So you stayed on?"

"Not exactly." I took a draught of Belgian beer, which is golden and sharp on the tongue, but I could not delay my answer forever. "I took to guiding English parties about the battle sites."

"Aye," he said briskly, "there'd be a market for that, I would imagine, if you know what you're doing, which I'll be bound you did."

"There was. Still is, so Planchon the landlord tells me. But I've no direct knowledge of it these days."

"You can afford to please yourself, then." He took another sip of his beer and grimaced. "I take it you're used to this stuff?"

"It's not like our English ale, certainly," I said, "but it becomes very palatable on better acquaintance. And Planchon keeps an excellent wine cellar."

"Does he? It's no use to me; I don't drink the stuff. I drink ale only when I've my doubts about the water, and not at all if there's any of my people to see. It sounds daft, but it sets an example. And, of course, we all want the Methodies for workers, for their sobriety."

"You need not fear the water here, I can assure you. But I take it that you are from a Dissenting family?"

"Aye. Unitarian, for the most part, though to be honest I go to chapel mainly to do business. Hetty wanted to be wed in church, and I'm not one to fuss over trifles like that. You're not married, Fairhurst?"

"I? No."

I was very grateful to hear the ladies' voices at that moment in the passage, for although I had taken to Barraclough more than I had expected to, he was the last man with whom I could have discussed my continuing bachelorhood. By now it wanted only a few minutes to noon, and the drizzle had gone off without leaving the streets disagreeably muddy. Mrs. Barraclough arranged her parasol, her sister's bonnet, and her husband's arm to her liking, and in the wake of her suggestion that Miss Durward likewise take my arm, we set out to view the town.

IN THE DREAM I came sudden and wet, like a man, but in the morning I woke curled round my own private, tight-clenched stickiness. It doesn't happen like that very often, asleep I mean. The first time it did I was a bit scared, thought there was something wrong with me, because nobody tells you it happens to girls. Even we don't talk about it. We talk and talk and talk about spots, periods, parents, boyfriends, dirty old men, puking young ones, even being pregnant—we talk about all the horrible things. Just not the nice ones. It's like nobody, not even us, thinks you should enjoy it without a boy doing it to you.

And one of the nice things is how sleep creeps up you afterwards like warm water, but I didn't actually get to sleep, because I thought suddenly, If I'm going to walk into the village and find out about buses then it wouldn't be so bad if I went now.

I got washed and dressed, and tidied up my clothes and makeup things a bit. The letters Crispin had given me were there too. What was his name? Yes, *Stephen Fairhurst*. He'd signed at the bottom of the first one, *your obedient servant, Stephen Fairhurst*. The black writing glinted as the light caught it. *My dear Miss—My dear—Miss Durward*, I read. *I was so very delighted to receive your letter. . . .*

Trying to make out the words, my eye had to follow the strokes and curves of the writing, tracking the pen, his pen, Stephen's pen. It was full of those curly *ands* and the *-st* and *-th* for the numbers tucked up high. And lots of long words, some of them fading, and the next word suddenly black and thick, as if the ink had run out and he'd dipped his pen again.

What with all the long words, and not always being able to work them out, it was hard to understand exactly what he was saying, except that after a while it started to be about army stuff, and a battle somewhere I couldn't read, Sab-something, and a windmill.

The men made an unflinching withdrawal from our own strong position across a plain held by a horde of French cavalry, to prevent the 7th from being cut off. . . .

I must end here for the present, so that I may be certain of these pages' safe dispatch towards their destination from the hand of your obedient servant   Stephen Fairhurst

My eyes ached a bit, with the ink fading in and out. I did want to find out what happened to Stephen next, but the second letter was much longer. And besides, I ought to get going while it was still cool. I put my sandals on.

Outside it was very quiet, the way it never is in a city, and the air was a little bit hazy. It felt as if this soft, silent light might show you all sorts of things through the veil, or as if someone might be watching you and you not know.

Eva'd said always to go through theirs to the road instead of down the drive, because of it being so much quicker, so I did, stepping round the edges of their clearing so they didn't have to see me from the stables if they didn't want to. Then if they did say hello, I'd know they meant it. The grass was wet round my toes. The windows had those small panes of glass, and they flashed in the sunlight so they were a pattern of diamonds, always seeming to shift and change from dark and glittering to see-through as you passed, and above them were the barley-sugar-stick chimneys.

Then one of the windows opened and Eva leaned out in her dressing gown. "Anna! Good morning! Are you in a hurry, or could we tempt you in with some coffee?" She did mean it, I could tell. And I knew suddenly that living at Kersey was going to be all right.

Eva's dressing gown was Chinese, million-colored dragons curling round her, a bit tatty, and with a pocket coming off, like she'd caught it on something. I was used to the coffee now, and anyway, Eva said this early she liked *café au lait*, which turned out to be the same coffee but with tons of hot milk in it, which was delicious except for thick bits of milk skin that she didn't bother to fish out. When I was little and had a cold Mum used to make me hot chocolate, and she always got the skin out before she gave it to me.

Eva went to get dressed. Theo was sitting at the kitchen table, just wearing trousers, drinking his coffee black and smoking. His body looked strong for someone as old as him, muscly in the shoulders and arms, and skin glittering with silver hairs and looking like he had been brown and tough forever.

"How are you enjoying life up at the Hall?"

"All right. They came and took away all the school things—the beds and desks and stuff—so it's very empty. But I don't bother to go into most of it. And Ray's very busy. I haven't seen much of him." I suddenly realized they probably didn't know about Belle, but somehow I couldn't think of a way to talk about her.

Theo was saying, "Closing down a business is never simple. And it has been a school for a long time."

"Has it?"

"Well, I think he bought it as—what is the English?—as a going concern sometime before we came here, and that was nearly two years ago. Perhaps he could not make it pay after all." He smiled at me suddenly, like someone coming into the room you're in and switching on the light. "You must be lonely there."

"It's okay," I said, though my throat ached with a sort of pleasedness, from him guessing how it really felt. I said quickly, "My—my grandmother's there. She's—she's called Belle. And there's Cecil."

He hesitated and then said, "Who is Cecil?"

"The little boy he looks after. Well, sort of. I think he runs pretty wild."

"I had no idea there was one," he said, taking a last, lazy puff and stubbing out his cigarette. Eva came back in wearing a silky, smoky blue dress. She wasn't skinny, but not fat either, kind of small but powerful. Mum would've said she was too old to be not wearing a bra, but somehow it didn't matter, it just looked cool and relaxed. "Eva," said Theo, "did you know that Ray has a little boy running wild up at the Hall?"

"No. But there are—were—so many children there. It is strange to hear it so quiet now. Although, come to think of it, I used to see one, rather smaller than the others. He liked to hide among the trees, but he didn't look very wild. I have not seen him for some time. I wonder where his mother is."

"I think she's ill, or something, or had a breakdown."

"That would explain it." She started filling up the coffeepot again. "Theo, shall we ask Anna?"

"Ask me what?"

"You say that you want a job?"

I nodded.

"Well, we wondered if you would be interested in working here."

"Here?"

"Filing, typing, answering the telephone," said Eva. "It's not very exciting, I'm afraid. But if you were prepared to learn, there would be work in the darkroom too. We could pay you a little more than the dole. And you would save money and time, compared to traveling further."

"Magnum handle most of my affairs," Theo said. "Eva does have an agency, but she prefers to keep the reins in her own hands."

I was so surprised that I didn't know what to say. They talked a bit more about what I'd be doing, and then Eva said suddenly, "But perhaps Anna doesn't want to do it, Theo." She looked hard at me. "What do you think?"

Want to? I didn't even need to think about it, but I did make myself take a deep breath before I said, "Yeah, okay!"

We had some more coffee to celebrate, then Eva said she was hungry and made us all some toast with strong-flavored, thin, dark bread and black cherry jam on it. Theo went down to the darkroom, and Eva started to show me how everything worked.

There was a machine that answered the phone when they were out and had a tape for messages, and a big filing cabinet full of papers. "See, these are the files," said Eva. "Invoices, assignments, letters to and from Simulacrum—that's my agency—teaching jobs, tear sheets filed by publication, lecturing, expenses for tax, expenses for reclaiming, insurance for the equipment, public liability insurance, model release forms." She pulled open the top drawer of the other cabinet. "This is Theo's. Not so much—most of it is at Magnum."

"Where are the photographs?"

"Downstairs," she said, picking up a big open diary from the desk.

"In the darkroom?"

She shook her head, still looking at the diary. "No, no, absolutely not. In the studio. You must not keep photographic materials anywhere near the chemicals. And they must be away from dust also, and filed in archival paper, and the temperature must be stable, which is why downstairs is good. And we keep film in the freezer."

"In the *freezer*? Whatever for?"

"Even film has a life, and we want to use it in its prime. The freezer slows its decay."

"It seems an awful lot of fuss. Does it all matter that much?"

"Technically? Or to me personally?" Eva said, looking up.

"I—I don't know."

"Technically, yes, it does. All photographic materials deteriorate. And transparencies and negatives are the most precious, because they cannot be remade. But personally? . . . I suppose . . . I want to keep my work well—for it to last—because . . . Well, I suppose that my work is the only proof—the only manifestation—of my existence."

I looked at her. The movement of the silk had brought her nipples into points, and her hair made rough, thick curls on her brown shoulders. Before, she had always had it shoved up into an elastic band. Either way, it was difficult to imagine Eva not existing.

She said, "Not after I'm dead—though I suppose we all have our vanities about our work being more than reportage. About posterity. But I really mean my existence now. Out there in the world. What I have seen—I, Eva Peres—and how I saw it—"

On the desk beside me the telephone rang like a firebell. She glanced at me, and I must have looked a bit panic-stricken because she grinned and reached across me to pick up the receiver. "Eva Peres . . . Crispin, hello! How's it going? . . . Crispin, I know, and if I could be in two places at once I would, but even if I grew my own wings I could not be back from Madrid before Tuesday lunchtime. . . . Could the Patrons' View not be Saturday? . . . Well, I would hate to come between Lady Raynham and a half-price Harrods mink, though how she can in this heat . . . Theo will have to be enough for them, if they insist on their exclusive view . . . Okay, Crispin. We shall speak before Monday. *Ciao!*" She turned to me. "Sorry about that. Now, where were we?"

"Posterity," I said, and her eyebrows went up like she was really surprised, and then we both laughed.

I learned to do office work because Mrs. Baxter, who ran the newsagent's I had a Saturday job in, said she'd pay me more if I could. I could already type a bit from rather feeble lessons they gave the girls at school, and Mum paid for some evening classes, because I might get to be one of those super-secretaries for a banker or a politician or something and get taken on expensive trips. She'd always wanted to be one, she said, and she didn't have to say it was having me that stopped her, because I knew. Holly's mum said, "Don't, because you'll be stuck as a secretary forever because women always are and their bosses never let them be anything more because of male chau-vinism." I don't know, but Mrs. Baxter paid me an extra 20p an hour to work in the office behind the shop. *Two bob*, she still called it, and I thought suddenly of Stephen Fairhurst's letters that would cost extra sixpences, and he hoped would be worth it. And I didn't have to put up with customers giving me looks when they bought *Playboy*. So I wasn't completely boggled by the kinds of things Eva and Theo needed doing. Eva gave me a stack of stuff to file, and later, between phone calls, she said, "If you read what you are filing you will learn a lot," and it was true. I was reading things anyway but after she said that I didn't have to pretend I wasn't.

Then suddenly it was lunchtime and Theo came upstairs and got salami and a sort of dark, soft ham and weird cheese out of the fridge. It wasn't really cooking, more organizing, but it was still him who did it while Eva went on signing letters. "If you have time, you must stay and eat with us," he said when I started to go. He broke French bread into jagged logs, all soft inside. "Or perhaps—are you busy this after-noon, or shall I show you how the darkroom works? I have a print to make." Of course I wasn't, and I said so. He made an enormous salad, not cucumber and tomatoes at all, but full of things like seeds and slivers of red cabbage, which he gave me a bit of to nibble from his chopping, raw and peppery, and then we all sat down to eat.

I did the washing-up, and Theo picked up a tea towel while Eva made coffee, but he only dried the big knives he'd used to make the salad and cut the ham. "The rest can drip," he said. "Now, shall I show you the studio?"

It was painted white and the floor was old bricks, dark and glossy with polish. The light came in from big windows, and the thick black curtains were pulled right back, so that everything smelled of sun on wood. There were several filing cabinets, which said things like "TB—1968–9" and "EP—Portraits—Fonteyn–Lorca," and rows of electric sockets, and big metal cupboards with locks that Theo said had cam-eras and lighting equipment in them.

"Eva works in here more than I do. It is not usually as tidy as this." He smiled and opened a drawer in one of the filing cabinets. "I am the tidy one." He pulled out a hanging file fat with folders and labeled "TB—1948, May, Berlin." "See? This is how we do it. Each folder has the contact sheet, the negs, and then any prints from that film." He pulled one out and showed me.

The contact sheet was tiny pictures all on one piece of shiny paper, like rows of little windows in a big modern building, and through them you could see aeroplanes like metal bees and men in overalls lugging big sacks and soldiers and women in headscarves. Then he opened a different drawer, right at the bottom of the cabinet. It said "TB & EP—Spain, 1936." He lifted out a folder, which was dog-eared and faded round the edges. "This is the one. Shall we go into the dark-room?"

I don't know what I'd been expecting, but the darkroom wasn't like it a bit. For a start, although it didn't have any windows it wasn't dark but white, and there were big strip lights in the ceiling. It was very warm, with big shallow sinks and trays with stains in the corners and shelves of chemicals in bottles and measuring cylinders on one side. On the other side—the dry side, Theo called it—there was just a wide flat shelf and three machines in cubbyholes painted black inside. It was like everything downstairs was either black or white.

"What're they?" I said, pointing at the machines.

"The enlargers. They project—" He stopped. "You will see."

He glanced at the contact sheet and held the sleeve of negatives up to the light with his eyes narrowed. Then he pulled one strip gently out of its slot. "Could you put out the white lights, please?"

"Safelight" Theo called the red light, and although it turned out he meant safe for the paper, I couldn't help thinking it felt safe for us too. It was like we were wrapped and tucked up in there, with the door closed tight and the trickle and slosh of water coming and going against the hum of the ventilator, safe, and warm, and red, and breathing.

Theo loaded a negative into an enlarger and switched it on, and suddenly there on the frame below it silvery ghosts were crouching in black sunshine that inked their faces and made pools of moonlight on the cobbles. A woman staring over sandbags with a long pale gun, and a young man thin against tall gray houses and his eyes on a sky that I couldn't see.

"So," said Theo, plonking a thing like a little microscope in the middle of the picture. "We check the focus. It must be sharp—we must be able to see the grain."

He bent over it and reached up with one hand to twist a wheel on the head of the enlarger. In the safelight I could see every bone in his spine so sharp that I could have counted them all. I looked at the curve where the corner of his jaw bent to meet the curl of his ear. His back stretched and shifted, and then he straightened up and smiled at me and switched off the enlarger light.

"Shall we make a print? Perhaps you would fetch the box of paper from that shelf. Glossy, ten by eight, resin-coated, grade two."

I found what he wanted eventually and he put a sheet into a frame. The enlarger clicked on and off, five times, while he uncovered more of the paper each time. "That's it."

"But there's nothing there," I said. "It's just white paper."

"Watch what happens in the developer."

He slipped it under the liquid in one of the trays, and stood with a finger hitched under the corner of the tray, lifting it gently, like rocking a cradle, so that the liquid rolled smoothly over the paper. "Look— here it comes." I looked. Coming out of the white at me was the woman's face, very pale now, and a dark, dusty cap, and sandbags like boulders in the sun. One end of the picture stayed pale and sunny, and each strip of time was a bit darker than the last, all the way to the far end, where the man's face was like a patch of cloud against night.

"That was the dev," said Theo and held the paper up with some tongs so that the last of the liquid slid down the wet surface back into the tray. "Stop bath—a few seconds—let it drip—fix—wash."

I switched on the white light when he told me and blinked.

"What do you think?" he said, and I peered into the big tray of washing water. I must have looked confused because he went on, "We must see detail—what is happening—in the brightest sunlight, and in the darkest shadows as well. Otherwise the image . . . well, is not complete, perhaps I should say. So, which piece of time is right?"

I looked up at him. He was watching me, not the strip. It wasn't a trick question. He really wanted to know what I thought, and his mouth, which was thin with curved little lines beyond the corners, was not quite smiling but almost.

I looked back at the strip. "The middle one?"

"Yes, I think you are right."

Just one click of the light, fifteen seconds feeling like forever while I held my breath, and then into the dev. I tried to see the woman, and it was as if she was shown to us by the developer itself, as pale as a ghost at first but not misty, because as soon as she was there at all, she was clear, staring out, waiting for the enemy forty years ago.

Stop. Fix. Wash, floating and swaying in the endlessly changing water.

"Look," said Theo as I came back to the wet side from switching on the white light. "The highlights have detail, except the girl's face. But what do you think of the shadows?"

"That black square? It looks—well, it looks like a bit missing."

"It is the window. Yes. Well done." For a moment more he studied it with his eyes narrowed as if he was staring into the distance. Then he said, "Light off, please, and I shall show you what we do on a fresh print." *Click*, and the enlarger light poured down, and after a while he held a piece of card in the way, holding back the light from the window. His hands were gentle, hovering. He was frowning a little with the concentrating, and faintly, I could smell his fresh sweat. The enlarger clicked off again. And then he set the timer to five more seconds and cupped his hands so that the light was caught in them like water and only a thin stream slipped through the crack between his palms, trickling the girl's face onto the paper.

"What was her name?" I asked when the print was in the fix and we stood watching the liquid rolling over it like the swell far out to sea.

"I never knew. One doesn't, most of the time. One waits and watches and shoots. I asked if they had any news. And when things were quiet again I gave them what cigarettes I had left, and moved on. We did not think beyond the telling of that moment. Who she was is not news, only what she was. We always moved on. We had to. Soon it becomes a habit."

"Yes," I said. "It does." I felt him looking at me. "Could she be dead?"

"Of course. It was only the beginning of the civil war. And few on either side liked *las milicianas*. But one cannot know." He picked the print out of the fix and held it for a breath and slid it into the wash. "War against ordinary people moves so fast. We had to tell. This at least was something that I could do."

I looked up at him, because he didn't sound like he was talking to me. And he didn't say any more, just stood staring at the girl slipping and bellying in the flow of water. It was as if he needed to make the picture—take the photo and now print it, miles and years later—and having done it, having shown what he had seen, there weren't any words left to say.

When the time was up, without him having to tell me to I went to switch on the white light and came back across the room to where he still stood, looking into the sink. Where the black square had been was a window opening inwards, and through the silky water I could just see a jug of wine and the face of an old woman.

I WENT BACK to the Hall with two pound notes in my pocket and met Cecil in the kitchen. He was lying on his tummy under the table and trying to make a little bunch of twigs prop each other up.

"Hello," he said as soon as he saw me, and came out from under the table.

"Were you playing a game?"

"I was burning a witch."

"Ugh! Listen, I've got a present for you."

"What is it?"

"Come and see," I said. "It's in my room." I went out, but it was a moment before I heard his bare feet padding along. There was a thud and voices from the study, Belle's scratchy and loud and Ray's very low, answering her. Suddenly Cecil was so close behind me that I could feel his breath on my back, but he didn't say anything.

We went up to my room and I gave him the water-painting book wrapped up tight in its bag. He turned the bag over and over almost as if he'd never seen such a thing before. It was only when the open end unfolded itself that he peeked quickly inside, and then up at me. "Go on, then, take it out," I said.

He did, and looked at it, and then said, "What is it?"

"It's a magic painting book," I said. Of course, probably he couldn't read. "You just need water."

He opened it. "It's empty."

"That's the magic," I said. "You just need a—oh." Of course, the cheapskate makers hadn't put a paintbrush with it, and I hadn't thought in the shop of needing one. "Shall we go and see if we can find a paintbrush somewhere in one of the classrooms?"

"No!" He started to back away from me, as if I'd been about to drag him into a dark forest. "I'm not allowed."

"Oh." There was nothing else for it. "You can have one of my makeup brushes. We'll just wash it clean."

We went to the bathroom and I washed the brush and filled a glass with water from the tap, and Cecil crouched on the floor and put a streak of water across one of the pages. Pale colors, like a rainy sunset, spread out from it.

Cecil squatted back on his haunches. "What is it?"

"Do some more, and we'll see. Only wipe the brush a bit so it's not so wet."

It turned out to be a rabbit with a basket of Easter eggs, and on the next page the water made a sailing boat and the one after was a rather damp and pale pink Father Christmas.

"I know him," Cecil said. "Susan said about him. He's nice."

"What are you doing here?" said Belle's voice behind us, and I could tell she was drunk. He jumped up and knocked over the glass of water, and she cuffed him round the ear, the way mothers do. "You stupid boy, look what you've done! Clear it up at once!"

"Don't worry, I'll do it," I said, picking up the painting book before the water got to it and dropping my towel into the not very big puddle.

"Go, back downstairs! You're a bad boy!" Belle said. I could smell her gin breath. Cecil shrank towards the door but he didn't go.

"I brought him up with me," I said. "I had a present for him."

"You shouldn't waste your money," she said, and her voice was shaking as if she was angry. "He'll only spoil it."

"He's doing it very nicely. He was enjoying it."

"Let's see," she said, holding out her hand. It was dark red and it shook too, she was so angry. I gave her the book.

"Not very educational," she said. "I'm afraid I don't think he should have this." Then she opened the book at the middle, tore it in half, and threw the pieces onto the floor.

She straightened up and stood, gripping her hands as if she wanted to stop them shaking. After a moment she said, in a careful sort of way, "Anna, please don't buy him things without asking me first. I'll tell you if it's a good idea. I'm sure you understand, you're very sensible. Now, I have a headache and I'm going up to lie down. Please make sure he goes downstairs at once. Don't let him up here again." She went out, and I heard her stumbling on the stairs. Cecil was looking sadly at the pages scattered round our feet. He crouched again and poked them about until he found the sailing boat and the rather smeary rabbit, but he gave up looking for Father Christmas. Then he suddenly dropped them, jumped up, and ran out. I heard his feet going down the first few lino stairs in soft little thuds and then I couldn't hear him anymore.

I felt as sick and angry as if she'd really hit him, but there wasn't anything I could do about it. Even if it was Ray who was the person looking after Cecil, not her. Supposed to be looking after him, anyway. I bent down and collected up the pages. I found Father Christmas: he was facedown but he had landed on the cork bath mat and not smudged very much at all. I piled the other pages together and put him on top and went back into my room. If Cecil didn't want me to stick the book back together again then I'd at least help him put some of the pictures up on his wall.

Where was the Sellotape? On the chest of drawers were Stephen's letters, lying where I'd left them.

You ask how I came to join the Army. . . . In short, I had very little choice in the matter. . . . Alas, within a year of my birth, both my parents succumbed to an inflammation of the lungs, & my great-uncle was persuaded by the Vicar & the Doctor, who had long known my mother's family, to pay for me to be cared for by one Mistress Malpas, a widow of the parish there in Dorset, until I was old enough to leave her house for good, and go away to school.

An ache was crawling up the back of my neck. I dropped the letters and found the Sellotape in the drawer. The edges of Cecil's pictures where Belle had torn them were jagged and the cheap paper was creased and swollen where she had gripped them. I felt almost frightened, and then the sadness came back, and made the ache tighten.

⚜

MY FRIENDS WERE pleased with the Grand Place, the Hôtel de Ville and Notre Dame du Sablon, and my carefully constructed tour was rewarded with an invitation to join them for dinner at L'Arc-en-ciel.

There Madame Planchon's table d'hôte proved as lavish as ever, and Miss Durward, I observed, was the only one of us not to take full advantage of it. As meringues and violet creams succeeded the turbot au sauce champenois and the capon stuffed with truffles in the warm, dim parlor, I was not surprised to observe how Barraclough's talk slowed as the beer sank in his glass—in the event, he had quickly developed the taste for it—nor how his wife's eyelids drooped above her flushed cheeks and drowsy mouth.

"Pray excuse me, Major," she said, rising. "I have a little headache, and am perhaps more tired from the journey than I had thought. Will you forgive me if I retire?"

"There is nothing to forgive," I said, opening the door for her. "I trust you will feel better in the morning."

Suddenly she held out her hand. "I am so glad that we are here. . . ." Barraclough rose with a stumble and came to the door. "No, no, George, thank you. I shall do very well on my own. Good night, Major. Good night, Lucy."

It was only a little after half past seven, and not yet dark. We spoke of this and that, and if Barraclough was sleepy he was not so ill-mannered, nor so uxorious, as to appear anxious to follow his wife. He and Miss Durward described the scenes at Dover, of which I had read in *Le Moniteur*, where they had been boarding their packet even as Queen Caroline came ashore to the riotous cheers of the new king's many ill-wishers.

"They were running alongside, throwing roses in at her carriage window," said Miss Durward. "The women most of all. . . ." She rubbed her brow. "How stuffy it is!"

She rose and went to the window, but the catch resisted her efforts to open it by pinching her finger, and she cried, "Drat the thing!" and stood rubbing the injury and glaring at the unyielding casement. "Why do they have to make it so difficult? All I wish for is some air!"

I went to her. "May I open it for you?"

"No, I can manage," she said and twisted the catch again. Another tug, a squawk of unaccustomed hinges, and at last it gave. Evening air rolled into the room and she leaned out, breathing deeply and watching the burghers of Brussels setting off on their evening stroll.

"No, it's not enough," she said, turning away from the window. "I must go out."

The parlor door opened, and an inn servant entered, bobbing a curtsy.

"Madame's compliments, Monsieur, and would you come to her room at once."

Barraclough started. "Oh, aye, very well," he said, getting to his feet. "Lucy, excuse me. Major, good to see you." He went out.

"Oh, bother! I had hoped to persuade him to go for a walk," she said. "I wonder what Hetty . . ."

"Perhaps she feels unwell after all."

"Yes." She took a turn about the room, as if to calm her temper. "Perhaps I am not being fair. Her spirits do require support. Well, I shall go out anyway. I cannot bear to be stuck in here on an evening such as this, and my first time out of England."

"Miss Durward—forgive me—but your sister . . . Only that she might fear your exposure to some insult."

She looked puzzled, then laughed. "Are you thinking that she would be concerned about my safety? Or about propriety? But you know Brussels better than any of us. *Is* it unsafe?"

"No more than any other city at this hour. But ladies that I am acquainted with do not go abroad unattended here, particularly if they are unmarried. . . ." My voice trailed off, for she had turned away from me and now went to the chair, onto which she had earlier tossed her things, and started to cram her sketchbook into her reticule. "Miss Durward, if you are determined to go out, will you accept my escort?"

"Well, better that than suffocate!" she said, tying the strings of her hat with such a jerk that she might almost have wrenched them off. "But I shall be stopping to draw. I wish you will not find it intolerably boring."

I caught up my cane and opened the door for her. "I could never find your company boring."

She stopped dead in the entry. "I'm sorry. That was shockingly ill-mannered of me. It is very kind of you, and I am grateful."

I would have offered her my arm but that she was already halfway down the passage. "Would you care to walk on the ramparts?" I said, catching up with her. "They afford a good view of both the town and the countryside. But it might be wise to take a shawl. It will be chilly when the sun sets, and that is earlier than you will be accustomed to in Lancashire."

"No. Shawls get in the way when I am working. But the ramparts sound promising."

She set off with a long, easy stride that made me recall Dora's gait in her eager youth, but my leg was already aching from the day's exercise, and even with my cane I had some difficulty in keeping pace. After a few hundred yards I said, "We have some little way to go: perhaps you would prefer it if I called a fiacre. They are open, so you will still be able to see the town."

"Oh, no. It's good to be able to walk at a sensible speed at last. I love Hetty dearly, but her dawdling along drives me to distraction. It does afford me the time for sketching, but then she disapproves when I have to run to catch up with her."

For some way our route lay along the same streets as it had that morning, but she looked about her as keenly as ever, so keenly that her replies to my conversation were decidedly random. It was only when she stopped before the Théâtre du Monnaie that I realized why this should be so, for without a word she dragged out her sketchbook and started to draw. In the daylight the prospect of the place du Monnaie and the new theater showed all the elegancies that modern civilization affords. Now, with rapid lines and scribbles, she set down the night that grew about the flaring gas lamps and glowing portico, the darkening roofs, the pits of blackness behind area railings, the shadows lying in a street-woman's skirts, and in a gentleman's eyes.

Miss Durward snapped her sketchbook shut and looked round. "Oh, there you are, Major. Which way do we go now?"

It was not the nearest part of the ramparts that was our goal, and by the time we reached it, it was all I could do to keep up with her. Now it was I who answered her questions at random. She asked about the billeting and mustering of the regiments in the Waterloo campaign and the Duchess of Richmond's famous ball, about the weather and the season. "As to the season," I said, leaning heavily on my cane as I followed her up the steps to the bastion that permitted the best view in all directions, "you have but to look about you. It was just this time of year. Would you care to rest on the parapet?"

It was a little high for her, but she shook her head at my proffered hand and hitched herself up backwards as easily as any schoolboy. When she was safely settled I got up in my turn. She sat, her hands still gripping the edge of the stone so that her shoulders were hunched, and gazed out over the countryside.

"It is difficult to imagine," she said eventually.

"What is?"

"All this . . ." She gestured to where the gardens of lilies and pink roses gave way to apple and peach trees, and thence to the massed green of new-grown fields and ancient woods. "All this, being fought over."

"Much of it was not fought over. At least, not in the sense that you mean. Beyond the battlefield itself, the chief effect was that with so vast an army quartered all around, the farmers and shopkeepers made more profit by supplying its needs during the Hundred Days than they might otherwise have made in a lifetime."

"And I suppose the other kinds of women also made a profit."

Startled, I half glanced at her, but she had none of the heightened color and lifted chin that very young ladies show when they have desired to shock. Her tone had been quite matter-of-fact, and after a moment, although I avoided her eye, I said, "Undoubtedly."

She turned on me. "Oh, Major Fairhurst, for heaven's sake, don't look so scandalized! You may write of such things, I suppose, but I may not speak of them. Is that it?"

"No—no—of course not. Have I not apologized for that letter?"

"You ought not have had to apologize: it is ridiculous. I was so angry with my mother's friends, but of course they did not understand. But with you at least I thought I need not be mealymouthed."

"Indeed you need not. If I appeared taken aback I am sorry for it. It is not for me to judge what you choose to say."

"How right you are! But I am sorry that I was cross. Shall we walk on?"

She slid off the parapet before I could help her, oblivious to the dust that adhered to her skirts, and as I followed I found that the rest had eased my leg, so that I was quite able to keep pace with her.

The warmth had gone from the air even as the last light had faded from the sky. Up on the city wall we were exposed to the evening breeze, and since the walkway was narrow I was close enough to Miss Durward to realize that she was shivering a little. I was entirely willing to offer her my coat, but to do so in anything less than a blizzard would have exposed her to some curious glances. I knew better by now than to say so, however, and merely asked, "Would you care for some refreshment? That coffeehouse down there is quite respectable, even at this hour."

"That would be delightful," she said, turning to go down the nearest set of steps. "I realize that we never had tea."

"Nor did we. We shall make up for the deficiency here, although I fear that the tea may not be quite as you find it at home." We made our way in and I set a chair for her at a table in the corner of the room. "But there is coffee, or perhaps a glass of wine?"

"A glass of wine! Now that is an excellent notion. Hetty has never cared for it, and of course George does not drink it at all."

"Knowing that, I thought it most courteous of him to offer to bespeak some for me at dinner. If I had thought that you would join me, I should have accepted it most readily."

She smiled at me. "Then next time we shall be companions in dissipation."

The waiter appeared at my elbow and I ordered a carafe of red wine. As soon as he had begun to attend to customers at another table, Miss Durward picked up her sketchbook and started to draw him where he stood patiently, waiting for them to decide between cognac and eau-de-vie. He was tall and very young, with fair Flemish hair sun-bleached almost white and skin burned brown like a farmer's, but I observed that my companion was setting down the figure in lines rather than the masses of dark and light that her pencil had conjured in the place du Monnaie.

I was saying as much when the wine was brought to our table.

"It is a question of whether it is the light that is interesting, or the subject," Miss Durward replied. She raised her glass. "Shall we say, to Brussels?"

"To Brussels!" I said, and we both drank. She was smiling, and then her eyes narrowed at something behind me. I turned to follow her gaze. The waiter was standing outside, trimming the flaring wick of one of the lamps that hung before the café. As I turned back, Miss Durward's gaze shifted to the open sketchbook before her, she snatched up her pencil, and drew in a dozen lines his light-flooded profile, his upstretched arms, his simple absorption in his task. Then she closed the book and sat back without speaking, as if the act of putting what she saw on paper was all that the moment required.

After a while, I said, "Was your journey into Staffordshire a success?"

She nodded, and then words came to her tongue. "Indeed it was. They were most welcoming. Mr. Wedgwood had taken the trouble to come back from his works at Etruria early only to show us his brother's work—sun-pictures, he called them. My father and I were fascinated, although it was not easy to make out the images, for they must be kept in the dark, lest they darken further, and may only be looked at by candlelight. Mr. Wedgwood explained how his brother brushed pa-

per or white leather with nitrate of silver—in solution, you understand—and then the object to be copied was placed on top of it, and
the whole put in the sun. It took only a few minutes, he said, if the
sunlight was strong enough." She pulled her chair close in, propped
her elbows on the table, and continued. "You see, the nitrate of silver
tarnishes by the agency of light, where the object does not protect it,
even to the degree of translucency of each part of the object."

"Rather as, when one lifts a long-fallen apple from the lawn, it
leaves its mark in the pallor of the grass below."

"Yes! And, of course, if the grass is again exposed, like the paper,
the light darkens it once more. Only the sun-pictures are done in a
matter of minutes, and they are so exact! Mr. Wedgwood showed us
one of a vine leaf. Every vein and stem was as clear as if I had drawn it,
only white, of course, on a darkened ground, like a white-line wood
engraving. My father was mainly interested in the precision of it, for
he has an idea of copying prints automatically by such a process, but
it was so beautiful too! There were some pictures of insect wings,
made through a sun-microscope so that they appeared larger than in
life. I almost feared that they would float off if I breathed too close."
She paused, as if the mere recollection caused her to stop her breath.

"And Mrs. Greenshaw—I should say, Mrs. Barraclough—she accompanied you?"

"Yes, for Tom was well enough by then to leave with my mother,
and it does Hetty good to get about. But she stayed in the drawing
room with Mrs. Wedgwood and some of her daughters. She said they
were charming, very easy and unaffected. But she could tell you more
of them than I." She drank a little wine. "My father was disappointed
because although Mr. Thomas Wedgwood did try to copy prints with
a camera obscura, time blurred the picture. My father and Mr. Wedgwood agreed that there being so many difficulties precludes any prof-
itable application of the process."

I refilled both our glasses. Even Miss Durward's concentration in
drawing had quite a sober quality; I had not seen her face so animated

since the most acute hours of her anxiety for Tom, and never with such eagerness. "Tom Wedgwood tried muriate of silver too, his brother said, which turns pale lavender, and violet at the darkest, and in a matter of seconds even in twilight. But it is not so readily applied, because it is not soluble in water."

A clatter from the back of the café made me aware that the waiter was lifting chairs onto tables, and that most of the other customers had departed. Miss Durward looked around her. "Goodness, it must be late."

"We should perhaps make our way back."

"I suppose we should," she said.

I signaled to the waiter and paid the reckoning. He followed us out and reached up once again, this time to extinguish the lamps altogether. I thought of Miss Durward's sketch, and to judge by her little nod and smile, so did she. Then she said, "The strangest thing was, to be able to make a picture of something real with no intervention—no agency—except the natural properties of the sun. The object creates its own image. Mr. Wedgwood referred to the image as a simulacrum—a replicant. And then suddenly it has an independent life."

"It is like a ghost," I said. "The object is—may be—long lost, in another time. Its image lives on, in a different place—" I could not continue, for suddenly the image of my love was too clearly before me for speech to be possible.

"Yes," said Miss Durward. She tucked her hand into my arm, and I felt the thin firmness of her through my sleeve. "But only when it is kept in the dark."

The cold doesn't let go. Toes and fingers die, and the men don't know it; they have to thaw before they rot. Shoes are sucked off by the icy mud. Lips freeze. Horses leave bloody hoofprints in the snow: their shoes are long gone. If they fall they are shot. If the enemy is near and silence is ordered, instead the man must beat his horse's brains out with a musket butt. The tears freeze on his cheeks before they can fall. I stumble over the body of a camp woman and her child. Wine trickles from their mouths, but they are dead. Their feet are bare, the blood frozen in the mud. We have had no food for three days. When we find food, the dysentery is worse, sucking the life from the mind. Three men are to be flogged; I must make sure it is done before the French come up.

The stones of the mountain track are sunk in mud and ice; a man slips and falls over the edge. The air is still and cold, so we hear the crunch of his body on stone, the rattle of his tin cup and musket, cracking ice and then smothered by snow, over and over again. Then silence. There is no time to find his body: he is one of so many. The road goes on, trampled to black.

My mind is emptied by pain. I cannot think beyond now, and now is agony. It would be so much easier to stop, give up, sleep forever in the snow.

❧ *III* ❧

I HAD ESCORTED MISS DURWARD AND THE BARRACLOUGHS on an expedition to Mechelin, but I was sufficiently out of practice as a guide to have failed to take note of the festival of St. Anthony of Padua, and the crowding of the Brussels streets with banners and penitents and bell-ringing priests delayed our carriage on our return so greatly that I did not reach the theater until halfway through the third act, and in a state of considerable weariness. At the start of the fourth act Katrijn looked up to where I sat and I lifted my hand in acknowledgment and apology, for, knowing that she resented the constant comings and goings of the fashionable people who were more concerned to be seen by their peers than to see the play, I had hitherto always arrived before curtain up. She turned aside and smiled at me, while the rest of the audience saw Elmire smiling at Tartuffe's hypocrisy.

By the time I reached her dressing room, she was putting on her hat. I bent to kiss her cheek. "Dearest, I'm so sorry. We were at Mechelin and I forgot about St. Anthony."

"No matter," she said, turning away to pick up her gloves. "It was not a good performance, in any case."

"Impossible!" I said heartily.

She did laugh at that. "What took you to Mechelin?"

"Miss Durward was anxious to see the cathedral. And Mrs. Barraclough desired to buy lace."

She nodded and allowed me to lay her cloak over her shoulders. As we left, I put my hand into my pocket to find a few coins for my customary tip to Sluter, the old stage doorman, and found as well the gift I had contrived to buy while my friends were resting after luncheon.

"Good night, M'moiselle, M'sieur le commandant," said Sluter. I opened the door for Katrijn. "Oh, by the way, M'sieur, I sent round to the box office as you asked. Thursday evening, box eight in the second tier."

Katrijn was looking back over her shoulder.

I thanked Sluter, tipped him, and hurried after Katrijn. "I brought you a gift from Mechelin."

She turned the soft parcel over in her hands. "Thank you, Stephen, that is sweet of you. Can I guess what it is? But perhaps I should open it when we are indoors."

"That might be wise," I said.

We spoke of small news, for it was a few days since we had seen each other, and then she said suddenly, "Box eight? I know the sight lines of yours are bad, but would it not be better just to move a little further round? Eight in the second tier is very far away."

"Oh, it is not for me," I said quickly, changing my stick into the other hand, so that I might take her arm in mine. "The Barracloughs were wishful to see the play. I thought they would prefer to be further from the pit."

"Of course. But I could have arranged it for you."

"I didn't like to trouble you over such a small matter," I said, and we crossed the road into the rue de l'Écuyer.

"So, what did your friends think of Mechelin?"

"They were most impressed, I think. Miss Durward would have stayed in Sint-Katelijnstraat and the Béguinage forever, sketching. She was interested too in the chapel of the Knights of the Golden Fleece in the cathedral, for she is considering making a series of prints of the Wars of the Roses. She says there is a great taste for tales of knights and chivalry in England."

"The Wars of the Roses? That sounds most romantic."

"Civil war is rarely romantic, whatever the author of *Waverley* may write. But I am a trifle worried, for I know little about the armies of that time, and I shall be in trouble if Miss Durward needs the kind of information about the Battle of Bosworth that I have been supplying her with for all these months about Salamanca and Waterloo."

"Have you?" Katrijn nodded to the concierge and we started upstairs. Meike had heard our arrival and was holding open the door to Katrijn's apartment.

"She needed the information for her work, and I could supply it because of mine. I have suggested to her that we might all go to Bruges for a few days."

"I see. And, yes, Bruges is very fine, if you like those old buildings." Katrijn put the package down on a side table and stripped off her gloves. "Now, what can this be?"

The hosier had scattered a few lavender flowers into the wrappings, so that their scent rose as she undid the ribbon. When she took up the stockings they streamed from her hand like fresh milk, a foam of lace still lying among the tissue paper. "Thank you, Stephen! They are beautiful!" she said, still holding the stockings as she touched my cheek to kiss me, so that the cool, soft silk caught, for I had not shaved since the morning.

"Not as beautiful as you," I said. "I wish you would allow me to give you more than such small gifts. You will not let me pay for your apartment, or your gowns." I took her in my arms and kissed her mouth.

"Stephen!"

I let go. "I'm sorry. Was I hurting you?"

"No—but I am famished."

"Of course," I said. I had dined with Miss Durward and the Barracloughs at one of my favorite inns, near Eppegem, which had a fine view of the castle of Het Steen, but I poured wine for us both, and helped Katrijn to some of the fruit and cake that was her customary supper.

She took a fig, and I watched her white teeth split the skin and bite down into the red, seed-thick flesh inside. When she had finished it, she wiped her fingers and said, "You must tell me what your friends think of *Tartuffe*. It is *Tartuffe* on Thursday, isn't it?"

"Yes."

She said that she was a little tired, but by no means too exhausted to deny me, and afterwards she fell asleep so deeply that when I rose at dawn she did not wake until I was almost dressed.

"Stephen?"

"I must go," I said, bending to kiss her sleep-smoothed brow. "I am sorry that I disturbed you."

"You did not," she said, stretching like a small brown kitten among the linen that still breathed our scent. "Must you leave so early? I don't have to be at rehearsal until ten." She sat up, and the sheet fell from her shoulders so that her creamy breasts with their brown nipples were soft and full in my hands and the camomile and cinnamon scent of her hair came to my nostrils.

"I must go," I said, my hands lingering. "I have engaged to be at L'Arc-en-ciel at nine, and I must change before that."

"Of course," she said, curling down again under the covers. "*À bientôt, chéri!*"

"*À bientôt!*"

When I reached L'Arc-en-ciel, shaved, washed, and changed, my friends were at the breakfast table, and as I opened the parlor door—for we had long since ceased to stand on ceremony—Mrs. Barraclough was saying, "If I had known, George, of course I would have asked you if I might spend that much. But you gave me no indication that you wished to limit the—"

"If your own good sense, Hetty—" began Barraclough, then stopped as I coughed loudly on the threshold. "Ah, Fairhurst, come in! We are a little behindhand this morning."

Mrs. Barraclough appeared pale and heavy-eyed behind the coffeepot, and said, a little fretfully, "I can't think where Lucy has got to. George, have you seen her?"

"No," he said, holding out his cup to her. "At no time of night does the dressing-room window command a view of your sister's comings and goings."

"Some coffee for you, Major?" said Mrs. Barraclough, hastily. "You must forgive us, we are at sixes and sevens this morning—paying for such a delightfully full day yesterday, you understand."

"I am glad you enjoyed it," I said, taking the cup she offered me. "I was afraid you and Miss Durward might be excessively tired. Do you still desire to go out today? We might easily put the expedition off."

"Oh, nothing tires Lucy! And I would not miss Waterloo for the world. Such tales of grandeur and heroism as you have told us!"

The door opened and Miss Durward entered. "Good morning, Major—George, Hetty," she said, in a voice so calm that I suspected that her thoughts were elsewhere.

"Where have you been?" Mrs. Barraclough said. "The coffee is almost cold, and here is the major, wishful to set off immediately."

"I'm sorry, I was working," was all that Miss Durward replied as she took a cup of the still steaming coffee. Silence fell, while Barraclough finished his ham and eggs. His wife pushed the coffee things away from her with a clatter.

"As to setting off immediately," I said, no more emollient a topic occurring to me, "we have no need to hurry. I await your convenience."

Miss Durward raised her head briefly from the single piece of toast that was her breakfast, caught my eye, and smiled.

I had suggested ordering an open carriage for our expedition, since the day promised to be fine and warm, and if the ladies did not wish to alight, they might see more of what was of interest from a barouche than from a chaise. But I had forgotten how the sudden shadow of the Forêt de Soignes fell across the road. After the bright sunlight it was as cold and dark as a thundercloud, and Mrs. Barraclough shivered. I felt familiar, sick, liquid fear churning in my guts.

Just as I had once learned to clamp such fear close within me by numbering my men and studying the ground, I later learned under the eyes of ladies and gentlemen to still the memory of it with a lively anecdote about the great Flemish oxen and their equally huge and ponderous drivers. I was about to do so again when Mrs. Barraclough shut her sunshade with a snap that echoed the brisk hoofbeats resounding among the trees.

"How tall the trees are!" exclaimed Miss Durward, before I could speak. "Are they all beeches?"

"For the most part," I said, recovering myself this time with talk of nature. "I believe there is also oak, and hazel. Chestnut too."

"And you marched in the dark?"

I nodded. "We left Brussels at about three, though my regiment had been ready since well before midnight, the call to arms having sounded at nine. A little after daybreak we reached the village where Lord Wellington and his staff had spent the night, barely a hamlet it was, which someone said was named Waterloo"—everybody always smiled at that—"and we had time to allow the men to stop for their breakfast. And then we marched on to Quatre Bras, to keep the road open between us and the Prussians. It wouldn't have done for Buonaparte to succeed in cutting our communications with our allies." Barraclough nodded. "He did his best, though, and in the event it turned into a regular battle. It is written of as a mere rehearsal for Waterloo, and I suppose in the eyes of history it was. But to those of us that were there, it was as bad as anything that came before or after. . . . I thought—if you like the idea—we would go there first, and follow the Allied army back towards where Lord Wellington placed our center at Mont St. Jean. We may cover in an hour or two what took us three days at the time." I smiled. "His lordship generally named his battles after where he spent the preceding night. But I had it from his secretary—Lord Fitzroy Somerset, you may know—that Lord Wellington's real opinion was that the English do not care to pronounce French names, such as Mont St. Jean, or even La Belle Alliance, which General Blücher wished it to be called. His lordship knew we would talk more, and more happily, of an honest Flemish place called Waterloo!"

The carriage at that moment arriving at a clearing, we were suddenly rinsed in sunshine. I smelled the green forest scents through which we had been driving, the clean dust that rose faintly in our wake as the birds began to fall into their midday quiet. A brief dip back into the deep shade of the trees, and then we were out in light again, breasting the ridge of Mont St. Jean, and rolling down the gentle slope towards the farm at La Haie Sainte.

I had bespoken a light luncheon at Quatre Bras, but although the inn there was better run than one might expect in so small a place, even Miss Durward ate more on this occasion than Mrs. Barraclough, who shook her head at almost every dish. Once or twice I saw her quietly press her handkerchief to her lips. It did not altogether surprise me, therefore, that as we rose, she swayed on her feet.

Barraclough and I caught her as she staggered.

"Thank you, Fairhurst," he said. "I'll take her now." I relinquished her to him and withdrew from the room.

It was at least half an hour before Miss Durward found me where I was sitting on a bench outside, hoping the sun's warmth would banish the weariness that had come on the heels of my earlier, remembered fear.

"I'm afraid my sister does not feel equal to coming with us this afternoon," she said as I rose.

"I had feared that such would be the case. I do hope that she is not seriously unwell?"

"Oh, no," she said. "She is lying down in one of the bedchambers, and I am sure she will be better presently."

"Would she not prefer to return immediately to Brussels? I have ordered the horses put to."

"No, not at all. We have settled all that," she said. "At least—if the plan is agreeable to you. Hetty wishes to rest for a while, but she has no particular need of female company, and I have persuaded George that he should stay with her. You will have to make do with me alone."

"That will be delightful," I said, with perhaps more emphasis than was entirely polite to the Barracloughs. However, I could not ignore my scruples. "But your sister—"

"Oh, she has not the least objection. I have said that we would return by dinnertime—is that right?—and if she is unwell, you say the landlady is respectable."

"Unquestionably."

"So, Major Fairhurst—what is it that the French say?"

"*En avant?*"

"Yes. *En avant!*"

The carriage was standing on the far side of the yard. I opened the door. "Also, they used to cry, '*L'Empereur recompensera ce qu'il avancera!*'"

"And did it work?" she asked as I handed her up. "Would they advance on the promise of reward?"

"Oh, yes. There was little Buonaparte didn't know about handling men. But the men loved him too, as ours never loved Lord Wellington." I got in beside her. "Excuse me, I am afraid of crushing your gown." She gathered the plain muslin into her lap without thought for creases, and I leaned forward to tell the driver to make for the crossroads at La Belle Alliance. He shook the reins so that the carriage started gently forward and turned out onto the road. Over the rattle of the wheels I said, "Is there any particular part of the field that you are interested to see?"

"Well, now that I have got rid of Hetty and George"—she tilted her bonnet to keep the sun from her eyes, for she carried no sunshade, and I thought her color was heightened—"that is, I think the lie of the land from Mont St. Jean is important," she continued. "But I would particularly like to see the Château d'Hougoumont and perhaps sketch a few perspectives there. But . . ." She hesitated. "As we were traveling from Brussels—through the Namur Gate and into the forest—you told us about marching along it that night, knowing what was to come. It has made me think about battlefields." She saw my puzzlement. "I mean, about the places where battles have happened—about how they appear to those who come after, with knowledge of the past."

"You said on the city ramparts that it was hard to imagine."

"Yes."

"Even if I described how we only checked Reille's corps over there?" I said, turning to gesture towards the cornfields behind us, "And how when the Duke of Brunswick was killed—he was quite young, for his father died at Jena—we thought we had met our match? It was only when General Cooke arrived with the Guards, from over there"—I pointed again—"that we regained control."

"I have read so much of such matters, and I can people the prospect in my imagination the better for having been here. But—but what of the place itself?" She frowned. "I shall use the knowledge—what you tell me, what I read—to draw a picture in my mind, and then on paper. In the end it is a matter of light, of form, shadow, texture, structure. Then I shall pick up my etching needle and watch it cut through the smoke and into the ground and down to the copper below." She pointed ahead. "There! That curve, where the brow of the hill drops, that will draw the eye down to meet the sunken road, I think. And then I can ask you who was before that ridge—"

"I can answer that without difficulty," I said, "for it was my own regiment."

She nodded and, without concluding her speech, took out her sketchbook and became instantly absorbed. The familiar road was ahead of me; I had traveled it many times, but rarely with a companion who sought out my company, demanded such exact memories of me, and then withdrew from the conversation so utterly. She peered

ahead, her eyes narrowed against the prospect, and down to her paper, and up again, and her thin hand, as ever faintly stained with ink
and the silvery shadow of pencil lead, moved about her work as a
saddler's or a gunsmith's does, in quiet certainty, without flourish or
hesitation.

We reached the Château d'Hougoumont, standing peacefully in
its gardens and orchards. "It's really no more than a comfortable
manor house." I smiled. "In the smoke—we once spoke of that before, I think—the French mistook that red-brick wall for a company
of Guards and fired upon it, furiously, they say."

She nodded, seemingly so absorbed in her drawing that I fell silent. "Go on, I'm listening."

"The light infantry were in the orchard, and they held them off for
a long time. Twelve thousand French, and some of their best men at
that. Twelve hundred of the Second and Third Guards inside. And
they held it. But in the end . . . It was only a handful of them that
marched out."

She nodded again.

At last, at my order, the carriage rolled forward again, across the
great killing field itself, where not long since the regiments had fought
on, blind with smoke and blood, till the very last man fell to close the
square of bodies.

Miss Durward dropped her sketchbook into her lap with a sharp
sigh. "I can draw it," she said. "I can sketch the lie of the land and the
trees and the houses. I can go home and look up the uniforms and
draw all the colors and buttons correctly—the public love uniforms. I
can show trained men doing what they do best. I can study anat-
omy—or, at least, that which the world will allow me to study. I can
draw the horses, and the wounds—not too appalling, of course, just
enough to make the buyer shiver. Then there is the excitement of
courage, danger, a little fear. In the printshop the customers' hearts
beat faster, their eyes grow wide and excited, their palms are damp,
almost as if they see a beautiful woman . . ." She stopped.

Through the headache that was gathering behind my eyes I tried to understand. "What you are saying is—is it?—that to look at a picture of war is the same as looking at a picture of passion, or loss, or fear. It breeds again the pity and the terror within one. In your work—as an actor does on stage—that is what you seek to conjure up."

"Of course," she said, turning on me and frowning, as if with the difficulty of articulating her thought. "But—should I? Is it not making money out of death?"

"There is no shame in memorials. They comfort those that are left behind, perhaps even reconcile them to their loss. And to be the means of transmitting news is honorable work. Citizens have the right to know what is done in their name."

"Yes, but I am not making memorials, and Waterloo is no longer news. I am making money from people's desire to taste horror, just for excitement's sake. I am selling the pleasure of fear. Look!" She leaned forward to call to the driver. *"Arrêtez-vous là, s'il vous plaît!"* He pulled up the horses and she scrambled out before I could assist her, only then turning back to me to say, "Shall we stop here? You must know this part of the field the best."

Indeed I did but struggled, as I had not on the day, to make my way through the heat towards the sandpit at the base of the knoll that we had been ordered to hold. Miss Durward climbed quickly up the small elevation and stood in the thin shade of the trees, looking about her. As I came up, she said, a little out of breath but as if there had been a few seconds, not several minutes, since she had spoken the first part of her thought, "If I could only draw it as I see it now, with the battle more vivid in my mind than it can ever be on a printing plate or a twelve-ounce paper . . . If only I could draw *this* scene so well that what is in my *mind* is conjured in the viewer's. That would be more honest! Do you understand?"

"I'm not sure I altogether do," I said, the heat beginning to hammer in my head.

She seized my shoulder to turn me towards the country spread out before her. "Look! Look at these hills and fields! Put them together with your memories! You will never see them thus in a gilt frame on a parlor wall!"

I looked as she demanded. The heat that day had been blistering, and now it seemed to waver before my eyes. Our savagery was numbered, chained, and uniformed, the brute harnessed and hardened. We were made little cogs in the machine, each turning another, I saw, and then clamor began to beat about me, and the stench of fear. The dust stung in my eyes, rasped my throat, clogged in my ears. I could not see, hear, breathe. There was blood in my eyes, sour and stinging. No breath—no sense—no thought. Only the machine, grinding.

IT WAS A broken branch that I first knew again, stinging where it pressed into my cheek, and then the high song of birds and the leaves' soft shifting, stilling the roar of blood in my ears. I opened my eyes, and observed with the clarity of extreme exhaustion how even the jagged end of the long-dead branch was smoothed and silvered with time and sunlight. Miss Durward was kneeling beside me.

"Are you all right? I'm so sorry."

"It's nothing," I mumbled, or thought I did. I tasted earth and then blood, and for a moment the darkness flickered before me again, but it was no more than a split lip. I found I was lying huddled on the ground, my arms about my head, and my legs cramped up to my chest. My boots scraped among the sandy soil. After a few moments I contrived, with an effort of will as much as of body, to straighten myself a little, then prop myself on my elbow. Miss Durward was looking anxious.

"I'm so sorry," she said. "You are ill—I had no notion—"

I did not reply, for all my little strength was concentrated on clinging to the light.

After a long time, she said suddenly, "This is the first time in my life that I have ever regretted not carrying salts, as my mother tells me to. But in any case, I am sure that you would prefer brandy."

"I would, and I have some," I said, sitting up after another small struggle, and feeling in the inner pocket of my coat. "It is my habit to carry it when escorting ladies." I held out the flask. "You have had a shock, and through my fault. May I offer you some?"

She took a good pull at it, wiped her mouth on the back of her hand like any urchin, and gave the flask back to me. "Thank you. Especially since your need is undoubtedly greater than mine."

The brandy having done its work on us both, it was not long before Miss Durward and I were making our way back towards the field gateway where the carriage had halted, but I could not have told you whose arm, as we walked slowly over the rough ground, was supporting whom.

"I think we should go back to the inn," said Miss Durward as we approached the barouche.

"I should not wish to curtail your visit," I said. "There must be more that you wish to see."

She stopped and glanced about her, almost dismissively, then turned towards me, her hand on the carriage door. "That is very kind of you, but I had not realized . . . Major, I am ashamed of myself. I did not think . . . all I thought of was of information, of what you could tell me. I said it was unimaginable, but you must see it all the time."

"Yes."

I said no more, for I could not have spoken of what I had seen, of how I felt it as I felt my vanished limb, my lost love: these things were no less real, no less alive, no less painful, for existing only in my mind. Nor could I speak of the stillness to which I had woken, the stillness of the jagged end of a broken branch, pressing into my cheek.

The carriage began to roll south again. I was startled to observe that the sun was already yellow and westering, for I had no sense of so much time having passed. I watched Miss Durward looking about her at the gilded land through which we traveled. After some time, I said, "I hope Mrs. Barraclough will be well enough for the journey home, but if she does not feel equal to it, I am sure you would be comfortable at the inn, though it's modest enough."

"I'm sure she will feel better. At least, if it is anything like last time." She went on, still staring hard out of the barouche. "Perhaps I ought not to speak of it, but you must have guessed—or I should tell you, I think." She hesitated.

"Tell me what?"

"Hetty is—she is in an interesting condition. And she is never well then—quite apart from her fears of—of what happened before. . . ."

Her voice trailed off, and what of her cheek I could see was decidedly pink.

I said quickly, "I quite understand. I shall take care not to urge her to any activity that she might find too strenuous."

"That is very thoughtful of you. Will you forgive me if I draw?"

"Yes, indeed," I said. "Is that not why we embarked on this outing?"

She smiled and pulled out her sketchbook. "Of course."

For all the pleasure of Miss Durward's company I asked nothing more than to be silent again. My spirits were still shaken by the clamor and stench that had reached out from the past to render me insensate for I knew not how long. And now how simple by contrast was the innocent joy and gentle apprehension implicit in Miss Durward's news! Before my eyes came an image of her sister's round, pale cheek, leaning on one hand at the luncheon table, and of the droop of her neck, drawing the eye down to where the pale cambric of her gown fell about her body. I no longer had any desire to marry Mrs. Barraclough, or any woman, and at the news that she was with child, I could not avoid feeling an ache whose cause was a lack within my memory, a grief for something that I had never known.

By the time I was aroused from my thoughts, by the carriage slowing to turn in to the inn yard at Quatre Bras, I had started to shiver in good earnest. Such was my state when we reached Brussels that the Barracloughs insisted on taking me straight to the rue de l'Écuyer, and as the carriage deposited me outside my lodgings, I mumbled apologies and farewells, and knew that the quinquina bark powder had failed, as it failed us all from time to time, and the fever was upon me.

ᏸᏉᏸ

WHEN I FIRST woke I was crouched under the sheet, shivering, with all the cold space pressing round me as if it was trying to get into my bones. I'd slept late, I realized. It wasn't sunny so maybe that was why I was cold. I was hungry, and I'd said I'd be at the stables at ten. I washed and dressed as quickly as I could, not bothering to put the radio on because it never seemed to make sense anymore: the talking came from too far away. There were Stephen's letters.

. . . *I was not there. My memories of the year '8 are of the horrors of the Light Division's ragged retreat to Vigo—dragging ourselves as bait to draw the French after us through ice & snow—& of our grief at hearing of the death at Corunna of the noble Sir John Moore, founding father & genius of our Regt. Such memories can never be erased. . . .*

The clock radio flipped over. 9:50. I was going to be late if I didn't get on with it. I picked up a comb from where it was lying on Cecil's water paintings, and suddenly I couldn't bear the thought of anyone else seeing Stephen's letters, his writing, his words. I slid them carefully into the drawer. Then I picked up Cecil's painting and the makeup brush and took them downstairs with me.

He wasn't in the kitchen, so after I'd had some toast I went to his room and put the pictures and the brush on his chest of drawers. There was a sweetish, wet smell coming from the bed. I wondered if Susan would've changed it for him.

There was a new painting on the wall. He'd spattered white paint like snow over a brown animal with long legs like a horse, lying down in a patch of white, with bright red paint smeared and stabbed all over its head and trickling down the wall onto the floor. He'd said he had bad dreams: perhaps it was one of those. Poor Cecil.

On the way out I almost bumped into Ray in the passage outside the kitchen. He was lugging a carrier bag full of bottles.

"Oh, hello, Anna. Off out again?"

"Theo and Eva have given me a job."

"*Have* they now," he said, passing a hand over his curdled-looking hair. "That's good news. Are you—are you working long hours?"

"I don't really know. It's sort of when they need me. Most mornings, I think." I made to get past him into the garden, and then thought I'd better say something about Cecil. "Um—I think Cecil's wet his bed."

"Oh, not *again!*" He sighed, with a sort of obvious heave of his chest and a let's-be-grown-ups-together grin at me. "He's got worse, I think. I suppose I'd better see to it. You wouldn't think he'd got a bathroom right next door, would you?"

"I suppose he's only little."

"Alas, yes." He glanced beyond me into the kitchen. "Which reminds me, Anna, Belle says you brought him upstairs yesterday."

"Yeah?"

"Well, of course you meant it kindly, but now that Belle's . . . I think it's better if he stays in his own quarters. He's so little, and this is such a big place, it's impossible to supervise him properly if he has the run of it, you know."

"He wasn't doing any harm. I was with him," I said. "And I don't think he would anyway."

"No, perhaps not. But—well—I thought I'd just drop a word in your ear. It wouldn't do for him to get used to being upstairs."

"Why not?"

"Well—as I say—did I?—he used to trot along in Susan's wake, but there's no one to supervise him, not now. And if he bumped into Belle . . . she doesn't like it."

I gave up. It wasn't as if I wanted Cecil to bump into Belle either, and it was the first time Ray'd asked me to do or not do anything. So I said, "Okay," and he said again, "Good news about the job." Then he squared his shoulders and sighed a bit, and went back into the kitchen, and I headed out and across the crunchy brown grass into the trees.

When I got to the stables Eva was sitting at the desk upstairs with a muddle of bits of paper in front of her.

"Oh, Anna, thank goodness! I am trying to make sense of these receipts and I really should be writing my paper for Madrid. Take some coffee for yourself and I'll show you what it is that needs to be done."

I sorted all the bits into the piles she said, equipment, materials, travel, accommodation, processing, professional fees, and so on, and wrote the amounts up as neatly as I could in all the right columns in a big ledger, and somehow I didn't mind that it ought to have been incredibly boring. The receipts said things like "Hotel Mamounia, Marrakech," and one said "Ernst Leitz Wetzlar Gmbh" and then had black squiggly handwriting like the stuff monks do. I had to ask Eva about that one. She glanced at it and said, "It's German. Repair of sand and impact damage. I dropped one of the Leicas off a pyramid. The strap broke."

"D'you mean Egypt?"

"Yes. It was a commission—you will find the invoice somewhere, for a flat fee. I think Time-Life. Anyway, Leicas can be repaired forever, thank God. Now, where was I?"

I went back to the pile of receipts. There were things that were closer to home but still got me wondering, like "British Museum," and a receipt from Fortnum & Mason, which said "Chocolates for Andrei Sakharov," in Eva's writing. I knew that name, I thought.

At last all that was left was the pile of things I didn't know what to do with. So I had to wait, trying not to look as if I was waiting, because she was on the phone again.

And then I heard the scrape of a match and the soft little *phut* noise people make with the first pull on a fresh cigarette and Theo came in, still blinking a bit from the daylight. There was a whiff of fix hanging round him, which his smoke cut through.

"You're staying for lunch, aren't you?" he said, almost as if it was automatic, and I said yes, please. Again it was Theo who got it ready.

We were about halfway through when I got up the nerve to ask, "Do you—do you need me this afternoon?" I didn't think it showed how much I hoped they did. I took another piece of the crumbly black bread, which was sour and smoky and alive in my mouth, and knew that I really, really didn't want to go back—I wouldn't say *home* but back to the Hall. But where else could I go, if Theo and Eva didn't want me?

"Theo, were you going to show Anna how to develop?"

He looked at me. "I was, but I'm afraid I have done it all."

Eva was using some French bread to mop up the last of the salad dressing straight from the bowl, and stuffing it into her mouth. "I tell you what, Theo, if we give her one of the F2s and a roll of HP4, she could take her own. She'll learn far more from looking at her own work than she ever will from watching you print yours."

"That is a good idea," said Theo. "Anna—what do you think?"

"What's an F2?"

"A Nikon—a camera," said Eva, "And HP4's a good amateur film—very tolerant. I use it quite a bit myself for some things. Even Theo agreed it wasn't bad, after he couldn't get anything else in Calcutta and had to use it or starve."

"Black-and-white?" I asked, leaning back and trying to sound like them. Their voices and their words smelled of aeroplanes and whiskey and typewriters, like *To Have and Have Not* and all those kinds of films.

"Yes," said Eva. "Everything starts there," and for a moment she reminded me of my history teacher Miss Hudson, only I didn't think Eva would let the boys give her a nervous breakdown. "Of course, color is important. Ever more so. But it is with light, form, shadow, texture, structure, that is where you will learn your trade." She pushed a bowl of peaches towards me. "Are you interested?"

While Theo made coffee, she put the camera into my hands. It was big and heavy, and the metal was scratched and the black bits worn smooth where fingers went. My fingers curled round the same places, and when I put it to my eye it fitted, resting half cold, half warm against my face. I could even smell Theo's smoke on it. Eva showed me how the camera worked. It was different from Mum's Instamatic—you had to turn dials and things. It was about what was sharp and what was blurred: what mattered in the picture and what didn't. Everything turned with a kind of big, solid smoothness, like the old Jaguar Mum's boyfriend lost when the bank pulled the plug, all thick leather and the doors shutting with a lovely deep *thud*. He was one of the ones I liked, I remembered, but he wasn't around for all that long. Mostly the nice ones weren't. I always hoped the next one would be, just like the next flat would be nice enough for Mum to want to stay put.

Eva put the strap round my neck, patted my shoulder, and stepped back. "There! Go and see what you can find. We'll be out this afternoon, but come back this evening and Theo can show you what to do with the film."

I went towards a place where I remembered you could see the Hall through the trees but behind the fence, looking like a picture. As I walked I could feel the camera lying just lightly against me, touching and letting go between my breasts.

I took the picture of the house, but then I couldn't think what else to photograph. I wasn't sure what would be the right sort of thing. I had thirty-six pictures, Eva said, so I spent some on not being sure. That felt odd. I climbed the fence, but the Hall just looked like a dolls' house. I tried going up close and filling up the picture with a side of one pillar, the stone all grubby and patchy-looking like old skin, not grand at all. But—yes! The window beyond it reflected two other pillars and the trees far away, all chopped into squares and a bit wobbly but there. I took one and then shifted about, looking hard, trying to get in the curly bit at the bottom of the pillar against the corner of the window frame.

There was a rattle on one of the windows by the front door. My mind was so empty of anything else, I'd been concentrating so hard, that I jumped out of my skin. I looked in the window and saw a shadow, saw Belle, peering at me and knocking. I pushed half of the front door open, with shock still stinging in my hands and feet and feeling the height of the door moving above me.

"What are you doing?" she said, which was a pretty stupid question to ask when I had a camera slung round my neck.

"Taking photographs." *Shot* and *shoot* Eva and Theo said always, I remembered.

The office door was open. I hadn't seen it since the furniture went, and now there was just a desk sitting in the space with a telephone and two chairs and some files spilling across the floor and rubbish thrown into the fireplace.

"Why?" she said.

"Eva's teaching me how to—to shoot," I said, "so I can help them better."

"But did I say that you could do so here?"

I was a bit surprised. It wasn't as if she'd been much interested in what I did. "I didn't know I had to ask."

"Of course you have to ask. I'm the head of the family."

"I won't photograph you if you don't want me to."

"That's not the point," said Belle. "You didn't ask permission. How can we make a fresh start as a family, if you persist in defying me?"

It was as if while I was taking the photographs my mind had been clear and clean. But her talking like that had wrinkled and stained the lovely clearness. Well, I thought suddenly, if that's her idea of family, I don't want it. Mum gets drunk sometimes, but at least she hugs me, drunk or sober. And she remembers my birthday, even if what she gives me depends on how much money the current boyfriend's got. That's family. Not this.

"Yes, it is the point!" I said, very loud, my voice filling up the space in the hall, like I was back at school, back at home, as if the last two days hadn't happened. "I'm not doing any harm. I won't shoot you, and if I want to do anything with any of the prints except look at them I'll ask Ray, because it's his house. Okay?"

She didn't say anything. There were spidery red lines in her putty-colored cheeks. And I suddenly saw how crooked her outline looked—limp, saggy-bottomed cotton skirt, scrawny arms with the skin hanging off them, shoes all stretched and with those white marks they get if they're soaked and you don't clean them. Even her hair managed to be crooked as well as floppy. Underneath and behind her were all the acres of black-and-white marble floor of the hall so that I saw her laid out in sags and wrinkles against the hard, ancient square-ness of the house. There were chips in the marble but the exactness was still there, the squares you could measure things by, things like people. This was Stephen's house once. He must have stood on this floor, walked up these stairs. His voice would have been in the air. *You ask how I came to join the Army,* he had said to Miss Durward. It was a sort of settling-down thing to say, a once-upon-a-time, with him sitting at a desk maybe, a big old desk in the room I could see behind Belle's shoulder now. Sitting, and writing as if he was talking to Miss Durward, knowing she'd be reading his words soon. There would've been the portrait hanging maybe above the fireplace, showing him with one of his letters—or maybe it was one of hers? And books and old furniture smelling of beeswax, like at the gallery. And at night he would have gone upstairs to bed, a four-poster maybe, and dreamed whatever soldiers dream. I thought suddenly of Theo's photographs.

Belle opened her mouth, and behind her I saw the swing-door beyond the foot of the stairs move a little bit and Cecil's face came round the edge. He saw me and smiled, then his eyes slid to Belle. His head disappeared and the door started to close just as slowly.

"Very well," she was saying, when there was a kind of yell, muffled but definitely Cecil, and she turned and called, "Boy! Stop that noise!"

I tried to push open the swing-door but he was plonked on the floor so close behind it that I could only just squeeze through. "What did you do?"

"The door went over my toe!" he howled.

"Show me." I squatted down with the camera swinging forward against my thighs.

"Don't worry about him," said Belle. She was so thin she'd squeezed through the gap much more easily than I had. "That's what happens to naughty boys who don't stay where they're told. Don't listen to him, Anna, he always makes the most ridiculous fuss. He just wants attention. Ray's been too soft with him, but we'll soon change that."

"It's bleeding!" yelled Cecil and it was, though not much, just a scrape—he hadn't hurt the nail that I could see.

"Shall we find you a plaster?" I said.

"Ye-es!"

Belle turned away and pushed out through the door, so it swung back onto me. I shoved it back the other way and yelled, "Where would I find some plasters?"

"I don't know," she said, and slammed the office door behind her.

"I think I've got some," I said. "Come on." Cecil got up and took my hand. He stomped up the stairs with such an exaggerated limp that I knew it couldn't be at all bad, because if it'd been really hurting he wouldn't have glanced up at me like he did to see what I thought. Belle must have heard him, but she didn't try to stop us.

At the top of the stairs he did catch his toe and stumbled and yelped with proper pain. "It hurts even worser now!" he said. "Will I have to have my leg off?"

"No, of course not."

"Uncle Ray says I will, only it's my arms when I put my elbows on the table."

"Oh, that's just one of those things grown-ups say to make you do what they want. He doesn't mean it."

"But they do cut legs off. I've heared it. Sawing, and it smells like meat burning. It hurts to screaming. I've heard the screaming."

We had reached my floor. "Was that in a dream?"

"I *think* so," he said. "Susan told me when things was a dream or not. But she's gone now. She was my friend."

I found a packet of plasters in my makeup bag and one of those antiseptic wipes. The antiseptic made him yelp again, and, like always, all the small plasters had been used up, but Cecil didn't seem to mind a big one, though he still looked a bit pale. "Come on, Long John Silver," I said, which Mum used to say, and then I remembered something else she used to do. "Shall we draw a face?"

"Yes!" he said, and I dug around in my handbag to find a biro. I drew a big smiley face on the plaster, and Cecil sat on my bed for a long time, looking at his toe and wiggling it like he and it were two people talking to each other.

Was there enough light? Yes. Cecil turned round at the second *ker-click* that Theo's camera made and I got two more of him looking straight at me, his pointy face still and his eyes wide open so you could imagine a hundred things going on in his mind, but you'd never know if what you imagined was true.

There was a shuffle along the passage. Cecil leapt off the bed and slid into the corner beyond the wardrobe. I could see Belle and Ray coming upstairs side by side, with their arms linked.

As soon as they were safely past, Cecil slipped out of his corner and was gone, like a small, pale ghost, so quietly that I couldn't have said when or where he went.

I opened the drawer and put the plasters away, and there were Stephen's letters, as if they were waiting for me. How did his story go on?

It was very quiet outside and hot, but when I sat on the bed where the light was good and read, my skin remembered the cold that morning and then the snow and the dead horse Cecil had painted.

The writing got easier and the reading got easier; it was like my eyes learned his handwriting and taught my mind to understand him, while my mind learned his words—his sentences—and taught my eyes to read them, until I didn't really think about reading them any more than you think about making your legs move when you want to walk down the road. I just read. It was like he was in the room with me, and I was listening to his voice. Miss Durward must have felt like that, reading like listening, so she could draw her pictures.

You ask, à propos of my account of our progress through France after Toulouse, whether I am content to have beaten my sword into a plough-share, & I can truly say that I am. With the harvest in, I feel that for the first time in my life I have been able to make more of what Fate has offered me: to bring good out of ill. . . .

. . . I ride about my green & peaceful acres on my old mare Dora, who has seen as much of war as I, & she too, I sometimes fancy, nods her head in contentment. I sit before the library fire of an evening, with a better glass of wine in my hand than I was ever able to get in the Peninsula, except I was in Porto itself, & I know that at last I have been able in some sort to make more & better of what has come into my grasp.

The next page was a drawing. The lines looked like pencil, I thought, they'd be silvery on the grain and creases of the real paper, but the photocopier's light had flickered off them and thrown their image like frayed black threads across this flimsy paper, two men in hats and half-length trousers and slouchy boots and jackets with big buttons. They had long mustaches and a sort of blanket round their shoulders, like Mexicans in a film, and one of them was holding the two plump fowls Stephen had written about. The drawing was clumsy-looking: *"with apologies for my draughtsmanship but in the confidence that yours will more than make up for my deficiency,"* he said. His hand couldn't draw what his eye saw, just the same as mine never could in art. Miss Durward must have been able to, like Eva could show what she'd seen. I thought suddenly of my photos, lying curled up in the camera. Would they show what I'd seen?

Through the page the photocopier light had picked up something that Stephen had written on the other side, but the writing was backward, of course, and I couldn't make it out except that, by the shape of the lines, it was the address. He must not have had envelopes—maybe they hadn't invented them. He must have folded the paper with the writing inside and stuck it up—sealing wax maybe, I thought, like in films—and then written the address on the outside.

Suddenly I couldn't bear to go on trying to work out what Stephen was saying to Miss Durward, without knowing even that little bit more about her. I took the page with the drawing to the mirror. The gray light from the window touched the back of the paper, and when I peered at the shadow in the glass I could just make out the words, the right way round.

MISS LUCY DURWARD
FALLOWFIELD HOUSE
DIDSBURY, LANCASHIRE

So, who was Lucy Durward, and why did she want to know the things he told her—the regiments and cavalry and now this stuff about stealing chickens? She must have, or he wouldn't have gone on, would he? She was drawing pictures or something, but what for? Perhaps she was being like a photojournalist, like Theo, only they didn't have photographs then, did they? Or perhaps they just wanted a reason to write to each other. But he'd said too, *"I like to think of you reading my small tales aloud in the evening,"* so perhaps she read them to the others, Master Tom, and—what was her name? Mrs. Greenshaw? I flipped back and found that now I could read that first page quite easily. *"Certainly a disability such as mine is not a negligible matter for a young lady . . ."* Who—what—what was it all about? I went back to where I'd got to.

I shall be taking this letter into Bury St. Edmunds myself to catch the Mail, & to hurry over those cobbled lanes is to court disaster . . . there is nothing like the loss of one leg to make a man cherish the health of the other.

I was so surprised I almost laughed, because of how he put it. Like he wanted to make a joke. He'd made a joke of other things, like about capturing the windmill, though now when I read it again, I thought how it must have been really frightening. But only having one leg really is—well, could be—funny. I wondered if Lucy thought it was funny. Perhaps he was trying to get the joke in before anyone else laughed at him, and sound cheerful before anyone might be sorry for him. Even about being a cripple. Even about not knowing when his birthday was. And about not having a father. Or a mother.

Some of the words I still didn't know, even when I could read them. Some of the stuff about Parliament didn't make much sense either, because I couldn't remember any history except Waterloo from whenever it was. And Bonaparte, when I remembered he was the same as Napoleon, though Stephen's spelling didn't look right. One sheet was a sort of map, with trenches and hills and regiments and towers marked. Most of it was writing, with the steady black words tramping along, drawing it on my mind, so that even when I didn't really understand what he was saying, I still felt he was telling me.

Ciudad Rodrigo . . . live shells, beams studded with nails, & finally a forest of swords so embedded as to spit each man as he advanced. Time & again officers formed up parties of men to lead them in clambering down the ladders into the ditch & towards the breach, under merciless and constant fire from the walls. Time & again we were repulsed, & left many of our number dead & dying, while we ourselves struggled back to climb the ladder. . . .

Each of us felt a private grief at the loss of a friend, & was unwilling to discuss it, or to remind himself that this is what, in the end, awaits us all.

I'D ALREADY LEARNED that film didn't have to be the plastic things Mum put into her Instamatic. This film was a little metal canister not much bigger than my thumb, and when Theo'd shown me how to open the camera, it dropped heavily into my palm and lay there fat and secret like a bomb.

And it turned out you don't deal with film in safelight, like paper, you deal with it in no light at all.

"I will load the film onto the spiral and into the tank this time. You will have to practice in the light first," said Theo, rummaging in a cupboard and bringing out a box of stuff. "So, we can get on with the developing. Could you please switch off the light?"

It was like someone had dropped a black-velvet bag over my head. I almost felt I shouldn't breathe, but there was the pull cord of the light switch tapping against me and small clinks and rustles and Theo whistling to himself under his breath, a tune I didn't know.

"There," he said, after what felt like hours. "It is safe. Would you please switch on the light?"

It was the same kinds of chemicals as for the prints, only times and temperatures and exactly how you shook the tank seemed to matter more. A bit like a chemistry lesson really, only Theo explained things better. Not as well as Eva, but I sort of understood it and then it wasn't boring at all. And there weren't any boys trying to brush up against our breasts in the practicals or girls seeing who could make Mr. Heller blush first.

"It must be washed for half an hour. There must be nothing left— none of the unexposed silver left to darken with time."

When we went upstairs I was surprised to see the light was coming in at the windows on the other side, all soft and yellow, sliding towards us from under piled-up clouds with tops that towered over the bruise-colored shadows in their depths.

"I should not be surprised if they are thunderclouds," said Theo. "And I think it is time for a drink, to welcome the weekend. Would you like a beer, or a glass of wine?"

I said white wine because I was afraid beer would make me sleepy. Theo brought it over to me where I was standing by the light box. It was white, but not like the Liebfraumilch that Mum got boyfriends to buy her—this was sharper and stronger, but not too bad, and sort of complicated-tasting, like once you were used to it you wanted to keep it in your mouth for longer to find out what all the tastes were.

Theo switched the box on so that all the slides scattered on it blinked at me like windows at dusk. "Put your glass somewhere well away, and come and see," he said. "Eva has been asked to go home, to give a lecture in Madrid—a very prestigious one—and she has been sorting out what she will take."

Quite a lot had labels on them saying things like "Fenton, Roger" and foreign names—"Stieglitz, Alfred" and "Kertész, André"—but some I thought might be Eva's. Next to the light box were some prints of different things. The top one was of a woman's body, naked, lying down. You couldn't see her face, just the curve of her side against black, sloping down to her waist and up again to the hip, with her back wide and pale like fields each side of a river of spine.

"Did you take that?"

"No, it is one of Eva's."

"Oh."

"What do you think of it?"

"It's—it's beautiful, but—well, it's kind of weird, thinking of her looking at—well—".

"As it would not be with a male photographer—is that what you are saying?"

"I suppose so."

"An image of a naked body need not be arousing, not in the sexual sense, at least. And the artist—even a male artist looking at a female nude—need not be in the business of feeling or provoking sexual interest. After all, one may photograph the same war to show the terror or boredom of a particular moment, or quite differently, because one wishes to describe the nature of man. So it is with the human body. It may be about sex—allowed, or transgressive and forbidden—but for the human mind, the body is also the measure of all things."

I couldn't make that last bit make sense, but I'd long ago stopped thinking he was trying to catch me out. And I knew if I asked things, he'd really want to explain them to me, like he cared that I understood and liked talking to me. I went back a bit. "So it doesn't have to be *Playboy*?"

"Certainly not. Besides, it is worth remembering that some of the best photographers of the female nude were—are—themselves homosexual. Of the opposite situation, I have less evidence."

"Of what?"

"Of homosexual women who shoot male nudes. No doubt the evidence exists, shut up in some cabinet of curiosities. The world is not that evenhanded yet."

"You mean, like lesbian?"

"Yes," he said. "Your film should be washed by now. Shall we inspect it?"

As we went downstairs he said, "There is always the possibility that something has gone wrong—that there are no pictures. I have been developing film for fifty years and I still feel it." And suddenly I could tell by the way he spoke and touched the tank that it was true even for my little film. He was a little bit excited and nervous like I was a lot, and my heart gave a sort of mini-thud like it used to a long time ago when an exam I cared about was being given back, or now when a boy I fancied came into the classroom.

Theo unscrewed the lid and showed me how the spiral of film was squatting under the water in the tank. He dripped in some stuff he called wetting agent, and fished out the spiral and reeled the film off it almost as if he was unrolling a ribbon in a shop, with the edges pressing into the pads of his fingers. He held it out for me to see against the light.

They were tiny of course, like all the other negs I'd looked at, but different because I was looking at them in one curling strip and all still wet. Clear lavender-colored shadows and dark skies, trees and pillars and windows and faces caught click after click, coiling and springing down the film one after the other so that all the distance and time between them was pressed into plain, pale bands of almost nothing.

❧✦❧

I ASKED THE concierge Permeke if his wife would find my store of quinquina powder and make up a dose, and in spite of my shivering I contrived to tug off my clothes and unbuckle my wooden leg before the cold fever began to shake me so much that my teeth clattered against the glass and the mixture stung on my split lip. All I desired was to lie still, but the tremor turned to convulsive jerks, as if my real and ghostly limbs, my entire body, were struggling to break free of the fever's icy hold, and shake off the bony, freezing fingers that clutched at my shoulders, ankles, hands, stomach, entrails.

The concierge's wife was as good as her word: she came at the hour I had requested to mix me another dose, and offered to bear a message to Katrijn, for all the concierges in the street knew the business of one another's houses. I thought that with matters thus settled I could bear the hot fever, but soon I knew that as ever I was wrong, when the fire began.

And then I reached the eye of the storm. A few minutes' grace, a time for rest, weak and battle weary, sipping water and observing that night had fallen and the watch was crying the early hours. How foolish I was to think that I had won! Yet I always did until, even as I swallowed yet more wine and bitter powder, I felt myself sucked into the mire of the sweating fever, breathing the poison, suffocating, drowning.

And in the dark swamp I saw a face but not a face, no eyes or lips, St. Luke grinning at me through rain that washed over him, as sticky as blood. And St. John, who would write nothing more, because his hands were gone.

The stinking air seemed to coil about me like the mists that hung about San Sebastian, dank and hot and heavy with all that they hid. In the fever fog I saw the girls: Mercedes sweaty with the night's work, trying to wash the kisses and clutches and semen of so many men from her body, which was no longer young; Izzaga nursing her whip-split face. I threw out the one that did it, but I could not mend her cheek. A man splits as easily, spilling his little life onto the ground: bread, meat, a prayer book, his water ration. He cannot be mended either.

I knew not if I were sinking, or if it were the mire swelling about me, seething, boiling, heaving, like the fire in the window of the church when I was a boy. I was not asleep; this was no nightmare to be banished by the rising sun. It was my waking eyes that saw the crushing rocks and fires and branding irons, and how a red-hot spear went in one man's mouth, and right through him. *It will all go on for-ever*, Mother Malpas said. *God will give sinners over to Satan. Only the good will be saved, and sinners like you, Stephen, you will burn for-ever.* Her cottage went up in flames, and she died screaming, said the vicar, when he wrote to tell me; she died screaming that she had been cursed. I got the letter at school, the only letter I had that year, and that was what it said. That was the year that Jess killed the rat in Farmer Vinney's barn. Jess was Pierce's dog, and the warrior that we boys longed to be. The dying rat whipped round like a snake and bit Jess deep in the muzzle. And still she held on until I smashed the rat with a stick, over and over again until it was nothing but pulp on the floor. But Jess died too, and her body that we buried came to me now in the poisonous mire of fever, sicked up by the soil as a battleground gives up bones to the plow every spring forever and ever, at Thermopylae and Towton and Malplaquet, so that the skulls look up at the plow-man with blank eyes, and who knows what those minds once were, for now they are only crawling worms and darkness.

The guns have stopped, ours and theirs. The silence holds. We must do nothing to betray our position to the watchers on the walls. We wait and wait, knowing what is coming. Then the advance is ordered. As steady as we are on parade, we march silently forward.

In the dark, the first few are spitted on the swords and nails filling the breach. We cannot get in, and each handful of us is presented for slaughter to the French. By the time we give up and retreat, there are dead men all around. Back, re-form with whoever can be found, advance again across the killing ground.

We are not thinking now, we have no sense to make. We just push forward, not seeing the live shells and limbs and brains spread across our path, not smelling the black powder and sour blood. I am wading through the bodies of men whom I led to the breach. Next to me as we go forward a cannonball knocks off a head. The men close the gap, ignoring the teeth and shards of skull that have buried in their own flesh.

A foot kicks my shin, begging: he has no arms to catch at me. Water? I have none. A hand: a friend whose pretty wife I've danced with. I must not spare a bullet for him, though he pleads, and I see his liver beating away his life by the light of a bloody flare that rises over our heads to show us the rest of the world.

PART THREE

So, as Balzac says, each body by nature is composed of a series of ghosts, laid on one another to infinity, layered by infinitesimal films. . . .

NADAR, *Quand j'étais photographe*, 1899

I

My dear Major Fairhurst,

We were so sorry to hear from your concierge that you have been so very unwell, & Mr. Barraclough & my sister join me in wishing you a speedy recovery from your indisposition. I do hope that you were well looked after; & that you would have called upon us for any further help that we could have given.

You will see from our direction that, my husband desiring to remove me from the noise & summer heat of Brussels, we have taken a house, the Château de l'Abbaye, here at Ixelles. We arrived yesterday & have taken it for 3 months. Had it been possible to consult you in the matter we would have been glad to do so, but Mr. Barraclough went into everything with the owner most carefully, & I think you would agree that we are very comfortably placed, off a pretty lane, & close enough to the post-road for the city to be only a short drive away.

Which brings me to my main purpose in writing this letter. Mr. Barraclough & I would be so pleased if you felt able to come to stay with us for as long as you care to, while you recover from your indisposition. The house is quietly situated with a large, sunny garden & shady orchard, & the servants seem to know their business, so that we are settled in already, & I can be reasonably confident of making you comfortable.

Of course, you may have engagements in the City which prevent your staying with us, & if that is the case then we should be delighted if you cared to call on us whenever it is convenient to

you; we have few engagements at present. But to be unwell in
lodgings in July seems to us a sad fate, & I do hope that I have so
persuaded you of the advantages of country air & home cooking
that you will feel able to accept this most heartfelt invitation from
your friend

Henrietta Barraclough

I let the letter fall onto my lap. The fever had overwhelmed me more completely than it ever had before, and I had only slowly begun to make a recovery. That day was the first on which I had dressed, and I was sitting in what passes in Belgium for an easy chair by the empty fireplace, with my crutch beside me, and the windows closed tight against what Madame Permeke called *l'air mauvais*. Certainly, to judge by the glaring gray skies and such city stench as crept through these defenses, she had some cause to call the air of Brussels bad, and by contrast, Mrs. Barraclough's description of the life at the Château de l'Abbaye was appealing indeed.

I picked up the letter again. I had until now seen only such examples of her hand as had directed a generous gift of fresh fruit, and another of wine. The writing was elegant, and not unlike her sister's, but I fancied it had something of a governess's copybook about its regularity, which Miss Durward's hand—swift and sometimes careless as it was—had altogether cast off. I reread the letter and placed it on top of two or three notes of Katrijn's, for though in her own interests I would not have allowed her to call at my lodgings, Katrijn too had sent good wishes—often, I guessed, scribbled in her dressing room between acts—and small gifts of food and flowers, which were generally addressed in Cousin Eloise's hand.

Indeed, it was solely the thought of Katrijn that held me back from writing immediately to accept Mrs. Barraclough's invitation, for although I had friends and acquaintances in Brussels enough, there was no other that could have kept me there with such an alternative offered to me. My indecision was interrupted by a rap on the door and the entrance of Madame Permeke bearing a tray.

"Your dinner, M'sieur." She put it down on the table at my elbow with a clatter and stood before me with her hands tucked under her apron, and an expectant expression on her broad face.

The smell of mutton stew rose rather too richly from the plate, and I took a sip of the lemonade that Meike had brought. "Thank you, Madame Permeke."

"There's a note for you."

I had already observed Katrijn's hand on the outside of a single sheet, and I took it up. Before I could undo the seal, Madame Permeke cleared her throat and went on, "Ah—M'sieur—I wanted to say, Permeke and I—we hoped you'd maybe think to engage a servant. If you're intending to stay, that is. We've been happy to help you out while you were so poorly, and you've been very generous, I know. But it's really more than I can manage, not being what I was engaged for. I'm not so young as I was, and with my girl Marie-Ange going back to my sister's for the harvest—" She stopped, more for want of breath I felt sure, than from the exhaustion of her arguments.

"Of course, Madame Permeke. I shall see to it immediately. Or— or it is possible that I shall be going to stay with friends out at Ixelles for a few weeks."

"Oh, that'll be nice for you—a bit of country air. Sometimes I think I should've done better to stay in the Haute Fagnes myself, not let Permeke persuade me. It takes it out of a woman, living in the city. But he's town-bred—couldn't see what I wanted with all those hills and cows. Would you be wishful to keep the rooms on, M'sieur? Only I should let the landlord know if you won't be."

"Oh, yes, I think I will keep them on. If I go, that is."

"That's good, then. And now I'll leave you to your dinner."

Desiring even more to hear from Katrijn than to put off eating the stew, I broke the seal on her note.

*Chéri—How are you today? I have just heard that my rehearsal
has been canceled. If you feel strong enough, come and have a
dish of tea with us this afternoon. I have missed you so much!*

K.

I scribbled an acceptance and rang for Marie-Ange to take it across
the road while I ate what I could stomach of the stew.

It took some little time for me to wash and make myself ready, for
my fingers were still slow and stupid, and faintness apt to threaten
at the least exertion, while the weight I had lost rendered my wooden
leg so ill-fitting that I was more than usually glad of my cane, and of
the brevity of the distance to Katrijn's apartment.

She too I thought had grown a little pale and a little thinner in the
face, in the week or so since I had seen her. I bowed, regretting the
necessity, since it made my head swim, and shook hands with Cousin
Eloise, who dismissed Meike and sat down before the teapot.

"And how are you, dear Commandant?" she said. "We were
so shocked to hear of your being unwell. Katrijn was quite out of
her mind with worry, but I said to her, 'Commandant Fairhurst
will be well looked after, you mark my words. He's not a stranger
here in Brussels, and the Permekes are good people—they'll help
him out.'"

"Indeed, they were most kind," I said.

"But I hear from that girl of the Permekes' that you'll be leaving us
soon. Meike was busy, you understand, so I answered the door myself—you must not think I commonly do so. Anyway, as I say, you
will be leaving Brussels?" continued Cousin Eloise. "Do have a pastry. I'm sure you need feeding up."

I looked up from the plate that she proffered, which was filled with
the finest that a French pastry cook could create, and saw Katrijn regarding me steadily. "Oh, as to that, nothing is settled," I said quickly.
"I only received the invitation this morning, and have not at all made
up my mind to accept it."

"The invitation?" said Katrijn.

"The Barracloughs have taken a place at Ixelles," I said. "For Mrs. Barraclough to escape the heat. She has not been well. And, thinking that I might be in need of such an escape myself, they asked—"

"Of course," she said, across my words, and after a moment asked, "and will you go?"

"Excuse me," said Cousin Eloise, getting up with a clatter. "I must speak to Meike about something. I had quite forgot! Please, Commandant, don't trouble about the door!"

I sank back with relief, and when the door had closed behind her cousin, Katrijn said, "Poor Eloise. She is so anxious not to get in our way." She stopped, and then said again, "So, will you go?"

"Not if you do not wish it."

"But you would prefer to be with those friends of yours."

I took her hand in mine, but even so little a gesture seemed to cost me effort. Katrijn let hers lie in my enfeebled hold. "I own, in my present condition, and in this weather, it would be very pleasant to be in the country. Nor . . . Dearest, it is so good to see you, but I cannot flatter myself that I shall be of much use to you, either as an escort, or in—other ways. The fear of the fever recurring makes me cowardly as I hope I never was before a human enemy."

"The company leaves for Namur next week," she said.

"So soon?"

"Yes. I think I have mentioned the date several times, Stephen."

"Forgive me—I have lost count of the days. Have you many rehearsals?"

She withdrew her hand and poured herself another cup of tea. After a moment she said, "And what would you do, if I said, yes, I shall be very busy? Would you go to Ixelles?"

"If you will be too busy for my staying in Brussels to be of use to you, then I shall accept Mrs. Barraclough's invitation."

"Then pray do so, dear Stephen. We may always write to each other."

"That is true, and I shall look forward to your letters. But are you sure that you want me to go?"

She rose, putting down her cup with a jingle of porcelain and silver. She went to stand with her back to the open window among the muslin curtains that hung without moving in the heat. As she looked at me the fever seemed to creep again from its hiding place, making my limbs shake and my body burn.

"And what if I said, no, I have no rehearsals? No, the plays from now until we close are short, foolish, old pieces that I could play in my sleep? No, I do not want you to go to Ixelles—I want you to stay with me? But I have my pride, Stephen! Oh, respectable people would not admit it. I am an actress, after all, a woman who exhibits herself for money. Why should I value my dignity so? To them I appear to be a lady like themselves, and yet I am the next best thing to a whore. How could I rather do without a man, than beg for one? But I would!"

"How can you speak thus—use such a word?" I said, my voice loud and trembling over the ringing in my ears. "That is not how I think of you! You are—I have always . . ."

"But you do not ask me to meet your friends. And you have not asked me to marry you. For us to share a bed may not transgress the law, but it transgresses the rules of your world. And so you keep silent."

It was true. I had been bewitched by the curve of her slim neck, the turn of her head, the spell that her voice cast over the theater, her quick kindness, her laughter, her brown eyes. I had worshipped these things, perhaps even loved them. Her ease and generosity of mind and body was of a piece with her world, the world I had so willingly entered. And yet I had not offered her a place in mine. Did I not think my damaged self worthy of her? Did I not think her worthy? Or was there, for all my delight in her company, too much of myself, my real existence, of which she could not know? I realized suddenly that I had not offered her a place in my life because that place was already filled by a presence—a love—so perfect that it was beyond my power, or my desire, to displace it with mere pleasure or friendship or bodily contentment.

I was silent for too long. She stepped from the window, so that the muslin curtains caught on her gown and tugged at her before falling away. "Stephen, your health demands that you do not stay in the city. My pride demands that I do not fall at your feet, and beg. Let us leave it at that."

"Katrijn, don't . . . What we have is too . . ." I tried to rise from my chair but could not, and sat powerless. "Katrijn—"

"There is no more to say, I think, is there? I cannot give up my profession; I could as well give up my soul, or you your acres. To demand such sacrifices of—each other would not be true to . . . to the happiness that we have known."

Through my swimming eyes I thought I saw that she tried to smile.

"Besides," she said, "I should be bored to death in Suffolk."

The fever ebbed, but a dreadful weakness rose in my throat. Then I felt her hand on my arm as she knelt by me.

"*Chéri*, I am sorry. I should not have let my distress get the better of me. I should have waited until you were well."

"I am sorry to have been the cause of it. You have every right to—to feel as you do," I said. "I wish . . . That I should be the author of your hurt!" I put my hand over hers. "If I have—if our association is likely to cause you any difficulty, among your acquaintance, you must tell me. I could not refuse in honor to set matters right."

She shook her bowed head but seemed unable to speak. At last she said, "That is like you, dearest Stephen. Thank you, but I have no expectation of such a difficulty. And having had your friendship, freely given . . . to know that you offered your hand only out of honor . . . Well, it would not be the same." I turned my hand under hers to grasp it, and she cleared her throat. After a moment she said, in an easier tone, "You are feverish—perhaps you should go home."

All at once, like an exhausted child, I longed to lie in her arms, my head on her warm breast. "I would rather stay. But only if you wish it. If you would rather I went, for now, or—or for good . . ."

Her eyes lifted to mine. "No, please stay." She smiled, and the lilt was back in her voice. "But—I think you should lie down."

"Perhaps that would be best," I said, and as I smiled too, my fingers recognized the warm, soft skin inside her wrist. "Although I would not wish to appear ill-mannered to your cousin. And I fear that I shall not—I doubt if—"

"I shall look after you," said Katrijn, getting up and holding out her hand. "You will have nothing to do but lie back."

THE CHÂTEAU DE L'ABBAYE was a small and charming manor house built of pale gray stone in the days of Louis Quatorze, in the upright French style, with tall windows and a mansard roof. It took its name from an ancient monastery that stood about a quarter of a mile away. The weather continuing sultry, on the first afternoon after I arrived I went to sit in the small orchard at the far end of the garden.

"This is so much more pleasant than the garden itself!" exclaimed Mrs. Barraclough as she seated herself briskly at the wrought iron table next to me, and picked up her tambour frame. The change of abode did appear to have wrought an improvement in her health.

"It is certainly shadier," I said, resuming my own seat, where I had already idled away a good hour in failing to read the newspaper.

"Oh, not only that. I cannot accustom myself to there being no lawns or spreading trees in the garden, only the gravel paths and all those stiff little box hedges and the clipped limes, like so many soldiers standing to attention." She caught my eye, and we both laughed. "It is all so formal, so old-fashioned. One might not be in the country at all. There is nothing of the natural, the picturesque, the romantic. The gardener must always be fighting against nature to keep it so, and Tom would have nowhere to play!"

Recalling my own childhood, I asked curiously, "Do you concern yourself with that? With how and where he plays?"

She nodded. "Oh, yes. For him to be safe, and yet free to explore nature—the world—is what I wish for him above all." She blinked, and then went on. "I know that my parents will keep him safe. But I hope that they will allow him that freedom too. It is the heart of all my care and love." She fixed her eyes on a nearby tree, as if she felt a little embarrassment at having spoken so feelingly to me. "But not here. He would ruin it in a week, and without the least intention of doing so. One could almost fancy that it would be easier to have the whole built of wood and green cloth, like a stage set, so that it might be repainted at will."

I smiled. "Which reminds me, what did you think of *Tartuffe?*"

"Oh, it was most amusing. I have long been meaning to thank you for arranging it, but what with your illness, and all the bustle of our removal from Brussels, I have not had the opportunity. We were only sorry that you could not be with us. Lucy, particularly." She bent her head to her work and picked up a fine white thread with her needle. "It has done her so much good to have you here, Major. Lucy and I love each other dearly, but I am too stupid and ignorant to enter into her chiefest concerns. You are able to do that for her. Besides, George and she . . . Well, he is not stupid at all, but he is of—of a practical turn of mind, and cannot understand how it can be that she does not care for her gowns, or for making pretty speeches, or that he has said her name three times while she is drawing and she has not heard him. He thinks only that she is ill-mannered, which she is not."

"No, indeed."

She laughed a little. "Mind you, they have plenty to talk of when it is about paper! They will discuss weights and—what is the word?—transparency for hours."

"My heart goes out to you, Mrs. Barraclough!" I exclaimed. "Such evenings you must have spent!"

"Well, at least now I have an excellent excuse for retiring to bed!" she said, then looked away as pink crept across her round cheek.

"Mrs. Barraclough, we are old friends," I said. "I would not embarrass you for the world, but may I say how delighted I am at the news? Truly delighted, for you both! This is the crown of all the happiness that I have wished for you."

Her color was still high, but she said, composedly enough, "Thank you, Major. I—Lucy said that she had told you, but I was uncertain, because of . . ."

"Because of the way in which we first became friends?"

"Yes, that is a good way to put it," she said, picking up another thread. "You are a very kind and thoughtful man, Major, and I thank you for—for your good wishes. I hope that Lucy—"

"Hetty!" Barraclough's voice came from the garden.

Mrs. Barraclough turned her head unhurriedly. "George, dear! Was Brussels horridly hot? I was just telling the major how much Lucy enjoys his being here."

"So I believe," said Barraclough, clasping my hand. "Please don't get up, Fairhurst. How d'you do? Sorry not to be here when you arrived, but it's good to see you, and not looking so ill, neither. All well here, Hetty?"

"Certainly. Lucy went out sketching after lunch, so I have put off dinner until six."

"Six? What good's that to a man who's tired and hot after a day in the city? You'll not make me a man of fashion by such means, Hetty."

"I have no desire to do so, George, only to make sure that we all sit down together on the major's first evening with us."

I watched as Barraclough got a grip on himself. Eventually, he said, "Oh, aye, fair enough. I think I'll go and change my shirt."

She rose. "Excuse me, Major. I should go and make sure that everything is in train for dinner. The servants are willing enough, but they are Flemish, and I am not always sure that they have understood my orders. Please, don't trouble to get up. You need to rest."

It was true enough. Even the effort of overseeing the packing of my things, and traveling by chaise the short distance to Ixelles, had exhausted me, and I was content to sit back and watch her claim her husband's arm to support her up the garden.

Perhaps I even slept a little after they had gone, among the dappled shade and the green scent of the orchard. In this waking sleep, so strong a sense had I of my love's presence, that it was as if she had but a moment before drifted out of sight among the trees. "Catalina!" I called, but there was no answer. There never was an answer, not by then, though for many months after we parted at Bera I had long, troubled dreams, in which we quarreled over and over again, as we had never done in life. Such dreams always ended in my waking anew to my grief. When at last these dreams gave way to a gentler knowledge of my loss, Catalina's voice in them gave way also, to silence.

I was wiping my eyes when the iron gate at the bottom of the orchard clanked open, and I saw Miss Durward striding through the trees towards me, bareheaded, her straw hat hanging down her back by its ribbons and the skirts of her gown thick with dust.

"Miss Durward! Did you find what you wanted?"

"Oh, yes," she said, dropping into the chair that her sister had vacated. "Well, I did not go in search of anything in particular, I confess. Rather, I sought exercise for my limbs, and my eyes, without the duty of conversation."

"You have not been sketching, then?"

"Oh—you are recalling my excuse to Hetty at lunch?" She pulled out her hat from where it had been squashed against the chair back. "Oh, this is crushed. You will not be offended, I know, if I say, no, I have barely drawn a thing. Tell me, is George returned?"

"Yes, about—well, some time ago." She nodded, but made no move. "We dine at six."

"And won't that please my dear brother-in-law!" She sighed and rubbed her eyes with a cuff, leaving a smear of dust across her brow. "I suppose that Hetty would say I should go and change my gown."

"There is time yet," I said, looking at my watch.

"Good." She sighed again, then took in a deep breath and stared fixedly at the small green apples on the nearest tree. "Major, I have something to ask of you, and I trust you will—will—you will not think . . . That is . . ." Her voice tailed off.

After a moment I said, "Perhaps it would be simplest just to ask me."

"Yes, of course. Major, I have some fear that—well, that since Hetty's indisposition, George has sought—companionship—else-where."

I did not pretend to misunderstand her. "And what makes you think so?"

She said slowly, "To be honest, I am not sure. But since we have been here, he has seemed to travel into the city more often than I would have expected. And—and returned dressed just a little care-lessly, perhaps. It is the kind of thing I cannot help but notice. And he is generally so very neat."

"True enough." I considered her words, and what it would be possible for me to discover, let alone communicate to her. "I have not yet seen enough of him to be able to offer an opinion. What is it that you wish me to do? He is my host, but—if I can serve you in any way . . ."

"I would not for the world ask you to betray his confidence, if you are in it—"

"I am not."

"—but I love Hetty dearly, and if I thought—I don't know. I would give a great deal to know that I am wrong. I do not believe in med-dling, but I could not stand by and watch Hetty made unhappy. Even, perhaps—I do not know much about such things—even ill?"

"I understand you," I said, looking full at her. "I shall do what I can. And I hope that I shall be able to reassure you."

"Thank you," said Miss Durward. She sat silent for a moment, running the tip of one finger round the iron tracery of the table at which we sat. "Do you know, I think I would not marry for anything in the world! I cannot be sorry for myself, as my mother and Hetty are for me." I must have looked enquiring. "However much George neglects her, Hetty cannot be free of him. She must keep his household, and—submit to him in all things. And if he so chooses, she will be sickly for nine months of each year and in mortal danger at the end of it. Think of his first wife!"

"I know that your sister and Barraclough entered into their contract . . . Well, in short, she was desirous of establishing herself. It was not a question of a passionate attachment," I said. "But I think perhaps you do him a little less than justice. He seems to be most considerate towards your sister, and speaks affectionately of Tom."

"Oh, yes," she said, "and if my suspicions prove unfounded, as I hope to God they do, then I have nothing at all to accuse him of. But—for *that*—for Hetty's life as I see it likely to be—for *that* to be accounted a good marriage! Can you wonder that I am not urgent to enter into such a one myself?"

"Perhaps not," I said slowly, for I had never considered the question in such a light. "But surely, for a lady, to have children is—"

"I suppose so," she said, and smiled suddenly. "But being an aunt is almost as good, and a great deal easier."

I laughed and glanced again at my watch. "Perhaps we should make our way indoors." I fumbled for my cane so that I might heave myself to my feet. "Which reminds me, have you had news of Tom lately?"

"Yes, indeed. My mother writes that he does nothing but play the Guards defending Hougoumont." We ducked under the apple trees and reached the gravel of the gardens. "Apparently one of the housemaids gave notice after he slammed the back door and caught her finger in the hinge—being Captain Macdonnell, ejecting the French infantry, you understand."

"Readily," I said. "And how was the casualty?"

"Oh, once the surgeon had set it and the pain was less, poor girl,

Tom was persuaded to apologize, and she was persuaded to take back her notice. My mother was relieved, she wrote, for it is not easy to keep servants in Cheshire. The manufactories pay better, when there is plenty of work, and the girls have so much more freedom than they do in service."

"More freedom," I said, "but less safety."

At that moment Mrs. Barraclough came out onto the terrace and Lucy swung the cartwheel of her hat in greeting.

THE THUNDER CAME in the night, thunder sounding like the sky splitting and great fat flashes of lightning, and I shrank into my bed, wishing I'd more than just a thin sheet all chilly and damp with my sweat between me and it. It was like guns were making the air shake, and the lightning lit the room as if suddenly you could see everything in the world, and then just as suddenly nothing at all. But if I closed my eyes then the light was still there over everything, red as blood, and I was still frightened.

Another wave of lightning and there was someone by my bed, small, his hair white and his face dark.

He didn't seem to see me and then the night closed down again.

Something pulled at the sheet, and even when I was still stinging with fright I knew it was Cecil by his warm earth smell.

"Anna—"

"What?"

"I don't like it."

I rolled over and flipped back the sheet. "Neither do I. Come and hop in. I'll get a blanket."

He snuggled down and I pulled a blanket out of the bottom of the cupboard and flapped it onto the bed, nice and thick. Then I got back in with him so that we lay like spoons with his back curled into my body and my arms round him just as lightning smashed down onto us again. The pause before the thunder hit was even less this time, but still there didn't sound to be a drop of rain, just the dry hot thunder and the cold lightning. After a while a tear slid onto my arm where Cecil's cheek lay on it.

"Don't cry, it's all right," I said, though I was hating it too. I always do, but at least when I was little I didn't have to go miles through a dark house to find a grown-up body to hold me. Sometimes two bodies, and I could pretend the other one was my dad. And now I was saying all the things to Cecil that Mum used to say to me. "It's all right, it won't hurt. Don't cry, Ciss, I'm here. It's all right, I won't leave you. I won't leave you, chick."

In the morning it was like it'd never happened, except that Cecil was still curled up against me with his thumb in his mouth and his eyelashes very pale against his sunburned cheeks.

Me moving woke him up and he said, "Susan?"

"It's me, Anna," I said. "Come on, Ciss, it's time to get up."

"There was thunder," he said, sitting up suddenly and completely awake and sliding off the bed. Most of the sheet and blanket slid off with him, so my bottom got a blast of chilly air.

"Yes, but it's all gone now," I said. I stretched and got up.

"Anna!" Belle's voice. "What on earth's going on?"

I tugged my nightie down. She was wearing a tatty pink candlewick dressing gown and I could smell sick. "Cecil didn't like the thunder, and he came and got into bed with me."

"You're a very naughty boy," she said, coming closer so I could see her red eyes and smell her yeasty breath, only last night's drink but she was still red and shaky, as if it wasn't just drink that made her be like this. Cecil hadn't been quick enough to hide and he was standing, pressed flat against the wall, looking at her like a rabbit in the headlights. "You're a bad boy. Go downstairs at once and don't you ever dare do such a thing again! You're a bad boy!"

"No, he's not!" I said, backing away. I was standing in front of Cecil, and the bed was between me and Belle. "He was frightened! You're allowed to be frightened of thunder when you're little. He was frightened, and he came all the way through the house in the dark to find me and I think that was really brave. And he's not going downstairs until *he* wants to. And I'm going to give him a bath! Somebody's got to!"

There was a long pause. Then Belle said, "Well, well, that's a very long speech you've made me, my girl. Does it occur to you that this is my house, and I am the head of the family? I tell you, what I say should happen *will* happen."

"Not when it's being nasty to someone smaller than you, it won't!" I put out a hand behind me. "And it's not your house. It's Ray's. Come on, Ciss, let's get you in the bath."

He glued himself to me all the time we were walking down the room, but he didn't try to stay behind. I hoped he couldn't feel how much I was shaking.

"Don't think I don't know what you're up to, my girl!" Belle said as we went past her, and I felt Cecil's hand tighten in mine, but I was between him and her and we were several arm's lengths away. "Your mother told Ray what sort you are. No sense of right and wrong, just a silly little tart. And now you're trying to poison his mind against Ray and me. Just to spite me."

I dragged Cecil into the bathroom and slammed the door behind us and dived into the cubicle I usually used and locked it.

"Am I having a bath now?" he said, looking big-eyed into it.

What Belle had said—it wasn't like that. Would Ray think it was like that? "Well—maybe not today," I said. "Maybe we should wait till Uncle Ray says you can."

"But I *want* one *now*," he said. "*Please*, Anna, may I have a bath? Susan gave me one sometimes, all bubbly. I made castles. *Please*, Anna?"

Why not? What Belle'd said—it wasn't true. She was wrong. It wasn't like that. I knew it, and Cecil would know it, though no one would ever ask him, I hoped, and surely Ray wouldn't think it, if he cared at all. And Cecil did need a bath.

I ran him the biggest, deepest, bubbliest bath I'd ever seen. When I pulled off his T-shirt he had a big bruise on his shoulder, like he'd fallen when he was climbing a tree or something. Then I helped him in and gave him the soap dish to play with and two flannels and two lolly sticks I'd found in a corner, and the little plastic pot my film came in. I left him to it while I washed and dressed. When I went back in, the soap dish was bobbing along a channel in the foam and the lolly sticks were standing in the film pot on board while Cecil waggled his knees to make the waves not quite sink the boat, shouting with excitement.

I washed his hair and helped him get out, though he didn't want to. When he was dry and I'd given his hair a rub and combed it with my own comb, I lent him one of my clean T-shirts and bent to pull out the plug.

And suddenly he wasn't there. I thought I heard small soft feet on the stairs but I couldn't be sure. I couldn't hear Belle around. It was like Cecil'd just had enough of being with me, like he'd stepped through a door and vanished.

I put the bed back together and sorted out my clothes and things. Even without opening the drawer, I could sort of feel Stephen's letters there. But I didn't want to read them when she might come in. So I left them and went down to the kitchen and got something to eat, but Cecil wasn't there. There were sticks under the table, Sellotaped into a sort of triangle, or a pyramid, really. I wondered what it was for.

Then I heard the bang of a door and grown-up footsteps and what Belle'd said came into my mind again. It was only a few days ago she was saying she wanted to start afresh. Join me into her family. It felt like so long ago, sitting on the coach, wondering if I could—hoping Ray would—wanting to be part of a family. Remembering *The Railway Children*. I should have known it wouldn't be like that. Nothing was ever how you hoped.

I rubbed my wrist under my nose, slid out of the back door, and headed for the stables, the tears aching in the edges of my eyes.

But it was so hot that by the time I turned to shut the gate in the fence the tears had cooled and dried. Once upon a time, I thought, the fence wouldn't have been there. The house and the stables and the yard round it would have been busy with servants and horses and dogs, and laborers in the fields and cows and sheep. And Stephen would have walked among them and known that he owned it, owned them almost. He was an orphan and a soldier, I knew now—no proper home, a visitor, polite, helpful, never belonging, never getting too fond of anyone, always moving on, never staying. He didn't even have a mum like I had, one person that he belonged with. Let alone what Lucy Durward had—a whole family, a sister and a nephew and so on, sitting round the fire and reading stories. He had no one. Then what was it like to suddenly be able to look round and see all this was his—his land under his feet, his earth, his brick and stone, his trees and his wheat? What was that like? To have a real, whole place you belonged to and it belonged to you? I couldn't imagine belonging anywhere that much.

Even if he'd been there, I wondered if I'd have had the nerve to ask him.

Theo and Eva were in the studio with files open all over the place. Eva was still in her dragon dressing gown.

"Ah, Anna, good morning," said Theo.

"I wasn't sure if you needed me today," I said.

"And on a Saturday too. How conscientious!" said Eva, but she was smiling. "I'm sorry, I should have said that we try not to work on the weekend. When both work at home it is too easy to let it take over one's life. But come and have some coffee, anyway."

Upstairs, Eva went to get dressed and Theo sat on the sofa and lit a cigarette. By now I knew how to work the coffeepot thing and I got it out and filled it. "Did you hear the thunder last night?" I said to him, switching on the electric ring.

"It was remarkable, for England. But there was no rain."

"I wish there had been. I hate it being like this, all gray and sweaty."

"Yes."

As I put the coffee on the low table he stubbed out his cigarette. "Would you like to print one of your negs this morning?"

"But I thought you didn't work on Saturdays," I said.

"This would not be work. There is talk of a book—that is what Eva and I were looking at. But it is not urgent. I should like to teach you to print."

"I'd like to learn," I said and put a spoonful of sugar into my coffee.

My film had dried straight and shiny and just slightly curved across its length, so when I cut it where Theo showed me, the strips lay on the worktop with their edges scraping a tiny bit, like the thinnest fingernails on someone's back. Then he helped me make the contact print, and there were my pictures, not running on and on but sorted out and squared off and numbered, as if we'd built a house out of time.

"Which would you like to print?"

When you looked close, lots of them were really boring. "The one of the Hall? The first one? It—it's the only one that looks like a real photograph. Like it was taken on purpose."

He helped me focus, do the test strip, everything. He left me peering at the proper print in the fix and went to put the white light on again.

"Do you still think it looks like a real photograph?" he said.

"Yeah. I mean—I know it's not much good. A bit fuzzy. But it looks—kind of meant."

"Frames do that."

"But it isn't framed."

"But with the trees and the fence, you have put a frame round the image of the Hall, within the picture. It says, 'Look! This is an image of something that has substance! Something important.' We are talking about composition here. Now, shall we do another?"

This time he just stood watching what I did. Once he reached past me to push the focus finder more into the middle as I bent towards it so that I felt my hair brush the inside of his arm. He didn't say much until we were back looking at it in the fix.

"That is the boy you spoke of?"

"Yes," I said, meeting Cecil's eyes as he came towards us on the paper. The light shaded round his cheeks and eyes so that in the red light I thought it was the shadows thickening as the time ticked past that made him look like himself.

"One more?" said Theo, when Cecil was in the wash.

I picked up the contact sheet by its corner. He came to stand at my shoulder and took the other corner. For a moment I could hear his breathing, rough in his throat but even. I felt him close behind and beside me, his smoky breath warm on my bare shoulder, and a thin cooler strip where the strap of my top was. I felt the slight in-and-out of his chest, warming and cooling and warming me, not sweaty, just the *being* of him, I thought suddenly, just the quiet smell of being.

"How about this one?" he said, pointing to one of the shots of the pillar and the window. It was one of the few that weren't pale and dull or splodgy with darkness. "I should like to see this one enlarged."

I couldn't get it right. If all the pits and scrapes on the big pillar showed then the reflections in the window were just gray and nothing-muchish—too soft, said Theo. When we printed it on harder paper, the pillar was just a slab of paleness down one side, but you could see the reflections and the waves and ripples of the glass. And through it, you could see someone was there, standing in the hall.

"So," said Theo, "which is more important? The detail of the pillar—the texture, the roundness—or the shadows and reflections in the glass?"

We had a couple more goes at it, and when he switched on the white light at last I rubbed my aching eyes.

"Have you a headache?" said Theo.

"A bit."

"You are not yet accustomed to the chemicals. We shall leave these in the wash, and you should go outside into the fresh air."

"D'you want me to clear up?"

"No, I shall do that, and put the prints to dry. Did the thunder keep you awake?"

"Sort of. I don't like it very much."

"Poor Anna. Go and have a rest."

I went towards the door. I was just reaching for the handle when there was a long knock. I jumped.

"Come in!" called Theo.

"How is it going?" said Eva as I opened the door. "If you have finished, Theo, I have found that contract you wanted to see." Theo nodded, and she half turned, and then turned back. "Oh, and Crispin telephoned. I have invited him to supper. Anna, would you like to come?"

I WANDERED INTO the woods. The sun was half coming out, and I didn't want to go back to the Hall. I didn't want to see any of them. Theo'd given me another roll of HP4 and helped me load it, but my eyes felt dead, as if they'd done enough thinking for the morning. In fact, all of me felt kind of dead. It wasn't just my head that ached.

There was a path from the stables that went the other way, not down to the lane, or the not-really path to the Hall. The trees were thick, stretching up tall and thin as if looking for the light had worn them out, but the path was clear so I wasn't going to get lost and I could walk along without worrying or looking back. It was hard earth with heaps of brambles either side and not much light getting through. The path started curving round to the left and I noticed there was much less noise from the road. And then I could see hills beyond the trees, and then I was standing on top of a bank covered with grass at the edge of the wood, looking out over the bone-colored fields with their black rims of hedges and broad single trees, like giants guarding them.

The sun was hot and I sat down on the bank. Here the grass was long enough and sheltered enough not to have dried out, and it was cool and soft round my ankles so that the sun didn't feel like it was going for me, just that it was there, it existed, as simple as that.

It was very quiet, and the silence felt full of things that might be, full of people who were not quite there, as if the shade had spaces, waiting for them. Stephen must have stood here, I thought slowly, stood here and looked at the fat ears of wheat and heard a bee hum. He wrote about the harvest, I remembered, about making more of what Fate had given him, about bringing good out of bad—*out of ill*, he said.

The air was clear, & the clouds piled high above the mountains were just beginning to be glossed with pink & gold rays from the early evening sun. And I knew suddenly that without taking a step or counting a second, I had yet reached some other world, that co-existed with my own.

I remembered what he'd said—what he'd seen—as clearly as if he was sitting next to me, and suddenly I knew what he meant too. It was a place he'd never seen before, *some other world*, and yet it was quite safe, he wasn't lost at all.

After a while I lay down so that my face was among the leafy-smelling grass. I watched an ant crawling up a grass stalk, and a tiny aeroplane, not any bigger, creeping across the sky. My mind felt quite clean, not lost any more than Stephen was, smelling and hearing everything but not arguing or working things out or being angry or sad, not empty either, just clean and safe.

⌘

ON ONE OF her walks Miss Durward had come across the remaining buildings of the Abbey of Cambre, and over dinner she expressed a desire to know how they had once appeared. "For what is left is all quite new—no more than a hundred years old, I would think. But the foundation itself is very ancient."

"No doubt one could find a picture of it, in some book," I said, taking a sip of burgundy. "Perhaps the shop where I bought your map of Waterloo would have a print."

"That is an excellent notion!" cried Mrs. Barraclough. Her health and her spirits continued to improve, and the candlelight added a brightness to her eye while the daylight that still came in at the tall windows showed clear color in her cheek. I realized that I could admire her looks without feeling the least regret. "Perhaps you could call in there, George, when you are next in town."

"Willingly," he said.

I gave him the shop's direction as the ladies took themselves off to the drawing room, and when he returned the next evening he assured me that he had had no difficulty in finding the place.

"Here's your print, Lucy," he said, handing her a large, flat parcel.

"Thank you so much, George," she said, laying it on her knees. We were sitting on the terrace, waiting for dinner to be announced, and I watched her intent expression as she picked the twine undone with her thin fingers, drew it from about the parcel, and opened the brown paper. "Oh, yes!" was all she said.

Mrs. Barraclough leaned sideways to look at it. "Oh, how charming!" she exclaimed. "Such ancient buildings—so picturesque! All those pointed windows and the stone mullions and the ivy. And the little nuns—see their headdresses! But how wicked for—whom did you say it was, Major, that destroyed it?"

"The Revolutionary Army."

"How could they? And just to leave the new buildings, all regular and dull!"

"You must tell me what I owe you for this, George," said Miss Durward.

"Oh—nothing at all, Lucy my dear. Call it a memento," he said.

"A most interesting place, that print shop, Fairhurst. I was glad that Lucy asked me to go there."

There was an air of expansiveness about him that evening, and Miss Durward was still looking at him when dinner was announced.

Later, over the port—for Barraclough had declared that the Belgian beer made him sleepy, and developed a taste for wine after all—he said, "Yes, an excellent place, your print shop. How well do you know it?"

"Oh, I have bought a few things there. And in my days as a guide I would recommend it."

"Aye. And I'll be bound they found what they wanted, and more," he said. "Some mighty pretty prints they had to show me."

"Prints?"

"Of actresses. Not the twopence-colored ones of the plays, the more artistic ones. There wasn't anyone else in the shop, so they had time to show me quite a few. Of other young ladies too."

"I understand you," I said and drained my glass to hide my feelings. It was not just Katrijn who did not deserve such calumnies, but most of her fellows, yet I could not protest, for fear that Barraclough might draw conclusions that trespassed upon ground I had no intention of yielding to him. Nor had I any desire to discuss the question more generally, although I had frequently directed gentlemen, married and single, as to the best place to find such pictures, and even to houses where they might meet the high-class young ladies themselves. Men are but flesh and blood, as I had written in that unguarded moment to Miss Durward. Certainly, if Barraclough were about to confide in me, I should then learn some of that which I had promised to discover for Miss Durward. And yet I should be unable to communicate the knowledge, for honor's sake as much from embarrassment. I saw his hand moving for the decanter and got up, although not as briskly as I should have liked, for the fever had left me easily tired, and with greater fatigue in my leg came sharper pain in the limb that I had lost. "Shall we join the ladies?"

My stratagem worked, and he withdrew his hand. "Oh, aye, if you will."

As I opened the drawing room door Mrs. Barraclough turned. "Ah, now we can ask them."

"Ask us what, Mrs. Barraclough?"

"A cup of tea, Major? Whether there is anything that would drive you into a monastery."

I tried to speak, but no words came. At my hesitation, Miss Durward gestured to where she had propped the print on the carved-stone mantelpiece. "We were talking of the abbey, and wondering that anyone could choose to shut themselves away from the world in that way."

It was a few seconds before I could frame a reply with any composure. "Well, some had little choice in those days," I said, taking the cup with great care. "They were given as children."

"How dreadful! How could any mother allow such a thing?" said Mrs. Barraclough.

"But what of grown men and women?" Miss Durward said. "What makes them do it?"

Mrs. Barraclough poured out a cup of tea for her husband. "If they've been bred up as Romans, then maybe it doesn't seem so strange. The church has its claws into them already. But to be shut away like that!"

"Perhaps—" I said. Everyone turned to regard me. The tea had done something to revive me, and I went on. "To belong to a company where everything is ordered, where the rules are known and the principles of command established. . . . It is very comfortable to know one's place in one's world. Particularly if one has never had a place to which one belongs—no true home—even as a child."

Mrs. Barraclough nodded, but Miss Durward said, "But never to be able to escape!"

"If one's sole desire is to be free, then perhaps it would be intolerable," I said. "But to live in a group is to have the same interests and experiences, and groups must have rules to live by. Perhaps the army is an extreme example, but consider the houses of the Béguines that we saw at Mechelin. Companionship of like minds and lives is an inestimable support, for women—of all classes—perhaps even more than for men. If one is not to have—has not had—the good fortune to find the greatest happiness of all . . ." Into my mind came a picture of the girls whose house I had shared in San Sebastian, Mercedes, Izzaga, and the others, women of less than no account in the world's judgment, but a community of women nonetheless, laughing and swearing at one another, crying and giggling, turning as one on the men who tried to injure them, sharing garments and tending hurts. My hand was still unsteady as I set down my cup.

"Nuns run away," said Barraclough, "usually into the arms of some man, and off they go to Gretna—or worse."

"Or they are running away from men when they enter," said Miss Durward, "from a forced marriage, from brutality, from betrayal—"

"It seems very cowardly to run away," said Mrs. Barraclough. "Surely one should stay, and try to make the best of things. Unless there is danger to life, of course."

"Danger to life may not come in the form of outright violence," I said, and my voice was suddenly hoarse, so that I had to drink some more tea before I could continue. "And yet there may still be no choice for them. The world turns its back on such women, without father or brother or husband. How can you despise . . . How can we despise one such, then, if she flees from us to a place that will take her in, and feed and clothe her? Where she may even find some measure of contentment and companionship? We who have a free and comfortable life, of all people, cannot condemn those whom society does not help, if they then accept help where it is offered."

"Poor dears," said Mrs. Barraclough. "You are quite right, we should not condemn what we can have no knowledge of. Dear Major, may I help you to some more tea?"

Perhaps, in my still-weakened state, my command over myself had been overstretched. In any case, this placid enquiry broke through my defenses as the image of high walls and faceless, voiceless nuns had not, and I had no strength left to control my feelings. Even my mumbled excuse betrayed me by the break in my voice as I rose, and I made for the French windows onto the terrace and gained the lawn without looking behind me.

It was not dark, for as the sun had set, so had the moon risen, but the cold, white light was splintered by the apple trees, and in my haste, my lost limb seeming as real as my present one, I all but fell twice. Only when I reached the gate at the far end did I halt, and stare out across the lane and over the dimming fields to where the moon itself was just breaking free of the branches of an elm.

The air was almost still. I was aching and empty with loss. The pain of this absence was worse than any wound could be, and if sheer longing could make a being corporeal, then I would have sensed the long grass bending to Catalina's step, known again the warmth of her hand on my arm, felt the vibration of her small, deep voice.

Querido? En qué estás pensando?

How was it possible, that she would not come to me? Even now I could smell her skin. Her lips were dark and sweet, and there was a mole on her shoulder that I touched and then kissed, as I did the soft, secret places that in her love she had yielded, and in which she had cradled the bitter fruit of our happiness. No, it was not possible. I would not believe it. While I had the power to long for her, she would be with me.

In the quiet, I heard the soft rattle of carriage wheels on the Brussels road. Then there was silence. It was so still in the lane that what was before my eyes might have been a woodcut print, the trees and hedges black, and the moonlit tips of cornstalks and branches and stones chipped and cut from the dark around them. Why, then, could not the light show me the small figure of my love, seeking me as I sought her, or perhaps unconscious of my regard, as she had been when I first caught sight of her? Surely my eyes could see her, if my heart and mind desired it strongly enough.

A dark figure was moving towards me, engraved by my longing against the pale road.

"Stephen?"

But it was not she. It was not Catalina. My longing had no more power than my ruined body had. Katrijn was walking slowly towards me along the lane in a rustle of silk.

"I'm sorry," she said. "I did not mean to startle you. Stephen, *chéri*, are you ill?"

"I thought . . ." Her hand in mine was warm and real, and in the bitterness of my disappointment I let it go. "What—what are you doing here?"

"I am on my way to Namur, and Meike heard from your Madame Permeke that there were letters for you. I was going to get my coachman to hand them in, but then I saw you here, in the garden." She reached up to touch my cheek. "But, tell me, *chéri*, how are you?"

I could not say: I could not speak. It was not she that I longed to hold, to kiss, to lie with.

"Stephen, you are ill?"

I pulled myself together. "No, just tired. I am better, but not well yet. I am sorry; won't you come in?" I opened the gate.

"Thank you." She stepped into the orchard.

"Would you care for some refreshment?"

"No, no, it is too late to call. Besides, I would not embarrass your friends for the world. I must be off in a moment. I have a rehearsal in the morning. How are you enjoying life in the country?"

"Very much, thank you. It has been most beneficial. Did you say that you have some letters?"

"Oh, yes, I beg your pardon." She fumbled a little as she took them from her reticule.

"Thank you." There were only a few, tradesmen's accounts for the most part by the look of them. I pushed them into my coat pocket.

"Stephen—" She stopped. In the moonlight she looked extraordinarily beautiful, the plume of her hat and the smooth wave of dark hair curving above her brow and eyes, her lips a little parted, the rich silk of her gown framing her honey-colored breast. I had possessed this beauty so many times, she had cried out in my arms, and yet I might have been staring at a painting—a confection of pigment and canvas—for all the desire I felt for her. The memory of taking her filled me suddenly with disgust, not for her, she was exquisite, but for myself, as a man does who hates himself as he takes a clean, pretty whore while he carries an image of his distant love close to his heart.

"Stephen . . . I was going to write to you from Namur, but now that I am here, it would be more honest . . . In short, I think we should end our association altogether. I cannot give up my profession, and you cannot give up your position, or your past. There is too much that we—we cannot share."

She seemed very far away in the moonlight and shadow in which we stood.

"Of course, if you wish to do so," I said, with a slight bow. I felt nothing at all. "It has been—oh, in every way delightful. But I have always known that such as I am cannot ever be worthy of you."

She came close to me. "No. Not that, Stephen. You must not think that. I thought I had cured you of doing so." She laughed a little, and I thought it strange that after so long she could still have no notion that what ailed me was beyond cure.

But then I had a sudden memory of her finger, pressed between my brows on that first evening. "You have done more than I had thought anyone could," I said, in a low voice. "Dearest Katrijn, I shall remember that for the rest of my days, and thank you. For that, and— for everything else." She smiled at me so sweetly that as I took her hand I wondered at the strength of my earlier disgust. "Please believe that the only thing I regret about our association is the ending of it."

"But it must end," she said, and her voice had a crack in it. "You once said, Lord Wellington showed not the least of his genius in retreat. Or perhaps I have that wrong. No doubt Miss Durward could quote chapter and verse. I am no genius, but an honorable retreat is within my power."

She turned away to the gate and I hobbled swiftly after her. "Katrijn—my dear——"

She stopped, and I took her in my arms; I could not help it. I had sought comfort there too often not to seek it now that my need was greater than ever.

She huddled close to me for an instant, then pulled away. "Please let me go, Stephen. Even actresses do not enjoy the parting of lovers in real life."

"Of course," I said, and opened the gate for her. As she passed me I smelled her perfume, and she was less surprised than I when I caught her to me again and kissed her. She returned my kiss with a pressure of her lips that awakened all my former delight, then pulled herself free, and walked up the lane to where her chaise was waiting before I could follow her.

I stood and listened to the click of the carriage door and the rumble of the wheels moving away in the summer dust. I seemed to feel little, as if the emotions of the past minutes had run so swiftly through me that they had left no mark on my soul; I felt only the deep, icy cold that leaves one insensate to other hurts. I turned my back to the gate and leaned on it, looking back up the garden to where the house glimmered through the trees. Dimly, I perceived a tall, pale figure standing on the terrace. It was Miss Durward, and as I watched, she started down the steps.

"Am I disturbing you, Major?"

"Not at all," I managed to say.

"Only I was . . . I was afraid, back there in the drawing room

. . . you were angry, or upset, but I have no notion by what. Please believe that none of us had that intention."

Good manners began to reclaim me. "No, of course not. It was merely a memory, awakened by—by that delightful picture, but too old to bear repeating."

"Not a memory—memories—like those of Waterloo? I still reproach myself for that."

"You need not, must not, reproach yourself. And tonight was nothing to do with soldiering."

She said nothing.

I could not be sure if she had seen Katrijn, and with the thought came a many-layered grief that swelled in my throat and held me silent.

Then she said, "Major, I am . . . I do not care to meddle in others' lives. When I asked you about George, I think that was the first time I have ever tried to do so. And I know"—she smiled—"well, Hetty says I go around blind for much of the time, blind to others' thoughts and feelings, that is. She says I care nothing for people's hearts, so long as I may draw their faces. But this time . . . I must say that if—if you want . . ." Her voice fell, but after a moment she continued. "Sometimes it helps to speak of things. And if it would, I should like to listen."

"You are very kind," I said. "But—"

"Even if you wish to speak of the lady I saw you with just now."

"I must apologize . . ."

"Why should you?" she said. "So few of us live readily by the rules that the world makes for itself, whether by law or custom. I do not—I transgress some rule every day by mistake, and would more, and deliberately, if I did not care for my family's feelings. And it is only your good breeding that hides the fact that you do not live within the rules either. Even Hetty has been known to exclaim against some dictate of propriety!"

I smiled.

"And," she continued, "if you do not know by now how difficult it is to shock me, then your perception is a great deal weaker than I have credited you with."

I smiled more broadly but said nothing, and after a moment she put out a hand. "I would not intrude on your feelings for anything in the world. You have but to say the word, and we need never discuss such things again. But in our letters we have spoken of so much of our lives that I feel . . . I observe only that you are not happy."

It was true, but I could only say, "On the contrary—"

She interrupted me: "I did not mean in your existence here. Although that lady . . ."

"That lady and I . . ." She was silent. "That lady and I no longer have an association. We have parted, by mutual agreement. I owe her a great deal."

"But even when an attachment between lovers comes to an end so quietly," she said calmly, "there is still much regret to be felt at its passing."

"Indeed." I said no more, and in my silence felt an easing of—of what? I did not know, only that it had come about by Miss Durward's agency.

After a while she said, "I'm sorry. It's none of my business. I should not try to meddle. God knows it does not come naturally!"

"No, please, you are quite right. It *is* regret that I feel—much re-gret . . . a great sorrow at the ending of a friendship. And yet it is not because of *her* that . . ." I could not continue.

"Then of whom?"

I looked at her. Her forehead was creased with a kind little frown between her brows. She was not thirsting for gossip or avid for a thrill-ing tale of grand passion and agonizing grief: she wished only to help me. For a moment, my heart lifted with the possibility of telling of those days in Bera, and San Sebastian.

Then I shook my head. "I cannot—it is so long ago. Forgive me." I turned towards the house and offered her my arm. "It grows chilly. Perhaps we should go in."

Miss Durward took my arm, but said nothing for a long time.

I GOT BACK to the stables at the same time as Crispin Cordner drove up in a very tatty little sports car with the roof down. He waved and got out holding a bottle of wine.

"Hello there, Anna! How nice to see you!" We shook hands. "Are they in?"

"I think so."

"I'm early—had to drop in on my sister, and it didn't seem worth going home. How are you getting on up at the Hall?"

"All right," I said. "I'm trying to be there as little as possible."

"Oh dear, that bad, is it?"

"It's all right, really," I said, because Ray was all right and for the rest of it I didn't know what felt so—so *wrong*. Just because they weren't . . . weren't what I'd maybe hoped for. And Belle wasn't any nastier to Cecil than lots of people are to children—at least not when she wasn't drunk. I'd lived in enough different places to know that.

"Well, don't let it mean that you allow Eva and Theo to work you too hard instead," he said. "They're so driven, each of them. Sometimes I fear it doesn't occur to them to make allowances. Or to notice what happens to the people around them."

"They're very nice to me," I said. He didn't say anything, so after a moment I said, "The letters are really interesting—all about Waterloo and things. Only I don't know enough about the history and stuff." I wasn't going to say that I didn't know all the words.

He stood back to let me through the door and upstairs. "I haven't ever had a chance to look at them properly. Is there much about Kersey?"

"Not so far, but I haven't read all of them. He does have a bit about how nice it is to be able to sit in front of the fire in the library. I wondered which room that was." Here at last was someone who really knew Kersey. Though it was me who knew Stephen. "You could imagine it better then. You can't tell from how it is now."

"The army had it in the war, I think, so goodness knows what they did to it. And it will have been hacked about more since it's been a school."

"But the one I've just read says Brussels not Kersey for where he was writing from."

"Perhaps he was on holiday. I know Brussels was full of English tourists during the Waterloo campaign. Are there letters dated 1815?"

"He puts ''19' and then ''20' for the date."

"1819? Peterloo—the Peterloo Massacre. Well, well. I wonder what he thought of it. Most of the landed gentry thought it was the beginning of the end for them. It was, I suppose, in some ways, with Chartism and so on. And places like Kersey end up as schools and offices."

I didn't know what he was talking about, but by that time we were upstairs. There was music playing, not the radio, I saw, but a record, slow sort of jazz. Eva got up from the sofa as we came in. "*Buenas noches*, Crispin!" He bent down to her and kissed her on both cheeks, which looked strange, because I knew they weren't lovers or anything. "And Anna—good!" She was wearing a silky tunic with Indian patterns all over it and black trousers and long, silvery earrings. Seeing her against Crispin I noticed for the first time how small she was, much smaller than me. "Theo is just taking a shower."

When he came in he was wearing an open-necked shirt and trousers like Crispin, and he was rolling up his sleeves as he went, which didn't surprise me because it was still hot, specially up under the roof, like we were. "Hello, Anna. Have you looked at your prints?" he said.

"Not yet."

"I should like to see them, if I may," said Eva.

I wanted her to see them but I wasn't sure about Crispin. Not that he wasn't nice, but just that, well, I felt shy of someone who ran an art gallery seeing my photos, a bit like playing a tune with one finger for Elton John. But Eva was looking at me, so I said, "Oh—okay, I'll go and get them."

They looked good, I thought, tramping back up the stairs with all the bits. They looked like real photographs.

Eva stretched out a hand for them. Then she said, "Mmm . . . Let's have a look at the negs." She switched on the light box and tossed them down onto it in their plastic-sleeve thing. "Hm. A bit thin. No wonder there is no detail in the shadows. And the composition— here, this first shot, of the Hall—is it this print? Yes. You are trying a frame, yes?"

"Yeah."

"A frame is a very strong compositional device. It dominates. But the risk is that it cuts off the viewer—it is static. It draws the eye in, but it does not encourage it to move around the picture. One look, and for the viewer that is that. The eye is bored, and it moves on. Do you see?"

"Yes," I whispered. I'd thought it was quite a good picture, till then.

There was a clank from the sink. Theo had started to cook the supper. I could smell garlic and butter melting and a nutty smell. I looked across to him so Eva wouldn't see my face going red. Oh, God, fish. And not just white fish either, which I could just about bear if I was starving and it was in fingers with lots of ketchup. This was fish with eyes. It was like Eva'd decided to make this evening as horrible as possible.

She dropped the print onto the coffee table and picked up the one of the pillar. "This is more interesting, compositionally," she said, "but you have camera shake. What was the shutter speed? Can you remember?" I shook my head. "Never mind. It all comes with practice. And this is the boy? Yes. Good. You have focused on the eyes. But you need less depth of field—the background is unimportant.

And it should be cropped here"—she slashed her thumb down just beyond his cheek—"and here"—under his chin—"it is messy as you have it. But this is a very good start, Anna. We must talk more about exposure, but I am impressed."

"You don't sound like you are," I said.

She laughed. "But I am, so I was taking your work seriously. I am sorry, I should have warned you."

"She's a hard woman, Anna. Don't take it personally," said Crispin, from where he was changing the record. "I promise you, she does like them. May I see the others?"

The new music was classical, violins and things. He came back and picked up the one of the pillar and the window. "This is interesting. You know, it looks like the original glass." He tilted it to the light. "Who is that I can see through the window?"

"My grandmother, it must be," I said. "There wasn't anyone else there."

"Oh, of course, though one could never be sure. It looks tall for a woman. And broad in the shoulder." He went on staring at the print, almost as if he was trying to look further into the window. "Strange how the less one can see of a figure, the more meaning—no, I think *import* is the word. One could imagine that figure to be almost anyone, from any time. It seems to mean more, because one can't see exactly what it is to know what it isn't. Strange." He smiled at me and took the last print gently from between my fingers. "Ah, now, let me guess. This is Cecil?"

"How did you know?"

"My niece Susan used to work at the Hall, when the school was open. She helped to look after him. She has a snapshot of him in her room. Odd little chap, he sounded to me. Ran pretty wild."

I was surprised. Suddenly there was a ferocious sizzling and spluttering from the stove and I jumped. Eva went to start laying the table and then said over her shoulder, "Crispin, would you get those candlesticks from the mantelpiece?"

I'd seen them on the first day, four of them, quite short, silver with little turquoise stones and tiny silver beads all round the rim and the base.

"These are charming," said Crispin. He picked up the bit of heavy flowery silk that they always stood on. "And this is delightful. Where did you get it?"

Eva looked up from where she was putting some dressing on the salad. "Oh, that was lying around when we moved in here. It seemed too pretty to throw out."

"It looks familiar, somehow. Chinese silk, I'd swear, but those flowers and fruit are English. The same sort of period as the candle-sticks, at a guess. A bed-hanging, perhaps. Pity it's faded."

"We had it on the windowsill for a while."

"Ah, light does so much damage. We coax it into our homes in our dull English climate, and then we deplore its effects."

"Except people who earn their living by it," I said. Everyone looked at me. "Like Theo and Eva."

"True!" said Theo, turning round with the frying pan in his hand. "How right you are, Anna. Now, where are the plates?"

I looked at the fish on my plate, and it looked back in a dead kind of way, and I didn't know where to begin, and I didn't want to either. But you can't hide a whole trout under your fork, or smear it round till it looks as if it's gone. I was wondering what to do when, by mistake, I caught Theo's eye. For a moment I thought he almost winked at me, though it might have been the candlelight, which was wobbling in the air from all the windows being open. Then he looked down at his plate, and very slowly stuck his fork into his fish's side. He put his knife flat into its back and cut it all the way down to the tail, and the whole side lifted off in a slab of pale brown that didn't seem so bad after all.

I did the same, and mangled it a bit but managed, and I found it wasn't that bad to eat either. There was lots of wine to wash it down with, and I saw Crispin dip a bit of his fish into the buttery juice, which had almonds in it as well, and I tried doing the same and that was nice. And the summer pudding we had afterwards was really good, everybody said so.

"Barbarous English food," said Eva. "If you had told me in Seville when I was a child that I should one day eat a dessert made of soggy bread and fruit so sour you must pour in a kilo of sugar, I should not have believed you. Not when I could climb the wall to steal apricots and almonds from the trees in the garden next door."

"But that was before I made it for her," said Theo. "Some more cream for you, Anna?" I took the jug, thinking how cool and sleek it was compared to the custard Mum would've made.

"So these things came more naturally to you?" said Crispin.

"Well, I do most of the cooking," said Theo. "But yes, I was brought up on all those desserts and pastries. And there was a sour cherry soup, which . . . Well, when I taste it now, it is as if I am again sitting on the counter in the kitchen of the Hotel Franz-Josef in Pest, watching my grandfather at work. And *csirke paprikas*, and *pala csinta*."

"But your mother was Czech, not Hungarian, wasn't she?" said Crispin.

"Oh, yes. And one of my father's grandmothers was Polish. There is some Lithuanian too, although I cannot remember where. I am a real *mitteleuropische* mongrel. Before the war we could stay with cousins anywhere from the Baltic to the Black Sea." He laughed. "Eva, now, is of the purest Sephardi blood. All Spaniards are obsessed with birth—you might say such families consider themselves the hidalgos of Spanish Jewry."

"So how did you meet?"

"In Spain," said Eva. "I had my first big commission." She smiled. "It was a piece about a nunnery. It had been an artillery barracks after the dissolution of the religious orders, but they were turning it into the municipal museum."

"I was working on a story about the effect of martial law in the Basque country," said Theo, smiling. "We argued till the café closed about what should be done with buildings that have lost their purpose. The Party's attitude was very utilitarian in those days—how you would have disapproved, Crispin!—but Eva saw it in terms of architecture."

"It is a little more drastic than a country house that becomes a school, certainly," said Crispin.

"When I went back to Madrid I found the man I'd been living with had moved in with someone else," said Eva, reaching forward to fill everyone's wineglass again. "Theo turned up on the doorstep two days later. He offered to console me."

"Successfully, it appears," said Crispin.

Eva laughed. "Most of the time. We swear undying love, and pick a country where we can live together. Then we have a row, and Theo flies off to Berlin, or Havana, and falls for some pretty little interpreter. And I decide to move out."

"Or the *Paris Review* invites Eva to New York to shoot some literary grande dame who has just published a muckraking memoir of her affair with Hemingway, and Eva and she end up in bed together and *I* have to get rid of the flat."

"It wasn't Hemingway!" said Eva. "It was Picasso!" and everyone laughed.

"But I gather that, these days, you don't bother to do the moving-out bit," said Crispin.

I hadn't been understanding it all, but suddenly I realized what they'd said. First, that they weren't faithful to each other, they both had sex with other people, and they didn't seem to mind, even made jokes about it. And second, that Eva was one of those.

I looked at her. The candlelight was all there was now, and it made her eyes black and sparkly, and the green silk of her dress was like smooth water lying over the aliveness of her. She was much older than

Mum, but I could easily imagine a man fancying her, and her fancying a man—Theo, for instance. Oh, yes, I could imagine that. But how could a woman fancy her? How could she touch another woman?

"There are two things you can't tell about a new man," Eva was saying. "How drunk he is, and when he's about to come. Wouldn't you say, Crispin?"

"Yes," he said, stretching back in his chair. "You have to get to know the man in question. Though as to how drunk he is—or one is oneself—there is one sure indicator, alas, is there not, Theo?"

Theo smiled and got up. "Perhaps it is so. Crispin—excuse me. I think I should see Anna home."

"Of course," said Crispin. He wasn't very drunk, I didn't think. He got up and came round the table to put a hand on my shoulder and actually kissed me on the cheek, just the way he'd kissed Eva earlier. "Good night, Anna. Do call in at the gallery next time you're passing. It would be lovely to see you. And let me know if you come across anything significant in the letters."

"I will," I said.

"Anna, I'm so glad you came this evening," said Eva. "I'm going to Madrid tomorrow—back on Tuesday. Theo knows what needs doing, if you want the work. I'll see you then."

I said good-bye and thank you, and Theo followed me downstairs. "I'm okay on my own, honest," I said.

"I know. But I should like to escort you some of the way. Besides, after so much food and drink it will be a pleasure to walk outside a little."

It was warm, but a breeze had got up in the dark and feeling it cool on my cheeks made me realize how hot I was. The sky was clearer than it had been for a couple of nights, darker even than the trees above our heads, and a few stars appeared and disappeared beyond the shifting leaves.

"Would I be offending you if I apologized for our conversation in there?" said Theo, after a moment. There were pine needles as well as soft grass under our feet.

"No. I mean—no, you don't have to apologize. I mean—no, I'm not offended."

"I am glad. I was afraid . . . Well, it is not easy to remember how young you are."

"Even when I can't get served in a pub?"

He laughed. "That still annoys you, doesn't it?"

"Sort of. A bit. Not really."

"But you were embarrassed in there."

"I—it's just stuff I—I don't know much about."

"There are so many rules about who may not sleep with whom. A few are necessary: of course the young must be protected. So many are not. And even when there is no law, *les bourgeois* think that ignorance will make up for it, will prevent sex that transgresses—that threatens their rules. So they keep silent."

"Doesn't mean you don't know what they say, though," I said, thinking of what I couldn't help knowing got said about anyone who went with boys at school. And about what Belle said. Did Mum really tell Ray? Say that? I shook my head to clear the thought away, and said, "Is—um—is Crispin a—a—"

"Homosexual? Yes. Does it bother you?"

"No—only—I've only ever known one."

"That you were aware of, at least. Old habits of discretion die hard. And, yes, Eva is bisexual. She loves women as well as men."

"I—I thought people were . . . I thought they loved either one or the other."

We had reached the gate out onto the playing fields. "Eva would say that there are very few either-ors about sex."

"What would you say?"

He stopped, with one hand on the top rail. "I would say . . . I would say that the mathematics of love defy arithmetic." He opened the gate for me. As I went through he reached and touched my shoulder. "Good night, Anna. Sleep well."

⤞⧓⤝

MISS DURWARD'S AND my chambers lay in opposite directions. So silent had she been that I was surprised when, as we reached the head of the stairs, she said quietly, "Forgive me, Major, I had not meant to offend you."

"Please do not apologize. I am not offended. On the contrary, I am touched by your concern for me." I reached and touched her hand. "Good night, Miss Durward."

"Good night, Major," she said. "I hope you will sleep well." She turned away, and went swiftly towards her chamber.

So powerful were the lingering remnants of my distress that it was only when I had reached my chamber, and put down my candle to take off my coat, that I remembered the letters Katrijn had brought. Three were tradesmen's accounts and one a note from an acquaintance bidding me to a card party on a date that was already past, so long had it taken to travel the few miles from Brussels. The last, I saw, had come from England, and after a moment of staring at it I recognized the rector's hand.

It was quite short. My bailiff Stebbing had suffered a stroke and, although in no immediate danger, was quite unable to manage my affairs. My tenants and upper servants were coping as best they could, with the assistance of the rector and my neighbors, but there was no escape for me: with the harvest imminent, I was called for at Kersey.

⁜

Two hundred and fifty lashes by beat of drum. There are ten drum taps between each lash, time to know the pain, and await the next. Three hundred and fifty still to come, unless he faints. The surgeon stands with his hand on the soldier's pulse, and nods to continue. The men of the regiment, lined up on parade to learn the lesson, cannot see Wat Bailey's face, only hear the screams, but it is a point of honor not to flinch. Some have been flogged so often there is no flesh left on their backs to take more. It will be their legs next time. But this back, this flesh, is sweet and new. The drummers are striking true with the lash; the wound is only a handspan high, and twice as long. I can smell the blood that runs down his trousers and over the wood of the triangle to the ground. I can see his face, black with screaming, and I remember him, a cheeky fellow who came from my own birthplace. We knew the same country, and I thought him likely for promotion in time, but I could not save him from being court-martialed for stealing four silver and turquoise candlesticks from a Lisbon merchant. He was in his cups, of course. His friend Campbell, sentenced to a thousand lashes for his being a second offense, drank vitriol and died in mortal agony rather than suffer them.

The youngest ensign goes aside and pukes. The surgeon holds up his hand. Three hundred and seventeen. Bailey is untied from the triangle and taken away to mend. When his back is healed he will be brought back for the rest. As he is carried past I can see the bones white and raw beneath welling blood. Later, under the surgeon's poultice, it will grow rotten. Maggots in it will writhe away from the light, burying themselves in the rotting flesh, feeding on corruption.

II

THERE WAS NO LACK OF BUSINESS TO OCCUPY ME IN THE FEW days that elapsed between the letter arriving from Kersey and my departure, but fortunately it necessitated only one visit to Brussels, where the heat grew more oppressive by the day and left me with no desire to linger in the city, while the orchard at Ixelles awaited me. I had already written to engage lodging and passage for my journey; in Brussels I paid my tradesmen's accounts, and spoke to my banker, but did not close my account with him, for I hoped that I might again have a use for it before many months had elapsed. There was little then left to do, except retrieve the last of my traps from my apartment and fulfill my promise to Miss Durward.

The print shop was my first object. The shopman recalled me easily, as a long-standing customer and a friend of their favorite Mademoiselle Métisse, and remembered Barraclough too, at my prompting, for his height and his Englishness. Suppressing my distaste for peering into another man's business, I put my hand into my pocket, and a generous number of francs elicited the information that I required: Barraclough had bought only a most innocuous handful of pictures of pretty young ladies, and made no attempt, there at least, to discover anything about such ladies in the flesh.

I went out again into the glaring heat of the street, and considered. I was reasonably certain that he would be too fastidious—not to say prudent—to pick up a street girl. That being the case, I repaired to the nearer of the two cafés that I knew he frequented and from thence to the further, and spent a garrulous hour or two in each, buying cognac with a lavish hand. If the habitués were surprised at my generosity, they were equally generous with their gossip in return.

IT WAS THUS on the eve of my departure for Suffolk that I was able to reassure Miss Durward that I had every reason to suppose her fears about her brother-in-law to be unfounded.

"I will not trouble you with the conversations I had, but I think I can assure you that Barraclough has no thought of, well, of seeking diversion elsewhere. Such tastes as he has are only of the most ordinary kind, which need cause you no concern. I think chiefly he sought the company of other men, and the passing urban acquaintanceships to which he must be accustomed in Liverpool, and that only a city can provide."

"I understand. Thank God! And I may leave well alone." She hesitated, turned from her contemplation of the sunlit garden, and looked me full in the face. Then she nodded. "I may trust you too."

"Trust me?"

"To speak the truth. There are men—many men—who would insult my reason in seeming to respect my sex."

"In what way?"

"By lying. By protecting a fellow man from censure, in pretending to protect me from such knowledge. You would not do so."

"I hope I would always protect a lady."

She waved a hand, as if such sentiments had no place in our discussion. "But not with dishonesty."

"No, not with dishonesty. Not you."

She said nothing but did not take up her sketchbook, as I had come to expect during her silences, even though the prospect from the terrace where we sat was charming enough to tempt any artist. The sun was still up, although we had lingered over dinner, and the soft light seemed to make the clipped limes and beds of late roses appear to be warm and swelling with life within their box hedges.

"What will you do at Kersey, after the harvest?" said Miss Durward.

"Oh, there is no want of occupation on a country estate," I said. "I shall be as busy as I described to you last year."

"I remember your letters well. To think that it must be a year too since that night in Manchester!"

"And Tom is quite recovered?"

"Oh, yes. But Hetty misses him so very much, and so do I. We thought to be home long before this."

"Do you have any notion of when you might return?"

"Hetty has been advised to wait until the fourth month."

"Of course."

Then Miss Durward did pick up her sketchbook and begin to lay down some lines. After a moment I realized that her gaze was not directed at the scene before us, but at me.

"You have no objection, Major?"

"Not at all—"

"Pray do not move your head," she said.

"I beg your pardon."

She made no reply; her gaze was quite impersonal. I could not see her paper, only hear the sound of her pencil—as light as the rustle of leaves at one moment and at the next as sharp and exact as a sword cut—above the calling of doves on the roof, and the trickle of water as the gardener went about his evening tasks. Her narrowed gaze flicked between my face and her paper, as a commander's does between his map and his battlefield. At the memory the muscles round my eyes recalled the strained attention we had all paid at such moments. Then, we sought to understand what the lines and symbols would mean on the morrow in cover, obstacles, artillery range, flesh broken, and blood spilled. Did Miss Durward, in observing my face, seek to understand the world that it mapped, or did she map the man which that world had formed?

She put down her pencil, and held the sketchbook at arm's length for a moment. Then she brought it close to her again, and I heard the few scratches of her final thoughts, as if she crossed a *t* and dotted a couple of *i*s on reading a letter through. She looked up, and her eyes met mine and engaged with them as they had not when it was their shape and shadow that she sought. But she said nothing and after a moment, glanced away.

"May I see your drawing?" I said.

"If you like." She put the open sketchbook on the table and pushed it towards me. Then she pulled up her shawl from where it had fallen, wrapped it round her shoulders—for the sun had slipped from us— and sat fiddling with the fringe.

For some seconds, all I could see was that the drawing was very like, even down to the twist at the outer corners of my eyebrows, for no man, of whom custom and propriety demand a clean-shaven chin, can be wholly surprised by his own appearance. But it was strange indeed to regard an image of myself formed not by the inherent, impersonal properties of light, glass, and metal, nor by the skill of a Norwich portrait painter, but by the hand of a friend. Her eye and mind had seen—had driven that hand to set down—what?

The image filled the sheet and yet appeared distant, the head a little averted, the gaze fixed beyond the confines of the page, with eyes and mouth narrowed into faint, habitual lines, so that the gray and silver marks that formed contour and shadow seemed to describe to me everything that my eyes and feelings already knew, but that reason could not apprehend until shown it by another.

Miss Durward was regarding me steadily. "Do you like it?" she said.

"I think so," I said slowly, and she laughed. Perhaps it was my indelible memory of that first morning in the print shop, conjured by these same words, that made me observe suddenly how quick and rough her laugh was, quite different from Katrijn's soft, low merriment.

"Perhaps you are a little taken aback?"

"Perhaps."

"You are not accustomed to think of how you appear to others?"

"I would not claim to be immune to vanity. I care for the cut of my coat as much as the next man. But here"—I put the sketchbook down on the table—"how is it that you have shown so much with these lines? Is *that* what you see?"

She smiled. "Yes. This evening, at any rate. But perhaps it is what I know, as well, that shapes the lines. Or perhaps it is what *you* know."

I could not answer her, and in the silence that followed I thought how often her words, as much as her art, took me aback. Was it more surprising to know that it was my very being that lay within those tightened eyes, or to know that it was she who had seen it, and cast it across the page in a net of silver lines?

She said suddenly, "I wish you were not leaving."

"I have no desire to leave, but I must. Besides, I have trespassed on your sister's hospitality too long already."

She sighed, and her shoulders seemed to sag with the exhalation. "The thought of all the evenings . . . Write to me, I beg you, Major! Write to me of battles, and horses, and men, so that I may not sink entirely into stupid woman's business, or end by murdering Hetty. She makes me so angry, and through no fault of hers. Write to me of men's business!"

"Even if men's business is death?"

"Even then," she said. "Better death than bonnets and servants and nervous headaches!"

"You would rather talk of murder, than poke-fronts and palpitations?"

She laughed. "Well, if you put it like that, perhaps not quite. And now that Hetty is so much better I have some hope of being able to go a little further afield. I would give a great deal to see something of France. I have not had your good fortune, you see."

I said nothing, although I might have said much, about the fortune that a man desirous of seeing foreign parts may find in a military career. But it was as if she read my thoughts, for she said suddenly, "Would you have had it otherwise? Knowing what you do now of war, would you have chosen to follow a different profession?"

I was still silent, for I did not know the answer. War had brought Catalina to me, and war had taken her away. Would I rather be without her presence in me, without so short a happiness, and so long a grief?

No, I had never wished the years of my love to have been one day shorter, any more than I would wish a road traveled with Catalina to have been one yard the less.

"I do not mean, do you regret what life has shown you of the world," said Miss Durward, "but, rather, do you regret your profession? A man's nature is formed and understood by what he does, as most women's are not."

"Until last summer," I said slowly, "I should have said, no, I regret nothing. Even the necessity of killing was just that: a necessity. War is ugly, but no one could have thought we ought not to oppose Buonaparte, and it was the army and the navy who were best fitted—who were the only means—to do it. How then could I refuse anything that my intellect and my body could do, in that service?"

"But not since Peterloo?"

"No. Not since then." I looked at the drawing again. Had what she showed in my eyes been there last summer? I remembered sharply the little room in Dickinson Street: Tom lying still and straight; the stricken, murmurous quiet beyond St. Peter's Field; Miss Durward's gaze in the candlelight as she touched her pencil so tenderly to the page, as if touching his pale cheek itself. "You would not get most of my friends to agree with me. But I saw how the brutality was unchained not by circumstance, but by design. And great men condone it! It should not have been a surprise, to one who has lived under his command, that the Duke of Wellington supports the magistrates' actions. But it was a surprise that he should condone the slaughter of such innocents . . . And none has been held to account for it! And now they pass laws to stifle true grievances and just complaint under the guise of the need for civil order."

"We none of us are unchanged, that saw Peterloo. How many other laws that we live under now seem iniquitous, or brutally expedient? But you were not part of it. *You* were only there by chance."

"But for *that* to be the freedom I was fighting for!" I said. "That . . . Oh, that is what haunts me! So many of us are dead—so many damaged beyond mending—and to what end?"

She said nothing but held out her hand, and I took it. To touch another creature steadied me, but by then I could not by any means stop myself, although I had never in my life thought to speak thus.

"I chose a profession of necessity, but the cause was just, and I offered to it what I had. So much was taken: bodily health and peace of mind, friends—even love! I lost my love! And now what we gave is betrayed, by drunken and licentious rulers, and a country that has enslaved its people by poverty if not law, and sold its soul for profit and political expediency! Perhaps I should not care for the ruin of my body and my peace, since I shall not love again. And for England . . ." I drew a deep breath. "Well, perhaps it is better so. Perhaps I have been spared some pain, for if I have no strength left to defend a just cause, then I should be glad that there is no just cause now left to defend!"

Miss Durward was silent for a long time, but her thin fingers gripped my hand so hard that I felt that the ink and paint stains might be pressed forever into mine.

Then she said, "Who was she?"

"Her name was Catalina."

Miss Durward nodded slowly. "Catalina."

She said no more but only continued to grip my hand. At last I said, "Forgive me—I cannot speak of it."

"No, of course not," said Miss Durward.

It was very quiet. The sun had quite set, and the light that lingered touched eyes and cheeks and lips without illuminating them, so that when I realized at last all that had been said, I had no means of determining its effect on her.

There was a faint rustle of silk from the open windows behind us, and Miss Durward's hand whisked out of mine and picked up her pencil.

"Forgive me, Major," said Mrs. Barraclough, "but I know you have an early start tomorrow, and I am about to retire. I could not go to bed without bidding you farewell."

"Nor I you," I said, getting to my feet. "My dear Mrs. Barraclough, how can I thank you enough?"

Behind me, I sensed rather than saw that Miss Durward had slipped away from us into the dimming garden.

"Oh, we are only sorry that you cannot stay longer," Mrs. Barraclough said. "I hope the journey may not set your recovery back."

"As to that, I feel entirely well, and it is all thanks to you."

She smiled, and made a little disclaimer with her hand. Then she said, "It is still quite warm. Will you take a turn about the terrace with me?" I offered her my arm, and we went a few steps. "Lucy will feel your absence so much," she said.

"I shall miss all of you."

She took a little breath, and said, "Major, you must forgive me, for I am a silly creature. George says that I cannot think of anything but gowns and gossip. But . . . Major, it cannot have escaped your notice how much pleasure Lucy has in your company."

"And I in hers," I said, then realized what Mrs. Barraclough was about. "That is, we are old friends, with the habit of easy intercourse, and some interests in common."

We had reached the far end of the terrace. "What better foundation could there be?" she said, turning so quickly that I all but stumbled. "I beg your pardon, Major. You will think me an interfering busybody."

"No, never that," I said, recovering my balance. "I know how devoted you are to each other's interests. But I am very sure that Miss Durward has no thought of—of such a matter."

"No?"

"She told me herself that she would not marry for anything in the world."

Mrs. Barraclough stopped so suddenly that, our arms being linked, I turned towards her perforce, to see her face lifted to mine in the twilight.

"Not marry for *anything*? Why ever not?"

Too late, I remembered Miss Durward's reasons. "Well, I think she felt that she would not be able to devote the time to her art that she is able to in her unattached state."

She sighed and began to walk again. "Dear Lucy! She always makes her drawing the excuse for following her own road. But could you not . . . you and she are so . . . If you asked her . . . ?"

It was I who stopped, in the middle of the terrace, and took both her hands. "My dear Mrs. Barraclough, I beg you to say no more. I know that you wish nothing but your sister's happiness. Would it serve to convince you, if I assured you that for all the affection and esteem in which I hold her, Miss Durward is not alone in . . . in realizing that marriage is not something to which all of us are suited?"

I thought she sighed, but she said quite calmly, "Then there is no more to be said. I shall not meddle anymore, however I might wish that matters would take such a course of their own accord." We resumed our walk, taking a few more steps before she went on. "The sky on the western horizon is as much green as blue, is it not, now that the sunset is gone? How few paintings show it thus."

We spoke a little on indifferent topics, but although Mrs. Barraclough kept her promise, and did not allude to the matter again, I realized, when at last I heard the faint crunch of gravel, and Miss Durward came back up the steps from the garden, that what had been said could not be unsaid. Mrs. Barraclough's quick glance from her sister to me seemed full of significance, and Miss Durward's fleeting

smile to each of us unfathomable. I had no notion if she knew anything of her sister's conversation, but I could not but ask myself
whether she had taken herself out of the way to ease Mrs. Barraclough's path, or out of refusal to follow it, or from a wholly innocent
desire to enjoy the dusk in solitude.

It came to me suddenly that perhaps this had been Mrs. Barraclough's motive for welcoming me to Ixelles, even for coming to Brussels at all. My fever-addled brain had seized on the fact of her
invitation to stay with them at the time, without pondering its origin;
now I realized that Katrijn had seen that there was more in the invitation, and in my accepting it, than I had dreamed of.

Mrs. Barraclough was on the point of retiring. Miss Durward suddenly declared that she too was weary, and would follow her sister.

"Of course," I said, although I had never known her to own to fatigue before. Painfully aware as I was of all that had been said, and not
said, I read into her admission—perhaps her untruth—embarrassment, and reluctance to be left alone with me. Our farewells in consequence had an awkwardness, a constraint, about them that did little
justice to the easy friendship we had hitherto known.

At dawn on the morrow I departed for Ostende, and in an un-
eventful journey to Felixstowe and thence to Bury St. Edmunds I had
all too many miles of sea and road in which to contemplate the prospect of life at Kersey unbroken by any correspondence with Miss
Durward.

MATTERS AT KERSEY were in no better order, but no worse, than I
had feared.

On the morning following my return I left my horse at the
Crown and walked through the ford and up the steep village street
to Stebbing's house. "Thank God you're back, sir," said Mrs. Stebbing, opening the door to me herself. "He's been fretting himself
to flinders about the estate and the harvest, and him not able to do
a thing about it. For Doctor said as how he's to do no business at

all. But you know what Stebbing is, sir, he's that conscientious, he'd worry himself into his grave, whether anyone tells him aught of what goes on or not."

Her voice shook a little, and I took her hand. "How do you do, Mrs. Stebbing? You've had an anxious time of it, I fear. But he's nothing to worry about now." I stepped over the threshold as she stood back, and set my hat on the table. "Which is not to say that I shan't value his counsel, when he's well enough to give it. May I see him?"

"Aye, and he'll be glad of it. If you'd just step this way, sir."

She led the way up the stairs and into the front bedchamber. Stebbing lay in bed by the long, low window, propped on many pillows. He had been a big man, strong, and quick moving when it was needed, for all he was already in his sixties when I first knew him. But now the flesh had fallen away from him, while the right side of his face was twisted into rigidity, and one shoulder and arm lay crooked and useless against the pillows. I grasped his left hand, as I had so often grasped the left hands of friends and men, and spoke of my sorrow at seeing him thus, and of how, although of course the estate missed his presence at the helm, matters were as well in train as could be expected.

"Aye, I know that," he said, his speech only a little slow and slurred. "I see what carts pass the window, and who's late for work, and who's sent to which field, and how the stock and the horses are keeping. But I can't be there to rub an ear of corn between my fingers and decide to start cutting. Sometimes I think I can feel the corn in my palm, or the tilth under my feet, or I dream of riding a hay cart back to the barn. But then I wake, and can barely lift my head, and even when I see the dawn in the sky at last it makes no odds, for it's not me that'll be getting up and about."

I could do little but grasp his hand again. I had never heard him speak of his feelings so; his anger was shaking in his wasted muscles, and it called up the anger in me that I had long thought all but gone, for I too knew what it was to feel in my body so exactly, so painfully, a world that I could not touch.

We talked a little more of crops and livestock, but I could see that he tired quickly, and it was not long before I judged it wise to bid him good-bye and promise to call in as soon as I might, to acquaint him with the progress of the harvest.

"But do not fear, Mrs. Stebbing," I said as we went downstairs, "I shall say nothing to agitate him."

"I think it would do him more good to see you, sir, and to feel as if he's still part of things, than all the medicine in the apothecary's. As he said, he knows what goes on, only he can do naught about it all. I got the boys to drag the bed over to the window, so he could see the street, for he's one who likes to be in the thick of things, and making things happen. He always was." She stopped in the middle of the room and brushed her hand across her eyes. "I think it was that caught my fancy about him. At the Michaelmas Fair in Bury, that was. Even now when I look at him it's as if I'm back there, more than forty year ago. He was so tall and strong, and doing his father's business as sharp as you like, for all he was only twenty. He was never one to stand back and let a chance pass him by. We waited ten year to be married, for he had his way to make. But never have I regretted it!" She was silent, staring into the heart of the fire in the range.

"I am only sorry that he has been brought so low," I said.

"Well, Doctor says he's in no danger now, if he takes things easy. And he's still my William, no matter what. If he was blind as well as lame—if he was quite gone in his mind—he'd still be mine, and I'd be his, till the Day of Judgment itself."

I rode back to the Hall, feeling the late summer sun on my cheek, and hearing Mrs. Stebbing's words in my ears.

Press of business kept me occupied into the small hours for some days, and by the time that I had dealt with the work that Stebbing's illness had left undone I was glad to exchange account books and title deeds for the rattle and smoke of the new threshing machine and the deep sleep of bodily exhaustion.

But once the corn harvest was done, there was less need of me in the fields, and the evenings lengthened. For a time I found pleasure in the soft mists and warm sunsets and in the quiet of the house that lay about me as I stood on the great black-and-white marble floor of the hall, or walked up the stairs, knowing that it was my home and my own land under my feet. When I felt restless I might go down to the stables, and if no groom was to hand, saddle my own horse with no more than a small pang of grief for Dora. And then the woods and lanes and meadows were mine for the riding over.

It was on one such afternoon, when the dull light in the estate office had driven me out to find fresh air and exercise, that I glimpsed the little lad for the first time since my return, perched in a big oak and peering down at me as I rode out of the yard on a new young horse, so that all I could see was a face like a thin moon among the leaves. To see a child playing on my land recalled Mrs. Barraclough's words. *For him to be safe, and yet free to explore nature—the world—is what I wish for him above all. . . . It is the heart of all my care and love.*

Bidassoa fussed and fretted as we approached the tree. "Hello there!" I called, and for a moment the boy looked as startled as a hare. "Who are you?"

He shook his head then, but still did not move.

"There's no need to be frightened!"

I saw how his face was tanned dark by the sun, which had also bleached the fair hair above it. Then he vanished; there was a slithering among the leaves and a crackle of twigs, and he was gone. I stayed where I was for a moment while Bidassoa grew calmer, before I turned him towards the avenue with the intention of trying his paces.

I saw the boy again a few days later. I had taken a gun out alone, more to have an object for my wanderings on a fine afternoon than in the expectation of any serious sport, for the calendar declared my proper game still unassailable.

I took a brace of pigeon on the edge of one of the furthest coppices, however, and as the light began to fade, observed half a dozen rabbits at their evening browse on the far side of the meadow. I reloaded while calling quietly to the dogs, lest they bound off in pursuit of this legitimate canine prey, and began to move in.

Two barrels accounted for two rabbits and I sent the dogs to retrieve them. Following at my leisure, I was surprised to see them swerve away from their task towards the hedge. Then Titus raised his head and set to barking.

Crouched on the ground, under the lee of the hedge, was the boy. For an instant I was gripped with fear that I had shot him, before I saw that he was trying desperately to back through the dense and thorny hedge, while Nell and Titus stood and bayed cheerfully at him, ears flat and tails wagging.

I called them off and went closer. The lad's eyes were wide with fright and my approach served only to make him redouble his efforts to escape.

"Don't be frightened!" I called. "They won't bite you! Tell me, are you hurt?"

He scrambled to his feet and shook his head, although I could see several scratches beginning to ooze a little blood. On the heels of my fear came anger.

"You stupid boy! Didn't you hear me firing earlier? What the devil do you mean by sneaking around like that? Don't you know you could have been shot? You young idiot! I've a good mind to tell your father to give you a thrashing! I could have killed you!"

But he seemed to be beyond reason or understanding. His body trembled as if he had an ague, and when he did open his mouth no sound came out. He wore only a shabby pair of trousers, and looked to be six or seven years old at the most.

"Well," I said, "there's no harm done this time. But who are you? What's your name?" He shook his head. "Your father isn't one of my tenants, is he?" Another shake. "Who's your mother, then?"

At that he made a convulsive heave, tore himself free from the thorns and brambles, and ran from me as fast as his childish legs could carry him over the rough grass, so that I could see his scratched and bloodied back.

"Wait!" I called, beginning to stumble towards him. "Are you lost? Let me help you. I can help you, but you must tell me who you are. Wait! I know you are lost. I can help you."

Two pheasant exploded out of the wood with a cry that sounded like a dozen rifles being cocked. At the noise the dogs forgot all their training and raced after the boy. He saw them coming, stood still for one split second of true horror, turned, scrambled through the hedge, and was gone. When I at last reached the hedge myself, there was no sign of him, although I could not see where he might have gone.

I shouted for the dogs while I took the shoulder strap from my gun with shaking hands, doubled it up, and thrashed them both there and then with the metal ends, on and on, my arm aching but my anger driving me beyond all bounds of proper discipline. I only ceased when I saw blood seeping out into the sweat on Nell's flank.

I clipped the strap back. There was a strange, ill sensation in the pit of my stomach. Battle was savage, army life little less so. But what had I come to, that so small—so absurd—an incident could awake such savagery in me? Was that what Miss Durward had seen?

I left the dead rabbits where they lay, picked up my game bag, and began to limp home, my head aching and my every limb weary, with Nell and Titus halting along behind me like frightened shadows.

It was the boy, I realized. I knew his fear as well as I knew myself. And I had wanted to help him, and he had fled.

My dear Major,

It has taken a few weeks of silence, & Hetty's confession, for me to realise that your good breeding demands that it is I who reassure you. At least, I trust it is good breeding, & not ill-wishing, that has silenced you.

No: I shall overcome my embarrassment & put the matter more bluntly. If you do not feel able to write to me, it is no more than Hetty—& I—deserve. But if you can find it in your heart to overcome what I fear may be a very natural anger, so that you may forgive Hetty for meddling, & me for being the reason for it, I should be so very grateful. I do not think that I can support many more days of life at Ixelles, without some small pieces of our former companionship to cling to. Even a paragraph on winter in the lines of Torres Vedras, or the price you are getting for corn in Suffolk this year, would serve to preserve my reason from breakfast until dinner.

We drove to Tournai last week, & in looking out from the cathedral tower towards Mons, I thought yet again how unimaginable it is, that this quiet Flanders landscape might be despoiled with such trenches & gun-emplacements as you described at Torres Vedras. But I would not for anything ask you to write of such things if you would not wish to. What of your life in Spain after the peace? You have spoken little of that, although you must have found your situation congenial, to have remained so long in San Sebastian.

I must end here, for I am under orders to accompany Hetty in making calls. We begin to know our neighbours, you understand, so the delights of halting conversation, fine china, & beribboned infants await us. Hetty is advised not to travel back to England for a few weeks yet, so all my dependence is on you to alleviate the tedium, if you can bring yourself to answer your friend

Lucy Durward

This letter had been placed on my desk when it arrived, and I found it on my return, weary and covered with dust from a day in the fields. I read it where I stood, and would have sat down to answer it immediately, but that dinner had been announced, and I knew that Miss Durward's apology deserved more than a hasty note.

More, the reply that I wrote that night did indeed prove to be, but still hasty, for as I wrote I realized that if I were to do justice to our friendship and her liberality of mind, by telling the truth, then I should have to write my story as I felt it, quickly, and if my memories transgressed propriety, then so be it.

My dear Miss Durward,

I was overjoyed to receive your letter, & were there anything in your sister's actions to forgive, I would do so most willingly, & at length, but my desire to return to our former correspondence overmasters all, & prompts me to suggest that we say no more about it. I feel, moreover, that I owe you an explanation for my behaviour on several occasions, & above all for—shall I say— the fruitlessness of your sister's self-imposed task.

I said, on my last evening at Ixelles, that her name was Catalina. She was a native of Castile, but lived at Bera, in the Basque country. The Light Division came to know the country thereabouts well in the summer of '13, & there was no fear of the novelty of a period of leisure in such fertile & picturesque surroundings—which old Peninsular hands recalled in less kindly seasons—bringing on the Regt.'s customary impatience with inaction, since the French were at all times within a couple of miles of our encampment on the heights of Sta. Barbara.

I saw her a few times in the marketplace at Bera without learning her name. She talked easily enough with her neighbours, yet held herself a little aloof. When the French shelled Bera, & I went in to withdraw our pickets, I saw her sitting on the ground among the smashed stalls, cradling a boy who lay with his bandaged head in her lap & what was left of his legs spread across the cobbles. His eyes were misting over, & he whispered, "Catalina!" I did not think much of this at the time. It was more urgent to get our men out, & all our thoughts & actions after that were taken up with the small disaster of the loss of the bridge into Bera, and 50 men with it.

The other officers were the best of fellows, & better companions in battle I could not have wished for, but I sometimes longed for solitude. Then I would push a volume of Virgil or Rousseau into my pocket & slip away, for I cannot find the latter's work any the less true, or affecting, for knowing the ill opinions heaped upon his character. The country was so thick with rocks & trees that I might soon find myself alone to enjoy my solitude & my reading, but on one hot afternoon I pressed on—at a speed that is now for me only a memory—until I reached a cleft in the hill where a little stream tumbled between the rocks, paused to form a pool of still water, & then threw itself down the hillside again in its hurry to join the Bidassoa river, so many hundreds of feet below. Stopping a little above the stream, I sat down, settled my back against a tree trunk, & opened my book.

I heard a soft footfall, & Catalina's dark head appeared. She wore a blue gown & carried a linen towel. When she reached the patch of flat turf that bordered the pool for the few yards between waterfalls, she paused, panting a little.

I had not intended to hide myself in choosing my position, but I had forgotten the calculated effect of my dark green Rifleman's uniform under the shade of the tree on a dull day, & it was evident that she had no idea of my presence. In honour I ought to have left, allowing her to know of my existence only as she was sure of my departure. On the other hand, some of my fellows would have made advances to her, & I had no reason to think that these would not be as welcome as they were to so many of the village girls. But my memory of her self-containment & self-possession in the noisy market, & the way in which she now moved, thinking herself unobserved, gave me pause. I told myself that I did not care to shatter that ease, to cast myself into embarrassment & her into distress, still less into the well-founded fear that any occupying soldiery, even an English officer, may arouse in the female breast. So I sat where I was, even as I realised by her movements that she intended to bathe.

I had swum in the Bidassoa many a time when I came off duty, & knew well how the cold struck, stripping the sweat & heat of the day from the flesh, & the weariness from the mind. She stepped into the pool & I saw her shiver of shock as the reflection of sky & mountains broke. She stood for a moment, & then moved forward, slipping downwards to submerge herself in what appeared to be a deeper part of the pool. She lay back & then reached up an arm as she swayed to & fro in the moving water. I could almost see how the drops hung from her skin as pearls hang from the ears of a lady. Then she reached & pulled the combs from her hair, tossing them onto the moss & letting the water ripple it outwards.

A stealthy retreat would now have been possible, as well as chivalrous, but that she rolled over, stood up in the shallows, & stepped out onto the shore.

A soldier is in the company of women more than might be imagined. Poverty is generally our lot, & obedience our duty, but chastity is not accounted a military virtue. I was perfectly accustomed to feminine company of every kind, but I had never yet watched a woman who had no consciousness of male regard. There was neither art nor fear in how Catalina dried and dressed herself. Rather, she was private in her own thoughts. Just as my skin could recall the icy kiss of those mountain rivers, so now I felt how the huckaback linen rasped the drops away from her. It was only afterwards that my thoughts turned to how trim & pleasing her figure was. Her ankle was shapely & her complexion of the soft gold which I had come to admire as much—perhaps more—than the white-&-rose of our own English beauties. Her hair was black & silken with the water: it hung down her back almost to her knees. She sat on a rock & swung it forward, squeezing out the water before rubbing it with her towel & running her fingers through to smooth it. Then she plaited it into a thick rope and pinned it up again. As she stood up I saw once again the girl of the marketplace. The front of her skirt was shadowed with the stain of the boy's blood where no amount of time or bleaching in the sun could fade it. He had been a brother, or a cousin, or perhaps a lover, for she wore no wedding ring. Now I longed to step forward, before she went downhill again to the town, but still I hung back. Though she was clothed & shod she would know what I had seen, & nothing that I could do or say would overcome her knowledge of my intrusion.

Finally she turned away, & I listened until her step on the stony track had faded among the trees. When I could hear only the birds & the stream & the wind in the trees I took my watch from my pocket & found that it had stopped. I had no idea how many minutes or hours had passed, but the sun, though misty, was low enough to tell me that the hour was advanced & that I should make all haste to return to camp & my duties.

From the very next time I saw Catalina, again at the stream, I was careful not to frighten her, or go one inch beyond what she welcomed for herself with all her heart. Her father had been a strict enough guardian, she said, in the Spanish style, but the death of her brother had broken his heart—at these words her own eyes darkened & her mouth trembled so that I was obliged to comfort her before she could continue—& he now paid little attention to her comings & goings provided that his dinner was on the table at the appointed hour. Of this inattention I was not ashamed to take advantage, but only because it afforded Catalina greater freedom from scolding & censure than would otherwise have been expected. I would never have done anything to make her seek her father's protection. But I had seen her when she was true to herself—when she was private—& that truth I loved more than I had thought I could love any human creature. When she gave herself to me, I gave my soul to her, & knew that she would have it for the rest of our lives.

Our life together, though, was brief. We had very nearly 3 weeks. We met when we could, in a barn on the mountainside, or such other shelter as we could find, & only occasionally, when he was absent, in her father's house. When in early Sept., the Army heard of the fall and sack of San Sebastian, I knew that we did not have long, & sure enough, my military duties increased as it became clear that we would soon be attacking the French in an attempt to drive them back over the border & beyond.

Catalina & I met less frequently; sometimes I was late, or unable to get away at all, but she never reproached me. Nor did she seem to have the least qualm of conscience about what she did; it was as if she too felt that our love was something beyond human rules, above the judgement of the curate as much as that of the butcher or the baker. It was our secret because none had the right to judge us but God, & I knew, without asking Him, or those who commonly consider themselves a mouthpiece of His authority, that nothing that Catalina & I did could be other than wholly good in His sight.

The battle of the Pyrenees took some weeks to be won, for we had to take each pass & many peaks, & though in the military sense it was a slow matter of much waiting in worsening weather, followed each time by the cruelty of yet another uphill assault, it soon carried the 95th beyond reach of Bera.

We had always known that one day we would be parted, & knew too that we would have no means of corresponding; letters from me would expose her to every vulgar calumny of which a small town is capable, & she would have no means of knowing where I could be reached. But so strong was our love that while we were in each other's arms, the future seemed infinitely distant.

One night I asked Catalina to be my wife, though I had precious little means to support her, & no stomach to see her in the brutal company of the camp. I asked her because I loved her with all my heart, & longed selfishly to take her with me, but I sought too to protect her from the wrath of her father & the stain that others would consider her honour to have suffered, should our love be discovered.

But Catalina said me nay, & said it steadfastly. She could not leave her father, & I could not leave my duty. The war might go on for years yet, & then there would doubtless be another, & what would become of her in the Army? she asked. How could she bear it if I neglected my duty because of her? Besides, she was not a lady, but I was an officer. She would not know how to go on, & I would be ashamed of her. In short, she would always be a drag on my advancement. Better to end now, she said, tears standing in her eyes, while we loved so perfectly that, however long we lived, we could wish for nothing more.

We spent the whole night together, for her father was away, & when we had loved, but talked little, for there was little to be said, & loved again, Catalina slept in my arms, so close that I can feel her there to this day.

Before sunrise I had to leave her. We arranged to meet by the stream that evening. But when I returned to camp, orders had been given: we were to march at noon. I had no means of seeing her, or bidding her good-bye. But there was not a victory in the rest of the war, not the battle for La Petite Rhune, not Bayonne, Tarbes or Toulouse, neither Quatre Bras nor Waterloo itself, that could burn the memory of Catalina from my heart.

I finished writing as the eastern sky paled to gray. My last candle was guttering, but it would serve to melt the wax. I folded the letter and wrote the direction, and sealed it without rereading it. Then I walked in my shirt through the dawn chill, feeling the tightly folded sheets heavy in my hand, and hearing the birds begin to try the new day with small, unpracticed songs.

In the stables some of the lads were going sleepily about their early tasks. The one I ordered to ride to Bury St. Edmunds went to saddle his horse. "Hurry!" I said as he put the letter into his pocket as if it were of no more account than a tradesman's bill. "You must catch the early mail if you can." For now that I had set my story down—given it an existence separate from my own—I needed above all to send it beyond recall, before my longing for Miss Durward's understanding could be vanquished by my fear of her disgust.

❦

NUMBERS FLOATED AROUND in my sleep, fractions of seconds wandering like scraps of dust in a sunbeam, *f*-numbers closing like knives around the dark pupil of the camera's eye: 250 was a shutter speed, though it should be a fraction, a two hundred and fiftieth of a second, a fragment of time; thousand was the same, a thousandth, a fragment of a fragment. But 317? What was that? Then the numbers made a triangle, Cecil's triangle of sticks, only bigger, big enough for a man.

When I woke, 317 was still writhing in my head, but the light was warm and quiet across my bed. I moved my legs to and fro. It'd been too hot last night for a nightie and now my bare body slipped around in the soft sheets as if they were water. I lifted an arm and watched the sheet flowing from it and the light glowing through the cotton in streaks and rumpling round my knees and hips as if my body was a stone in a stream and I was watching from the shadows.

Somewhere there was a church bell going, just one—*ding, ding, ding*, pause, *ding, ding, ding*. I couldn't tell where it was coming from; it sounded far away and very quiet, as if the sound was softened by all the time it traveled through to get to me. I'd forgotten it was Sunday. I'd lost track, just felt like there'd been days and days of new people and sky and trees and faces, with the time between them almost nothing. Days and days since I'd met Theo.

The air was actually cool. I washed and put on shorts and a suntop and slung a sweatshirt round my shoulders. I took my camera—Theo's camera—because if the light was coming in like that onto my bed, then I wanted to see how it lay among the pillars and the pine trees and the clearing round the stables. Thinking about them I thought of Stephen. There were two more letters left. I took one, because I wanted to know what happened next, and left the last one tucked in the drawer, so that the ending would be safe. If there was an ending. Because of course even though Stephen had endings to the stories he wanted to tell, the letters might not tell me the end of the story of him and Miss Durward.

Outside it was as if the sun was making the day be Sunday morning, and instead of shut shops and hangovers, for this time—this place—it'd decided to make quiet. It'd made a faint mist too, to pale the shadows and soften what it knew was its own dazzle, so that the straight beams touched the pillars and grass stems and hills and hollows gently, stroking their curves.

And then I saw Cecil. He was curled in a corner of the portico among the dry dust and ancient leaves, and he was asleep. The light slid in between the pillars and touched his bare back. It was scratched and pricked all over and the blood had beaded and smeared, as if he'd been in among the bramble bushes, and he had a new bruise high up on each arm.

He shivered and curled up tighter but he didn't wake. Was sleeping out better than his room? Had he been locked out and nobody noticed he wasn't safe in bed?

I slid my sweatshirt off my shoulders and laid it over him. His hand came up and curled round the sleeve and I wondered if I'd woken him when all I'd wanted was to make him sleep better. Or should I wake him up properly, take him indoors? He looked small and lost and damaged, lying on the stone. But then his thumb slid into his mouth, and with the little sucking noises the tightness went out of his curled-up back. Whatever he was dreaming must be friendly and warm enough. I stepped away as quietly as I could and went over the grass, as if the light was cushioning my footsteps too. When I turned to look back at the house I saw how the beads of light that the dew-drops caught were crushed into darkness where I had trodden.

I took a few shots, but it was so quiet even the shutter seemed too noisy. In the woods the light made the mist lie like pale blue and gold velvet, pleated by the trees and falling into a pool in a little gap in the undergrowth. Just looking at it didn't seem enough: I wanted to touch the light, live in it, just for a little. I sat down with my back against one of the tree trunks so that flecks of sun were falling about my knees and onto Stephen's writing. He'd written it from Kersey, I saw, from home. And what about her? And then I saw that this time I wouldn't need the shadow in the glass. This letter was so long that he'd written on the back of the last sheet too, and left the least space he could for the outside and the address.

MLLE LUCY DURWARD

CHÂTEAU DE L'ABBAYE

IXELLES, BRUXELLES, BELGIUM

Bruxelles was Brussels. So Lucy went there too. At the same time? Was there a time when instead of letters they could talk to each other? I hadn't really noticed the dates—I'd need the other letters to work them out. But now Stephen was back here at Kersey and she was in Brussels. What did he need to tell her then that they couldn't talk about face-to-face?

The writing was open and quick, like a horse leaping straight into a gallop.

My dear Miss Durward, I was overjoyed to receive your letter. . . . I said, on my last evening at Ixelles, that her name was Catalina. She was a native of Castile, but lived at Bera, in the Basque country. . . .

I had no means of seeing her, or bidding her good-bye. But there was not a victory in the rest of the war, not the battle for La Petite Rhune, not Bayonne, Tarbes or Toulouse, neither Quatre Bras nor Waterloo itself, that could burn the memory of Catalina from my heart.

A CAR WENT away down the lane, rattly like a taxi. My shorts were damp from the dew, and the light had moved away. When I got up I was stiff from sitting so long. I was still thinking of Stephen and Catalina, and wondering what Lucy felt about her, and him, when I reached the clearing and looked across to the stables, and saw Theo.

He was sitting on the tree trunk in the sun, his bare back against the brick of the stables, watching the smoke from his cigarette trickling upwards to the sky. The light gleamed on his chest and shoulders, and I almost thought I could smell the scent of his smoke and his skin, mixed in with the smell of the pines and the woods and the green grass of the clearing. If I could just get closer, just fill the frame with him. . . .

The *ker-clunk* of the shutter made him turn his head. "Anna! You're awake early."

"It's such a lovely day."

"It is, isn't it? I got up to see Eva off, and I could not bear to go back indoors."

"You don't mind me photo—shooting you?"

"Mind? No, of course not. If you want to." He laughed. "I shall remind myself of what Constable the painter wrote. Do you know it? Crispin read it to me once. He wrote: 'There is nothing ugly; I never saw an ugly thing in my life: for let the form of an object be what it may,—light, shade and perspective will always make it beautiful.' " He stopped, and I thought about it and then laughed while he went on, "He is the local boy, you know? He was born at East Bergholt."

I shook my head. "I haven't been there. In fact, I haven't been anywhere. Except the village."

"I have an idea," said Theo, and did a long drag on his cigarette, then stubbed it out on a stone. "We shall go upstairs and have some breakfast—or have you eaten?"

"Um—no."

"Good. And then I shall take you on a tour. Though of course we have one of the prettiest places on our very doorstep."

"Have we?" I said, following him upstairs.

"You will see Kersey on more calendars, as Eva says, than any village this side of Finchingfield," he said, flicking his cigarette butt into the bin. "Except perhaps for the Guildhall at Lavenham."

"I didn't notice the village."

"You will," he said. "Now, how about croissants for breakfast?"

KERSEY WAS PRETTY, Theo was right, and I couldn't understand now why I hadn't noticed on the first day I was there. Too busy being hot and cross, maybe. It seemed ages since then. Theo drove slowly down the main street: the only street, it was really. The houses were all black beams and plaster painted white and pink and pale toffee-colored. They sat all settled-looking, nothing quite square or straight but very old and solid, down the slope to the ford at the bottom. There wasn't even enough water in the ford for the ducks to get their feet wet, though Theo said in winter it was often high enough to make people with fancier cars than his think twice before they went through it. "I saw a horse and trap go through it once. Much easier," he said, and I could almost hear the splosh of hoofs and the rattle of wheels. Strange to live when Stephen did, when that was all the noise there was. How did a cannon firing sound—how did it feel—when hoofs and wheels were all you'd ever heard?

"If no one has gone through it for a while it's quite still," Theo was saying. "You can see the sky and the church tower reflected in it." The tower was made of split and whole flints, white and blue-black like a chessboard in the sun. I looked up and saw there were birds flying round it and shrieking, small but with wings curved like black swords slicing through the air. "Swifts," Theo said. "They are like swallows, only bigger."

We drove with all the windows down. Theo held his cigarette outside so that the fat hedges almost brushed it away in the narrower lanes, and he asked me about Mum and Dave and school and I said much more than I usually did, because I was sitting so easily with him in the big car with the sky all round us—so much sky, there was—and the fields rolling away like cushions, and cool tree-shade splashing over us now and again. We drove through villages and past cottages with little windows and hens and gray-muzzled dogs not bothering to bark. And he was listening so carefully and quietly, and I was saying about how it is when Mum gets dumped, and when we move. The new place and Mum's new boyfriend, and sometimes a new school in the middle of term when everybody's already friends. And suddenly I found I was telling him about the time I was lost, years ago, when we'd just moved to one of those estates where it's all walkways and underpasses. Mum sent me down to the shop for milk—I must have been six or seven, not much bigger than Cecil. And I bought the milk, I was quite used to doing that. But I couldn't find my way back. I couldn't find anywhere I even recognized. Just blank concrete walls and blind alleys. One corner I turned and saw a stranger in the distance across some empty, dog-shitty grass, but I couldn't see their face. Then I realized I couldn't remember the name of our block or the number of our flat. I started to run, not with a plan, just anywhere, just because if I tried enough places one of them might turn out to be right, only I ran and ran and got more and more lost until I began to wonder if I'd been in the right place, near home, at the beginning and hadn't known it. Only I couldn't find my way back there either, and then I knew that I was lost forever. And I tripped on a crack in the concrete path and fell down and skinned my knees and my hands, and the milk bottle smashed.

I was saying all this to Theo, stuff I thought I'd forgotten. And how it was like that all over again when they went through the gate at the airport, and I turned away.

I thought it didn't show but I started to cry, which is something I don't do, I really don't, but this time I did.

It was only a bit. I just slid my hand up my cheek every now and again, and under my nose with my wrist. But Theo knew, and he stopped the car in a field gateway and pulled a big hankie out of his pocket and shook out its folds and gave it to me. It smelled of clean washing and his tobacco and him, close up against my face. He said, "Poor Anna. Poor old Anna. That is tough," and after that I couldn't have stopped crying if I'd been offered the whole world to do it.

It must have been ages, because I saw afterwards that there were three more cigarette ends in the car's ashtray, but at the time all I knew was this great hard aching lump of something was swelling up out of my belly and roaring in my ears and bursting out of my eyes and nose and mouth, and some of the ache was for losing Holly and Tanya, and some was for losing Mum, and even Dave sort of, and some wasn't for a person at all, but for a not-person, a nothing, where my lost dad should have been.

It was like the ache infected all my bones and muscles, so the whole of me was tired and sore from it swelling up and pouring out of me. In the end I lay back because I was too tired to stay all hunched round my belly, and there was Theo's arm behind me, so even with the ache running through me and out of my hands and shoulders and legs like ice in the sun, I could feel not all of me would melt and I wouldn't quite go to nothing. There would be something left after it had all gone—the something that Theo was holding on to, stroking my hair, almost like rocking, and murmuring, humming to-and-fro, to-and-fro, while I grew more sure that there was something left, that I only needed to rest there, against Theo's shoulder, and then I wouldn't be so lost ever again.

"Shall we drive to find some lunch?" said Theo at last.

I pushed my hair away from where it had stuck to my face, and sat up a bit and sniffed. "Yeah. Please. I'm sorry."

He reached his cigarettes off the dashboard and started the car with the other hand, dipping his head to light up before he got into gear. "You must not apologize. I think perhaps that has been a long time coming."

"I suppose so. I mean, I don't often . . . well, not like that. . . ."

"The ones who don't often, it is they who need it most. Eva is the same." I wondered what he meant exactly but I felt too tired to ask. He glanced sideways at me, and after a moment went on: "She has lived through a great deal. Her parents . . . the Falangists . . . Well, when people know that I am a Hungarian Jew, they go carefully. Civilized people, anyway. But everyone forgets about Spain. Afterwards, it appeared to be just an understudy rehearsal. And when she tried to find a way through, by making photographs—well, it is hard as a woman. Think of Gerda Taro."

I didn't really get what he was talking about, except it was about the war. "Who's she?"

"Exactly. A wonderful photographer that so few have heard of. She was killed by a Republican tank. But if she is spoken of at all now, it is as Capa's girlfriend. Lee Miller is another—Man Ray saw to that—and then Penrose, in a sense. At least Eva's and my work are very different from each other, but even so . . ." He was silent for a moment. "I'm sorry, such names do not yet mean much to you."

"Not really. I'm sorry." I thought suddenly of Lucy Durward. If they were in Brussels together, did Stephen tell her more stories? Show her where it all happened—where people were killed, where he was wounded? Did she listen, and look round her and try to imagine it, imagine him there?

Theo didn't say anything more, and after a bit I said, "What about you?"

"What about me?"

"What do you do—with stuff? All the shit?" I said, and wondered why you can talk about those kinds of things when you're side by side in a car, when you couldn't possibly face-to-face.

He hesitated, as if he was deciding how to answer me, flicking ash out of the window and looking ahead. Then he said, "It depends. Some of it is in the pictures of the shit. Once it is on paper it exists alongside me, not in me. And I can always choose to move on. And choose what to do next. Guernica—what happened to Eva in Seville—it made me go to Berlin. What happened to my family . . . it sent me in the end to the Golan Heights. But some stays inside." He smiled. "When Capa—Robert, not Cornell—when he ran out of film on D-day and went back to England, they offered to fly him to London to speak about it on the BBC and be interviewed by all the newspapers. 'But,' he said, 'I remembered the night enough,' and he got changed and stocked up with film, and took the first boat back to Normandy. Some things . . . Some nights we all remember enough. . . . Here we are."

We were driving up the main street of a big village, and he suddenly hauled the car round and squeezed it up a little lane between houses, and into a market square.

The whole of one side was taken up by a great long half-timbered building with those sparkling diamond windows and a big door and twisted chimneys. All round the other sides were a mixture of little half-timbered houses, and pretty brick ones with lots of symmetrical windows.

Theo waved at the big building as he turned off the engine. "That is the Guildhall."

"Why's it not properly black-and-white?"

"I believe they never were," he said. "Not in the sixteenth century. They were limewashed all over. The white just fades with time and light until the beams show again, that silver color. But Crispin could tell you far more about it than I."

"I like Crispin."

"So do I. And he is a good friend. Now, this is where I thought we would go."

He locked up the car and led the way towards the corner of the square where there was a big old pub, white and flat fronted with patterns standing out from the plaster so that the light caught in them: a shield and those heraldic sorts of flowers.

"I think you would like a drink," said Theo.

"Yeah, but, well, last time—"

"We shall sit in the garden, of course, on this fine day," said Theo, with a sideways look at me, and we went round the corner to where there was a gate straight into it, and while he went to the bar I dived through the back door into the loo and did what I could to my face and hair. By the time he came out with my lager and his bitter and a bar menu tucked under his arm I was sitting at one of the tables in the garden, watching the sparrows hopping about.

We had crisps, and I had a ham sandwich and he had a chicken one, and he told me about Watergate. We were halfway down our second drink when he glanced at the sky. "The light will not be on the front of the Guildhall for much longer." I looked up. "At least, I am sorry, are you thinking of taking photographs? Since you have brought your camera with you?"

I had brought it, but only really because it had become a habit. Now I picked it up from the table. "Yeah, but . . ."

"Well? What?"

"It's only silly stuff. If it's not a bother. I won't take long. The wood, and those patterns in the plaster."

"It is not silly. No subject is silly. 'There is nothing ugly,' Constable said, but silly will do." Theo grinned. "He probably said it in this very pub, getting drunk with his friends from his school days, when he came back to see his parents. Maybe your Stephen Fairhurst was sitting at the next table. No doubt Constable's old schoolmaster sat him down and told him how he was wasting his talents on hay carts and river barges when he might be winning prizes with the rape of the Sabines, or the death of Actaeon."

"Who?"

"He was turned into a stag by the goddess Diana, for seeing her bathing in a stream, and then his own hounds tore him to pieces," Theo said, with a grin that made me laugh back. "See how the gods punish voyeurs?"

"Yuk!"

"Yes. And they wondered that Constable preferred to paint a thatched cottage with trees and clouds around it, or the brown river water that curls round the carthorse's haunches when he begins to leap the weir."

"But you don't."

"Don't what?"

"Eva shoots trees and clouds and beautiful buildings and nudes. 'The measure of all things,' you said they were. But you don't."

"No." He looked into his nearly empty glass, and twisted it round a few times, staring through it at the rough sun- and rain-cracked wood. "No. Unlike Eva, I cannot find salvation in form, even the forms of nature. And I cannot turn away. Nor give up hope—not altogether—that if I show the world what it does to itself, something will change." He smiled, sort of. "I am like the faithful wife of a philanderer. I cannot stop hoping that if I love well enough—honestly enough—someday it will all be all right."

"But . . . Does it never make you—all the shit, I mean—does it never make you stop hoping? I mean, you *know* everything goes bad. I mean, it always does. Wars happen. People die. Even stuff like, things always cost too much. People leave, or they dump you, or both. Before or after they screw you. It . . . it hurts. Why go on hoping it won't this time?"

He put his hand over mine, where I was fiddling with the camera strap. "Anna. Is that what you feel?"

I nodded.

"Always?"

"I think so," I said, and thought suddenly of Stephen and his Catalina. "Yeah."

He was looking at me without moving, like Cecil looked at me that time, so you could see he was thinking all sorts of things, without knowing what. "Don't move," I said, and slid my hand and the camera out from under his, and took the picture. As I lowered the camera my cheeks went hot. "I'm sorry. You don't mind, do you?"

"No, not at all. You say to yourself not, What do I say now? You think only, Quick, I must get that shot! I'm delighted."

He said it quite friendlily but I wasn't sure if he was annoyed. Then he said again, "I *am* delighted. . . . If you want to catch the light, we should go."

In the little post office and gift shop opposite there were tea towels and biscuit tins with bright pictures of the Guildhall printed on them, neat and black-and-white and stripy and not like it really was at all.

"Like a zebra crossing," I said to Theo, and he laughed.

I turned round to look across the square at the real thing, at the way the sun caught and faded the limewash, and splintered across the grain of the beams and lay on the tiled roof and colored each face of the building differently, so that it looked solid and full. "When—how old did you say it was?"

"Early sixteenth century, according to Crispin. Tudor, I think, in your English terms."

"Was it a house?"

"Not exactly. It was a meeting hall, for the guilds, apparently. The craftsmen and merchants and so on, arranging prices for wool or spices or ironwork, and judging those whose skills were good enough to admit as master leatherworkers or corn chandlers."

"You can almost imagine it," I said. "Behind those windows. You can't see, so you can imagine. Like at the Hall, like Crispin said. Stephen, or whoever. He stood on the same floor, he went up and down the same stairs, almost it's like he's breathing the same air, like it really was him in my photo of the window. Like in the negs, the space between the times is such a little bit. Sometimes it feels like almost nothing."

"Almost nothing," repeated Theo, and was silent.

We drove on when I'd shot what I wanted, back over the great open fields, high and flat, with tall church towers that stood up from them, and then suddenly there'd be a break in the plateau with a river at the bottom, or a village with people walking off their Sunday lunch, or a farm tucked down among the trees with paint peeling off plaster that said 1573 and children riding bikes and pausing to stare and wave.

When we got back to the stables Theo stopped the car on the weedy gravel and we got out. "Coming?" was all he said, and we went upstairs and I put the coffeepot on. Theo talked about this lecture Eva was giving, all about photography and death.

"Death? You mean, like war photography?" I looked at the photograph Eva had of him on her desk, in army clothes, with beaten-up cameras slung round his neck, and one sleeve torn open and a mucky-looking bandage on his arm and an aeroplane with propellers behind him. He was younger then, but not different, still dark and thin and tough, and about to laugh.

"Eva talks about how all photographs are about death, really, and time: about preserving a moment in silver and chemicals, when life itself is never preserved, when every cell of everything is already decaying, and being replaced, and decaying again. The subject and the image coexist for the moment that the shutter opens and closes. And then the subject decays but the image lives on unchanged."

"It makes it sound like a ghost."

He grinned at me. "Oh, Anna, does the idea give you gooseflesh all over? But Eva would say that a photograph does prevent something—somebody—from being laid to rest."

I thought about it for a while, but I still wasn't sure I understood. I moved a little, and felt the slight, hot roughness where my shoulders were newly brown. I looked down and saw that the image of the dark straps of my top was printed pale by the sun.

Theo was sitting on one of the big sofas with a thin curl of steam rising in front of his face from his cup.

My camera said I had a few frames left. "May I?" I said, picking it up.

He nodded. The light from the window stroked his cheek, and caught on his lip where it touched the cup as gently as a kiss. I got one of him stooping his head to sip coffee, and then another of just his hands.

His shirt was unbuttoned at the top and the edges of it sprang open so the white cotton collar stood away from his neck, away from the sinews and muscles and the tough, brown skin where the tendons lifted to the sides of his skull. The fine silver stubble that glittered in the light had grown since that morning, hours showing there like years did in his face. Years of talk and silence in the grooves from nose to mouth. Years of looking in the fan of light-cut creases at the corners of his eyes. Years of seeing, in the pinch between his brows and the lines that ran like telegraph wires across his forehead, full of too much knowing. I looked and looked, and in my hands the shutter snatched at what I saw, but I wasn't sure whether it caught what he had seen, or what his seeing had done to him.

His hands still cradled his cup. It was small and white and breakable.

My film was finished. I laid the camera in my lap and started to rewind it. When I'd finished I realized Theo was still watching me. He smiled, and I would have smiled back only something in my chest—something deep inside the cage of my ribs—started to grow. It wasn't really happiness, it hurt too much for happiness, only I didn't have another word for it, not for the strange, soft balloon that I felt swelling up and filling my chest and my belly and my throat, and bursting out of me at last, in a great smile that went on and on like crying.

The French are not long gone as we enter Pernes. The people look like walking corpses, their skin yellow and withered over their bones. In air that shakes with the blaze of the sun, they poke over the putrefying rubbish piled in the lanes, pushing at the stinking body of a mule to find brothers and children who have slipped beyond walking or breathing forever. A dead girl lies in the street, blood on her belly and legs. Her mother sits at the window, herself big with child and rocking to and fro with the pain of a sabre slash, at her breast, sobbing that the soldiers didn't stop, not even when she died.

The few shops are empty, no bread or corn or meat. All has been taken by the French. Our men find a wineshop, but we don't have to post a sentry to stop them drinking, for there is nothing left but one barrel of wine, and that is green and oily. A soldier kicks the staves, and a black and bloated hand floats to the top. There is a smell of smoke and burning flesh: behind the shop we see flickers of fire. I take a moment to run upstairs in case there is anyone to be got out. Only a boy, smooth and young, pinned to the wall with a spontoon and left to die. Dropped at his feet is a baby wrapped in a rag. The baby is dead too, no wound, but with thin gray skin hanging loose from its skeleton.

A bundle of uniform in an alley is a French dragoon. He has been slit open from navel to neck and his entrails wrapped round his throat. His companion, crumpled in a doorway, has been castrated and left alive. Our allies the guerrilleros have done this. The stench of shit fills the alley. An old man shuffles past, and spits in both men's faces.

❧ *III* ❧

ALTHOUGH THE GAME SEASON HAD OPENED, AND ON MORE than one occasion I found an excuse in estate business to travel up to London, in the weeks that followed its dispatch, I could not by any means prevent my thoughts dwelling on Miss Durward's reading my letter. From one day to the next the almost bodily lightness that had filled me as I set my tale onto paper, would be replaced by a sick dread of her disgust or incomprehension that made food taste sour and friends seem distant. That I had not told all the tale, that I had withheld what I realized suddenly she might regard as the most significant part of it—though I did not so regard it—added to my apprehension. And then on the morrow my spirits might rise again, as far as I could make out for no better reason than a fine sunrise seen as I shaved, or a joke of Stebbing's as we sat on each side of his fireplace and I watched the side of his face that was still alive brooding over some problem of men or markets that I had brought him. I saw the boy several times, and wondered yet again if he had a home, and someone to care for him.

But for the most part, my thoughts were elsewhere. I had not copied my letter before sending it to Miss Durward, but I knew that in the deep silence of the country night, when only the scuffle of a rat or the hoot of an owl breaks the dark, I had written more plainly—more honestly—than I had ever had cause, or confidence, to write before.

The stable hands were not best pleased to learn that one of their number must go to Bury each day, that I might have my letters before me when I came in from my morning ride, rather than waiting for the carrier to bring them to the village. But even as I awaited the arrival of Miss Durward's reply with an eagerness that did not suppress fear, along the same road came news from a wholly unexpected quarter.

For all my anxiety, I could not rest, nor feel sure that the course of action upon which this news had made me decide was right, until I had set down for her my reasons for embarking upon it.

> *My dear Miss Durward,*
>
> *I make no apology for writing again so soon, when my last can but barely have reached you, & you will have had no chance to reply, even if you wish to. But I have an irrational sense that what has occurred since I wrote last has in some way been brought about by my setting down of my tale. It is as if some strange power can work across the distance of years & thousands of miles.*
>
> *I can most easily explain what has occurred, & the course of action on which I am determined, by taking up my story at the point where I left off. You know already how I came to leave the Army & find a congenial living in escorting travellers about the battlefields. This employment took me back in due course to Portugal & thence to Spain, & were it not for the demands of those who rightly considered that their entertainment & welfare ought to be my chiefest concern, I should have begun to search for Catalina immediately, sparing no effort or cost to find her. As it was, I was dependent on my employers' whims & their purses, & so it was some months before I had sufficient time & money to travel to Bera.*
>
> *The house was empty. Where all had once been trim & cared for, I saw now a shutter flapping loose from one hinge, & weeds growing between the roof tiles. In mist & rain I made my way from house to house, in a pilgrimage whose goal I did not dare to contemplate. But if my Spanish was once again fluent, for the most part theirs was not. That her father was dead, & the family*

gone, I soon gathered. They kept themselves to themselves, those castellanos. The girl? Who knows? Perhaps the priest? It was so long ago, in the war, when things changed & moved so quickly. & now, times were hard, Señor Inglés, & they had work to do.

The priest lived in a small, dark house by the church. An ill-kempt housekeeper admitted me with a bob, & shuffled off to announce me to her master. & of what followed, though it is 3½ years ago, I can remember every word.

To my relief he spoke the Spanish of Castile, but as I explained the nature of my search, his face stiffened, & he enquired why an English soldier was so interested in a Spanish girl. I had conned my lines carefully on the long journey from Lisbon. "I came to know the family well in the time my Regiment spent here, Padre, & after the death of her brother, & now, I am told, her father, I should like to assure myself that she is safe & well cared-for."

The people of Spain, he observed, had not fared well at the hands of the English Army in the war, still less had their womenfolk.

Before I could bite my tongue, I retorted that the hands of the French were no cleaner nor less brutal. But arousing his enmity was not at all my intention, so I softened my tone & said how all war is an ugly business, Padre, & it makes men ugly too. All I sought to know, I said, was that Señorita Maura was happy & safe. He might think, if he chose, that I was trying to make a little reparation for that which innocent people suffered in our shared efforts to rid the world of the Corsican Monster.

He was silent, & I tried to discern if a heart beat under his black buttoned gown. He was not old; his face was plump although in the house I had seen no evidence of good living, & his hands were folded in his lap. Eventually he spoke.

"Señorita Maura is safe, & she ought to be happy. Her father died just before the Feast of the Purification, of the following year. His daughter left to enter the Dominican Convent of San Telmo

in San Sebastian a few days later. The mother superior wrote to tell me that she had completed her noviciate & taken her final vows. As far as I am aware, she is there still."

I know not what unexpressed hopes I had cherished until that moment, but I stared at him as if they had all been snatched away. He raised his brows at my continued silence, but I had no intention of allowing him to think that I desired to know more. I rose, thanked him for setting my mind at rest, & wished him good morning.

He rose also, & rang the bell, & then his hand went up for a moment & he muttered a Latin blessing to which I did not trouble to listen. The housekeeper held the study door open for me.

As I went out, the priest said, "What became of the child, I know not."

I stopped. "The child?"

"She was with child when she left Bera," he said, & bade me farewell.

The housekeeper appeared unmoved. Perhaps she spoke no Spanish. As I left I hesitated by the box outside the front door, which was marked PARA LOS POBRES, but instead I pushed the coins into the hand of the first beggar that I saw.

& so it was that I came to San Sebastian. My first intention was to seek my love & her child. I stood before the iron-banded convent door, set in a long, stone front with few windows & those barred & high, & raised my hand to pull the bell. But doubt overcame me. Catalina had vowed to remain within these walls for the rest of her life, that much I knew. How willingly she had done so I could not know, but taken her vows she had, & her conscience & her Pope forbade their breaking. Were she to know of my return, I feared that her sorrow at the separation from her child, the depths of which I had seen in other women, might flower again, & bring such pain as I would not have inflicted on her for all the world. Knowing that I had returned, might she

even crave release herself from her vows? With the certainty of
this I could not flatter myself, but I knew suddenly that I must not
risk even the possibility. I turned & walked away. She had found
asylum, found a place in the world in the leaving of it, & though
I longed to see her face & hear her voice, or if that were denied
me, to know simply that she did move & breathe inside these
high stone walls, it would have been cruel & selfish to seek such
crumbs for my own comfort when by so doing I might destroy hers.
Even merely to seek to know the fate of her child might endanger
what I hoped so greatly was her serenity.

To calm my disordered thoughts I entered a small coffeehouse
across the plaza from the convent, & when I had ordered
delectable Spanish coffee rather than deplorable Spanish brandy
I fell into conversation with the girl who served me. I took little
interest in what we said, save as a distraction from my inner
distress, until she mentioned that one of her aunts was a lay-sister
at the convent, & was frequently permitted to leave it on errands
to the market, the doctor, or the priest.

You will realise that, for all the frankness with which I have
described my love for Catalina, it is not easy to set down for a
lady to read in plain English the circumstances in which I now
found myself. But in order to do justice to your trust in my
honesty, & to explain events, & the decisions to which I came,
I must set down the facts. If it is not possible to do so without
offending, I ask your pardon beforehand, & hope to be forgiven
for having taken you at your word.

I think the girl Mercedes understood something of my
situation, but with a discretion which at the time I recall thinking
is not commonly associated with females of any kind, she made
no enquiry. Day by day, as we became friends, she relayed her
aunt's gossip in the form of answers to my careful curiosity. By
calculating dates I realised that Sister Andoni, who was so kind
& gentle & did such beautiful needlework, was my love. She had

taken the name of St. Anthony, to whom Papists pray when they
desire to find something lost.

It happened that in the same week that Mercedes introduced
me to some of her friends, my landlady gave me notice that her
married daughter was coming to live with her & my room would
be preferable to my rent. Lacking a roof, & fast running out of
money, I accepted Mercedes & Izzaga's suggestion that I might
like to share their accommodation, for which, in return for the
appearance of masculine protection and proper ordering afforded
by my presence, they would be pleased to accept a peppercorn
rent. I wrote to all my patrons & such colleagues as Monsieur
Planchon of L'Arc-en-ciel, to advise them that I had taken up a
new abode in order that I might be still better able to conduct the
discriminating student of modern warfare, & England's glorious
part in it, around the exemplary sites & noble scenery nearby.

If Mercedes, or at one remove her aunt, thought my interest in
women's reasons for entering the conventual life curious, she did
not say so, & I could not risk gossip about Sister Andoni's
history, nor the exposure of my feelings, by being more explicit.
But the talk over dinner among the girls, which my careful
questions set going when we were alone, made me realise that, far
from being light-minded or merely careless of their virtue, all four
had an acute apprehension of the realities of this world, which
leaves females so little choice in their lives. I said nothing, but it
seemed that they, more than I, could judge the decision to take
the veil as merely one of those few possibilities. I could only see
high, blank walls & a life within of poverty & obedience to
Popish command. But Arrage spoke in her rough Basque voice of
a means, though not her own, of fulfilling material need, & of
how, to a good daughter of the Church, or a repentant sinner, the
demands of such a life were different, but not so strange.

"A repentant sinner?" I enquired, for of course any church
would see my Catalina in that censorious light.

I fancied that Mercedes avoided my eye as she said, "Sister Andoni, for example. My aunt says that she had a child before she entered, although she was unwed. But the Sisters of San Telmo are famous for their compassion."

I asked, with a little difficulty, what had happened to the child.

"She was given to the Sant' Águeda foundling home at Bilbao, but after that I don't know, though I think my aunt would have heard if she'd died. So many die in such places—one sickens, & then many. It is sad, when their mothers must hope they are giving them into a better life."

If the girls considered that my precipitate departure from the table was due to my having taken too much wine, I did not disabuse them of such a notion.

The rule of Catalina's order did not allow her to go outside the convent building, nor any man who was not a father, brother, or doctor, to enter so much as the doors. Only priests, as consecrated guarantors of the place's proper ordering, might penetrate beyond the visitors' parlour. & yet in the months that followed I could not bring myself to leave San Sebastian, although I soon knew all there was to be known of Catalina. I did travel to Bilbao, & contrived, with some expense, to discover discreetly the fate of Catalina's child. She was named Idoia, & she had indeed survived the dangers of babyhood, being by then almost four years old. She was no lost or abandoned child: the orphanage was large & well run, to judge by what I heard, & I had no fear that she would not be well cared for.

Knowing your love for Tom, & your parents' love for you & your sister, I would venture that you are wondering that I did not seek Idoia out directly. I did consider doing so, but my reasons for leaving her in Bilbao were like a pale but true image of my reasons not to disturb my love. The child was well; it would be unkind to unsettle her, & I would not for the world risk

reawakening the pain in Catalina that she must have felt at the
giving up of her daughter. & what had I to offer such a child,
most especially a little girl? No fixed home, no woman's love &
care, only a rootless, impecunious existence wandering about
Europe at the beck & call of a series of travellers whose purses
commanded all.

Nonetheless, when the English mail in the spring of the year
'18 brought a letter from my cousin's attorney, with the startling
tidings that, on the death of my cousin without issue a few weeks
since, I was heir to my great-grandfather's property at Kersey, I
felt no small reluctance to leave Spain. But the attorney wrote
that the estate had been much neglected as a result of my cousin's
long illness, & when I demurred wrote again, & at greater length.
I realised finally, as the summer drew to a close, that it was my
inescapable duty to return to England & attempt to put things
right.

I had no knowledge of the management of land, or taste for
the company of country squires who yearn for the days of Queen
Anne when they are not talking of horses, & I had little relish for
the damp climate & its likely effect on my constitution. But it
could not be avoided, & as I went aboard at San Sebastian it
was with no expectation of returning there, except in my dreams.

I paused at this point, my pen in my hand, watching how the afternoon light, lying on my words, made them appear clear and sharp as
they ran across page after page.

A drop of ink fell from my nib onto the letter, and I reached for the
blotting paper. Ought I to go on? I knew, without rereading it, that my
apology to Miss Durward was not at all sufficient for the matter that
followed it, but, I reflected, no apology would be sufficient, were I to
consider society's rules, and were I considering them, I would not then
be able to write to her of anything at all that was close to my heart.

The letter that had arrived that morning from Spain was on my desk before me. The neat, unknown, clerkly hand had given me no warning: I had thought it to be some tradesman's account that I had overlooked on my departure from San Sebastian, forwarded by a busy merchant who had only recently troubled to discover my direction. I had put down my coffee cup and broken the seal, not idly, for any news from Spain conjured memories that could, for a moment, overcome me, but without the least apprehension of what lay within.

Now I sat at my desk, the ink drying to iridescence on my pen and San Sebastian thick in my senses: tobacco, incense, seagulls crying, salt cod drying in the wind, the clip of mule hoofs, the resinous mist rolling down from the pine-hung mountains, golden stone baking in the slanting sun. These memories were part of me, and I could no more deny them, by omission or direct falsehood, than I could deny that I was a cripple. And yet, I could not bring myself to court them again.

Nonetheless, it was with some hesitation that I dipped my pen in the standish and began, slowly, to explain.

You know much of what followed. A modest advance on my inheritance reached my banker in San Sebastian, which was sufficient to establish the security of my friends, & render any more of my exertions on behalf of the travellers of Europe superfluous. Some few days it was necessary for me to pass in London, for much had to be explained to me, who knew nothing of the estate of which I was the inheritor, by my cousin's man of business, & still more business awaited my decision or my signature. At last I was able to board the mail to Bury St. Edmunds, where my cousin's coachman met me, & drove me to Kersey Hall.

For some time, my life at Kersey was congenial; the climate, which I had feared, proved to be drier than that of San Sebastian, & the brandy better too, & my neighbours agreeable enough. It was after the harvest was in, & dark days & winter idleness were enforced upon me, that I realised that it had only

been unceasing activity that had hitherto served to keep at
bay the grief of my days & terror of my nights. Eventually I
was driven to seek the advice of the rector, the result of which I
cannot regret, since it led to my friendship with you. My departure
for Brussels too was born of a recrudescence of my earlier
unhappiness, &, as you know, were it not for my duty to Kersey,
I should be there yet. I still hope to return to Brussels, when
Stebbing is sufficiently recovered, or a successor settled well
enough in his place, to allow me to do so.

But this morning I have received a letter from Bilbao. The
orphanage at Sant' Águeda is in need of funds, since the poverty
& dislocation of the Spanish people, consequent upon the late
European war & more especially the naval blockades, has greatly
increased the number of children being brought to their door. The
Reverend Mother is appealing to all who might feel some interest
in or obligation towards the place, to assist them, &, Catalina
having given my name as Idoia's father at the time of her birth,
they have found out my direction with the assistance of the Army
List kept by the British Consul at Santander.

You, of all people, will have some idea of the confusion of mind
into which this news has thrown me. Not least, it has made me
realise that I ought, in duty, to enquire more closely into the
circumstances of my daughter's upbringing, & if it is suffering, for
want of funds at the orphanage, to consider putting some money
towards the support of Sant' Águeda. My first impulse was
indeed to travel immediately to Spain. & yet, I still fear the
consequences of disturbing Idoia's life there. Still more powerfully,
I know I must not disturb Catalina, & yet I fear that were she to
hear that I had come to Spain without writing to her—& there
are many links between San Telmo & Sant' Águeda by which the
news might travel—it would be too great an insult to the love that
has sustained me for so many years. I cannot risk that.

*Thus I think it best to send funds anonymously, or at least
with a stipulation that none other than the Reverend Mother is
told of their source. Such a course smacks of shame at Catalina's
love, & at Idoia's existence, & I am reluctant to behave as if I
feel such shame, when I do not. But I am still more reluctant to
disturb Catalina's peace, & my settled existence. I have no doubt
that I may enquire closely enough into my daughter's well-being
without—*

I was interrupted at this point by Nell, who leaped up from where
she was lying with her head on my feet and ran, barking, to the library
window.

A carriage was coming up the drive. The horses were strange, the
postilions well splashed with mud, and the whole had the worn but
serviceable look of a turnout hired from a large and busy coaching
inn. I was in no mood for visitors, although on another day I might
well have gone forward to admit them myself, and allowed my butler
Prescott to stay sunk in his afternoon somnolence. But as it was, I
hushed Nell in an urgent whisper and withdrew to the furthest re-
cesses of the library. I was pretending interest in Clarendon's *History
of the Rebellion* when Prescott entered. "A Mr. and Mrs. Barraclough
have called, sir," he said. "Are you at home?"

There could be but one answer to that. Nell trotted out after him
to investigate while I hastily folded the letter and pushed it into my
pocket, and on hurrying into the hall, found that my hopes were fulfilled. Miss Durward was standing there, looking about her exactly as
I had so often seen her do elsewhere, observing the fall of light and
shadow in the hall and the movement of figures against marble and
oak, while she pulled gently at Nell's ears.

When I had expressed my delight at their arrival, I sent the servants bustling for tea, and set a match to the library fire myself, for the
afternoon warmth was fading. "I am only sorry that the drawing room

is under holland covers," I said, "but until now it has not seemed worth the trouble to keep all the rooms open when I have so few lady visitors."

"But this is a delightful room," said Mrs. Barraclough. "And in any case, we would not want to put you to so much trouble. You must understand that I had been dreading the long road from Dover. Then George realized that to sail to Felixstowe would shorten the journey to Lancashire by a good deal. And once we were in Suffolk, Lucy was sure that you would pardon us for descending on you, were you not, Lucy?"

Miss Durward was looking at the portrait that hung above the library fire. "What, Hetty?"

"I said, you were sure the major would pardon us for descending on him."

Her gaze did not move. "Oh, yes. It is a good likeness, Major."

"So I am told. Certainly the painter was well recommended."

"I am not surprised. But how curious it is that the measure of such a work should be its fidelity to some aspects of the sitter's countenance—those twists to your eyebrows, for instance—and not to others."

"Others?" I said as Mrs. Prescott appeared, her cap only a little askew, to escort the ladies upstairs.

Mrs. Barraclough rose. "Lucy?"

Miss Durward started and, without another word, turned away from the portrait and hurried out in the wake of her sister.

The fire had caught and was going nicely by the time they returned. Soon everyone was sat down and provided with tea and such refreshment as my cook could send up at ten minutes' notice. As I saw my guests comfortably established, and sat down myself, I felt again the letter in my pocket.

"How long are you able to stay?" I said, and Miss Durward looked sharply up from where she had been stroking Titus's belly and regarded me with narrowed eyes.

"We thought to reach Bishop's Stortford tonight," said Barra-clough.

"But you must at least stay for a night or two," I said. "Much lon-ger, if you can. It is the least I can offer you after your hospitality in Brussels."

"Well," began Mrs. Barraclough, "it is most kind of you. George, what do you think? I *am* very tired after so much traveling, but I long to see Tom as soon as possible."

"It is as you wish, my dear, but you must take care of yourself. If Fairhurst is so good as to offer his hospitality, perhaps we should ac-cept, for a day or two, at least."

"That is decided, then!" cried Miss Durward, getting up like a spring released, at which Titus looked reproachfully round. I went to ring the bell.

I was pleased to observe that my household was not dismayed, as it would have been a year earlier, to be told that we would be enter-taining for an indefinite number of days a party that included two ladies—one in delicate health—and a maid. It was therefore with rea-sonable hopes of a dinner being sent up that would not disgrace me, and with the Barracloughs taken up with matters of baggage and bed-chambers, that I was able to accede to Miss Durward's request for a tour of the grounds.

"They are not extensive," I said as we stepped down into the shrubbery. "The estate as a whole is nothing compared to Holkham or Audley End. Nor are the grounds in very good order. My cousin was more interested in his coverts than his gardens, and I cannot bring myself to set strong men clipping lawns when they might be till-ing fields."

"Your military instincts do not demand that every last blade of grass be polished?" she said, looking about her.

I laughed. "Not when it is my income that would pay for the pol-ishing, and only my eye that is offended by the lack of it."

"No, indeed!" She said nothing more, and so taken up were my thoughts with the news from Spain that I could think of no further conversation. I had also to decide what to do about the letter that still hid, hastily folded, in my pocket. I had written freely because I felt safe in the knowledge that some days and many miles lay between my telling my story, and her reading it. Now I was no longer safe thus, and the simplest course—perhaps the only course that I could face— would be to say nothing, and wait until they had departed to post it to Manchester.

I had just decided to do that, when Miss Durward cleared her throat and then said, "I would have spoken of it earlier, had we been private, but we were not. I was most honored—touched—by your letter."

"But I fear that you were shocked—"

She stopped, and actually stamped her foot, grasping my arm with her strong fingers. "Stephen! Listen to me! We are friends, are we not?" I nodded. "Friends tell each other the truth. If the world is shocking, then I accept being shocked. It is not for you to defend me from it. But there was nothing in your letter to do so. Nothing at all! Only . . . Well, I cannot put it into words, except to say, I understand. And I honor you for it."

"Thank you," I managed to say as we began to walk again. When we had gone a few steps, I went on, "I confess, I had not thought— until I started to write, that is—I had not thought to find so much re- lief in setting it down."

"You ended your tale with your leaving Spain with the army. Did you never contemplate going back to find Catalina?"

I hesitated.

"Forgive me," she said quickly, "I should not have asked."

"No, no. It is only that I have had some news." I felt in my pocket. "I was writing to you when you arrived. Here: please read it."

"Now?"

"Yes . . . If you feel able to do so. It explains matters. But it is not finished, you must understand that. I have not finished it."

"Of course," she said and held out her hand, so that our fingers touched as she took the folded sheets from me.

Then I walked away and fixed my eyes on the western sky, where ivory clouds lay above a horizon streaked with rose and gold and turquoise, so that there was distance in my mind, if no longer in time or space, between the last part of my story, and her knowing it.

Only by the sudden departure of two sparrows, which had been hopping about in the quiet for some time, near where I sat on the brick edge of the ditch that kept the cattle from the gardens, did I know that Miss Durward approached.

"So, you are not going to Spain," was all she said.

I shook my head, wordless for fear that the immediacy of the situation of which I had written might have awakened a disgust that she had hitherto been able to hide.

She crouched and sat beside me. "I cannot say that I would not have suggested coming to Kersey, had I known. But you must go to Spain, and as soon as possible."

I was taken aback by her vehemence. "That was my first thought too. But . . . but I would not disturb Catalina for anything in the world."

"No, and I do understand your reluctance. But Idoia . . . Stephen—Major, I know a little of such places. My mother has had to do with one in Rochdale. They are necessary. But Idoia cannot be truly happy. We shall leave tomorrow morning."

"I would not have you do so for anything in the world and, besides, there is no need. I am sure that I may do all that is necessary from here."

She did not answer me directly, but said, "If you do not wish to be seen to change your plans, we shall stay until the day after tomorrow, as you so kindly offered. But we shall be gone as early on that day as we may."

"I should thank you," I said. "I do thank you, for your consideration, but I think that you don't understand. I shall make certain that Idoia is well enough, but I cannot risk disturbing Catalina's peace."

She took a deep breath and was silent for a moment. Then she said, "Would Catalina not wish to know that you care for her child's welfare? She too lives under the authority of the Roman Church. It would perhaps be difficult for her to question its provisions, as you may. That is, should you wish to do so."

I wondered for a moment at how simply she saw the matter, before I realized that she could not know that at the thought of traveling to Spain, of being so close to Catalina, I felt joy, which I knew could have no fulfillment, and terror of disturbing the love that had formed my life. Against these two, my duty to my daughter weighed something, but so much less.

Miss Durward shifted a little as she pulled the hem of her gown out from where it had caught under her as she sat. Then she said, "Forgive me. I, of all people, should know that you are not one who needs his duty explained to him. You must understand that it is only the thought of a child, your child . . ."

I was silent as her voice tailed off, and then realized with no little surprise that I was thinking of Tom, lost and trampled, and of Miss Durward, sitting down so suddenly in the little parlor, and weeping as if even her strength could not prevent fear overwhelming her, fear for a child not even her own.

"You are right," I said. "I must go to Bilbao, and as soon as I may. But I wish you might stay longer. I have wanted you—all of you—to see Kersey for such a long time. And I very much dislike appearing so inhospitable to your sister. . . . Yes, you must stay longer. It will make very little difference."

"Except to you. I would love to stay longer, but how can I demand—even request—that you stay, merely to provide me, and Hetty, with some pleasant hours? It is true that someday I should very much like to see more of Kersey. But on this occasion we shall be gone on the day after tomorrow."

"You are very good."

We sat on the wall, side by side, watching the sunset, for some time. For once, she had no sketchbook in her hand, and her attention seemed to be given to the scene before us, where the clouds moved slowly about in the light, and a heron that had contrived to evade the guns of the local fishermen glided in from afar and flicked its wings upwards before landing on delicate legs among the sedge that bordered the stream. Nonetheless I was not surprised when she spoke again.

"Thank you for telling me the rest of the story."

"I should have waited for your reply to my first, but that I needed to tell you of what has happened. And I had no notion that you might be reading of it here."

"My reply to your first is no doubt sitting in a sack in the hold of a Dover packet-boat." She stopped, and after a moment turned towards me. "No, I shall not wait for paper and ink to say it for me at a safe distance. My reply says that if you ever desire to reach Catalina, that . . . that if there is anything I can do to help—whatever you hope for from her—I shall do it. And now . . ." She smiled, an awkward, unpracticed smile that might have been the first, not the thousandth, that had ever illuminated her face. "Before today, I might have repented of such an offer to meddle. But now you are going to find your child."

"Yes. I have a duty to her. And"—I spoke with some hesitation, for my resolution was but newly formed—"I think that, for all I have said, it might be well for Catalina . . . that she might, as you say, wish to know that I am caring for her—our—daughter. . . . Yes, she might wish to know that."

"In her place, I should wish to know it," said Miss Durward. "But will you be able to speak to her?"

"I think not. I shall have to find some intermediary. If I did not fear that the rule of her order permits others to read her letters, I should write. Above all, I should wish her to hear from me privately, and before I go to Sant' Águeda."

She nodded, but I could not make out her expression in the fading light. The evening noises of birds and leaves were quietened, as if the setting of the sun snuffed out sound and movement as well as sight. Miss Durward herself was very still, but not, I thought, from quietness of mind.

"Is it too chilly for you?" I said. "I hope your gown is not damp from the grass."

She scrambled up. "Not in the least. But perhaps I should go back to Hetty and George. Hetty at least will need no urging to leave when we have engaged to, for she longs for Tom."

I began to get up. "What does Tom think of his stepfather?" As I spoke I thought it strange that the question had not occurred to me before.

"Oh, he likes George well enough," said Miss Durward, reaching down to help me to my feet. "He barely recalls his own father, after all. And he's approaching the age where he may look to a man to introduce him to that of the world that Hetty cannot. But he is accustomed to have his mother to himself. It is not easy for a child of that age to understand, when the fundamentals of his world change."

"No," I said as we started to stroll back towards the Hall. I had felt her arm in mine, thin and firm, so many times, and supported by it, I spoke a thought that I had never uttered before. "A child of six understands so little."

IT WAS LIKE the space between Theo and me had no time in it. The air was plain, pale, almost nothing, but full of everything that I'd never seen, never even known could be there.

He put his cup down in its saucer. "Would you like to process that film?"

"Yes," I said, and I only said when we were halfway down to the darkroom, "if it's not a nuisance."

He stopped with his hand about to push open the door. "Anna, you are not to think that. You are never a nuisance. Do you hear me? Never!"

Suddenly I started to laugh. I couldn't help it, even though it felt sort of like crying too. And then so did he, and it was just as well he was standing right close next to me all the time I was doing the film because I'd never have got it right otherwise, probably would have ruined it. And when I'd pushed the hose down into the tank and twisted the tap to and fro till the water began to trickle out round the edges, and dried my hands and turned, all he said was "I need a cigarette." But it was he who remembered to glance at the clock before we went towards the door.

He lit one as soon as the darkroom door swung shut behind us, dragging the smoke in hard and letting it out in a sharp breath as we walked out into the sun. We sat side by side on the tree trunk, and there didn't seem to be very much to talk about until the film was done. Theo smoked his second cigarette more slowly, and when I said that a cloud that was drifting towards us over the clearing looked like a witch on a broomstick he tilted his head on one side and said, "Or a dragon, if you look at it this way."

"Or a swan. Look, it's stretching its wings up like it's about to land."

We watched the swan till it started to break up altogether, as if there was much more wind up there than the small breeze that stirred the leaves but hardly seemed to touch us where we sat with the brick breathing sun-warmth at our backs. Then the half hour was up and we went back in.

When I undid the tank my heart was banging around in my chest so hard you'd have thought it was my first ever film that Theo pulled so gently from the spiral, so that the water clung to his fingers and ran inch by inch down the inside of his wrist as he held the strip up to the light.

I couldn't see it well enough from where I was, so I went closer and took it from him. The long tail of Lavenham uncurled itself almost to the floor, but he caught it from behind by the edges just in time, so his arms were each side of me and his chest was so close to my back I could feel him breathing.

"What do you think?"

"I . . . I can't tell, really," I said, after a long time.

"No. One never can. The images are there, and properly exposed, and beyond that it is necessary to see them in the enlarger, or at least on the light box. Shall we have something to eat while it dries?"

He opened a bottle of red wine and made what he called *csirke paprikas*, with chicken and spices and cream, and dark bread to dip in the sauce. It was delicious, but there didn't seem to be much room inside me for food. The windows were all still open upstairs, and the air that came in had that warm, baked smell of places that have been soaking in the sun for hours, a sweet smell like newly made bread, the sort of smell you could live on. Theo filled up our glasses again and said, "Shall we have a look at your film? I have the chemicals I mixed yesterday, if you would like to print one or two."

Going into the darkroom was like a sort of going home, like I always wanted going home to be. I felt we belonged there, safe and not quiet exactly, because we talked about things, about the pictures and what we were doing, but quiet because there was nothing else going on, we were both doing the same thing, and equal, because although he knew more about what to do, I knew more about what I wanted.

There weren't many shots that really worked. The one in the pub garden of Theo looking at me was out of focus. One that did work was of the corner of the Guildhall where the different faces of the building came together and the corner-post was carved into the figure of a saint, all worn now, so the features were blurred, as if they'd been under water for all the years since someone had carved each fold of stuff and where it creased at the elbows and crumpled round her feet.

"Did he make it like someone he knew, do you think?" I said. "His wife, or his sister, or someone?"

"Perhaps," said Theo. "Crispin would know."

"It's a pity the face has gone."

"There are very few figures with faces left round here. The Puritans smashed them."

"You'd have thought they'd take down the whole thing."

"Perhaps they were in a hurry, hurrying to change the world. They thought that without faces the images lost their power, so it was enough."

I left the print lying in the wash. "Can I do another?"

"Of course."

There was only one that I really wanted, the last one. No face, just Theo's hands holding his coffee, just his hands, and his shirt out of focus, soft gray and white in the background. In the bends of his fingers the shadows were sharp and you could see the skin was quite thin; it was the muscles beneath it that made them look so strong round the china. The rim of the cup pressed into the pad of one of his forefingers, sharp as well, and I suddenly knew how the cup hung in his hold with its weight and heat not quite touching the curve of his palm, and his hands so careful round it. The light caught his fingers so that you could see the jointing of each knuckle, and the lengths of them making chevrons against the white, and on the far side just the tips of his thumbs on the rim and their bases twin swells of dark muscle that branched away from each other in the shadow below the cup.

I did that print myself. Theo sat on one of the high stools in the safelight and he didn't say anything, just watched me looking and thinking and cropping the image and focusing. Like always, I found I was holding my breath for the exposure, and when the enlarger clicked off and I let my breath go again it was loud against the hum of the ventilator, and he laughed just a tiny bit, deep in his throat. He didn't get up to see the print in the dev even, just sat there till I slipped it into the fix.

As I went past him to get to the light switch he half rose and put his hand on my arm. It was hot, almost burning against my skin. I stopped, but he didn't say anything. Then he dropped his hand and said, "Well done," and I went and switched the light on.

The print wasn't far off what I wanted. "That's where I should crop it," I said, drawing a line in the air above the fix. "Burn in the background so it's less bright and important, and crop out your sleeves, so it's just skin—your hands and the cup, and your wrists a bit softer where they're going out of focus." He nodded, but he didn't say anything, so after a moment I went back to the enlarger and changed the crop and refocused and did a new test strip, all properly, the way he'd taught me. And then when I crossed to the wet side with the exposed paper and slid it into the dev, I looked at him again, and he was looking at me, and I knew all of a sudden what he was thinking about.

After miles of time he said, in a rough sort of voice, "You should put it in the stop," so I did and stood rocking it with one finger, watching it not him. But, of course, the print was him too, and I dropped it into the fix and then the wash and stood there staring down and not moving, with a hot feeling in my back and spreading all through me until I thought my chest was going to burst.

"Anna . . ."

I turned, and deep in my belly, I felt something somersault with love, but still when I moved it felt like I was stepping over something—some threshold. I went to him and he put one hand hard on my waist and the other between my shoulder blades and I reached and pulled him towards me so that my arms met round the back of his neck and my face was buried in his shoulder with the heat of his skin against my cheek.

I think we stayed like that a long time, not wanting any more, just being there. Gently he rubbed his face in my hair, over and over again. Then he moved away and his hands dropped to my hips and then let go, almost as if he was trying to push me away.

I looked at him.

"I'm sorry, Anna."

"What for?"

"For doing that."

I wondered why people say "I'm sorry" when they don't mean it. It's so smug, so "I know better than you." I hadn't thought Theo was like that.

Or perhaps it was just he was playing the game.

I looked at him sideways. "I'm not sorry."

He blinked. I dropped my lower lip just a tiny bit till it was full and soft, and tilted my head, holding his gaze for a second, and then went to the door. "Coming?"

He followed me upstairs, close, I thought, his gaze seeping into the way I was walking. And when we got to the sitting room I stopped and turned and just looked at him, so that it would be him who had to make the last move.

He did, of course. They always do. I smiled up at him. His hands touched my shoulders, trembling a bit, his thumbs sliding under the straps of my top. But then he stopped. "No, Anna. It is not like that."

"Not like what?"

"Not . . . This is not what you are. Not what I want so much."

The room was full of shadows. I started to feel sick and it was safer to be further away from him, but I still couldn't stop the crying from squeezing up my throat and into my eyes. "Then you don't want me?"

"Oh, sweet Anna—" He was still far away. Then he was there.

It seemed very simple after that. He kissed me very long and so gently I could feel the quick rise and fall of his breathing and then we took each other's hand and walked to the bedroom.

He pulled his shirt over his head and slid off his trousers. He was naked underneath and I just watched because his skin was like old gold leaf pressed over his muscles and bones, burnished and tarnished, with little breaks and creases but warmer and more real because of them. Then he came to me where I was sitting on the end of the bed and crouched down and slid the straps of my top and my bra off my shoulders and pushed them down.

"Yes," he whispered, as if he was agreeing to keep a secret. Then he dipped his head and kissed my breast while he cradled the other with his hand.

When he raised his head his face was all flushed and blurred-looking and I took it in my hands and kissed him. He put his arms round me. His open palms were hot on my back, and then he half stood so that I let go and pulled off my shorts myself and my top and undid my bra, and moved up the bed till my head was on the pillow. He followed me, but only halfway, and then he bent his head and kissed me between my legs like he had on my mouth, sweet and gentle and warm. It wasn't like hands—not my own, or anyone else's—it wasn't like anything I'd ever felt, because it was so kind, it was so good. I curled my fingers into his hair and felt how his head moved as he found each of my dark places one by one, and kissed them.

Feeling his lips and tongue made me want to kiss him myself.

"Theo?"

He raised his head, and I cupped my hand round the back of his neck so that he slid himself up towards me.

It was strange to smell my own stickiness all over his mouth. For a moment I wasn't sure if I liked it, tasting myself, but then I thought, in a hazy sort of way, that it was Theo that found it—found me and gave me to myself—so it must be all right, more than all right, it was wonderful that he did that.

The wonder of it carried me down. I kissed each nipple in passing, they were neat and hard and where his chest muscles dipped in the center there was a thin, rough stream of hair that tasted sweet and salt. I rested there, small against his breadth, and then moved on, my face falling off the cliff of his ribs onto his stomach, quiet and smelling of sun with a pulse from somewhere deep inside him beating against my cheek. I circled his belly button with my tongue once and went on, because for the first time in my life I really wanted to, not just because it was the quickest way to get it over with.

The softest, finest skin in the world, I thought, and it was even softer and sweeter because of the hardness I could taste insisting within it, though when I looked up Theo wasn't insisting, he was lying with his eyes closed, and there were only his hands gripping in my hair and him leaping in my mouth to tell me what he was feeling.

Then his hands tugged harder and I let go and pulled myself up between his thighs until we were kissing each other again, length to length, lips and tongues, chest, belly, hips all fitting together. His hands were stroking each curve of my bottom and waist, over and over, as if he wanted to learn their softness by heart, and then he slid his fingers into the heat between my legs and stroked me there until I couldn't bear to wait any longer and rolled off him onto my back, looking into his eyes all the time, so that he turned onto his side with his hand resting on my belly.

Then he said, "Anna, are you sure?"

I nodded, holding my breath, because I wanted him so much that the crying might come back. He moved to be above me, not heavy, just right, parting my legs with his, feeling his way into me, blunt and gentle. And then he stopped, as suddenly as if he'd slammed a gate against himself, and behind it I could feel the whole of him, every muscle straining to hold himself in, even his teeth gritted, and through them he said again, "Anna, are you sure?"

And I didn't even have time to nod, I just put my hands on him and pulled him all the way deep inside me.

For a moment it was enough. We were completely still.

And then it wasn't enough, I wanted more, I wanted everything, I wanted him to find me completely, and he wanted me, and we were taking as well as giving, taking and giving, until we didn't mean anything, our bodies meant it all, more and more. My back started to curl and my mind and my guts closed down around him.

Everything was dark like being underwater. Then I felt Theo again. His head went back with letting go, and then the whole of him drove into me for the last time.

It was Theo's smell I woke to, stronger than before but the same, salt and sweet and smoky where my nose was pressed into the dip in his collarbone. His arm was round me and I thought he was asleep.

It was quiet and very dark. I couldn't really see the room, only feel bedclothes. Theo must have put them over us while I slept. An owl hooted, not very far away. I lay in the crook of his arm with my head on his shoulder, like lying in a hammock, feeling the small sway of our breathing.

But I did need to pee. I moved out from his arm and stood up.

"All right?" said Theo, from his sleep.

"Yes," I said, and went out of the open bedroom door. There was the faintest grayish light from the passage window, enough for me to find the bathroom. In there it was too dark to see. I shut the door and the light pull banged against the back of my hand before I managed to tug it.

Through my sleepy blinks everything glared at me. There was shampoo and toothpaste and Eva's makeup and Theo's shaving things side by side on a shelf. The room smelled of her as well as him. On the back of the door hung her dragon dressing gown.

She couldn't mind, could she? She slept with other people too. They both did. She wouldn't mind. Theo wouldn't have . . . So I didn't have to worry, did I?

I turned away. I peed and dried myself and found I was tender there, not sore, but extrasensitive, heavy and awake.

When I went out into the passage I could see there was light outside, splashing down from a moon I couldn't see and showing me a child. It was Cecil. He was standing at the edges of the trees, looking up at the window, and he was wearing my sweatshirt. It came down almost to his knees, and the sleeves dangled beyond his hands. I waved, but he didn't wave back, just went on looking, as if I wasn't there, then suddenly turned and skipped back into the woods, as if someone in the shadows had called to him and he'd gone quite happily.

Theo was lying on his side. The faint light picked out the tiny curls on the back of his neck, and the swell of his shoulder and arm muscles like a range of faraway hills. But it was too chilly to stand looking at him, and when I slid into bed he reached and drew me in so my body was curled within his and his arms were warm round my stomach and breasts. His drowsy breath on the back of my neck was like a kiss putting me to sleep so I could stay there with him, for a hundred years.

❦

MY GROOM HAVING returned with the news that the *Unicorn* would sail out of Portsmouth two days hence, bound for San Sebastian, and that my passage on her was booked, I had only to deal with the business of putting all in order before I left Kersey, without revealing my reasons for doing so to the Barracloughs, and while attending to their needs and desires as well as I might. It was a wearying business, and there was little opportunity for private talk with Miss Durward to brighten it. I almost looked forward to the solitary tedium of a post chaise, but in the event the road was long and dull indeed, and it was not only because I was anxious to embark on the next stage of my journey that the sight of the great ships-of-the-line, rising like cathedrals above the wharves and terraces of Portsmouth, raised my spirits.

The *Unicorn* was due to sail on the evening tide, at eight o'clock. I bespoke dinner at the George Inn, arranged for my baggage to be taken on board, then set out to stretch my legs along the seawall.

It was a fine afternoon of cloud and some sunshine, and a large part of the population seemed intent on doing the same, so it was fortunate that, having spent much of the journey pondering what lay ahead of me, I was eager to be distracted. Naval uniforms abounded:

within a stride you might be blinded by the flash of gold braid that caught the sun, and brushed past by a master-mate's shoulder clad more in darn than in cloth. Tarry pigtails conferred with flowered bonnets over the choice of a street vendor's ballads; a master carpenter and a gunsmith had stopped and were drawing limbers on the flat of the parapet with a stump of chalk; a midshipman no higher than my elbow paraded in his new uniform, his snowy linen and well-scrubbed face betraying his mother's tearful pride. There were rear admirals' wives with weather-beaten faces, their Canton shawls plucked at by the sea wind and their gait bred by the Atlantic swell, and a pair of pale seamstresses blinked red-rimmed eyes in the air, while a porter shouldered by with a by-your-leave-Miss, balancing on his head a towering basket of fresh-caught eels.

I walked on, almost to the very far end of the seawall, where the bastion looked out to the main channel to the sea and to all the creeks and islets that guarded it. Sitting on the far side of the parapet, legs dangling above the incoming tide like any truanting lad catching dabs, sketchbook and pencil in hand, was Miss Durward.

My delight at seeing her was only heightened by my astonishment. She, on the other hand, to judge by the calm turn of her head and her smile, felt no great surprise. She swung herself back to the landward side and jumped to her feet.

"What lucky chance has brought you here?" I asked as we shook hands.

She seemed to hesitate. "Well, it was not precisely chance," she said. "I had not meant you to know until . . . until we went on board. I have booked a passage on the *Unicorn*, to San Sebastian."

"What?"

"I am going to San Sebastian."

I struggled for words against delight and dismay, and all that I could bring forth from my confusion was "Why?"

"I thought I might be able to help."

"But your sister? Your mother?"

"They think I have gone to stay with an old friend near Wilton. I left Hetty and George at Wolverhampton. I said that I would write when I was certain of my plans. Not that I care for propriety, but they do, and I do try not to cause them distress when it can be avoided, even if it means telling an untruth."

"But—but this is not a question of propriety. This is . . . this is simply impossible!"

She did not answer me directly, but tucked her hand into my arm, so that I was obliged to accompany her back along the walkway. Then she said, "You cannot prevent me going on board."

"Short of violence, I suppose that is true. If the circumstances were otherwise—if Mrs. Barraclough or Mrs. Durward were with you— I should have nothing but pleasure in your company. And if the object of my journey were something other than it is . . . But you are alone, and I am heading into who knows what sordid or distressing situation."

"Your love for Catalina was not sordid, and that it bore fruit could never be anything other than wholly natural and right."

I was silenced, not only by the truth of these words but also by her saying them in so gentle and simple a manner.

"Major, I think I can help you. Your . . . your respect for the past, and for your obligations to it, is admirable. As your friend, I would help you to do what you feel is right. You said yourself that you will need an intermediary. Why not me? You might even, for the first time in my life, make me grateful that I am not a man."

"But—"

"What the world thinks of me is my affair," she said, with a smile, "and I doubt if it will think anything very much. For one thing, who in England is to know?"

"You may call me selfish—"

"Stephen—never that!" she said suddenly and pressed my hand, a little awkwardly on account of the sketchbook she was still holding.

"But perhaps, in this case, I am," I said, "for I have no wish to figure as the author of your disgrace. Miss Durward, please do not ask this of me, for what we know of the true circumstances of our traveling together will have no influence on what others will be determined to think."

She took a quick breath, and loosened her hold on my arm to look up at me quite seriously. But after a moment she said, "You need not acknowledge me, you know, not until we reach San Telmo. And not then, if you truly find you have no need of me. I am quite capable of ordering my journey myself." She laughed. "If we should happen to take a turn about the deck at the same hour, you may raise your hat to me with the blankest of well-bred glances, and I shall bow my head only very slightly in return, to depress your pretensions!"

I could not help smiling at the picture. "I fear we shall be in the wrong season for turns about the deck to be pleasurable. Not that Biscay is a pleasure to cross at any time of year." I recollected myself. "But you must realize that I cannot allow you to come, for both our sakes. I am sorry if I appear ungallant, but so it must be."

"Gallantry is not the point," she said, with an air of great patience. "You cannot prevent me boarding the *Unicorn*, and you will not. If you do not wish to ignore me altogether, would it serve if we were to be brother and sister? Half-brother and -sister, if you like, since our names are not the same."

"Perhaps," I said, for I could not deny it. Nor could I deny, even to myself, that her presence would be welcome in dealing with the convent, and that her companionship would render the journey there and back infinitely less tedious. "But I still—"

"If our being brother and sister can overcome your scruples as to my reputation, then there is nothing to worry about." She stopped, and I turned to her, but it was only after a moment that she continued. "Nonetheless, you must tell me truly—now, once and for all—if, thinking simply of what lies ahead of you, you do not wish me to come. Tell me that my presence would be a hindrance, not a help, as ungallantly as you wish, and I shall get on the next mail to Manchester."

I looked at her. Our eyes were almost on a level, and hers were very blue in her thin face; her mouth was firm and red.

She looked away, and then her eye was caught by a clipper that was slipping down the main channel towards the sea, flags snapping in the wind, sailors scrambling upwards, and boxes and barrels roped and stowed on deck with a thoroughness and care that spoke of a long voyage ahead: round the Cape, perhaps, or to Jamaica by way of the Azores. I recalled how eagerly she had explored Brussels with me, how impatient she had been with the limits imposed on her by her sister's ill health, and I thought that her desire to come to Spain might be bred in part by her simple thirst to see the world. It was her longing to go beyond her present horizon that reached my heart.

With a strange sensation that we were crossing a threshold together, I took her hand, and said, "Very well, Miss Durward, and without the least gallantry, I do wish you to come with me to Spain."

"Thank you, Stephen," she said.

We turned, and she tucked her arm again into mine. Her touch was so familiar that it was a moment before I realized that even this simple gesture had been changed, in its significance, by what had been decided.

We walked thus for some time. But the throng thickened as we headed towards the inn, and I was seized by a conviction of the madness of the course on which we had set ourselves. What had we done? We were setting ourselves up to be spoken of as a lady disgraced in name, and a man who truly was, in one sense, the author of her ruin. These unknown faces through which we made our way would feel entitled, did they but know what we intended, to show disapproval of our apparent transgression, to express sorrow, disgust, or worst of all, a prurience as offensive to my companion as it would be disagreeable to me. I could not even comfort myself with the thought of those who would smile on what they thought a passionate—if irregular—adventure, for they too would be mistaking the facts. We were not what they called us, and we had no thought of such a thing. True, I had once contemplated contracting an alliance with her sister, but I was painfully conscious that I could not have given Miss Durward the free heart that she so much deserved. In any case, Miss Durward had said that she had no desire to receive any man's heart at all. And yet no true facts, I knew, would serve to diminish the world's conviction that because we should shortly go aboard the same ship, eat meals at the same table, say good night and good morning, travel in the same carriage and sleep at the same inn, we must be lovers.

But I still could not deny that I wished for her company, more so perhaps than ever. Contemplating the days that lay ahead of me, seeing old griefs to be revived and new difficulties to be confronted, I knew that I would want her quick understanding and observant eye, her unjudging view of the world, her ready desire to help, and her detachment that would allow her to stand back as readily, should I have no need of that help. And I could have none of this, which I most urgently wished for, without the certain risk—if not the certainty itself—of ruin for her and defamation for me.

"You know," said Miss Durward suddenly, looking up at me, her hand gripping my arm more tightly, "if we are to be brother and sister, you must call me Lucy."

We will sleep where we stand, a single line left from five thousand men, our mouths still screaming with thirst from heat and powder. The light is fading, but we can see our dead bedfellows. It is difficult to walk without treading on the slain. Some look as if they merely sleep too soon. Some lie in their own guts and their horses' blood. Here are many of ours; there the whole of the 27th, a regiment of corpses, dead in their square, bodies tumbled on torn bodies like dolls on a bloody nursery floor.

My boot slips on the pulp of an arm. I stumble over the smashed muzzle of a mule. We must count our dead, but how much quicker it would be to count the living!

I ordered the enemy ammunition wagon to be cut up for firewood, but a sword must have struck a nail. The explosion is worse than any gun. The two men are blown into the air, higher than a house, and fall, then jerk into the air again, and down like puppets, before they drop finally to earth. We run forward. They are just alive, burned naked and black, skins blistered and eyes red and staring, but they cannot speak, stand, walk. Four of the men carry them away. They will not live long, and it was my order. I turn back. We must count, and name, and bury our friends. Here, by the rags of the hedge that was all our shelter, the gunners are dead at their posts. I step forward among the broken horses, limbers, traces, ammunition boxes, shells. My foot slips again. The explosion cracks my ears, and I think, How strange. The wagon blew up a second time.

The surgeon has been working all day and all the night before. He will take my leg off. He must. I am lucky he can do it now, before the fever sets in. "Don't worry, sir, he's a fast worker, and he does the new cut," says the orderly, and reaches for the saw resting on the dusty windowsill. I feel it cutting through flesh. There is blood everywhere, even on my face. Then I hear it. The saw-cuts judder within the agony, so fast I smell hot bone. It is this or die.

I will not die.

PART FOUR

*It is not merely the likeness which is precious in such cases—
but the association, and the sense of nearness involved in the
thing . . . the fact of the very shadow of the person lying there
fixed for ever!*

ELIZABETH BARRETT BROWNING

{ *I* }

I HAD THE LENGTH OF A GOOD DINNER AT THE GEORGE TO accustom myself to addressing Miss Durward by her Christian name, and by the time we went aboard, it rose to my tongue without too conspicuous a hesitation. She was rather silent as we made our way to the quayside. It was I who engaged the seaman at the foot of the gangway in conversation and learned, among circumlocutions, that the *Unicorn* was a three-masted brig carrying a mixed cargo of which the bulk was Lancashire cotton and fine china bound ultimately for Madrid, and returning with tobacco, cacao, and maize. Passengers, the purser explained, as he led us below, were lodged, most commodiously, aft of the mast on the main deck. He bowed Lucy into her cabin and led me on to mine. Commodious was not the word that I would have used, but it was clean, and furnished with everything necessary for a few days at sea, and when I met Lucy in the companionway, she agreed that hers was no different.

The light was going, and the movement of the tethered ship under our feet was changing as the tide turned, like a horse suddenly restless in its stall. The sound of orders and oaths that flew about us where we stood by the side was as familiar to me as an old song, for all these concerned foresails and main braces. Even the oaths had no great animosity to them, and although Lucy seemed not entirely at ease on board, she did not flinch, except at my anxious glance towards her.

At a few minutes after eight o'clock we cast off, and the *Unicorn* began to slip from the quay. As we dipped and swayed away from the shelter of the harbor Lucy shivered a little.

"Is it too cold for you, with the sea breeze? Would you prefer to go below? The saloon appears comfortable enough."

"No, I thank you, I am quite warm."

We spoke little after that, resting our elbows on the side, listening to the leadsman calling the soundings, and looking out at the dim land falling away from each side of the Channel, until we could see nothing but points of lamplight in distant cottage windows and the buoys marking our passage south and eastward round the Isle of Wight and towards the open sea. Only when there was nothing but the sweeping flash of the Foreland Lighthouse to breach the darkness about us, and even the sails swelling above our heads could be only partly seen by the small glow of the lamps swinging at the crosstrees, did Lucy decide to go below.

"I shall see you in the morning, Stephen."

"Good night," I said. "I hope that you sleep well."

"Thank you," she said, and as I moved towards the head of the companionway, which was extremely steep even by naval standards, and offered her my hand, she went on, "No, I can manage."

I went below myself not long afterwards, although I feared that the inevitable discomforts of maritime life, and my anxiety about what lay ahead of me in Spain, not to mention the necessity of ensuring Lucy's well-being, would combine to make for a restless night indeed. But at least so confined a space was an advantage to a one-legged man, I reflected, for everything I might require was within arm's reach. Indeed, I really had no need to prop my crutch ready to hand simply in order to get about, but my habit of defending myself against the too-vivid life of my missing limb was of long standing. I got into my bunk, trying to imagine how Lucy was faring, for she had said that this would be the longest sea journey she had yet made. Already the ship was pitching as the Atlantic swell, squeezing up the Channel, met us head-on, but Lucy would not be daunted by the prospect of storms or foreign lands, I knew, nor even irritated by such plain, cramped quarters. And realizing that, I went, after all, quickly and dreamlessly to sleep.

The master had every expectation, he said, of making San Sebastian in good time. We should not be more than four days at sea, all being well, he went on, and I welcomed the news, not only from anxiety to reach our destination, but also from a fear that our deception might be revealed, and from a growing knowledge of our fellow passengers. There were only three: a clergyman and his nephew on their way from the West Riding to minister to the Anglican inhabitants of Barcelona, and a middle-aged man whose complexion declared a lifetime spent in India, and whose voice confirmed him as a Scot. Thus it was that Lucy was the only lady to sit down at the saloon table where our meals were served. To my relief our fellows appeared to accept her as my half-sister, but I could not be easy while the conversation was general, for there were innumerable moments when either of us might have betrayed us both.

Shipboard life is generally compounded of boredom, seasickness, and the necessity of keeping one's feet. On this occasion, the seas were generally as moderate as Biscay ever chooses to be, and the clergyman's unfortunate nephew suffered all the seasickness that the whole party might have expected, while the others sought to relieve the boredom with, on the one hand, anecdotes of a life spent shipping opium into China, and on the other, reflections on the sad decline of England's moral fiber since the introduction of the spinning jenny. At her request, I did teach Lucy some words of Spanish, but for the most part she escaped from the saloon whenever she could—for despite her skirts, she had the least trouble of any of us in keeping her footing—and was generally to be found tucked into an obscure corner of the deck, with the hood of her boat cloak pulled forward about her face.

At my step she looked up, her expression much like Nell's on being discovered in a favorite but forbidden chair.

"Oh, it's you!" She smiled and put back her hood. "I was afraid I should have to hear yet more about the wickedness of Dissenting preachers in stirring up discontent."

"Well, I can promise not to talk about that!" I said, sitting down beside her on the canvas-covered hatch. "What were you thinking of at breakfast when I caught your eye? I thought you about to burst out laughing."

"I was. If you had not turned aside to take more coffee I fear I should have done so. It was not kind of me, but I suddenly saw that, if I were to paint our fellow passengers, I should need my whole color box. At least, it wants only you to be blue with cold, for where Mr. Bradshaw is red—a good cellar, his vicarage must possess—and his poor nephew is green, Mr. Campbell is decidedly yellow!"

I laughed and laughed, and with my laughter her own amusement was revived, so that it was some minutes before we were quiet. When she took up her pencil, I drew a volume of *Guy Mannering* from my pocket. "Shall I disturb you if I stay here?"

"No, indeed," she said, settling herself with her back against a barrel. "And if you are reading, the others may stay away. For some reason they think they may interrupt my drawing as they would not dream of interrupting a man with a book or a newspaper. Do you suppose that they do so because of my occupation, or because of my sex?"

I considered the question. Did the difference lie between man and woman, or between reading and drawing? "Both, I should imagine," I concluded at last, opening my book, and we stayed side by side, absorbed in our respective pleasures, for a long time.

Early on the morrow, I was standing on the poop deck, talking to the master, when Lucy appeared on the main deck and looked about her.

"Good morning, ma'am," called the master to her. "Care to join us? Military men are always welcome to come up here, unlike some passengers, and their ladies the same."

Lucy had picked up her skirts and climbed the ladder before I could go to her aid, and as she reached us the master continued. "I was just saying to your brother here as we should make port tonight. Providing we're not thrown off course, that is, for we've got a squall on the way."

"Oh, have we?" she said quickly. "How can you tell? It appears fine enough to me."

She was right, for the sea was moderate and the clouds that chased one another across the pale blue sky were a soft and innocent white.

"Well, can't expect a lady to tell these things," said the master.

"Perhaps if you would allow my sister to look through your glass," I said.

"Certainly," he said and handed it to Lucy most readily. "If you look over there—oh, you have it, ma'am. Sou'-west by west, which is as you'd expect for the time of year."

She looked through the telescope. I had done the same only a few minutes earlier, and had seen steely shadows in the master's glass, clouds piled into a few degrees of the horizon, the dark, spreading patch of sea slashed with foam, and the air between stained with gray rain.

Lucy looked for so long a time that I could not but speculate as to what she was thinking. Then she took the glass from her eye, and gave it back. "Thank you, Master."

"If you'll excuse me, ma'am, sir . . . ," he said, and moved aside to speak to the helmsman.

"Am I foolish to be dismayed?" Lucy said as we descended to the main deck, for already there were sailors running to the side and swinging themselves up into the rigging.

"Things may become a little uncomfortable," I said, "but I am sure he knows his business."

She nodded, and though the seas grew heavier under us, she stayed, wedged into a corner so that her hands were free, watching and drawing. The storm took an hour or so to grow from a patch on

the horizon that one might blot out with one's thumb to one that even
my two palms could not cover, any more than they could stop the
thunder reaching my ears, or the lightning my eyes. The ship pitched
and rolled, so that I was forced to grip the side, and as the gusting
wind began to throw rain as well as sea spray into our faces and onto
the pages of Lucy's sketchbook, a sailor shouted across to us, "Master's
compliments, miss, sir, and he'd be obliged if you'd be so good as to
go below. Looks like it's going to be rougher than we thought."

The loudest crack of thunder yet came from directly overhead. In-
voluntarily, we both looked up. Above us was a pale luminescence,
faint blue against the black and swelling clouds, flickering about the
mainmast like an icy halo.

"Saint Elmo's fire!" exclaimed Lucy. "How I have longed to
see—"

Her words were bitten off as the ship plunged as if it fell into a pit.
I lost my grip and my footing and was thrown sprawling across the
deck.

"Stephen!" Lucy crouched, anchoring herself with a belaying pin,
and grabbed for my hand. My wet fingers all but slipped through hers
as the ship gave another heave, but her grip tightened and her strength
held, until mine returned, and I could reach my knees, then my feet.

Inch by inch we made our way within. I was still somewhat shaken
when we finally got to the saloon, and only too willing to sit down on
one of the padded benches that ran round the outer three sides, while
Lucy tugged at the strings of her cloak and cast it aside. Such light as
came in through the low windows was dim, and although the big lantern that hung above the table had been lit, it swung so wildly that it
was of little assistance in reading her face.

The other passengers were not to be seen, although we had heard
faint, distressing sounds on passing the cabin of the Reverend Mr.
Bradshaw's nephew. We could not even obtain the tea that we both
desired, for Lucy's enquiry was met with the news that all fires were
ordered put out, and that only ale or brandy were to be had, sir, if

wanted. We did not want either, so we settled back and tried to talk of other things against the groans of the ship's body, the thunder, and all about us the howl of the wind.

Lucy's replies came increasingly at random, until she fell silent. I was just thinking that perhaps the movement of the ship had finally begun to affect her—for even I was finding it necessary to steady my stomach deliberately—when a particularly violent heave flung the ship into a solid, dark green wall of water, which struck the windows hard by Lucy's shoulder.

She screamed, then clapped her hand to her mouth. As the ship righted herself she said, "I'm sorry."

"That was a shock," I said.

She nodded, and then as the ship dropped suddenly and the sea hit us again with still greater force, her face crumpled with terror. I could see her teeth biting down into the flesh of her hand in an effort not to scream again. Her eyes were half closed, and with her other hand she gripped the back of the bench.

"Come away from that side," I said, half rose and held out my hand, so that I might help her to move round to the far side of the saloon.

She nodded and started to shuffle herself along the bench into the opposite corner as the ship plummeted again. I sat down, perforce, as another wall of sea-darkness hit us, and she was thrown, with a half-smothered cry, into my arms.

For some minutes it took all my strength and attention to keep us both safe, for in her distress she could not prevent her body being flung about as easily as a rag doll in the hands of a giant. I held her to me, feeling her now silent sobs heaving within her slight frame. Her face was buried in my shoulder, and she held on to me as tightly as I did to her.

It was some time before I realized that the ship was no longer dropping quite so far or so fast each time into the pit beneath us, nor staggering quite so steeply out of it, although my grip on the bench back was still all that prevented us being thrown, together, onto the floor. Lucy raised her head from my shoulder, so that her hair brushed against my chin, and I felt cool air where her cheek had been pressed against my coat.

"I'm s-sorry. I . . . It is the only thing that frightens me beyond all reason." Another wave, smaller, but solid enough, smashed into the far side of the ship, and she flinched. I gathered her against me again. She spoke as soon as she could, as if her words could make her certain when her thoughts could not. "I *know* that we are safe, that we are safer here than on deck, that ships sail unharmed through such squalls every day. It is foolish to be so frightened. I hate myself for being so weak and silly!"

"If you are frightened, you are frightened," I said. "There is no shame in it. We all have our own, particular terrors."

She looked up at me.

Then she blinked, and averted her eyes, and color crept into the pallor of her cheek as we let go of one another in confusion.

When the steward came in to announce that the galley fire was lit again, and we were welcome to our tea now, if we still wished for it, we were sitting at the long table, discussing with some urgency the disposition of the French fleet at the Battle of Copenhagen.

The weather moderating as swiftly as it had worsened, we were glad, after dinner had been served to those of us who could contemplate it, to make our way out of the stuffy saloon and on deck. The storm had not, we were told, sent us off course to any great degree, and the stiff salt wind, which whistled through the rigging and snatched indifferently at sails and cloaks, drove the ship forward. It was still not easy to make one's way along the shifting deck, but the clouds were lifting, and even beginning to break up. Our southern latitude was evident in the speed with which a higher sun promised to fall to an earlier twilight, but it was still warm enough for it to be very pleasant to reach a small, sheltered spot, and watch the white-flecked waves racing past, the shore growing before us, and the sun setting behind us on the starboard side.

For some few seconds we sat in silence. My forearm was cool where Lucy had relinquished it on our sitting down, and her hands gripped together in her lap. Her fingers were pale with cold, and I knew an impulse to take them in mine.

She said, "Did I . . . did I tell you of our expedition into Burgundy?"

"No."

"Truly, did I not do so?"

I turned my thoughts towards her words. "You wrote only that you had made it to see this fellow Nièce."

"Niépce," she said. "Monsieur Joseph-Nicéphore Niépce." She stopped, and I felt the quick catch of her breath before she went on. "He—he makes sun-pictures like Mr. Thomas Wedgwood, only by quite a different method. But I should start at the beginning. Did I say that I went to your print shop to buy some prints of Bruges and Mechelin, to take home?" I shook my head. "Well, I fell into conversation with the manager, about cameras obscura, and he remarked that he had seen sun-pictures taken by their agency." The ship gave a lurch, and she hesitated, her hands clutching at the edge of the hatch, so that for a moment her wrist was taut against my knee. "He—he is a native of Burgundy, not Belgian at all."

"What was this different method?" I asked, grateful that our position side by side on the hatch made it easy to avoid her eye.

"Monsieur Niépce has been able to protect his images from darkening in the light, to some degree, by means of nitric acid. And he uses muriate of silver, which tarnishes so much more quickly than nitrate of silver. He tried to make printing-stones, too. It was with the promise of seeing those that I persuaded George that we should travel to Gras to find out more, if only on my father's behalf. With his camera obscura Monsieur Niépce has made images of the view from win-

dows—roofs, and a dovecote." Her voice was beginning to alter from
the flat, hurried tone in which she had begun, to the eagerness that I
knew so well. "But the images were not very clear, and, of course, like
Mr. Wedgwood's they were reversed: what is light in life is black, and
what is dark, white. Somehow it appeared strange, as it did not with
Mr. Wedgwood's feathers and insects. He was reticent about the ac-
tual processes, though, until George went out of the room. Then he
became quite forthcoming. Perhaps I have discovered another advantage of my sex."

I clenched my hands.

She went on. "He is not a young man, but he is still so eager for
new ideas. He used to experiment with his brother. He was stationed
at the barracks at Caligari in the days of the Republic, and his brother
was a naval officer with the French fleet there." She smiled up
at me in the old way, as if speaking thus of that friendship, that
easy companionship in shared interests and enquiries, kindled again
our own.

Even as I thought this, however, I realized that there was by now
no going back to our own old, simple friendship. I cleared my throat,
and we both looked aside. After a moment she said, "Now he is ex-
perimenting with substances that harden in the light, rather than
darkening, for it should be easier, once they have been exposed, to
wash away the areas where the light has not fallen, and then etch them.
But he has yet to discover the right substance."

It was not easy to remember, against my almost painful awareness
of her presence so close to me, what she had told me about etching,
but I had to make the attempt. "So, if he can discover it, it is the lines
and shadows that will be formed by the acid, and then take the ink, to
make the picture."

"Yes!" she said, and we smiled at each other until my cheeks grew
hot, and yet again I looked away, only to catch sight of the great twin
rocks, with the Isle of Santa Clara held between them, that I had not

seen for many years, but which were engraved on my memory by my love, and fixed there by time itself.

"There it is!" I got to my feet and went to the side. "San Sebastian!"

Soon the ship began to bustle, and not long after that the master took the trouble to roll over to us and say that we should be in, in an hour or two. "And I hope that there little squall didn't trouble you too much, ma'am," he went on. "Not that it was more than a storm in a teacup, as they say."

"Oh, no," said Lucy. "It barely troubled us at all."

<hr/>

I DIDN'T DREAM, not all night. I just slept in the soft dark, slept like lying in a cloud. I only woke in the end because Theo gave a little snore and then his arm tightened round me and my eyes flicked open and I remembered everything.

"Mmm?" I said. I turned round in his hold so I could kiss him.

After a moment he kissed me back, and then his eyes opened.

"Sweet Anna," was all he said, and he put up his hand to smooth my hair away from my face, over and over again.

I turned my head and kissed his palm, and then I licked it, and bit just a little into the dark flesh at the base of his thumb. It was strong between my teeth and suddenly I wanted him so badly, as badly as I had last night.

I could tell he felt my body pressing into his and the heat that washed up me, and his arm tightened. But then he let go, almost he moved away, and there was cold morning air rushing into the warm space where we had touched. But he didn't get up to go to the bathroom or anything, just lay there, looking at me, with the little lines between his eyebrows gone deep, like he was worried.

"What is it?" I said in the end, and the happiness in my stomach began to go queasy. "What's the matter?"

I think he heard the shakiness getting into my voice, because he picked up my hand and suddenly smiled, a bit crookedly but like he understood, and pulled me close to him again and started to kiss me, and we were pressing together, fitting together, closer and closer, as if we wanted to be in the same body.

It was quite early still, but the light and the birds singing and even a combine-harvester purring far away made everything more awake than the endless dark of last night, like we had the day waiting for us. Theo slid down the bed and kissed me between my legs. Almost straightaway, wanting swamped everything in my mind, even loving him, and I tugged at his shoulders, and when he entered me all the love came back like I was being hit with it, even before everything exploded in us both, even before my happiness came out as tears.

"Anna?" he said, raising his head from where it was buried in my neck. "Sweet Anna, are you all right?"

I nodded.

"Don't cry," he said, and took one of his hands from behind my shoulders and wiped the tears from my cheeks with his forefinger and traced the outline of my smile. "What's the matter? Did I hurt you?"

"No, oh, no," I said, because how could he ever hurt me? And the memory of him coming inside me meant I couldn't stop myself, and I said, "I love you."

He was very still. He didn't even breathe. Then he rolled off me and hugged me close, and kissed me on the forehead, and then rested his cheek against it.

"Oh, Anna," he said, "oh, sweet Anna."

After a moment I said, "It's all right, you know. You don't have to—to do anything. It's just . . . how I feel."

He took my face in his hands and looked straight into my eyes. Then he said, "It is a great honor, what you have told me." He didn't say anything else and after ages of looking I kissed him and snuggled back into his arms with my nose pressed into his neck and the pillow under my cheek smelling of me and him so mixed up that it was like together we made a whole new person.

I could have stayed there forever but a while later the telephone in the big room started to ring. We both jumped. Then Theo kissed my forehead again and rolled out of bed and went to pick up the phone.

"Hello? . . . Good morning, Crispin!" A longer pause. "Okay. We shall be there at five. . . . No, that is good. . . . Yes, of course. . . . *Ciao!*"

I sat up in bed. Theo put down the phone and came back into the bedroom. He started to pull on his trousers. "I took your prints out of the wash, by the way."

"God, I forgot about them. When did you do that?"

"Oh, when they were ready. You were fast asleep. I am glad I did not wake you."

"Was that when you put the blanket over us?"

He smiled. "Yes. I did not want you to be cold." He didn't bother looking for a shirt but went out into the big room, saying over his shoulder, "You are coming to the Patrons' View, are you not? It starts at seven, but Crispin has to go to the printer's to collect the leaflets. I have a lot to do this morning, but I have said I can be there at five to help with the last preparations. Will it suit you to come with me then?"

"Fine!" I got up and started looking for my knickers.

"How about some coffee? And then I expect you would like to go back to the Hall to change."

"I suppose I'd better," I said, but for the first time ever I thought, I don't want to wash, I want to go on smelling and feeling Theo on me and in me forever. It must have shown in my voice that I didn't want to go back, but of course, he mistook why.

"Poor Anna, is it that bad?"

"Sort of. I mean, Ray's okay. Kind, mostly, and he wants me to have a nice time, I'm sure. But he's busy. He doesn't even look after Cecil, not properly. Cecil's just sort of strange. Even his name—it's like he doesn't belong to now. And Belle's . . ." For a moment I couldn't say it, but then I went on. "I mean, I know she's my grand-mother and everything, but she's . . . She doesn't really live there, any more than I do. She keeps saying she wants me to be like family. But she's nasty to Cecil—really nasty. And if I don't do what she wants . . . It's sort of frightening. At least, when she's drunk it's fright-ening. And—and last time—she said things about—about me that weren't true."

He screwed the top onto the coffeepot. "That is not nice. Can you keep out of her way? You do not have to be there too much; there is always here." The way he smiled made it all suddenly all right. "We have run out of croissants, but would you like some toast?"

I was hungry, and I cut bread for both of us, yesterday's French bread, cut on the slant like he did it, and put it under the grill. I had to reach right past him to do it, and he moved aside, and said, "So, where is your mother staying in Spain?" while he poured out the coffee and put hot milk into mine.

"It's called Mijas but you say it Mihas. Dave says it's small but pretty—rather posh, kind of olde-worlde."

"I know Mijas," he said, saying it properly, "and your Dave is right."

"They decided to stay in the big hotel there, only it's not very big, to get an idea of what kind of people go and so on. Then they're going to buy one themselves. Dave's owned hotels before, so he knows what he's doing."

"It certainly sounds like it. Now, how is the toast?"

I had managed not to burn it even though I was smelling and feel-ing every move he made far more than I was watching the grill, while he went to and fro past me putting butter and jam and plates on the table. It was that sort of tingle between my shoulder blades again, like in the darkroom, as if my body was looking at him, even though my eyes couldn't.

We were just finishing the washing-up when the phone rang again.

Theo went to it. "Hello?" His face lit up. The receiver crackled with talking. For an awful moment I wondered if it was Eva. Not that she'd mind. I knew that.

"Kajik!" he said, and went on in a foreign language, excited, frowning, waving the hand that wasn't holding the receiver, and sometimes the hand that was.

I'd run out of fingers to dry with the tea towel and Theo was scrawling on the back of an envelope with the receiver wedged between his ear and his shoulder. Watching him jotting down foreign names and strange addresses, even some Russian writing, so quick and neat, made my heart somersault. I hadn't made a sound but he looked up and said in English, "Kajik! Forgive me! May I call you back later?"

"Don't worry," I said. "I'll go. I need to change like you said."

He said, "Kajik, hold on for a moment," and laid the receiver on the desk and put his arms round me and kissed me. "Sweet Anna. I'll see you later."

I kissed him quickly back on the mouth and hung my camera round my neck and went out and down the stairs as he picked up the receiver again. "Kajik?"

It was warm outside compared to the stables but it wasn't sunny, and I walked across the clearing and into the trees quite slowly. The air was still and humid. My skin breathed the sweat and smoke of Theo, and my own salt muskiness, and as I walked I felt the heavy warmth just inside me, not sore but fullness, filledness, feeling him there again with every step. I went through the green and light and shade of the trees and when I got to the gate the Hall looked tired and old, squatting in the middle of all the mangy brown grass. But it didn't matter because I had Theo. The tingle between my shoulder blades was almost like having Theo's breath there, like feeling him with me, and I pushed open the gate and marched across the grass and opened the back door.

Somewhere, Cecil was crying, loud but far away, on and on. I hurried down the passage to his room.

Sometime, he'd painted two people in black paint on the wall, lying down, as high in the air as he could reach. But he wasn't there. The crying wasn't stopping—it was almost like screaming, louder and louder as I ran through the kitchen and on through the swing door.

Belle was in the hall. She was bent over, holding Cecil by the arm, and she was punching his back and his head, over and over with her fist while he jerked like a puppet in her grip. The door flapped shut behind me. She half straightened and threw him across the floor. He stopped screaming and lay there. Then she turned and saw me.

I ran past her so close she staggered back. Cecil was whimpering, curled up by the double door with his arms over his head, and each sob seemed to hurt him. When I touched him he screamed, but it was a tired sort of scream, as if he'd given up. I stood up and looked round.

Ray was outside, watching through the window. Through the old glass I thought I saw tears running down his cheeks.

I whipped round. Belle had gone.

I bent over Cecil. "Ciss?" He half nodded. "I'm going to try to sit you up." I took his arm as gently as I could. He screamed, and then his belly heaved and he was sick all over the marble.

Beside me, the front door opened. Ray came in. He was gray and shaking, and he was pulling off his cardigan. "Don't try to move him. Is he all right?"

"No."

"I . . . Does he need a doctor?"

"I don't know. Yes. I think his arm might be broken."

He knelt down in the sick without even noticing, and laid his cardigan over Cecil. Then he began to check him all over, talking to him and touching him gently but in a purposeful first-aid sort of way even though his hands were shaking. "Can you hear me, Ciss? I'm just going to look in your eyes. Can you tell me where it hurts? Here? And here? Is that all right?" After a while Cecil stopped whimpering and lay still, but his eyes were open and followed Ray when he sat back on his heels. "I think you're right about the arm, poor little fellow. I'd better take him to Casualty. It'll be quicker than ringing for an ambulance—they take forever in the country. Can you stay with him while I go and get everything?"

"What if Belle comes back?"

His eyes flinched. "I . . . don't know. She won't. I don't think. I'll be quick. Keep talking to him, just quietly. Keep him with us." He stumbled across the marble and up the stairs.

I turned back to Cecil. "Ciss? It's Anna. Can you hear me?"

"Sick like the dog," he said, in a tiny little voice, as if he was ill as well as hurt. "And dead people and worms. Hot. Burning hot."

"Not anymore, pet," I said. "Uncle Ray's going to take you to hospital and they'll make you all better."

Then I thought, Ray didn't stop Belle. He just stood there, like he couldn't move, watching and crying, like a child. Will Cecil be safe with him?

There was a sound on the landing, and I looked round. After a moment I saw it was Ray coming downstairs. He had an armful of blankets and a big red first-aid bag. I stood up so I was between him and Cecil as he came across the hall. He stopped.

"I'll come with you," I said.

"Thank you, but I can manage."

"I think I should."

He was silent for a long moment. Then he took a deep breath. "Oh. Oh, I see. . . . Anna, I don't blame you. I can't—I couldn't stop her. I can't explain. . . . But I wouldn't hurt Cecil for anything in the world. I'd give anything for this not to have happened. He's my—he's like my son. I love him."

And I don't know why—maybe it was the way he'd touched Cecil, the way he hadn't even noticed the sick—but I did believe him, and knew that Cecil would be safe: he wouldn't need me. He asked me to hold Cecil's bad arm tight to his chest, so he couldn't move it, while he wound a bandage round and round to keep it there, and then I took the blankets and went out to pad the floor of the minibus because he'd be safer there than on the seat, Ray said. Behind me he picked Cecil up as carefully as he could, carried him out and laid him in the sort of nest I'd made with most of the blankets and covered him up with another.

Then he started the engine and drove very slowly away. Even when all I could hear was silence I still stood there with the windows of the house behind me, watching them go.

The air was hot already and I could smell Theo on my skin. Only now I wanted to wash, to get rid of everything I'd seen. I went back in.

The hall stank of vomit. Belle came out of the study. To think that she'd been in there all the time we'd been looking after Cecil made my skin crawl.

"So you've done what you came for."

For a minute I thought I was going to throw up at last: Cecil's sick and her vile smell were so strong in my nose and throat. I didn't want to talk to her but I felt sick and dirty and I wanted to find Theo and I had to get clean first. What I'd seen seemed to be burned on my eyes. I started straight upstairs without looking at her but the air was thick and shadowy.

When I got undressed I found Stephen's letter about Catalina in the pocket of my shorts and I put it safely with the others. I had a bath as hot as I could bear, scrubbing and scrubbing till at last I felt clean. I washed my hair and put on my last clean bra and knickers, and a tiered skirt and a flowery top I'd been saving up for nothing in particular. They were all the clean clothes I had left, and thank goodness, they would do for the evening too. But I didn't put on any makeup. I didn't want to look in a mirror.

I put my camera over my shoulder and went out onto the landing. Belle was coming upstairs, walking as if it hurt her and clinging to the banisters so hard her hand looked like a bloody claw. She stood right in my way.

"You don't want to be part of the family, do you? You go and make friends with strangers—foreigners—and you just come back to make trouble."

My hands wanted to hit her, to hurt her, the way she had Cecil. "That's nothing to do with it! It isn't me who broke his arm!"

She came right up close to me, panting as if even that was too much walking for her, and I could smell everything, sour and putrid.

"Your mother told Ray she couldn't leave you on your own. I know why. Because you're a little tart, that's why. You'd open your legs for anyone. As if you didn't get it from her. Your father was only the first—did you know? And when his family wouldn't help she ran away. And now she's sent you to split us up. But you won't do it. Ray'd never abandon me. He's mine. Not Nancy's. Not yours. Not the brat's. Mine. He's never looked at anyone else. Even all the time when he was here and I was away . . . Just because some slut pretended he'd fathered the brat, and he's too decent to deny it . . . But he's mine. He always has been. He wouldn't dare disobey me."

A horrible taste was rising in my throat, sick and shaky, because now I knew what it was all about. What had happened.

"You—that's what you did. To Ray! You hit him, and now you hit Cecil. No wonder Mum wouldn't stay. Did you hit her too? No wonder she had to leave and manage on her own. You're old and horrible and you make me want to puke."

"What's your precious Theo, then?" she yelled. I stopped dead. "I can smell him on you! Does he like bedding schoolgirls?" She grabbed my top and tried to pull me into her stink. "Tell me, what do you two do? What does it feel like, to be screwed by a man older than your father?"

Her hand went back and turned into a fist, and I wrenched myself free and ran away down the stairs. She staggered and swayed above the drop of the stairs and screamed, "Slut!"

I ran down the next flight and past Cecil's sick, wrenched open the front door and ran out. Halfway down the steps I realized what she'd said. *Even all the time when he was here and I was away . . . Just because some little slut pretended he'd fathered the brat, and he's too decent to deny it . . . But he's mine. He always has been.*

Ray was Cecil's father. Or he said he was. I thought further back, trying to make my mind just glance, not see it all.

He's my—he's like my son. I love him. And that was Cecil. I knew it was true even while I was thinking it. Ray'd sent her away, or whatever—and the drink, of course—and come here on his own. And he'd ended up with Cecil, not whoever the mother was for some reason, maybe she was mad or something. And now he didn't have the money to keep Belle there, and when she came back she found Cecil, and Ray didn't—couldn't—wouldn't—stop her.

I ran all the way to the stables with my skirt dragging round my legs and my camera banging against my side and the air rushing cold through my wet hair, without thinking of anything except I had to get to Theo.

He was upstairs sitting at the big desk. He saw me panting in the doorway and got up quickly and came to me with his hands out. "Anna! What's the matter? What is it?"

For a moment, because of the things Belle'd said, he looked to me almost like someone else. He had deep lines on his face, tough old skin; even his muscles fell sort of slackly from his bones until he moved. I thought, How could I have held him, wanted him, made love with him? Perhaps that was why everything about me smelled of sick. And if I did smell like that, how could he want to hold me? How could we be together?

But then he was holding me, and I thought, No, he's here. He wants me, whatever I'm like, wherever I come from. However lost I am, he'll find me. He is Theo, and I love him.

But, like always, someone being nice to you makes it impossible to keep going. I started to cry in a choking, coughing sort of way. He pulled a hankie out of his pocket and gave it to me to mop my eyes and blow my nose, so that after a bit I managed to stop.

Then he said, "What is it? Anna? Can you tell me?"

I shook my head. It was all muddled. I wanted to tell what had happened, but it was mixed up with what Belle had said, which I never could tell, not to Theo, never to Theo. It was like my head was all stuffed up with it, like I had a cold and my eyes were streaming and my nose was blocked so I couldn't breathe for all the stuff in my mind.

He held me away from him and looked at me, and I just stood there sniffing. "Is it . . . ? No, let us go for a walk."

We took the path away from the road and the Hall, and for a while we didn't say anything, just walked between the trees with the grass and pine needles and last year's leaves under our feet and the hot, thick air breathing against us as we moved through it.

When we came to the edge of the trees I saw that the wheatfield had been cut. The stubble stretched away, scruffy and dark yellow, with the fallen stalks heaped in straight straw ribs and waiting for the farmer to light it. There weren't even any larks. It was like they'd been cut down too.

We sat on the bank and Theo put his arm round me, and when we were comfortable he said, "Do you want to tell me?"

I told him about Belle hurting Cecil, and Cecil having to go to hospital, and by then all the anger seemed to have leaked out of me and I just felt incredibly tired and sad.

"But Ray is taking him to hospital?"

"Yes, but . . . Things he said. And Belle said. Ray's Cecil's father."

He nodded. "We did wonder. So often nothing is said. Does it upset you?"

I thought about it. "No, not really. Apart from wondering who his mother is, I suppose. It's—I can't imagine not having a mother. How could she leave him? Unless—oh, I don't know. But no, it doesn't upset me. It's just what happens, the kind of thing old-fashioned people think shouldn't happen, like sex before you're married, or having a colored boyfriend or whatever. But—it's—When Belle was beating Cecil . . . Ray didn't help him. He just let her hit him."

"What?"

"He just let her do it. He was outside. Watching through the glass. He was there. But he didn't do anything." I looked up at him. He was frowning, but him knowing too made me feel a little bit lighter and softer. "He didn't . . . he was sad. Crying. It wasn't that thing when people enjoy watching. Voyeurism. Just like he couldn't do anything else. Sort of paralyzed."

"When someone is damaged enough . . . they cease to believe they can fight back. I have seen it, how they just . . . let it happen. As if they are helpless. I have seen it."

"I think Cecil was okay before Belle came. And Ray tried to keep him out of her way. But then everything went wrong with the school and he had to have her back. And he can't stop her. Now I know why Mum left as soon as she could. Everything she's done since, she's done on her own. And she never said. She didn't think Belle would be here. She thought the school would be going and there'd be people. But Belle—she called me . . . names. She said my mum said. Mum wouldn't do that! Just because I sometimes . . . Not to Ray. Belle made it up. But she said anyway, horrible things about me."

He turned so he was looking at me and said, "Anna, Belle is wrong. She has her own problems and it is they that drive her. You of all people could never be horrible. You are sweet, and lovely, and infinitely desirable. And nothing that sick woman can do or say makes the least difference to that."

He was so calm, so clear and quiet about it, I started to feel clean, but I couldn't be, not really clean, not until I'd said everything, pulled it out of me and put it into the light so it could melt away. "And she said horrible things about us too, about me and you, about you being older than my—" I stopped.

For a long time he didn't speak, but his hands clenched suddenly on nothing. I sat and tried not to feel that he was moving away from me.

At last he said, "I had not thought . . . But is that how you see it? It is how *you* see it that matters."

"No. I don't see it like that."

"Truly, no?"

"Truly. What I see is you. And I love you."

"But?"

"It's just . . . I can't get her voice out of my ears. It's like—it's like some horrible smell." He smiled. "Don't tell me you can't have a smell in your ears. That's what it feels like."

"I know that you can," he said. "That is how it feels."

"I can't get rid of it. Even thinking about her makes me feel sick."

"Then don't think about her. Think about something else. That is possible. Most of the time, at least," he said, looking at his watch. "Remember that you are the only person who can judge whether what you do is good or bad, and then come with me, and we shall go and lunch somewhere."

"But haven't you got work to do? You said you were busy."

"You are more important," Theo said, and we walked back through the woods and I got into the car while Theo went up and got his suit for later, and then we drove away from Kersey.

I DIDN'T KNOW the places we drove through. It was the other way from before, and we ended up at what looked like a pub but was really a hotel, so they still did food even though it was gone two o'clock by the time we got there, and it didn't shut at three either. There weren't many people, being a Monday, mostly old couples and their friends, and some men who looked like salesmen, with red cheeks from the beer and loud voices. We took our coffee into the gardens and sat on the grass by the river. There was a pair of swans and a few ducks, and one of the swans decided to do his displaying thing, all wings stretched upwards and sailing about watching his mate watching him, and I grabbed my camera and photographed them both. A breeze had got up, which moved the heavy air about and blew bits of my hair across my face. The coffee was thin and stale; just part of being in England, Theo said, like the greenness and the ducks.

"I don't think I would've noticed before," I said. "In fact, I would've preferred it like this. But now I've got used to your kind of coffee."

"An English girl who knows good coffee from bad," Theo said. "Well, that's one good thing to come out of all of this."

It was cold by the river. I said, "Only one?"

He put up his hand and smoothed the strand of hair away from my face. "No, sweet Anna. Not only one," and by the way his fingers touched my cheek, and the way his eyes smiled, I knew that it was true. Suddenly he leaned forward and kissed me.

Behind us I heard the sort of up-and-down quacking voices we used to hear when Holly got a crew cut to go with her dungarees. Old-fashioned voices, who thought they could stop us. Theo's eyes flickered. He looked up, and then back at me, and then we moved together and kissed longer, and harder, and closer, until the voices went away. By the time we were back in the car I wanted him so much it hurt.

"We should probably head straight to the gallery," said Theo.

"But I need to put some makeup on," I said, and Theo laughed.

"I know that if I say you look fine, which you do, it won't make the slightest difference, so let us stop at the next chemist we see, and you can buy what you need. Do you have enough money on you, or may I lend you some?"

Theo waited in the car while I poked around among the blue eye shadows and pink blushers in the chemist, but in the end I found some black mascara and okay foundation and bought a comb, and some earrings from a rack of cheap jewelery.

When we got to the gallery Crispin was rushing around. "And d'you know, the printers delivered after all? So I needn't have dragged you in early. I did ring, and left a message on your machine, but you were out. I'm sorry."

"It doesn't matter in the least," said Theo. "I'll get changed, and then what can we do to help?"

We set out red wine and cartons of orange juice and glasses, and squeezed as much white wine as we could into the wheezy old fridge in the office, and I changed two lightbulbs, and Theo put paper in the toilets, and we all put out the leaflets listing the photographs and their prices. When we were down to picking imaginary bits of fluff off the floors and straightening the glasses and looking at our watches, Crispin said, "How is life at Kersey Hall, then, Anna?"

"Oh, all right," I said. "Theo's been teaching me to print."

"Has he, now? You hadn't done it before?"

"Not printing, no."

He looked at me, and then at Theo, and I wondered if he'd guessed. It made me feel hot but happy, because Crispin was friends with Theo and he would understand.

I said, "I must go and get ready," and I went up to the ladies' and had a bit of a wash and put plenty of makeup on because I was going to need it to cope with all these people. The eye shadow I'd found was quite a nice deep bronzy violet and the lipstick was properly dark red. Then I combed out my hair and put in the earrings. They were big crystals and you couldn't see they were just junk, once they mixed up with my hair and sparkled there among the dark.

When I came downstairs Crispin was saying, "I think the Fairhursts have more or less died out, but those local gentry families usually married pretty efficiently. The Jocelyns are related in some way—the brewing family in Bury, you know. One of them married a Fairhurst daughter, I think, and there've been plenty of sons in *that* family, so the genes go on, if not the name. But Kersey was sold for a school after the war, and it's changed hands several times, I think. So many of the big houses went that way then, when the taxes became punitive. Though recently there have been one or two which have opened as hotels. The portrait of Stephen Fairhurst is the best of what we have, but there are the letters, and I've bought a few things when I came across them at sales. Photographs, for the most part. There seem to be a lot of those around for some reason."

They turned to the portrait just as I reached the foot of the stairs. Stephen's eyes met mine. I could feel Theo's gaze on my cheek.

There was a dead silence.

"Anna, my love!" said Crispin. "You look wonderful!"

Theo just smiled at me, on and on, and I smiled back, feeling Stephen watching us both. After ages Theo looked back at Stephen and said, "It is quite a good portrait, I think. But, Crispin, do you have an acquisitions budget? I thought you were only funded for exhibitions."

"Sometimes I can't resist buying things for myself, particularly pictures, and photographs. There's something about seeing what a place looked like . . . And seeing too how the artist saw it, which is a different matter altogether. And the old photographic plates are so beautiful. They're not like film negatives, are they? They've a substance of their own, a presence. Daguerreotypes most of all, of course. It's as if the very existence of the subject shimmers within the glass—"

There was a brisk thump on the front door. "That should be Penny," he said. "You haven't met my sister, have you, Anna? Penny Stamford? And my niece Susan?"

Penny was tall and thin like Crispin, and just as nice. Susan was helping with the drinks, she said, with another girl who wasn't here yet. "So you're staying with Ray Holman at Kersey Hall?"

"He's my uncle," I said, which was about all I could manage without starting to shake.

"Susan used to work there, you know."

"Yes, Crispin said. And Cecil."

"Cecil's an odd little scrap, I thought. He must be old enough to have joined in with the school, but I think Ray felt he was too shy to cope with it. I suppose he knows. He's an experienced teacher after all, even if he wasn't a headmaster until he bought the school. The far side of Bury, isn't that where your family came from? But you must know more than I do."

"Not really. And I don't know Ray very well either."

She said nothing for a moment, and then, "It's a fine old place, the Hall. Quite impractical for a private house now, of course. Times change." She laughed. "In his heart of hearts, I think Crispin wishes they didn't. That's why he collects photographs of how it all used to be."

I thought suddenly of Stephen, and what he didn't really say, and Cecil's nightmares. "Even with—all the bad things that used to happen? I mean, at least we have doctors, and medicines, and people don't starve. And votes and things. Even—even places I've lived—it's not as bad as then. Mostly."

She smiled. "At least you know that it's only mostly. I'm a juvenile magistrate, and I know it too. But most of the people you'll see here tonight don't have the first idea of it. And yet they're not bad people. Just lucky. Come and meet Susan."

Susan wasn't tall and thin, she was plump and smiley in a white shirt and black skirt, and she was only a bit older than me. I told her I knew Cecil, and she beamed and said, "How is he? We were friends. But I couldn't go on working there. The school closed and the children went away."

"He's all right," I said. "He does talk about you a lot."

"Does he? I miss him," she said, and then people started to arrive and want drinks and she bustled off to do it. It was only seeing her with other people that made me notice she had those funny eyes.

Theo was at my elbow. I could feel the heat of him through my blouse. "Is she a mongol?" I whispered.

"Yes, but Penny and Crispin always call it by its proper name. Susan has Down's syndrome," he said. "She's sweet, isn't she?" He picked up a glass of white wine and held it out to me. "How about some of this? And then I shall introduce you to people."

"Must you?"

He laughed and closed my hands round the wine. "You will be fine!"

I looked up and saw Crispin watching us. After a moment he moved to stand in the arch between the two rooms and clinked two glasses together several times. When everybody'd shushed everybody else, he made a speech about the generosity of patrons and local councils, and the need for places like the gallery, and the importance of Theo and Eva's work, and then it was Theo's turn.

"Thank you so very much for coming this evening," he said, and I watched how his head and both hands moved as he spoke, old gold against his white shirt and dark suit and his eyes dark too and spar-kling in the light. "Eva Peres has asked me to offer her apologies. She is so very sorry not to be here, but she has been asked to give a most prestigious lecture in Madrid. She is returning to her homeland and her family—she has been invited to return—for the first time in forty years. Nothing is certain there, but she has hope. I know that those of you who are also exiles, who have had to leave everything that you love behind . . . you at least will understand what that means to her, and forgive her."

People murmured agreement but I thought how lost Theo looked, in the join between the rooms with everyone standing back. The people were all black ties and long smart skirts, and they looked like they had clean, blond children and Labradors left at home. How many of them knew what Theo meant, about leaving everything behind?

Stephen did.

Before sunrise I had to leave her. We arranged to meet by the stream that evening. But when I returned to camp, orders had been given: we were to march at noon. I had no means of seeing her, or bidding her good-bye.

But Theo was saying, "So, enjoy the pictures, and the friends, and this beautiful gallery, and thank you for coming." Everybody applauded properly then, only a bit awkwardly because of their wineglasses, and then Theo came back into the crowd. "Come on, Anna," he said, and led me up to a group and just slotted us in, quite easily.

"May I introduce Anna Ware to you?" he said. "Anna is assisting Eva and me." People were quite friendly and said wasn't it hot, and asked about how I got the job. I just said I lived nearby, and no one asked more than that, because they weren't really interested, which for once I was grateful for, but it killed that bit of the conversation so they went on by asking what did I think of the pictures?

That was easy. The pictures were wonderful. It was more or less dark by then and in the lights, instead of seeming like windows to outside, they leapt at you, telling you to look at them, making you look at them. Too much sometimes: I saw several people peer at the burned-out screaming man and turn away quickly. But mostly they had their backs to the pictures and were yakking away to one another. They only looked properly at them on their way to get more drinks; it was like they had to earn the drink, and then they could get back to talking.

A couple of people got me new drinks, and then I saw some others were starting to go. Penny came over. Crispin had told her so much about me, she said.

"Me?"

"Why not? He said you had the makings of a good photographer."

I looked at Penny hard, but she didn't sound like she was being sarcastic. It was like the only time a teacher ever said to the whole class I'd written a good essay, and meant it. And Crispin had said that! Not just to me to be nice, but to her. Then she said, "Perhaps . . . Susan misses Cecil so much. Would you and he like to come to tea someday?"

"That'd be great!" I said. Then all the awfulness came slithering back into my mind. But I couldn't say that. "Though Cecil's a bit shy. I don't know . . ."

"Well, we'll see," she said. "If Susan came with me to pick you up, perhaps he'd—Oh, hello, Crispin. Congratulations! One of your best, I think."

"Almost all done," he said. "Every time, I wonder how two hours can be quite so exhausting."

"There's all the organizing before," I said, watching Theo shaking hands and laughing with two oldish men, who looked dark and faintly foreign, like him. With the chatter softening around us I realized they weren't talking English. One of them must have told a joke, because as I watched, Theo's head tilted as he laughed out loud, and I felt the arch and flex of his back like a lovely punch in my stomach. Then they all shook hands and kissed cheeks like the French, and the men went, and Theo came over to us.

"Crispin! A success, I think. I see a few SOLD stickers already. So, are we going to go to find something to eat?"

Penny shook her head. "I'd love to, but I promised I'd drop Susan at her boyfriend's for the night, and that's over towards Hadleigh. And I'm sitting at Chelmsford in the morning. Another time, please, Theo."

"Her boyfriend's?" said Theo.

"Yes. I know most people would disapprove, old-fashioned people anyway. But . . . They met at the day center, and they do seem, well, sensible. His mother's a very nice woman."

"Well, good luck to them," said Crispin into an awkward sort of silence. Penny looked at me. "Anna, very nice to meet you. And if you need any help or anything . . . Or Cecil does. I know how busy Ray must be. We're in the phone book, under Stamford. Just ring. I mean it. Anytime."

Before I could answer she nodded to us all and made for the door but turned back just as she got there. "By the way, apparently the electricity's out over your way, Theo. That couple from Needham

Market—the architect—they said everybody's out between Hadleigh and the Waldingfields."

"Again!" said Theo as the door closed behind her. "The penalty of living in the country. Crispin, are you coming with us?"

Crispin glanced from Theo to me, and back again. "Would you think me very churlish if I said no? By the time I've done the last jobs and locked up I fear I shall be fit for nothing but my bed."

So Theo and I went alone, past Stephen and out into the street. We walked past the car towards a restaurant he knew. It was incredibly quiet, but I could feel him and me still buzzing with all the talk and wine and people.

"So, that was all right, wasn't it?" he said.

"Yes, it was fine."

"It was good to introduce you to people." He laughed. "I used to think you were well named—so wary, you were, when you came first to the stables, Anna Ware!" I looked up, and kissed him. "But now— do you have another name? A middle name?"

"Jocelyn," I said, making a face.

"It's good. About joy, isn't it?"

"I don't know. I've never really thought about it. Perhaps it is."

And he kissed me, and then we were there.

The restaurant was dark and full of candlelight. The menu was written up on a blackboard and I knew in a vague way that the food was nice, but I couldn't have remembered after five minutes what it was, because all I was really thinking about all through dinner was Theo's eyes and hands, and how much I wanted him and how much I loved him.

The car was parked under a streetlight and he stopped to feel for his keys and I said something, laughing, about how one of the patrons had said the silvery log Eva'd shot had obviously not been dealt with by a trained tree surgeon, and he went quite still, as if I'd hit him across the face.

We couldn't breathe, looking at each other in the space. Everything about him was still, as if he was afraid of what would happen if he moved. And then we were crushed together, kissing, grabbing to hold on, Theo kissing my face and eyes and neck and me arching under his mouth and hands, bent back against the side of the car.

He was kissing my collarbone and I stretched my neck against his mouth, turning my head in the swimming light. Not ten feet away Crispin, his keys in his hand, was watching us. Then he walked away up the street.

We only stopped because we had to. We got into the car and drove home with the old engine roaring through the hot black night and the smell of burning straw and warm earth rolling in through the open windows. All the streetlights were out and only candlelight flickered in a few cottage windows. Theo didn't even light a cigarette. He just drove very fast with one hand on the wheel and the other hot on my thigh with the ruffled cotton all rucked up.

The clearing and the stables were still and quiet. We went straight through the door without stopping to shut it, and then upstairs, and then Theo was pulling at the strings of my top and I was tugging at the buttons of his shirt because I wanted his golden skin against mine, and we didn't even bother with my skirt, we just went down on the sofa, snatching nips and licks and scratches, hands and mouths everywhere, until all our heat exploded.

Theo lay like the dead on top of me. I felt his quick breathing, our sweat mixed together, the breadth of his chest on mine, his weight on every inch of me, pressing down, and I knew that I would never be lost again.

There was a tiny sound by my shoulder. Drowsily I turned my head.

Cecil was standing there like a pale shadow among bigger, darker shadows. There was a splash of white across his chest, where his arm was in a sling. His eyes were like big black shadows in his pale face. He said, "I can't find Uncle Ray. Something happened."

❧❧❧

SAN SEBASTIAN IS not a large town for one so important to the region. I engaged a couple of porters and offered Lucy my arm as we passed through the harbor gate, the cobbles seeming to sway a little beneath our feet, and made our way to the San Cristóbal inn. It was nine by the harbormaster's clock, and the sign on the door of the inn declared COMPLETO in Basque as well as Spanish. It was only to be expected of the best inn the town afforded, but Lucy's arm sagged a little in mine. She was tired, I could tell, and still shaken by the voyage.

"I had no time to write ahead," I said, "but there are several other respectable inns we may try."

"To be frank, all I desire is to sleep. Short of bedbugs, I care nothing for where it is, provided I may do so."

I pressed her hand. "With luck, we shall need to go no further. I know the landlord of old. Let us go inside."

The landlord, Moyúa, recalled my face immediately and my name before I could utter it. Although he was disappointed that I had not come to revive our former association, he made an amendment in his ledger, dispossessing two travelers who had not yet arrived, and conducted us upstairs with a flourish. If he was surprised by the appearance of a half-sister of whom I had made no mention in former days, he gave no hint of it.

Our bedchambers were on different floors, and we reached Lucy's first. She turned in the doorway. "Stephen, will you forgive me if I retire immediately? I am so very tired."

"Of course," I said, taking her hand. There were shadows in her eyes, and such was the confusion of my own feelings that I could not by any means prevent myself raising her hand to my lips, and kissing it.

I too was tired, but I knew that had I gone to bed, I should not have slept. Besides, for all her avowed acceptance of the world, I preferred that Lucy had no knowledge of the visit I was about to make.

I WAS SURE that Arrage and Mercedes would be in their parlor, for their house was regulated by the town's bells as completely as the nuns' was, or as soldiers' lives are by bugle calls, and I was not disappointed. They leaped to their feet as I was ushered in by a smart young page. There was a new girl too. Business must be good, I reflected. Mercedes flung herself into my arms and kissed me soundly. Arrage had a bruise on her arm that powder only partly concealed.

"And the others?" I said.

"Dolores's mother fell ill with the stone," said Arrage, "so she has gone to Santander to be near her, and take over her girls. This is Pilar." The new girl was clad in white muslin with her hair dressed in childish ringlets, and carried a doll, but it was as much pretense as the glass jewels and the lacing that makes worn bodies seem young: I knew Mercedes would not have taken her on if she were less than twelve. "And Izzaga is upstairs with the mayor."

"And Iragarte?"

Arrage said, "She died, and the baby with her. Every Saturday I light a candle before Our Lady of the Annunciation, because she was named for her."

I pressed her hand but made no comment, and after a moment, brought out the pint of cognac that I had bought at the San Cristóbal, for a price that, had I not known Moyúa of old, I should have assumed had been forced upon him by actually paying duty at the French border. We settled on the sofa, and I was just pouring us all a second measure when a client called, and then another. A tiny movement of Mercedes's head, and Arrage and Pilar slipped off to work.

Mercedes raised her glass and breathed the scent of the cognac. "I thought we might see you back. I heard Sant' Águeda were in want of cash. That Mother Agustín's a terror for getting money out of people, my aunt says."

"You always knew," I said.

She nodded. My arm about her shoulders told me that she was still warm, and plump, and, underneath her perfume, not particularly clean, but wonderfully kind and comfortable. I recalled the night she told me—indirectly—that Catalina's child might have died. At the thought of Catalina's grief I had stumbled up from the table, quite unable to speak, and when, much later, Mercedes surprised me by coming to my room, she had played off no arts to attract or arouse me, although she was most expert when she chose, but simply held me in her arms until at last I fell asleep. In the morning she was gone.

She drank again. "So is it the child brings you back, or your Sister Andoni?"

"The child, in the main. I must make sure she is well. But I could not come here, and not tell Catalina—Sister Andoni. And I would know that she too is well."

After a moment she said, "You'd not—not be seeking to see her, or anything like that, would you? They're strict, you know. She's taken all her vows."

"No . . . I seek nothing from her. I know she has taken her final vows. I have a—my half-sister with me, who will see her on my behalf. And unless Catalina doesn't wish it, we shall travel to Bilbao. I seek—" I looked down at her, and she raised her brows. "Truly, I seek nothing else. Nothing will change, only that I shall have peace of mind, and Catalina will know that I have a care for her daughter."

She did not answer me directly but ran her fingertips up and down my thigh. It occurred to me that, of all the women I had known, she was the only one whose disgust I had never feared. "I never knew you had a half-sister. You'll not fancy an hour or two with me, then? For old times' sake? I'll warrant you manage even better now with your missing leg than you learned to with me. I can tell you've had plenty of practice since."

"I'm very tired," I said, taking her hand before it could go any further and kissing it. But it was a crooked smile that I gave her, for I was overtaken with astonishment that I had not before acknowledged—in denying it—that I might seek more than peace of mind from Catalina. "We ran into a storm, and it has been a long day." I had a sudden memory of Lucy in my arms, her face pressed into my shoulder and her heart thudding against mine, the scent of salt and ink in her hair, her small white teeth biting so fiercely on the flesh of her hand.

Mercedes, of course, saw at once what I tried not to acknowledge but, understandably, mistook the cause. "You can't tell me you don't fancy coming upstairs," she said. "Just for old times' sake?"

As I walked back through the straight, dark streets, I reflected that I could no longer ignore the feelings my body had made plain. And yet such emotion had no outlet; no possibility of satisfaction. To seek anything from Lucy was . . . impossible, and it was this bleak impossibility that had all but driven me to seek comfort of Mercedes. I so very nearly did seek comfort there. That I did not was thanks to, of all people, the mayor, who, stumbling down the stairs as he complained of his wife's frigidity and extravagance, suddenly aroused in me a distaste for the whole business, which, though fleeting, served to chill my desire sufficiently for fatigue to overmaster it. And with the cooling of my heat had come Lucy's words. They came from far away, from long ago, but her voice was clear.

I may trust you too . . . to speak the truth.

It occurred suddenly to me how well she was named, for she cast a clear light on all that she spoke of, and by her agency perhaps I could see my way.

Wondering at these things, I walked without paying attention to my road, for I knew the whole city too well to need to do so. And then I looked up and saw that I must have forgotten more than I thought, for without realizing, I had wandered from Mercedes's house to that of the nuns of San Telmo.

When I first came to San Sebastian, after that first day I had returned only occasionally to stand in the plaza and contemplate the plain stone walls and the closed, iron-banded door, and to question if my decision had been the right one. Now, in the dark, the walls looked as high as those of any citadel that I had been ordered to assault, and infinitely long, as they stretched away along the deep, narrow street on one side, and on the other stood rooted to the rock that rose up to the fort above. And yet these same walls appeared quite insubstantial in the wavering light from the lamps that lit only the corners, as if a breath of wind might scatter them to nothing and reveal the life within.

Was Catalina sleeping? Or praying alone in her cell, or kneeling in some dim chapel thick with incense? I had no idea, none at all. What did I know of her now? Nor could I any longer guess at what she was thinking about. Did she ever think of me? She must surely think of her child. To have carried a child for nine months, brought her forth in pain, given her up . . . I knew only that I could not know what she felt. It was beyond my power of imagining. And yet Catalina was my love: there was a time when I knew what each tremor of her mouth or smile in her eyes betokened. I had longed for her in silence for so many years, and now I had returned. . . . For what purpose?

I turned and walked away, and as I limped down the side street that led to the inn, I glanced up. Lucy's window was dark, the shutters open, and through the glass that enclosed the balcony, I thought that I could make out a pale figure, sitting at the window, looking down into the street.

It is a mild day, and the fever is gone. The surgeon is pleased with my progress; the new cut takes longer to heal but will be more comfortable in the end. There is nothing to worry about, he says, that getting out and about will not cure.

I must do it. I cannot hide forever.

Hanging between my crutches, I drag along my own dead weight.

My good leg tires quickly, and the foot that is not there jumps and twitches, feeling each step, each cobblestone, even as the pain cries out my loss.

Two boys rush past, laughing, with stolen apples in their hands. One knocks against me, and I spin, and fall on to my damaged knee. I think my new-mended flesh has split, so sharp is the pain. I cannot get my breath for it, or reach my second crutch, and then one of the boys laughs again, and kicks it further beyond my grasp.

A woman comes to my aid. She is strong enough to get me to my feet. "It's the barrels, you know, I keep a café. Come by for a cognac, when you've finished your walk. I've a soft spot for a soldier, for my boy was killed at Borodino."

I go on, because I will not go back, though my hands, soft through their long idleness, are chafed almost beyond bearing by the handles of my crutches, and there are blisters under my arms. The wind is cold, and yet I am sweating. It has taken me ten minutes to reach the end of this street, and I have nowhere to go after that.

When I am awake, I can think of Catalina. Sometimes she is even granted to me in my sleep, in place of the dreams that I dread. But if I go out I cannot hold her close to me, for I must keep watch with every slow step that I take. I can withstand nothing: there are running boys and drunken men, there are dogs that jump up and handcarts that push through a crowd. There are crooked stones and slippery mud, and ladies that sigh over my soldierly bearing and my broken body, so that their escorts are charmed by seeing pity in such blue eyes, and delicate horror on soft red lips.

To them, I am a pitiable object. To them, I am a cripple.

{ *II* }

THE QUESTION OF HOW BEST TO APPROACH CATALINA, SO AS to cause her neither pain nor embarrassment, had occupied me since I left Kersey, but it was the sight of Lucy at her window on the previous night that brought home to me how strange and uncomfortable the burden was that I—albeit at her urging—was about to place upon her shoulders.

We met on the morrow in the coffee room, and if she did not appear to have slept any better than I, she did not admit to it. But her eyes brightened at the appearance of the cups of rich, sweet chocolate and basket of rolls and pastries that are the Spanish breakfast, although I saw that she ate little more than she ever did. Such fare was familiar to me, but none the less welcome for that.

For some time, neither of us spoke, and when she did, even though I was watching her, her voice made me start. "So, what is it that you need me to do?"

"I think I should write to her, if you would be so good as to take the letter. And if it's possible—if you are willing—you might bring back her answer." She was engaged in pouring a little more chocolate into her cup, and I could not make out her expression. I said, "But you must say if you don't wish to do it. I realize that it is not . . . not a simple task."

"Of course I wish to do it," she said, very readily, finishing her chocolate and setting down her cup. "And I shall not mention the letter, except to her. There is then less risk of their insisting on my handing it over." She put her napkin on the table and rose. "I should like to explore the town, so shall we meet at, say, noon? The light will be too harsh by then."

And with that she smiled, took up her sketchbook and hat, and went out without another word, although whether her reticence was born of an instinct to leave me to be private with my task, or of an unexpressed distaste for what I had told her of hers, I had no means of discerning.

My own task was not distasteful, but neither was it happy. I limped upstairs and sat at the table in the window of my bedchamber. I wrote in Spanish, but what was intended to make the letter easier for Catalina to read made it harder for me to write. I cursed the clatter of brooms outside and barrels below, that made it difficult to think but did nothing to lighten the silent oppression of my memories. I wrote pages of my past sorrows, and tore them up, for had I not come to Spain simply to arrange Idoia's care? True, I had an obligation to tell Catalina that I was doing so, but for that a few lines should suffice, and would be wisest, since I feared that to write anything more would disturb my love.

But as I sat, with the sounds and smells of San Sebastian pouring in through the open window, I wondered at how I had deceived myself—or, rather, at how I had refused to know that my coming here would awaken feelings that I had thought long laid to rest. That I loved Catalina still was an article of faith, but now that I was so near to her, now that I must put my intentions into words, I wondered that I could have traveled so far under such a misapprehension of my own state of mind. It was as if I had embarked on a year's campaign with only the simplest of commands. Certainly, my concern for her child, though real enough, was the least of it: merely an hour and a compass bearing. What power, then, had given me these sealed orders, so secret that I had not known they existed, so important that only now were they opened for me?

Was Mercedes right? Had I, in my secret heart, thought to be reunited with Catalina against the rule she had accepted? Or did I seek her forgiveness, and, if so, for what? And what of the storm? I stared down at the writing paper on which my hand rested. Soon, her small brown hands would hold it. The distress and confusion of my feelings at that thought, compared to the simplicity of my former longing, made any words that I might write seem fraught with unintended meaning and equivocation.

At last, it was as much my fear of inconveniencing Lucy, as the difficulty of being faithful to love as well as to honesty, that led me to toss all my efforts into the stove and write only the plainest of tales.

Mi corazón—

My friend Miss Durward has agreed to carry this letter to you. You may speak frankly to her if you wish: she is a lady in whom I have an absolute trust.

I pray that you will forgive me for disturbing what I so dearly hope is your tranquillity, but when I heard that those who care for Idoia were in need of funds, I felt obliged to come to Spain, to assure myself of her well-being.

I think you do not know that as soon as I was able after the war, I returned to Bera, & was told by the priest of your entering San Telmo, & of your having been with child. I came to San Sebastian & spent many months here, hearing news of you, but never seeking to tell you that I was here, nor seeking out Idoia. Oh, my love, can you forgive me? Did I do what was right? I have been haunted ever since by the thought that you might have wished to know that I had at least come in search of you. But your peace of mind I cared for above all else, & knowing your chosen fate, I shrank from awakening in you all the grief & doubt that I so hoped had been laid to rest. When I heard that I had inherited land in England, I was forced to return there, but nothing has erased you from my heart.

Dearest, I have not been so selfish as to hope that I have held an equal—& equally sorrowful—place in yours. Can you find it

in your heart to forgive me? I pray that you may, for I seek your
agreement to my travelling to Sant' Águeda. I must see Idoia, &
know that she is well, for she is all that is left of you in the world.
But if for any reason you do not wish me to go, you have only to
say so.

Catalina, my love for you grows no less, with the passing of
the years. To know that you are happy is all that I ask of you, for
you could have no greater place than you already do in my heart.

Stephen

I looked up and saw that the sun was high and harsh. That all my
struggles could have resulted in so short a letter amazed me, and although there were many words that I had not set down, on reading it
over they seemed to be present too, between the marks of what I had
written.

I was reading through my words yet again when there was a knock
at the door. It was Lucy, her hat awry and her face flushed with the
sun. "Am I disturbing you?"

"No," I said, rising, "I have just finished. What do you think of San
Sebastian?"

"It is charming, though I am surprised to find so much of it new-
built, and the rest so very damaged."

I sealed the letter. "It was all but burned to the ground after we
took it from the French. I wrote to you of Badajoz, so you may imagine the scene."

She nodded, and was silent, her thoughts seemingly elsewhere.
Then she looked up at me and said, "Perhaps we should go."

I did not move, for to turn away from the writing desk to the door
seemed suddenly as momentous an act as crossing the River Nivelles
into France had once been.

"Or would you rather wait?" she said.

"No. It is only . . . a natural apprehension."

She moved, so that she might look full into my eyes, then nodded. "Of course."

But the expression of my fears had weakened them. I picked up the letter. "The portress will understand you if you speak of Catalina as Sister Andoni." Lucy took the letter. "Will you give it into Catalina's hand? She speaks English. At least, she once did. You may explain your coming, and the rest is in the letter. And I have written that you are my friend, in whom I have an absolute trust."

She put the letter into her reticule and spoke without looking up. "I understand. Thank you."

As we started through the narrow streets, between houses so tall and close-pressed that one might have been walking at the bottom of a ravine, she still looked about her, at the bustle of men and women carrying food and fuel, at mules stepping neatly over the cobbles under great, swaying baskets of fish or corn, at the high windows with shutters ready to close against sun or storm, at the dim interiors of shops stocked with bread, cooking pots, prints, linen, holy images, wine. "War is not so difficult to imagine, somehow, among streets, as it is in the fields," she said suddenly. "Perhaps because towns too are man-made. Were you here? At the sack, I mean?"

"No, it was Graham's division; we were at Bera."

"I have never forgotten what you wrote of Badajoz." She hesitated. "Or, rather, what you did not write, but I can picture."

"Can you? Should I hope that you cannot?"

"To be a civilian—to be a woman, a child—in such a place . . . One should remember that we too are part of what war is. We are not safe. And so often we have nowhere to go."

"I know," I said. "What I have seen . . ." But even to Lucy I could not give words to such things. A few more yards, and we had reached the wide plaza where stood San Telmo. Lucy stopped, and gripped her reticule to her.

The place was so familiar to me, the stones painted with so many memories, that I had not thought how the blank walls and heavy door of the convent must appear to her. A clear picture came to me, of her sitting silently at her window last night. Had she been kept awake by thinking of this task? Had the storm changed her desire to help me reach Catalina? "You need not do this," I said. "I cannot ask it of you."

"You did not," she said. "I offered myself."

My memory of the storm gave her words a meaning that she had not intended, and in the sudden confusion of my feelings I took her arm so that I might turn us both away. "No, I shall send the letter. I have no right to——"

She would not follow me. "No, you have no rights over me. But I choose to help you, if you choose to let me. Stephen," she went on quickly, "I shall meet you in"—she looked across to the corner of the plaza—"in that coffeehouse over there."

It was the place, had she but known it, where I had first encountered Mercedes. She grasped my hand. "Please do not worry if it is some time before I return. I must make myself understood, and even then it may be a while before she is free to speak to me."

Suddenly I understood the courage that she had found to do this task, but with this understanding I felt no surprise: I knew her too well. Rather, it was that my reason only now acknowledged yet more of what my feelings had long since apprehended.

I pressed her hand. She returned the pressure but immediately withdrew it, walked up to the great door, and pulled the bell.

It clanged within the walls, and after a long time a shutter opened in the door. Lucy spoke, and listened, and spoke again. Then a small door cut in the great one opened. I caught a glimpse of greenery and whitewash and stone, and a black robe, then Lucy stepped over the threshold, and the door closed behind her.

There was no more that I could do. Try as I would to be calm, I could not help but imagine what was happening within the convent walls, and a fear bred of uncertainty rose insistently in my throat. I went into the coffeehouse. It had not changed either; it was dim after the bright light outside, and the sanded floor was gritty under my halting step. I ordered a glass of brandy, sat down at a scuffed table by the window, and waited.

What would Catalina think? A strange Englishwoman, come to speak to her in a half-forgotten language, of her most painful and, for all I knew, secret past. Would she think . . . dear God! Even Catalina might think that Lucy was my mistress. Were it true, I could scarcely have offered her a worse insult. That it was not true exposed Lucy too to insult.

"Señor?" said the girl. I avoided her eye, and desired her to bring me more brandy.

The plain fact was, I could not know what Catalina would think. For so many years I had heard the tone of her voice without her words, seen again the tears that stood in her eyes without seeing her face, and even these were only pictures that I carried with me. Once, I could imagine her with me, fancy that I heard her small, deep voice, but now I had only a sense of her, for the images were darkened and worn away by time.

Lucy would speak carefully, I knew, watching Catalina's face for understanding, her own thin body still and taut with concentration, looking at my love, seeing how the light fell on her face, how her eyes flickered with grief or happiness. That, I could see so clearly. But Catalina herself had no face in my imagining. She appeared as a figure in a dream: I knew who she was without being able to see her.

Would she weep, or rage, to know that I had been so close to her for so long? Would she be indifferent? No, never that, please God. She could not be indifferent. We loved too well, too perfectly for that. And there was the child.

To be a woman—in such a place . . . One should remember that we too are part of what war is. We are not safe. And so often we have nowhere to go, Lucy had said. I understood suddenly, with a stab of fear, what she had perhaps meant. Catalina had sought safety, away from the world and its wars. But somewhere, in Bera, on the road, here in a blackened and burned-out San Sebastian not so many weeks after the war had moved on . . . Could she have suffered as so many women suffer at the hands of soldiers, and of the native scum that follow always in their wake? Could some man—Oh, God! . . . I had seen many such things.

To think of her violated made me rise clumsily to my feet and stumble outside. And then, as I vomited into the gutter, I thought, Perhaps Idoia is not my child. Perhaps she was made not of our love but of the seed of violence, of Catalina's terror and pain. If it were so, I thought, leaning my forehead against a wall, perhaps Idoia would have been better dead.

Perhaps I should have left well alone, for in coming here I had indeed endangered everything that had sustained me for so long.

I knew not how long I stood with my forehead pressed to the stones, but when someone tapped my shoulder, though I had not carried a pistol for five years, I whirled round with my hand at my side, my wooden leg catching between the stones and wrenching my stump so sharply that I cried out.

"Señor, are you ill?" said the girl from the coffeehouse.

I allowed her to coax me back inside, and give me coffee and a glass of water, for I had no wish for more brandy, even to dull the pain in my leg. Bitter and poisonous my thoughts remained, however, so much so that when I saw the convent door open, and Lucy step out into the street, I longed more than anything that we might not speak of it ever again.

As she came near enough for me to make out her expression, I saw that she was smiling, although her eyes were wet and red.

I rose and went out to her. "You saw her?"

"Yes," she said, "I saw her. I should have been here sooner, but that she desired to write to you." She fumbled in her reticule, pulled out her sketchbook, laughed a little, and at last found the letter.

It was folded merely, not sealed, and after a moment I realized that it was written on pages torn from Lucy's sketchbook.

"There was no paper, for we were sitting in the cloister garden, and she was not . . . she did not wish to go in search of some."

"Was she well?" I asked. "Did she . . . did she understand your coming? I had feared . . ."

"Of course she understood," said Lucy. "Now, shall I go away, while you read her letter?"

I had longed for news of Catalina for so many years, but such was the horror still in my thoughts that I knew that I could not receive it here, so close to the convent, cramped and closed in by the bustle of the town and the memories of fire and bloodshed. At my request, Lucy came with me, out through the harbor gate and away from the quays, to where the sand of the bay curves round from Monte Urgull and the town, towards Monte Igueldo, so that the two great green-clad rocks seem like hands, holding the Isle of Santa Clara between their fingertips.

The yellow sand was fine and dry, and difficult to walk on. After a few yards I was glad to sit down on a rock. Lucy went a little further, sat down on the sand with her skirts crumpled about her, and pulled out her sketchbook. For a moment, I smiled to realize that, for her, the two movements were one. Then I looked at Catalina's letter.

She had written only *Stephen* on the outside. I turned it over. I had to read it, and it could not be worse than my imaginings. Was this not what I had wished for—dreamed of—for so long?

I looked up again, to see that Lucy was settled, and as I watched her I thought how the small movements of her head, as she gazed first at her subject and then at her paper, over and over again, were as familiar to me as her smile or her thin, ink-stained fingers, or the grip of her arm within mine. She would leave me to make what I wished of Catalina's letter for as long as I needed.

Querido—

I can hardly write for the joy of knowing that you are alive. I had feared you killed at Waterloo, or before, & now you are here!

You will forgive me for writing in Spanish, for my English is out of practice, & I must make you understand about Idoia. It was not long after you left that I realized I was with child. For all my joy, I did not know what to do. I could not feel it a disgrace to carry your child, but my father would have killed me & your child in my womb, if he had known. But God was merciful: my father died without the grief of knowing his name disgraced. You know that we had never made many friends among our neighbours. I had to go to the priest, though I knew what he would say. I inherited a little money from my father, not enough to live on, but enough to dower me as a religious. The priest arranged for me to go to a house near the orphanage at Sant' Águeda until my baby was born, & then to enter San Telmo.

She was born on 16ᵗʰ June. I trust I shall never know another sorrow like that I suffered when they took her away. Days & nights I spent on my knees, praying for the strength to bear it, & finding none. If what you & I did was a sin, I could have received no greater punishment.

The rest you know. I have been here ever since. You were here before, you tell me. I do not know what I should have done, if you had come to me then. I know that I should have tried to see you, against the rule of our order. Now I see that God is wiser than we are, for had I known three years ago that you were here— had we met then—I fear I should have yearned to break my vows altogether. Now that I am older, I know the strength & happiness that the religious life brings. So, for all the great love I bear you, I could not wish it to be otherwise. I know that I have already been granted more joy in the world than many of my sisters. I am happy to have such joys & sorrows as memories, & to spend the rest of my days here, within the walls of San Telmo.

I beg you to go to Idoia. I know that whatever you decide to do will be wise. Your friend has told me a little of your meeting, & your friendship, & I know that she will help you. I have also given her a letter for Mother Agustín, who is the Mistress of Sant' Águeda, for although I have no rights over Idoia, they know that you are her father, & I would beg them to help you to do whatever is best for her.

I should say that when she was born, I was permitted to name her, & at my request she was baptised in memory of the Virgin. Our Blest Lady appeared to humble people, centuries ago, at a lake high in the mountains here in the Basque country, & she took the old Basque name for a pool or stream: Idoia. I knew that, if you ever heard of our child, you would understand.

Querido, we have grieved enough, you & I. Now we must accept the mercy that God has shown us. I have found peace here with my sisters, & from what your friend tells me, I may hope that you have found peace in the world. I pray for you & for our child every day—I have always done so. Now I can offer thanks, to the end of my days, for He has answered me.

Ad majorem Dei gloriam

Sister Andoni

When I tried to read Catalina's letter again, her words swam in my eyes until they filled my vision. It had been many years since I had wept so, but now, for a long time, I allowed all these sorrows, old and new, to overcome me.

When at last I raised my head from my knees, so great were the emotions that had passed through me that I felt something like astonishment to see the Isle of Santa Clara still lying in the bay, the waves still rolling past to peter out in the sand at my feet, the sentinel rocks still guarding the shore where we sat. The wind was fresh, but I did not shiver: rather, I felt the promise of it on my cheek as a sailor does. Against the indifferent elements of sea and sky I measured my sorrow, and found it less, as if time and light and the movement of the waters had worn my jagged griefs smooth, and laid them gently down at the bottom of my soul. They were not gone, but they were stilled, and to touch them brought not pain, but only its memory.

When I looked up, Lucy was no longer drawing, but watching me. My eyes caught hers. She glanced away and busied herself with her pencil again, sketching a mule cart that I had not seen before, halted close by on the wet sand while two peasants loaded it with driftwood. After a moment or two she ceased drawing, then rose, and came towards me.

"Dearest Stephen." She knelt in the sand before me and continued, in her quick voice, "Is there anything I may do to help? Or would you wish me to go back to the inn? Or to England?"

I said nothing. She hesitated, and then said, fumbling with her sketchbook, "I—she said she did not mind—I thought Idoia might like it. . . ."

She had drawn Catalina.

I wondered that I could ever have been unable to recall my love's face. Even with the white linen set like a frame about her brow and throat, even with the dark veil hiding her beautiful waves of black hair, I could not have mistaken her, though it would take many words to set down the half of what I saw in the fraction of a second in her portrait. Her round black eyes, and full, dark lips I had kissed, dreamed of, wept for. But there were lines about her eyes and mouth that I did not remember; her high cheekbones stood out above cheeks that were no longer plump and smooth. She looked older, as my looking glass told me I did also, and she looked most certainly like a nun.

"I can copy it for Idoia, if you wish to keep this one," said Lucy after a long time, and I thought her tone almost fearful, as if for her the offer, or my reply to it, had some significance.

"No," I said. "It is beautiful, and Idoia shall have it."

I thought she grew easier. After a moment she said, "So now all that remains is to go to Bilbao?"

"I suppose that is true." I got to my feet. "Even though I shall not see Catalina again, I can make sure that her daughter is well. Will you come with me?"

She took my hand, rose, then smiled as we turned our steps back towards the town.

❧❀☙

THEO HEARD CECIL too. He raised his head, looking almost drugged, and rolled sideways, and I sat up, my arms across my front. "What is it, Ciss? Are you hurt?"

"I can't find Uncle Ray. I woke up. In the minibus. My arm hurt."

"What about in the house?"

He shook his head. His eyes were enormous. "*She* might be there. I wanted to find you."

I felt around for my top. Theo sat up and pulled on his trousers. I could smell him, on him and on me, and feel a stream of his stickiness and my own running down between my legs. Then he went to the light switch, but of course it didn't work. He swore under his breath, something foreign. "Anna, would you like me to go to see what has happened?"

The way he spoke, I knew I could have left it to him. Everything would have been okay. Someone else to cope with it all. But I couldn't leave it. Cecil was family, and I needed to know, whatever it was. No one could do that for me.

I crouched down. "Ciss, can you stay here? This is Theo's house. Theo's a friend of mine. You'll be quite safe here."

Theo was pulling on his shoes. Cecil shook his head again. He was shivering. "Look," I said, "you should be in bed." I glanced at Theo, and he nodded. "How about here, while we go and sort things out? Go and find Uncle Ray for you?" Cecil frowned. I held out my hand. "Come and see. It's a nice big bed. Lots of room for you."

With a bit of persuading he did agree to be tucked up, with my sweater to cuddle, when I'd promised him that I'd be back really soon.

Even in the open the air was hot and thick, with peppery stubble smoke hanging in it. I thought I could almost hear the crackling, sort of sluggish way those fires are, like they can't be bothered to try too hard.

As we got closer to the Hall I could see a dark, golden slash of light coming through the open front doors, wavering on the stone of the porch, breaking over the steps, and fraying to nothing on the lawn. We walked towards it, quiet over the grass, not talking. The beam of Theo's torch was bright and sharp and silvery. As we started up the first step it crossed with the thin fringes of gold from the doorway and I saw his fingers go to the torch switch, but he didn't turn it off.

There was a stumbling sort of crash. The gold scattered into the dark.

I was pressed up against a pillar, smelling sharp old stone. Theo's body was hot against my back, and his heart and mine were beating in great whip cracks, slamming against each other. I couldn't see anything at all because Theo's arms were round me.

He whispered, "Are you all right?"

I nodded, scraping my cheek against the pillar.

He peeled himself off me. "Ssh! Stay where you are."

But I couldn't. My heart was slowing and I pulled away from the pillar and followed him. I was just behind his shoulder when he reached the open doors.

Dark shadows and gold ones stood and moved across the floor and up and down the stairs. At the foot of the stairs something was crumpled on the black-and-white like a stain. There was a broken lamp beside it, and a flicker of oily gold flame ran like blood across the marble. A couple of candles on the mantelpiece still burned steadily. Then I saw that the stain was Belle.

"Anna, stay here." Theo started forward, walking carefully. "Don't touch anything." He bent and pressed his fingers against her neck.

The flame shrank and died.

The swing-door opened towards us with a crash and a light flashed across my eyes. "Anna?" It was Ray. He sounded drunk. "What's happened? Has something happened? I was cleaning up Cecil's room. Where's Belle?"

Theo stood up and turned round. His torch-beam crossed with Ray's. "I am afraid that she is dead. If you wish, we could try to resuscitate her but . . . I think it would not work. Other than that, we must leave everything just as it is, and telephone for an ambulance."

THE ELECTRICITY CAME back on with a thud. It was like a flash-gun, printing everything across my brain, the colors too bright but dirty, and Cecil's sick half-dried on the floor by the door. Over and over I saw it all, the moving shadows suddenly black and dead, and everything dark and grubby yellow and red and brown, and a messy lump, which was Ray and then Theo, bending over Belle in turn and trying to revive her on the measuring marble squares. There wasn't anything for me to do, but I couldn't go away, just stood there. Over and over I thought, She'll get up in a minute and turn the lights on and talk and walk. Only we all knew she wouldn't, but they kept going till the ambulance men took over.

I couldn't get the crash out of my mind. It kept splitting my thoughts up, so that I could see what was happening, but I couldn't make it into a proper picture, into something that made sense.

One of the ambulance men reached out and closed her eyes, and stood up.

Her nose was so sharp, I saw, and her arms and legs lying on the marble were sort of snapped-looking. Where her face should have been was just bones and empty skin like a crumpled paper bag and her eyes were unseeing, blind, dead. What she'd been, what she'd done—to Cecil, to Ray, to Mum—all of it had leaked away, and there was nothing left.

An ambulance man started to put a blanket over her, but he held the top back, looking up. Ray went forward and stood there for a long time, staring at her, but what he was trying to see, I couldn't tell.

Suddenly he spoke.

"She said to me once, 'We were children. We were supposed to be safe. Away from the war. I wasn't even a woman. Not really. But I wasn't safe. And I had nowhere to go.' That was the only time she said anything. . . ."

He shook his head, as if it was all beyond him, and turned away, and the ambulance man laid the blanket gently down, over her face.

By that time there were policemen in uniforms and Theo was in the study phoning Penny to come and keep an eye on Cecil at the stables. Then I realized how drunk Ray was, but the way he talked was more than that, sort of dulled, dead-sounding, as if nothing was real. But he had got things sorted out into a story that made sense, and one of the policemen was making notes.

"Cecil fell out of a tree, the big one by the stables, you know, Anna," Ray said. "I was afraid his arm was broken. We had to wait in Casualty—Bury St. Edmunds General, Officer—and the X-ray took ages and then they had to set his arm. I'd thought we could go after that, but they wanted to observe Cecil, said he was concussed. Only he was very upset—distressed by being in hospital. So they said they were pretty sure he was all right, and I could bring him home if I watched him. He went to sleep in the minibus on the way back, and I didn't want to disturb him. And I had to sort his room out if I was going to sleep there with him. I haven't had time . . . lately. I know it's not been very . . . Anyway I kept checking on him. I thought he might wake, but I didn't think he'd get out. Not in the dark."

The undertakers when they came didn't wear uniforms, just black suits, and they were almost invisible and almost silent and I didn't want to look. They carried Belle out of the front door to their van. All that was left were a few blackish oily smears across the marble. I wondered how somewhere could feel so empty, when only a person who wasn't a person anymore had gone.

The police let Ray go with Belle. I should have been angry with him because Cecil hadn't fallen out of a tree and Ray must have told him to lie too. But I could see there wasn't really any point in saying anything, and besides, the police had started talking to us.

Theo sat absolutely still while he talked. His face was blank and unmoving except when he had to answer them, but the hand that held his cigarette was shaking and I thought, suddenly, He doesn't like police. He's afraid of them. Does he think they'll say it was us? Or is it from long ago, Nazis and things? Or from all the times you see in films, East Germany, things like *The Looking Glass War*? Was he there?

But these police weren't nasty, just bored, and a bit impatient with me saying it was Anna, not Anne, and Jocelyn without an S, and Ware, and they didn't look or talk as if they thought I'd done anything, or Theo, but the study was full of uniforms and smelled of men and sweat and still I couldn't stop seeing the oil flame and Belle all crumpled and Theo's face, and wondering if we were going to be all right. I know a bit about what can happen in police cells and the backs of vans. They went on, over and over, about where we'd been that day, and who'd seen us when, and where was Ray, and when did he take Cecil to Bury, and had we heard the minibus coming back, and did Theo go out at any time that night, or did I, and was I sure about where Ray was, and what had Belle and Ray been like, and did they drink, and when had I last been at the Hall? And where had Ray been? And where had we been? And where had Ray been? I managed to keep saying that Theo and I'd been talking at the stables when Cecil came in, and then they told Theo to stay in the study, and made me show them where everywhere was, the minibus and the kitchen and Cecil's bedroom. And then they said they needed to go upstairs.

Suddenly it was like the whole evening was cracked across—the Patrons' View and Theo's face when I came downstairs and the restaurant and the car roaring through the hot smoky dark—everything good I'd ever had . . . It was all ground down into the dirt and trampled on, and I started to cry because I was so tired I couldn't stop myself.

The swing-door banged open. Penny came into the middle of the hall. She took one look round and said, not loud but very clearly, "Good evening, Officers. I'm afraid I think Anna's had enough," in the kind of voice that makes even policemen do what they're told, though they pretended they hadn't been told, by making a great fuss when she said she would show them round and I could go back and keep an eye on Cecil because he knew me better. But she said, "That's all right, Anna, off you go," and I turned and walked down the stairs and out of the front door, and they didn't try to stop me.

It was almost morning and Theo was waiting for me outside on the lawn in the thin gray light, standing still, all hunched round his cigarette. We didn't say much on the way back and he felt very far away.

Cecil hadn't woken, but when I crept in to see him he stirred and whimpered like a baby rabbit among the blankets and his eyes opened. "Anna?"

"Ssh. It's all right," I said, sitting down on the bed and taking his hand. It was warm and soft, not feverish at all. "I'm here."

He closed his eyes again but he didn't let go of my hand, and seeing him all drowsy I felt sleep hit me too, like a wave, and it rolled me over and into bed, curled up, with Cecil nestled in the curve of my body.

I WOKE UP but the dream of what had happened didn't slip away from me, it was mine, and it stayed printed against my eyelids, yellow and red. I opened my eyes to wipe the dream away, but there was Cecil lying next to me in Theo's bed with his plastered arm awkward and lumpy lying on his chest and I knew all over again what had happened.

I slid out of bed. My skirt was creased; I hadn't even got undressed. Everything was strange and horrible, but Theo would make it be all right. I turned the door handle very gently and went out to the bathroom. From the sitting room came the smell of coffee and hot milk, the way I liked it, but on the way back I saw through the open passage window that the shadows were stretched out in the yellow light. It was late afternoon. And then, from outside, I heard Eva say, "So what happened next?"

She was back. My heart hit me so hard I couldn't move. I went close to the window and looked out. Theo was answering her. I couldn't hear the words, though I guessed they were sitting on the tree trunk against the wall, and I thought how the way his voice moved was like the lines of his face, or the feel of his fingers on my cheek. Each time, what I saw or heard or felt was like a big new print taken from the tiny, perfect image I had inside my head.

Eva was saying, "But I thought it was nearly one in the morning?"

I found if I leaned forward almost out of the window I could see them.

"It was," Theo said. "We had been out to dinner after the view. Well, you know what it's like after these affairs. And she had worked so hard. I wanted to say thank you."

I saw him stretch forward to pick up the coffeepot from the grass and pour them each some more. Then he put his arm round her and hugged her shoulders, just the way I might squeeze Cecil's, and he said, "I am glad that you are back."

"I also," said Eva.

I was holding my breath, and my heart was slamming against my chest. I couldn't think enough even to know what I was afraid of, or what I was hoping for.

Then she said, "You know that she has a crush on you, don't you?"

"Yes."

"You will have to go carefully."

"Yes."

"Oh, well, I expect it will blow over." She was drinking coffee with one hand and running the fingers of the other through the short hair at the back of his neck. My hand had touched him there, and now hers did. He had his hand on her thigh. Her fingers and his skin were the same color, lined and tough. She said, "What will happen to her?"

"Ray has telephoned Anna's mother, and she is flying back. She will have Cecil too, I think. Penny is coming to pick them up this evening and keep them until then."

"Thank God for Penny. But there is much that Anna still has to find out, I suspect. And not all of it easy."

"I know. But I am sure that she will be all right," said Theo. "She is intelligent. And she is brave."

I could feel a smile spreading all the way through me.

Eva jumped up and smashed her coffee cup into his face. "*Hijo de puta! Bastardo!* You slept with *her!*"

The cup hit Theo between the eyes and fell onto the grass. "Yes," he said, after a moment.

"How could you? You—you . . . How could you sleep with her? Here?"

He took out his handkerchief and wiped the coffee from his face. Then he got up and went to where she was standing. When he took her shoulders I saw how much smaller she was than him.

"Eva—*milácvku*—I know it should not have been here. I am so sorry. That was wrong."

"Yes, it was. But that's not important. Theo, how could you do that to Anna? How could you? Have you lived with me for so many years, and you still do not know what it does to a girl that age?"

"Eva, I know, but she is not—was not—"

"So that makes it better, does it? Just because she's fumbled around with so many boys, just because there's nothing better to do with her life, no other power that she has? Just because you would never force her, so that's all right? Well, I tell you, Todos Besnyö, it is not all right! Nobody forced me, did they? Not really, not after the first times. You don't have to force a girl who worships the ground you tread on. But it still isn't right."

"No, I know," said Theo, so low I could hardly hear him. He was sitting on the tree trunk again, hunched up with his elbows on his knees. He hadn't even lit a cigarette.

"Has she said that she loves you yet?"

I thought that he nodded, and something lurched with delight inside me, all in among the fear.

"Of course she has, God help her," said Eva. "*Mierda!* How could you? Have you any idea how she'll feel now it's finished? What she might do? When you have proved you don't love her in return?"

He was silent.

"Did you know that she is under age? Oh, of course you did. That day in the pub . . . And not even the thought of going to gaol stopped you? You don't care even if you break the law, as well as what is right?"

"It did not occur to me."

"Evidently." Eva turned and walked away from him, towards the trees. Theo just sat there, bowed over.

"Anna?" I heard Cecil calling, a bit panicky.

I went back into the bedroom. He was sitting up with the sheet wound round him. His face was pink and soft-looking and he smiled at me.

I smiled at him, but I couldn't stop myself going straight to the window. I didn't even think to worry that they might see me.

Eva had turned and was walking back. As she got near to Theo she held out a hand. He pulled a packet of cigarettes from his trouser pocket, shook one out, and gave it to her. Neither of them spoke. He shook another out for himself. Eva sat down by him on the tree trunk, and Theo struck a match and lit both cigarettes with one flame.

❧❧❧

"HOW LONG IS the journey to Bilbao?" said Lucy as we passed the fisherwomen, where they sat mending their nets on the quayside.

"About sixteen hours by road. Even with a Basque pilot, it is between six and twenty-four by sea."

"Let us go by road," she said, so quickly that I could not forbear to smile. She smiled in return. "I'm sorry."

"It is a magnificent road," I said, gripping her hand in acknowledgment of her apology, "but little better as to its condition than any other in Spain. You will be sadly tired."

"That is not important," said Lucy.

Our ostensible relationship demanded that I pay our reckoning at the inn, but as soon as we had taken our places in an open chaise, not long after dining at midday, Lucy took out her purse and repaid her share to me.

"That is generous of you," I said, the money still in my hand.

"No, only fair," she said as our baggage was loaded behind. "Although the world would also say that it would be most improper for you to pay my bills." She laughed. "For once, propriety and reason march together."

We had the intention of halting for the night at an inn that I knew of at Motrico. The road from San Sebastian passes for some little time through the steep valleys and green wooded hills that are characteristic of the region, and for that distance we spoke of the history of the Basque country and of Wellington and his army's journey through it. But for all Lucy's interest in the subject, I could not easily support my accustomed role of knowledgeable guide. So much had changed since I had read Catalina's letter that thought and feeling alike were in disarray within me. All I knew for certain, as Lucy and I set off on the road to Bilbao, was that Catalina had bade me farewell as completely as if she had that day breathed her last.

And yet I was grateful for Lucy's enquiries about roads and regiments, for they forced me to keep some control over the confusion that threatened to overwhelm my mind. In her replies she did not, uncharacteristically, always appear to have understood the finer points of whatever matter was under discussion, but such was my state of mind that I was uncertain whether it was my explanations or her comprehension of them that was at fault.

We stopped to change horses at Zarautz, and since the afternoon was advancing, and we did not wish to find ourselves driving the more precipitous road that I knew was ahead of us in failing light, we stayed no longer than it took to pole up a fresh team.

I was glad, as the road wound out of Zarautz, twisting its way up each rock, and curving round cliff faces, that I had suggested such haste. Following Lucy's gaze I observed how the afternoon light made the black slate crags appear like the redoubts of some great fort of a race of giants. The sun had gone in since the morning, although there was no sign of rain, and the piled clouds resembled so closely the rocks above which they moved that the view appeared as mountains do when reflected in still water, where that which is real and enduring, and that which is merely an image to be broken and scattered by the first breeze or leaping fish, seem to coalesce for a moment to form one true whole.

I looked again at Lucy. She was gazing about her. She had not even taken out her sketchbook, although our progress was slow enough, the road being sun-hardened into deep ruts and rendered slippery by more recent rain, for her to have laid down several quick lines describing a view, had she wished to. But, rather, it was as if her whole being had become merely the servant of her looking, and had no need of occupation for itself. I could have sworn that she had forgotten my existence.

I had not forgotten hers: it would not have been possible for me to do so. I had held her on the ship, and ever since then—long before then—into the friendship that I had been able to acknowledge, had been mixed a desire that I could not allow, on her account certainly, but as much, and perhaps more disturbingly, on my own. As so often before, I saw the turn of her head and curve of her mouth, felt her thin shoulder swaying against mine, the heat of her body, the fall of her plain gray traveling gown and the touch of her thigh against mine as the carriage lurched to and fro. As so often before, I tried to turn my mind to other things, but Catalina's letter was the only other matter on which my feelings would allow my mind to dwell.

I am happy to have such joys & sorrows as memories, & to spend the rest of my days here, within the walls of San Telmo. The words came to me, running through my heart like a stream swollen with the spring rains.

With a start that seemed to shake me as bodily as the road did, I knew that I was no longer bound to Catalina. She had given me my freedom.

We spoke little. Lucy seemed too absorbed in seeing to form words, and I knew the road of old. While it never failed to astonish me with its magnificence, I found my former delight as nothing to what I now felt, for in watching Lucy it was as if I saw the slanting slabs of now golden rock, the thick, rough green of the trees gripping it, the sea foam curling like lace about the base of the cliffs below us, all anew. As for Lucy, I fancied that so absolute was her absorption that I might have seen every wisp of cloud, every stream and wet, jewel-like pebble, reflected in her eyes.

The road rounded a shoulder of rock and the view out to sea was obscured by pine and chestnut. The sudden cool that fell across the carriage penetrated Lucy's reverie and she turned her head and smiled slowly, almost drowsily, as in the aftermath of passion. "Oh, Stephen, thank you," she said, picked up my hand, and kissed it.

I barely spoke until the road took its last twist and rolled down the hill towards Motrico.

The inn that was our destination was as I had remembered it, not large or luxurious, but clean, and bright with flowers at the windows. The landlady, I realized, as she showed us to our bedchambers, was quite incurious as to our relationship. We were lodged across a small courtyard, both our doors giving directly onto it. Grateful for the touch of cold water, I washed while I watched the doves cooing and circling about their dovecote, then went to meet Lucy in the empty coffee room, where was set out good wine, bread, and cold home-cured ham. Lucy ate more than I had come to expect of her, although her manner was still somewhat abstracted. I could eat little for the turmoil of my thoughts, and I feared that she might remark upon my lack of appetite. A glass of wine, however, was welcome, and it was rather more calmly that I could then agree to Lucy's suggestion of a walk.

Although the sky had cleared, and still showed more turquoise than indigo, the daylight was fading already in the valley, while the crags above us glinted in the last rays of the sun. The town clung to the rock about a natural harbor, a small bay so steep that half the cobbled streets were staircases, and the other half sufficiently precipitous to demand the utmost care in walking. At that hour only a few inhabitants were to be seen going about their business, feeding chickens or chopping wood. We left by the harbor gateway and walked along the shore, away from the town towards the headland, while over the shoulder of the cliffs to the east rose the moon.

The sandy shore before us was irresistible, and the tide being at the furthest ebb, for the most part we could walk arm in arm along the newly revealed sand as easily as along a pavement. It was with some surprise, therefore, that, on turning to look back whence we had come, we saw, by the moonlight that engraved the rocks and ever-shifting sea in inky black and silver, that we had come so far from any human habitation as to feel ourselves entirely alone.

We walked on, and stopped when we could go no further, out of sight of the town, towards the point where the cliffs curved round and plunged into the sea, so that the waves crashed against the rocks. There we found a resting place on the tip of a tongue of rock that ran out onto the sand and down towards the low-water mark. For the last few yards the going had been more difficult; my leg was aching, my thoughts were confused, and I was not surprised, when Lucy spoke, to hear a rough edge of breathlessness in her voice.

"We have come a long way."

"You are not too tired?" I asked, propping my stick against the rock.

"No, not at all. To have traveled so far, so urgently—until this evening, at least—and reached even a temporary destination, makes me feel—" She broke off, and waved her hands, as if no words were adequate to her sensation. I saw the quick beat of a pulse in her pale throat as she turned towards me. "Do you feel it, Stephen?"

"Feel what, precisely?" was all that I replied. I was afraid that, were I to say any more, I was liable to betray myself.

The rock was narrow: the warmth of her arm pressed against mine, and her skirts lapped against my leg.

"I suppose . . . that now what is past is behind us, all our powers—of feeling as well as thought—may be directed at what lies ahead."

I could not answer, but she mistook the cause of my silence.

"Oh, Stephen, I'm so sorry. That was unforgivable. I have no right to assume anything about . . . about what the past still means—" She broke off again, pressing her hands to her cheeks. "Forgive me, I am making bad worse."

"No—"

"I think that all this grandeur must have unhinged my mind. Pray forget it, and forgive me."

"There is nothing to forgive," I said, and if my words were ordinary enough, I saw by her startled expression that my tone was not. I felt suddenly that it was enormously important that she understand the truth I now knew. I must make her understand, now, or nothing would ever be truly easy again between us. I turned towards her and took both her hands. "Since this morning, since last night, perhaps, I have known that the past is . . . past. And . . ."

I could not say more. She was holding my hands as tightly as I was hers, but she neither moved nor spoke.

As the present swelled about me it was her fingers that seemed strong enough to make me able to continue. "My love for Catalina is in my past. I shall always love her in my memory, but memories are only reflections."

Lucy's hands gave a convulsive tremor, but her eyes held mine.

"Throw a stone into the pool," I said, "and they are gone."

I thought that she nodded. I looked at her. How had I not known, for so long, that I loved her? For love her I did, and the knowledge roared in my head. My body had known it before my mind would; now it was all that I could do not to pull her into my arms.

But she must not know. I must not tell her, for if I did, it would place too great a burden on her, in the enforced proximity of this journey. Provided that I kept silent, I might still have her friendship.

So I withdrew my hands, releasing hers. Then I rose from the rock, with some difficulty, and said, "Perhaps we should start back, before we lose the moonlight."

She rose immediately, and took a few quick steps, not back along the shore but down, to where the sea ran up the sand towards us and slipped away again. She stayed there, staring at the horizon.

She appeared to me as a silhouette against the silver, thin and black and taut.

After a long time I saw that she had turned and was walking back. I could not make out her expression, for the bright sea was behind her, but I knew that she was not smiling. For a moment she stood before me. Her hand went out to me, then she snatched a breath, put her arms about my neck, and kissed me.

So complete was this fulfillment of all the desires that I had yet acknowledged that, for a long moment, neither my mind nor my heart could find a voice to object. It was only when she took herself out of my arms that my reason was able to fight back against the sensation of her mouth on mine, of her fingers, of the heat of her breast and body. By the time she spoke, however, I was in command of myself.

"Now I must beg you to forgive me," she said.

"No!" I could say no more.

"At least I know you too well to fear that you will think of me as some would."

"You do me a great honor," I said. "But I fear that it has been my . . . well, the shadows in my past, that . . . that have engaged your pity."

"Stephen!" she said, and only the sand prevented me hearing her foot stamp. "Stephen, I love you."

No shadows now, but a great certainty overcame me, as vast and irresistible as the world's turning beneath us. It made me say, "I love you."

Her gaze was as open, as sure, as I had ever seen it, and her lack of hesitation melted my own. Such was my joy, and wonder, that I could no more have stopped myself taking her into my arms than I could have stopped the sun rising.

It was the chill of seawater curling about our feet that roused us. Lucy looked down and laughed at the advancing tide. "Are we about to be cut off? Perhaps we shall have to scramble back across the cliffs." My arms were still about her waist, and hers about my neck, and I felt a little surge through her at the notion. As we moved up the beach to escape the immediate danger of a wetting, I tried to consider the ground over which we had come, but I had been so preoccupied that I could not recall whether the high-water mark was hard against the cliffs at any point. "I am sure that we shall be safe enough on the sand, if we start back now," was all I could say.

"Given the darkness, I suppose we should settle for safety," she said, and it was my turn to laugh at her obvious, if not wholly serious, regret at such prudence. She laughed back, and our delight found its expression again in kisses. She was almost as tall as I, and though slight in my arms, I could feel the strength that she was made of, the eagerness that matched my own.

Our delight was not spent when we were at last compelled by the tide to release each other, but I found that my joy was not lessened by such an intervention of the elements, for this love, I realized, as Lucy pointed to how the cliffs across the bay also curved down to meet the sea, did not depend on propinquity, or circumstance, or the opportune waxing of a moon. It seemed quite natural to discuss the geological formation of the cliffs—about which Lucy knew a good deal more than I—as we started back along the shore, as natural as it did to find that my arm fitted about her waist and hers about mine as easily as if it had been the thousandth time and not the first that we had walked thus. It felt natural too to express my content with kisses.

But through my delight I heard a dog barking, and a man whistling to it. I let go of Lucy. She was surprised, even when she realized the cause of my withdrawal, but linked her arm readily and decorously into mine. Decorum notwithstanding, I could not forbear to grip her close to me, so that I could feel her every movement as we made our way.

"Never mind," she said, lacing her fingers into mine. "We shall be much more comfortable back at the inn. And we have the whole night before us."

"What?"

After a moment she said, "You are thinking, I suppose, that I ought not to have said that."

I did not pretend to misunderstand her. "No, perhaps not. Although I should not like to think that there is anything we ought not to say to each other. A few kisses, here on the shore, in the dark, are . . . well, you would not believe me if I said I was unwilling, would you? But such a thing as you suggest ought not to be thought of."

"Why not?"

"Because . . . Must I spell it out?"

"You said yourself that there is nothing we ought not to say to each other. And you know that you cannot shock me."

I said nothing, for how could I begin to explain? Ignorant of the world and the creatures in it she was not; I saw that her innocence was of a more fundamental sort, for she spoke only as if it were a question of transgressing society's rules. She had no idea of the true nature of what she suggested. Young men at such a moment allow themselves to acknowledge no loss of innocence, only the claiming of their masculine birthright. But I had seen in Catalina, in the sisters, the wives, the mistresses of friends, in Mercedes and each new girl who arrived, how no woman remains unchanged when she gives up that innocence, whether it is willingly or unwillingly, with benefit of clergy or unobserved, among the chaos of war.

My thoughts having fortified me thus, my defenses were promptly breached from within by my own desire. My arm tightened about her, and she turned into my grip with all her eagerness so renewed that, had I been ten years younger, I should have pulled her down with me onto the sand and sought to fulfill our desires there and then. It was fortunate for us both, I realized, that I was old enough to know that no degree of passion can be wholly sustained on rocks and sand, in a cold wind, with salt water approaching. I laughed at the thought.

She was looking at me with narrowed eyes, and then she too laughed. "No, I know. You are quite right. We shall be far better off in a comfortable bed back at the inn."

"No!" I said, moving away from her, since her presence in my embrace seemed so disastrous to my resolution. "I will not do it. You cannot ask it of me."

"I can ask it of you, and you may refuse me," she said, and held out her hand. "Dearest love, let us not quarrel about it."

"Quarrel? Not for the world," I said, taking her hand in both of mine. She was smiling, and I longed to kiss her black lashes, to outline her red lips, feel her white teeth and her tongue on my fingertips. But I held her at arm's length and found just enough release in kissing her hand to be able to say, after a moment, "Though I should still love you, if we quarreled from now until doomsday."

She laughed and started to walk again. "Good. Then I need have no fear that you will cease to love me if I say that I see no reason why—while we are here in Spain—we should not live as man and wife."

I had not been expecting a renewed attack, and my guard was in disorder. For some moments I could muster no more formidable a response than yet another *no*.

She continued. "Were we in England, your scruples about my reputation, and yours, would be understandable. Besides, I have no desire to offend, only to be allowed to order my own life as I think best. But while we are here, who is to know?"

We were walking along the harbor's edge. Already the moon was lying just above the further cliff, and we would be plunged into full night as soon as we started up the lane to the inn.

"Dearest, you can have no idea of what you are suggesting," I said. "If I thought that you would marry me . . ." The image that came to me with these words, of her standing in the hall at Kersey looking about her, was so strong, so much, I knew suddenly, at the heart of my love for her, that I could not continue, but in my confusion, this strange conversation seemed no more substantial than that image: both were painfully vivid, and yet no more real than dreams. It was only my continued, halting step on the cobbles that reassured me that I was still in the world.

She gave a small laugh, it seemed of embarrassment. "Oh, are you remembering what I said of—of marriage at Ixelles? You must make allowance for, well, for irritation of nerves. How I contrived, in all those months, not to murder my brother-in-law, and dear Hetty with him, I shall never know." She stopped, then went on, with a little constraint in her voice. "It is some time since I have realized that . . . that a marriage need not be as theirs is. I have seen that a marriage is made by the parties to it, not by the society that appears to rule what such an alliance should be. If a man and a woman decide that their lives will be better spent together than apart, and are left alone to decide for themselves on what terms they wish to live with each other . . . I can see that a marriage like that could bring great happiness."

It took me some yards—some moments—to comprehend Lucy's meaning, but when I did, I hesitated only for as long as it took me to grasp her hand, and ask her to be my wife.

She stopped walking, and turned towards me, but for a long moment she said nothing, and fear began to shake me. I loved her so much, she was so necessary, I knew now, to my happiness, that were she to refuse me, I should lose all hope of finding peace. No new cities or old friends, no ceaseless journeying, no work, no wine, no woman, no child . . . none of these would fortify me against the tide of darkness that awaited me beyond her nay. I could not believe in the heaven or hell that I was taught, I knew not what would come, only that even oblivion would be preferable to continuing this life, if she were to refuse me.

"Stephen?" She was staring at me, frowning.

I could bear it no longer. "If—if you are to refuse me, I pray you to do so. It need make no . . . no difference to our journey. I hope our friendship is too old to feel any embarrassment. But, please, tell me, if you are decided."

"I must make you understand." Her words did nothing to reassure me, although she still gripped my hands, and in that gesture I tried to find hope. Then after a moment, she continued. "My hesitation is only—Oh, I have not the words!" In her gesture of exasperation she dropped my hands. "Women are not allowed to draw the human form as it is made—" Even in my fear, I could not help but laugh at her choice of words. She knew the cause of my amusement, but continued. "And, likewise, I have no means to speak directly—practically—of such matters in marriage, either."

"Are you afraid of what marriage entails?" I said, my voice unsteady.

She took one of my hands and squeezed it. "Dear Stephen! Not afraid, not exactly. It is only that . . . Well, I would rather know everything of what being a wife means before I consent to be one, even yours, dearest love. Then we shall be equal in our desire to be married."

"I understand you," I said, and I did, but understood too that to win her, for whom I would have laid down my life, I must ruin her. And if I not only ruined her, but disgusted or even frightened her, perhaps I should lose her forever.

We saw no one as we made our way back up the lane, for we had been longer on the seashore than I had thought, and there were few lights still showing in the windows. At the inn, a lad in the taproom nodded sleepily to us, but we saw no other as we made our way through into the courtyard.

We were still in the open when she said softly, "Well?"

I tried to collect myself. The thought of what she proposed had all but overwhelmed me, but now that we confronted the moment, not her fear but mine flooded me, fear of her disgust at the sight and touch of my maimed body.

All my chivalry, I thought suddenly, all my scruples as a man of honor . . . did they come to this, that I would not lie with the woman I loved, because I feared her shrinking? Mrs. Barraclough's words forced themselves into my mind. Even the thought of my wounds had been more than she could face.

"Dearest, consider," I said, in a low tone, for though we spoke in English, I could not avoid the sensation that we were overheard. "Consider, and forgive me, for I must be frank. I would . . . I could never forgive myself, if I caused you distress, or pain. The first time is—is not always easy."

"No, I know," she said. "Hetty said . . ." She turned away and put her other hand out to open the door of her bedchamber. "Oh, Stephen, I am not setting you some sort of test. If you are truly unwilling . . . if it will make you unhappy—"

"Not unhappy!" I burst out. "How could I be unhappy, if I had you?"

She took a few steps into her chamber, drawing me with her. "Nor unwilling?"

I allowed her to lead me. "No. Except . . . Well, we have spoken much of what war does—"

She turned to look back at me, and the light from the courtyard lantern fell on her face. She smiled and said, "I love you. Nothing, of what you are, will change that."

"Oh, my love," I said, and took her in my arms. "If you are willing, I have not the strength to say no. Nor the desire," I went on, between kisses. "You are all that I desire."

For all the ease and friendship that had grown between us in the past few days, I nonetheless feared embarrassment for her as well as myself, but found none, and when our growing desire could not be satisfied by simple kisses in the candlelight, I sat beside her, on the edge of the bed, and put a hand to the lacing at the back of her gown. "May I?"

She nodded, and I kissed the back of her neck, where as always many soft strands of hair had escaped their pins since that morning, while I plucked her laces undone and parted the edges of her gown. My passion was born of my love, I thought, so I had no fear that it would overcome my care for her comfort.

She stood, stepped out of her gown and petticoats, and turned away to fling them over a chair with no more coquetry than if she had been alone. As I went to her she reached up and unpinned her hair so that it fell about her shoulders and my hands and down her back, breathing salt and sea air and her own warmth. She turned in my arms and our mouths met. My hands went to the fastening of her stays. I thought that she started, but then she laughed a little, and her hands went in their turn to the buttons of my coat, so that we were equally engaged.

With Mercedes's help I had long overcome any practical difficulties of my disability. But now my earlier fears, suppressed by joy, became once more insistent. "What is it, Stephen?" said Lucy, from where she lay, wearing only her chemise, propped on one elbow among the pillows. I had sat down to remove my boots. "What are you worried about?"

"Only . . ." I could not say it. To cover my confusion I pulled off one boot, and tossed it across the room. Lucy glanced down.

"Is it your leg?"

I nodded.

She put her hand on my thigh, as tenderly as a mother touches her child's brow. "Come and lie with me, Stephen."

Slowly, I took off the other boot, trousers and drawers, unbuckled the straps of my wooden leg, and pulled off the sock that clothed my stump. She did not flinch. Nor, when I pulled off my shirt, did she blink or blush, even for a different reason, but moved to make space for me beside her. I slid in under the covers, keeping my leg away from her.

"Love, you need not hide your wound from me," she said.

"It is not pretty."

"But I must know all of you," she said, and knelt in the middle of the bed, her chemise crumpled about her and slipping from one shoulder. Then she turned back the covers and looked at my damaged leg.

For a long time she did not move, and for all that the image of her face had filled my nights as well as my days for so many weeks, I could not read her thoughts. Perhaps she had none: her regard was as exact, as impersonal, as I had ever seen it when she gazed at a face, or a rock, or a battlefield.

Then she reached out, and touched each mark, one by one. She touched the straight lines of the surgeon's cuts, and the ridges and furrows of damaged flesh that had healed as best it might, each scar faded by time from bloody darkness to broken silver. She touched all these, quite gently, but with the same sureness in her fingers as in her gaze. Then her hands came to rest on the calloused stump, thick and dark and ugly, and yet what wood and leather could grip, and make my life possible. She sat, in silence, holding the stump, cradling the form and image of my wounds.

She looked up, and saw the tears standing in my eyes. "I have not hurt you?"

"No, oh, no," was all I could say. "No one . . . I had not thought it possible."

She smiled, and I saw that the points of candlelight in her eyes were so very bright on account of her own tears. I held out my hand. "Dearest love, let me kiss you."

She lay back against the pillows beside me.

I had thought my passion too much formed by my love to go beyond what she wished. But as I held her, love itself all but overwhelmed me. The lawn of her chemise might have been cobwebs for all it formed a barrier; she might have been as naked as I. I could not prevent myself pulling her body to me.

My urgency startled her, and I drew away.

"I'm sorry," I said, but the candlelight that fell on her face as I moved showed me no shrinking or distaste in her expression. The lines about her mouth, and about her narrowed, observant artist's eyes, had softened, and she smiled.

Passion demanded that I take her on the instant. To possess her wholly was all that I desired. But what I had learned of gentleness with Catalina held me back, and what I had learned of woman's pleasure from Katrijn came to my rescue. If I could show Lucy what pleasure there could be for her, if I could order and control my own desire, then how much greater my delight would be when I brought hers to match it.

Gently, while kissing her, I stroked her neck, her shoulders, the firmness of her arms, her thin wrists. Gently, I kissed her ink-stained palms, and she touched my lips and ran her fingers through my hair. Gently, I unlaced her chemise and parted the yielding cloth.

Her breasts were slight. When I first brushed them casually, as if in passing, she gasped, and her eyes opened where they had been half shut. She smiled, uncertainly.

"Do you wish me to stop?" I said.

It was only a small movement with which she shook her head, and so it was very slowly that I slid my hands round once more to touch her breasts. Her eyes were closed again, her breath slow, but when I bent my head to kiss her there, she gave a small sigh, and brought her arm round to hold me, until my head was resting in the crook of it.

Her skin was fine-grained, her body no soft, voluptuous pillow for a man to lay his head on, but firm under my hands, each muscle close-coupled to the bone, and the flesh a taut, neat covering. She in her turn ran her hands over me as if they were eyes, feeling curves and hollows, bones and skin, in my shoulder, my cheek, my arm.

She knew well enough what I would be about. What she had not expected, I realized, was that I should use my hands as I had learned to do. I approached slowly, adoring the slight swell of her belly, and then for a long time I simply held her there. When I began to stroke her, she started, then slowly stirred, puzzled but accepting, and then breath by breath, eager in this strange new country, as she was in all the others I had shown her.

My longing to possess her was almost unbearable, yet I dreaded causing her pain. But I might not have her without doing so. At least I could first make it as easy for her as I knew how. Only when I felt her open to my fingers, only when I felt her breathing surge and quicken, and looked up to see her face drowsy and absorbed in her own pleasure, did I enter her.

She did not cry out, but her head turned convulsively from side to side on the pillow, over and over again. I withdrew.

"Don't stop," she said, and raised her head to kiss me.

"But I cannot bring myself to hurt you."

"It is done, or almost done. And I wanted it."

"My love, are you sure?"

She nodded, but I could feel that all the eagerness and delight had gone from her. Her body was once again firm and cool, and when I approached her again, there could be no mistaking that she braced herself.

It was, as she said, done, or almost. But I could not bear to try to possess her thus again, unhappy as she was, and filled with the fear of more pain. I kissed her gently, and knelt back.

There was blood on her flesh.

So little blood, I thought, for so great a change. But it must not stay on her. Wounds must be helped to heal.

I bent, and kissed the blood away from her, as gently as I might. It was almost sweet on my lips. She gasped, but soon I felt her softening. Her skin warmed, and her breathing quickened as she moved and opened beneath my kisses.

Sooner than I would have thought it possible, her body seemed to understand, and then to be so wholly overtaken by sensation that it was in some haste that I wiped the sweetness from my lips and returned to her.

This time she welcomed me, her kisses my reward for my gentleness, her growing passion license for my own. When at last I possessed her completely, I allowed joy to overcome me, so that, before I was overwhelmed, I was filled with wonder that she and I could have found such happiness.

The roar of cheers and crash of music in my ears is solid and unwavering, like the haze of sweat and sooty dust through which we all move. I stumble, in trying to get between solid human bodies and iron railings.

Cavalry. From the southwest. On they come, all order lost, their sabers out, cutting at whatever man, woman, or child is within range. Among the hoofs a lad falls, a girl goes down screaming, I try to seize a bridle, but the rider's eyes are blank. He does not see me. I am knocked aside like a shadow by a huge man seeking weapons, and I fall.

I can see nothing but the burning dark, and feel nothing but blows.

I struggle to my knees, into a hail of cobbles, bricks, and iron bars. There is a woman lying on the hard stones, her hands pressed to her breast and blood oozing. Her face is turned away, but I am certain it is Catalina's, it must be. I cannot touch her. I cannot help her.

Then she rises, and I see her truly.

It is Lucy, and she is whole and smiling.

"Stephen?" She holds out her ink- and paint-stained hand. "Did you not know? The child is found."

III

THE CLANK AND SPLASH OF THE COURTYARD WELL WOKE ME from a dreamless sleep into early light and the soft patter of rain. I raised myself on one elbow and saw that Lucy slept still, lying close to me on her side, with her nose pressed into the pillow and her chemise creased about her. Her unbound hair spilt over the linen in dark strands and tangles. For a long time I was content to watch her sleep, feeling the warmth of her and the rise and fall of her slackened breath, smelling smoke in her hair, and the faint tang of salt that recalled the ship, while the light grew brighter and the rain moved off.

She stirred, then stopped, as if the movement hurt her, and a little frown of puzzlement flickered across her brow.

I lay down again, that I might hold my love close and comfort her.

She stirred again at my touch, a small but deliberate movement, as if she sought to understand what she felt. Was it pain? Was it repulsion? Fear?

Oh, God! What had I done? What madness had overcome me? For madness it must have been: I could not call it love, that could do her such an injury.

She felt my withdrawal and dragged herself to sit upright, pulling her chemise down about her as she looked at me where I lay. Had I not feared to disgust her still further, I would have tried to draw her into my arms and kiss away her doubt. As it was, I too sat up, and we regarded each other.

Finally I said, "Last night . . . I fear that I hurt you."

"Only for a moment," she said, but there was still doubt in her eyes and retreat in her body. Suddenly she said, "But in the light of day you are regretting it."

"Only because I love you," I said, my voice shaking. "I have done you a great injury."

"Is it . . . Is it only that?" She said no more, and then she looked away, seeming to shrink against the bedhead, and continued in a low tone, "Now that I am no longer . . . I fear that everything is changed between us."

She appeared so thin and uncertain in the light that was beginning to creep through the shutters that I found I was holding my hand out to her, palm upward, although whether I was reassuring her, or begging her, I could not have said.

"Lucy, everything has changed, and nothing. I love you, and long more than ever to be married to you." Still she looked silently at me. "But it is for you to say how we are to go on. If you would prefer not to . . ." Fear suspended my voice.

She began to laugh, so suddenly that I started. "Oh, dearest Stephen, you are a fool! You have shown me a new land, and yet you still fear that I regret it!"

There was no more to be said. We celebrated our betrothal by taking possession of each other, with no pain, but only joy, as the inn and the village woke around us.

The journey to Bilbao was long, and the showers that came in from the Atlantic made us stop for the hood to be put up more than once, but it was far from tedious. The road clings higher on the cliffs as it runs west, and the grandeur of the scene through which we drove did now call Lucy's sketchbook forth. I watched as her gaze took it all in: an ancient chapel standing hermitlike on a rock out to sea; sun falling like rain between the straight trunks of pine trees; a river that cut its way through a ravine, only to open into a wide green delta and run placidly into the bay. The presence of the driver on the box made gestures of affection much beyond smiles ineligible, but my content in her company—whether she spoke, or simply drew unceasingly—was too great for me to trouble to resent the restrictions of propriety. Not even my newfound eagerness for nightfall could make me enjoy these hours the less.

We dined on the road, at Guernica, and arrived in Bilbao at too late an hour to do more than direct the driver to seek out the inn—comfortable, but private—which I knew would be most suitable to our needs. He began to urge the tired horses down the last hill and through the gate into the twisting streets of the old town.

Lucy was peering down an alleyway towards a lighted plaza. "Is that the cathedral?"

"Yes. We must therefore also be near Sant' Águeda."

After a moment she said, "It is no small matter, going to find your daughter, I think."

"Certainly, it is my urgent duty," I said, and only on hearing them spoken thought that my words sounded cold, although they were true to my feelings. I was glad to look up and see that we had reached the church of Sant' Anton, which stood guard by the bridge that led to the newer, quieter part of the town, and to the inn at the sign of El Moro that was our goal.

Our bedchambers were next to each other. Lucy welcomed me into hers and, when we had loved, fell asleep in my arms as readily as a child, with her naked back curled into my body, and her hair tickling my chest. But I could not sleep, for on the morrow I would see Idoia.

For all these years, I had known that I had once begotten a child rather as I knew that I had once had a mother: their absence was all the knowledge that I had of their existence. It was as Catalina's child, as my last link with my love, with Spain, with so much of my history, that Idoia found what little place in my mind she had held. It was my duty as her father to make sure that she was cared for, just as it was my duty to care for my land and my people at Kersey, and Lucy had made me see that I could not properly discharge my duty to her from a distance, any more than I could leave Kersey forever. Then I had read

Catalina's words of such grief, bred of such love, that I had felt some of that grief, and that love, stir within me. Idoia lived in my mind now, as only Catalina had lived there when I had resolved to come to Spain. I lay, feeling Lucy's breath brushing my hand, and I could no longer deny that I had both feared and hoped that love of Catalina would divide me from the wintry nights of my duty to Kersey, and keep me in Spain. Perhaps that had, after all, been the true cause of my deciding to come to San Sebastian, and perhaps Lucy had known it. And yet for all the love that I now knew she felt, she had come to Spain to help me. Had she wished only, selflessly, to promote my happiness, as well as Idoia's? Or had she known—as I had not—that it was only in returning to Catalina that I had any hope of laying my old love to rest, so that this new love might grow in its place?

The conviction that this was so came over me, as a man looking out of a window may himself be suddenly immersed in sunlight. Everything about me and beyond me appeared changed by that light, and I knew that its cause was sleeping in my arms.

As if my thought penetrated her sleep, Lucy moved, and I gathered her to me with a thrill of joy that she was mine, and of fear that I now had so much happiness to lose. I longed to take her home to Kersey, as I had never longed to go there alone, and yet these clandestine days of Spanish freedom were like wine to my senses. I longed to get her with child, to feel our love stirring within her, and yet I would know always that I had another child far away.

It was long hours before I slept. But when sleep did come it was as if I held a powerful talisman. Lucy lay breathing softly in my arms, and no dreams came to trouble the rest that I found with her.

I was awoken on the morrow by all the racket that a city inn can make in the early morning: milk churns, seagulls, hawkers, carriage wheels, hoofbeats, the cry of a diligence driver, dogs barking. I was reminded of L'Arc-en-ciel and marveled at the changes that so few months had wrought in my life, and in Lucy's.

Her eyes were still closed, but under my hands I felt her body awaken, and then her back arched in a stretch as easy as a cat's as she turned to face me. I kissed her on the nose. "Good morning, my love."

She kissed me in return and then reached her arms above her head to stretch again. I moved a little away from her warmth and the curve and flex of her body, and turned onto my back, for I would not on any account oblige her to acknowledge my desire if she did not wish to.

She did acknowledge it, however, moving towards me again, and then sliding one long leg over me. The silk of her inner thigh as it slipped over mine was more than I could bear, and I would have set about engaging her own desire, if she had not astonished me by moving to lie bodily on my chest.

I was taken aback, for until now she had been in the main the recipient of my attentions, rather than the instigator of her own. For a moment we lay together, while the pressure of her breasts and hips on me, the touch of soft, warm curves and creases that I might now explore more easily, flooded me with such desire that she felt it, and laughed.

Her laughter stopped. Instantly I stayed my hands, but she looked only thoughtful, almost intent. Then she moved, in a flurry of her thin limbs, so that before I could determine what she was about, she was kneeling above me. She appeared a little surprised at herself, but welcomed my hands, and it was not long before the quickening of our desire demanded its fulfillment. Gently, I showed her what was possible. Gently, enquiringly, like a beautiful cat stepping beyond a newly unlocked gate, she took possession of me, her body understanding so soon what she was about that I could watch and feel her courting her own desire and mine, gaze at her flushed face, her tousled hair, her arching body, until she claimed her delight with a cry of triumph.

When we awoke again it was full day. I kissed her brow and each of her drowsy eyelids, then sat on the edge of the bed, strapped on my wooden leg, and put on only as many of my discarded garments as would serve to get me back to my room, and leave her to be private. I was accustomed to women's lives, from living with Mercedes and the girls—for they had soon forgotten to shelter me from the women's matters from which many men shrink—but Lucy had not even brothers. What had passed between us, I reflected, my fingers shaking on my buttons at the memory of her face, and her tangled hair, gave me no right to embarrass her.

"Is it time to go already?" said Lucy, sitting up. "I shall dress as quickly as I may."

"I am going only to bespeak some breakfast, and leave you to your toilet," I said. "But there is no need for you to dress at all, should you not wish to do so."

She stood up. "You do not wish me to go with you to the orphanage?"

I halted, my hand on the door. "I would not ask it of you."

"But if I said I were willing, that I should like to?"

"We shall be speaking in Spanish. I fear that you would be bored."

"I could not be bored in a matter that so closely concerns you and Idoia. But if you would prefer me not to be there, then I shall go out drawing." She pushed back the sheets that had covered us, and her bare feet struck the floorboards with a thud. As she stood up, the light from the window slanted across her unembarrassed nakedness. She was all bone and muscle, and the tendons in her neck stood out like whipcord as she caught sight of my expression. "What is wrong with that?"

"I confess, the streets are so busy, and the population so mixed—this is a port, after all, and a manufacturing town—that it would be safer for you not to go about unescorted. I fear that you might find yourself in some difficulties."

"Are you telling me that I must not go out at all? We are not Mohammedans."

"No, indeed," I said, smiling at her, but she did not smile back.

"Then let me come with you."

I looked at her, and her narrowed eyes met mine and held them.

To look away was to capitulate, and then I would be lost, for I must not let her go with me, but I could not tell her why.

"Stephen?"

I shook my head.

"Then I shall go out drawing," she repeated, and went past me to where her discarded garments lay across a chair.

I wanted to reach out, grip her arms, make her understand that I would not—could not—let the world do her harm. I wanted to shake sense into her body and her brain. I moved towards her, and she flinched backwards, putting up her arms with a gasp to ward me off.

What was I doing? What had I done? I backed away, stumbling, for I knew I must not be near her, for fear of what I might do.

She reached for her chemise with shaking hands. Only when she had put it on did she speak again.

"Why will you not let me come?" Her voice was calm, as if she refused to acknowledge that I had injured her in thought if not in deed.

"As I say, we shall be speaking in Spanish," I repeated, but my voice sounded lame even in my own ears.

"It is not that. You have only just thought of that. No: it is that you do not wish to appear to the nuns—the guardians of your child—with a lady who might be taken for your mistress. You fear that they will not believe me to be your sister."

I would not agree, and I could not in honesty deny it. Dumb, I remained by the door.

"I knew it!" she cried. "You cannot just love me. I cannot simply be your love, as you are mine. You must give me a name that the world will understand. I am not a wife, so I must be a mistress, a secret, shameful female, kept hidden lest anyone set eyes on me that might be offended." She snatched up her stays and stood fastening them as fiercely as if they were the cause of her anger. "Well, Stephen, I do not wish to live hidden, even until we are married."

I tried to marshal my wits. "Of course not, I had no idea of such a thing," I said, coming back into the room. "I thought only that, since to enquire after Idoia's well-being requires some delicacy, it would be wise to approach the orphanage with as simple an account of myself as possible."

She dropped her petticoat over her head, wrenching the strings to tie it as she turned on me. "So, my existence complicates the matter, does it? The world may be allowed to decide what I am? Oh, can no one simply see, without judging? Though we say nothing, for it is no one's business but our own, they must still do their sordid calculations of place and time, and condemn me—me, mind, not you—as a fallen woman, not fit to breathe the same air, not worthy to be seen or listened to. And you . . . you allow it! You play their game. You would hide me, *me*, whose breasts you kissed, in whose arms you cried out. You are ashamed of our love. You allow them to make you so!"

The anger that I had hitherto almost held in check suddenly flared, fueled by the sweet memories she had taken to use. My arms hurt, my palms stung, and from my guts surged a great anger at her folly, at her thin limbs that she must learn were not invulnerable, at the slight, soft swell of her belly that she would not call tender. She must know her own weakness. I grasped her arm, and wrenched her round so hard that she cried out as I seized and held the other with all my strength.

"So, what would you have me do?" I shook her then. "I cannot change the world, however much you wish me to. I cannot do that. I love you, I would do whatever you want, but we do not live in a desert. Do you wish the nuns to condemn me as unfit to know of my daughter? Do you wish to be slighted, to be scorned?"

"At least we would be honest!"

"But what would you have me do?" I cried. My fingers bit into her flesh and bone, and I made no attempt to stop them, though she tried to pull herself away. "To lose Idoia *honestly*? To expose you *honestly* to the spite of the whole world? To watch other men thinking they may eye you, follow you, touch you? I tell you, you cannot ask it of me! You cannot come with me to Spain, travel in my company, share my bed, give me joy beyond all expression . . . and then betray the purpose of our journey, and refuse my love and my care for you. I tell you, I cannot do it. I am not made thus. If you want my love, if you want me to help Idoia, you cannot deny my care for either of you."

"If your care means my living hidden, then I do not want your love," she said, and wrenched herself out of my suddenly slackened grasp. A great fear welled up within me as she stood, rubbing her arms. I could see the red marks of my fingers. Soon they would be bruises, and I had made them.

At last I said, "What do you want? What would you have me do?" She looked up, her face somber. "I cannot cease to love you, or to care for you, but short of that, you may command me as you wish, to leave, or stay."

She came a little nearer, still holding her arms, so that her fingers appeared livid gray against the dark bruises that my anger had printed on her flesh. I remembered the blood on Nell's flank and knew some of my anger—my brutality, I must call it—to be born of my own fear. And with the memory came remorse. I had injured my love because she would not accept my protection from the injuries of others.

At this thought the last hot dregs of my fighting rage leaked away, leaving me sick with bitter mirth. I made to take her hand, and she did not resist me.

Lucy seemed to sense my amusement, such as it was, though I did not utter it, and she looked at me uncertainly. In her glance I saw what my anger and incomprehension had not before allowed me to know: that she too was frightened. At last, she said slowly, "Go, and find Idoia. Take my drawing. I shall be here when you return."

For a moment I looked into her eyes. "You will stay? Until then?"

"Yes. You have my word."

I bowed and kissed her hand, took up the picture in its boards, and went out.

I did not stay to break my fast but dressed, disarranged my bed as if I had indeed spent the night there, and set out at once, limping my way through the crowded streets. There was some distance to go, back across the bridge and into the old town, and fear that I had lost Lucy forever dragged at my halting steps and blurred my vision. For some time the crowds seemed nothing but an impediment to my progress, but as bodily movement steadied the turmoil within me, I could not help but begin to notice again the crimson and scarlet and yellow of vegetables heaped upon a cart, the black hats like horns of two priests who stood and gossiped against the pale gold of the cathedral wall, the flash of doves in the morning light, wheeling about a bell tower. These were things I had learned to see through Lucy's eyes, I realized, with a pang that cut through my confused thoughts, just as I had learned to observe the ripples of bright ribbon stitched about a gypsy's skirt, the red and brown of the brick and timbered houses with their wooden arcades below, the mules with their bowed heads, the shadows in the empty cheeks of a beggar. Lucy had taught me to see such things, and if this were the last day that I ever saw her, she would still have changed me forever.

The orphanage of Sant' Águeda was a large, old building built of gray stone, with thick walls, from which came no sound of children. It was difficult to believe that Catalina's child lived and breathed within. I presented my card and asked to speak to the religious to whom Catalina's letter was addressed, Mother Agustín. Without much delay I was led for some way down a red-tiled corridor and into a small office where sat a tall, black-clad nun at a large desk, with almost as large a ledger open before her. Hung on the wall above her was a crucifix of moderate size, and in a corner stood a small prie-dieu.

I bowed, introduced myself, and presented Catalina's letter. My Spanish had improved with recent practice, and I described fluently enough how, although the exigencies of war and my duty as a British officer had separated me from my daughter before I knew of her existence, I felt obliged to assure myself of her well-being, although—I bowed again to Mother Agustín—now that I was here, I felt sure all was well. And, of course, I should like to discuss the question of assisting the orphanage in its work.

"It would be a pleasure to discuss such a matter. And, of course, we hope that you will find your daughter to be satisfactorily cared for," she said. "If you wish it, I shall call for her to be brought to you, and you shall see for yourself."

I had not thought that so simple a request could so unnerve me. "Yes. That is, I think I should see her, if it is possible."

"Certainly," she said, and reached for a small bell that stood on her desk. While we waited for it to be answered, I listened with only a tithe of my attention to her account of the system of endowment and patronage that supported the orphanage, for I could not escape the knowledge that within a few minutes, at my request, it would be Catalina's daughter—my daughter, my child—who would step over the threshold and into this room. And one part of my mind and heart could do nothing but circle about the emptiness that would be all I could look forward to if I lost Lucy.

Mother Agustín was describing the criteria for admission, and the education of the girls in the Christian—by which she meant, of course, Roman—religion and in domestic skills. "We have a hundred girls here, but we could take in half as many again, were it possible," she said, peering at the ledger before her. "Let me see. Idoia Maura was born on the twenty-third of June."

In my surprise I said baldly, "I understood that she was born on the sixteenth."

"That is the date of parturition, yes. We record that when we have it. But at Sant' Águeda we count their lives from the day of their arrival here. Many are foundlings, and for the rest . . . well, we regard each child as a tabula rasa on which we trust that God will inscribe faith and obedience. They leave us at the age of twelve, and you may be sure that they go to work in good, respectable households or as lay-sisters to other houses of our order. Your daughter will be taught all that she should know for such a life. Some have dowers, of course, and they stay here until they are married or enter the religious life."

She might have been discussing livestock rotation on a large and well-ordered farm, and yet it was my daughter's fate of which she spoke. Mrs. Barraclough's voice, so like Lucy's, and yet so different, rose in my mind. *For him to be safe, and yet free to explore nature—the world—is what I wish for him above all.*

For a moment, I was unable to speak, so overwhelmed was I by the knowledge that I might have destroyed my right to call Lucy mine, but the necessity of matching Mother Agustín's businesslike tone steadied me. "Indeed," I said. "I should like to discuss the possibility of my supporting her in such a way. A dowry, certainly, and meanwhile—"

She rose. "Perhaps you would like to see the orphanage? You might then gain a clearer idea of the work that our endowments support." A young lay-sister opened the door. "Oh, we do not need you after all, Sister," said Mother Agustín. "Thank you." She turned to me. "I shall not keep you long; I am sure you have other business to attend to."

I was conscious of a small relief, that Idoia would not be entering the room. But I saw too that it was wrong, that Mother Agustín would not try to dissuade me from departing without seeing her. If she who stood in the relationship of a parent to my daughter could not realize how necessary it was that Idoia should know of her father and mother, and that they cared for her fate, then it must be I who took on that duty.

"I should still like to see my daughter."

"Certainly." She glanced at a large clock, which hung opposite her desk. "They will be at dinner. Please come this way, Major Fairhurst."

I had no great interest in the inhabitants of the orphanage beyond Idoia herself, and that of my mind which was not concerned with her was still taken up with fear and uncertainty over Lucy. But I had no desire either to appear discourteous, and, I reflected as we reached a pair of heavy doors at the end of the long corridor, even if such a tour chafed my feelings with the delay, I should at least gain a better notion of the circumstances in which my daughter lived. Nurseries, dormitories, schoolrooms, and sewing rooms were passed under review. Each shone with polish and sweeping, and the ranks of beds, tables, desks, and chairs were as exactly placed as any drill sergeant could demand. Even the flowers and candles that stood before the innumerable images of saints seemed to have been marshaled and inspected before they might be permitted to fulfill their offerers' votive purpose. Everything was ordered, I saw from a chart pinned to a wall, even each minute of the day. That of the chapel that I might see was plainly furnished, although gold and candlelight gleamed beyond the screen.

"Your daughter has, of course, been raised as a true daughter of the Church, and she will make her first communion next year. You are not of the Faith, I take it," said Mother Agustín, when she had genuflected towards the invisible altar and crossed herself.

"No."

"Ah, well, God may yet be merciful."

My senses were swimming a little in the hot scent of candle wax and incense but I could not feel that the mercy of this God of Rome, at least as Catalina described it, was much to be grateful for, although I must be so for her sake, I thought: grateful for anything that had comforted her in a sorrow that was beyond my imagining.

It was with that thought still aching within me that I followed Mother Agustín into the refectory. At yet more rows of tables and benches one hundred gray-clad girls ate in silence while a nun, standing in a pulpit, read to them from a small, old book. Each child had a bowl of stew, a cup of well-watered wine, and a spoon. By each left hand was a piece of gray bread. Each child who had finished laid down her spoon in her empty bowl and dropped her hands into her aproned lap as neatly as any soldier commanded to stand at ease. Which of these, I thought, looking at the rows of dark-haired, white-capped heads, was Catalina's child?

Then the reading nun closed her book, crossed herself, and all the children rose, whether they had finished their meal or not. Grace was said, and still silent, each row of children filed out of the refectory and into a courtyard beyond.

"They have half an hour of free play before afternoon duties," said Mother Agustín. "I shall ask for your daughter to be brought to us."

"Perhaps we might go and find her in the yard," I said.

"Certainly, if you wish it," she said, "You will see that we do not encourage wild spirits or particular friendships, but a little exercise and fresh air is beneficial to all creatures."

We reached the playground. All about the gray-walled, empty yard the creatures were hopping, chattering, skipping, and whispering. They seemed lively and healthy enough, and a few stopped to look at us with wide eyes. Mother Agustín beckoned to the nun who stood, hands hidden in her sleeves, overseeing the children.

"Mother, would you be so good as to show us which is Idoia Maura? I wish to speak to her."

Through the throng the nun went unerringly towards one small gray figure that stood in a far corner, watching her fellows. As she approached, the child pushed something into the pocket of her apron and stood as if to attention. Then, as the nun turned, she followed.

It was written in my heart that Catalina's child was six years old, but until now I had not carried any image of her in my mind. She had her mother's black eyes, and waving black hair dragged into neatness under her cap, but thin, straight eyebrows with a little kink at the outer ends that I realized, with a shock, I knew from my own looking glass. She was my child too. Her soft, dark red lips were closed to narrowness, as if they had no cause to part or smile, and her hands gripped together against the rough linen of her apron. My hand went out to her, but her hands only gripped each other tighter.

"Make your curtsy to your visitor, Idoia," said Mother Agustín, "and *then* to me," and a little haltingly, Idoia did as she was told. "Now, you may come with us, for your visitor wishes to speak to you."

We made our way in near silence back through the refectory, up staircases and down passageways, to Mother Agustín's office. She gestured that I should sit, then did so herself, so that Idoia stood between us, her hands folded.

"Now, Idoia, I must tell you that this is your father, who has come all the way from England to see you and make sure that you are growing up a good girl."

"From . . . from England?" said Idoia. Her Spanish had the Basque tang to it, but was clear enough.

"Yes, from England," I said. "My name is Stephen Fairhurst, and I am English." I held out my hand. *"Encantado de conocerle."*

Idoia cast a glance at Mother Agustín, who nodded. Then my daughter put her hand into mine, a little reluctantly. *"Encantada, Señor."*

"Well," said Mother Agustín, "Is there anything else that you wish to know? If not, perhaps your daughter should return to her duties. The orphanage always welcomes any assistance with God's work, most especially in our present need. In the matter of your daughter's future, I can recommend a notary who has experience of such arrangements."

She rose again, and against her black habit Idoia seemed smaller still.

I pulled myself together. "Is there somewhere that Idoia and I could be private? I should like to get to know her, and I would not wish to discommode you. I am sure that you are very busy."

"The affairs of an institution such as this are certainly time-consuming," she said. "If you wish to have a little more time with her, I think St. Catherine of Siena is not being used at the moment."

Thus it was that Catalina's daughter—my daughter—and I found ourselves sitting on opposite sides of a small table in an otherwise empty room, the window too high to see out of, with a crucified Christ looking down on us, while in the corner St. Catherine, as Idoia informed me, displayed her holy stigmata.

I had asked her about the figure, since I could think of nothing else with which to start the conversation. "And are you happy?" I continued. "Are the nuns kind to you?" She nodded, her hands still folded in her lap. "I'm afraid it must have been a shock to you, to be introduced to your father in such a way."

She gave a little giggle, I thought of embarrassment, and clapped her hands to her mouth, as if she did not know how to answer this. I tried again. "Do you know . . . did the nuns tell you about your mother?"

"Only that she is now a religious herself, Señor."

From the pocket of my coat I brought forth Lucy's drawing of Catalina and parted the boards that kept it safe. "This is your mother. It was made only yesterday. Her name is Catalina Maura, but in religion she is named Sister Andoni."

"I pray to St. Anthony when I have lost my slate pencil." She took the paper, and gazed at it, sitting quite still. I saw how the short, strong nose, the high cheekbones, the round cheeks were echoed to and fro between mother and daughter, young and old, as if the drawing were a looking glass placed where time divided, so that the past was laid over the future, and the future laid over the past, until which was which, I had no means of discerning.

After a long time she looked up, and held the paper out to me.

"You may have it, if you wish," I said. "It was drawn for you to keep."

"Please take it," she said. Her voice was deep for her years. "They won't let me keep it, because my mother was a whore and I am a bastard."

My anger was lit by so vile a word for Catalina, but still less did her child deserve to live under as dark a name. Was it only the other girls, in their innocent brutality, who had called her thus, or was it those whose duty it should have been to love and care for her? Was it this that had narrowed her lips and stilled her hands? My rage blazed, but she appeared so still and small in this chamber, which was meant for adult interviews, that I would not have let her feel it for anything in the world.

"What is it that you have in your pocket?" I asked, when I had controlled myself.

She looked at me as Titus did, when he feared I might take a favorite stick from him. "I will not tell anyone," I said.

Slowly, keeping her eyes on me, she put her hand into her pocket and brought out a small doll made of linen rags, with black wool stitched to her head, and a face, somewhat smeared, drawn in ink.

"Does she have a name?" I said.

"I called her Estefanía."

I was silenced. Then, as she began to look frightened, I managed to say, "But you are allowed to keep her?"

"Until I am seven. Then I shall be too old."

"And when will that be?" I asked, although I knew the date that she would give me.

"On the eve of the feast of St. John," she said. "There are fireworks on my birthday."

"That is very lucky. But what will happen to Estefanía then?"

"She will be given to the poor children," said Idoia. "They will need her more than I shall." She stopped, then said, "I want to keep her. She will be all alone in the basket for the poor children. She will be lost."

"You do not wish her to be lost?"

She shook her head, as if the matter were beyond words, and I fancied that for the first time she looked at me as on a faint hope of help, and with eyes so like Catalina's that I felt an impulse to rise and take her in my arms. But we were strangers still, so instead, I said, "But you are not lost. You have lived here all your life."

"Yes," she said. "But when I leave, where shall I go?"

It was not something that I could answer. "I am sure that Mother Agustín will arrange what is best," I said.

"Yes," was all that Idoia replied.

"And now I must go," I said, stumbling as I rose. "I am making arrangements for your future. You will be looked after. May I come and see you again, before I return to England?"

She nodded, putting the doll back into her pocket. "Why are you going to England?"

"Because that is my home. I have a house, and farms, and I have to look after them."

She nodded again. "Good-bye, Señor."

"I shall be here on the morrow, or certainly the next day. No later than that." She looked steadily at me. "I give you my word. Now, we must go back to Mother Agustín." I held out my hand, and she slipped hers into it. It was warm and square, the fingertips a little roughened with work, but the palm young and soft. I was suddenly overwhelmed with the memory of Catalina's hands, bigger, but not different.

I opened the door. Outside in the corridor a young nun was waiting. Idoia's hand dropped from mine.

"I shall not interrupt Mother Agustín," I said. "I am sure that she is busy. Would you be so good as to let her know that I shall call again to see my daughter in the next day or two?" Now that my own folly— brutality—had driven my love from me, I knew, I could have had no other certainty, beyond that.

"Certainly, Señor," said the nun. "Come, Idoia."

Feeling suddenly wearied almost beyond standing, I watched Idoia walk down the corridor in front of her escort, growing smaller with each short step, until the dark double doors closed behind her.

⁂

IT WASN'T ANY GOOD. I'd known that ever since I saw Eva and Theo out of the window. I'd hardly made any dreams, just lived in my loving him. And now I couldn't live there anymore.

Penny offered to come with me when I went back to the Hall to get my stuff. "You must have a suitcase or something. We'll take the car. And I must pick up Cecil's things. I don't suppose from what you say there's much, but he might as well have some familiar things around him, poor lamb." I climbed in, and thought how it even made it a tiny bit better to have someone helping me do the things I needed to do.

She stopped the car outside the back door of the Hall.

"Does Ray mind us taking him?" I said, and realized I'd hardly thought of Ray at all since I'd woken up. My mind wouldn't work properly because it was full of Theo.

"No. He knows . . . he knows it's best. He's in no state to look after him at the moment. Or . . . Well, we'll see. And your mother will be here soon."

"Will Cecil miss him, do you think? Miss here?"

"Probably." She got out. "Children do, when it's all they know."

The back door wasn't locked. "I spoke to Ray while you were asleep," said Penny. "He's very distressed still, and he was a bit vague. She seems to have had a heart attack. She probably felt ill, and tried to come downstairs to find help. Or maybe something startled her, with the electricity off. Something in the shadows. Anyway, she fell."

Dark shadows and gold ones, standing and moving across the floor and up and down the stairs. *Something happened*, Cecil had said from the shadows.

"I don't—it's—going upstairs . . ." I didn't know what I was frightened of.

But Penny just said, "No, of course not," quite calmly. "I'll come with you." I remembered she was a magistrate. No wonder the police did what she said, more than they ever would've for Mum or Theo. It was funny to think of, somehow; she seemed so normal and nice. Funny to think that even being almost like a judge, she was still on my side.

"I'm afraid I had no idea of . . . that anything like this might happen," she went on. "Ray was decent enough to Susan, and the school seemed reasonably well run. And though he never seemed to take much notice of Cecil, I don't think he was ever unkind to him. Certainly there wasn't anything that I would have felt I ought to report."

For a moment I saw Belle's red, twisted face. And Ray's, through the glass. "I don't want to see Ray. Maybe I should. But I don't. It's . . . I can't explain."

"Don't worry. I'll be there."

I opened the door into the passage and knew suddenly that Belle was dead. My grandmother was dead. My mother's mother. It was a sort of thud in my stomach. Yesterday she was alive. Then something in the shadows startled her, smashed her on the black-and-white squares. I could still see it, printed inside my eyes. A person smashed, along with everything else.

When we went into Cecil's room I saw Ray had done some tidying up.

Penny looked round quickly at the paintings on the wall, then opened a drawer and started to drop Cecil's clothes into a plastic bag. The sheets had gone from the bed, but Ray hadn't put clean ones on. He must have meant to.

"I'd no idea that it was like this," Penny was saying. "It was always rather bleak, but when the school was running—when Susan was here—it was at least clean and tidy. Ray always said they were going to rebuild at the back here, so it wasn't worth redecorating. And now, this."

I nodded, looking at Cecil's paintings glaring at me from the walls, the dead horse, the snow spotted with blood, the burned bodies in the air. I remembered the tower he said he'd dreamt, and the red that flared across my sleep. Stephen had written to Miss Durward about a siege, I remembered, and ice and snow. Was it Stephen who'd dreamt the things Cecil painted? His dreams—his nightmares—his soldier's dreams . . . Were they so thick in the air, so strong, that they'd soaked into the wood and stone?

For a moment I felt as if a hot and cold fever was crawling over me and gripping at my throat. *Sick like a dog,* Cecil said, *and dead people and worms. Hot. Burning hot.*

Then Penny closed the last drawer with a bang, and opened the curtains wide so that the light fell into the room. Her hand hesitated at the window catch, as if she would've liked to open it wide too and let the air in. But we were leaving.

"Would you like a hand to round up your things?" she said.

If it hadn't been for going upstairs and Ray being there I'd have said no because it wasn't like I needed someone to do my packing for me, but then I thought again about going through the hall and upstairs and I said yes. So we went out of Cecil's room and Penny dropped the bags of his stuff by the back door, and then we went through the kitchen and on.

The swing-door was heavy, as if I was pushing it open against everything that had ever happened in the house. But actually walking through it wasn't too bad.

The hall was empty and clean, just black-and-white, stretching away.

"He's cleared up," I said, and felt a stupid lump of crying swell in my throat.

"Yes," said Penny. She put an arm round me and gave my shoulders a squeeze. "Poor old Anna. But your mother will be here tomorrow."

"I suppose so," I said, because I couldn't see how it would help.

And then I thought of her at my age, walking away. Not from the Hall, they didn't live here then, but I couldn't help seeing her there. My mother, lugging a suitcase with her along the drive just the way I would, walking away alone, with a child deep in her belly. And now she was coming back to find me.

I suddenly remembered the time I got lost when I was little, the time I told Theo about. In the end Mum came to look for me. She found me sitting in the puddle of milk and broken glass and crying and she was a bit cross because milk was expensive but she carried me upstairs, even though I wasn't so much smaller than her, and washed my knees and hands and made us both cocoa without milk but with lots of sugar.

The marble was hard and cold and solid under my feet. Where it happened was the same as all the other squares. The house was full of things like that, things that had once happened, Stephen's and everybody else's, things that hung in the space or settled on you, like specks of dust in the sun. Last night was only a picture, I thought. I saw it in my mind's eye, but it lived outside my head.

My bed still had the blankets pushed back from where I'd got up so early on that beautiful morning, and taken Stephen's letter about Catalina with me, and read it in the streams of light that fell through the trees, and then seen Theo, sitting in the sun against the brick of the stables and smoking.

"Can I help at all?" said Penny, from the door. I was still staring at the bed, and remembering. "Are you all right?" she said.

I wondered if she knew about me and Theo. But she didn't say anything and I couldn't think of a way to ask her without giving it away and crying, and once I started crying I knew I wouldn't be able to stop.

"I'm okay."

She looked at me for a moment longer, then nodded and went away. I heard her footsteps going upstairs, heavy and quick. She must be going to see Ray.

I got my shampoo and things from the bathroom, and then I pulled my suitcases out from under the cupboard and stuffed all my dirty clothes into them. There weren't any clean ones left. I found the cards Holly and Tanya had sent. I'd never answered them. What could I write now? I knew somehow I could never explain what had really happened, how it had really been. They were too far away, it was like they lived in another time. And no postcard from Mum, let alone a letter. She had been too far away too. If one came, it would be after I'd gone. Mum would get here before her letter did. I wondered if that had ever happened to Stephen and Lucy, and suddenly wished I could ask him.

I pulled the sheets off my bed and folded them. Then I took down the pictures I'd stuck up: Paul Newman and the polar bear and John

Curry. I opened the drawers and found Stephen's letters. On top lay the last one.

At first his writing was slow, as if his hand was stiff, as if he was thinking while he wrote.

I can most easily explain what has occurred . . . by taking up my story at the point where I left off. . . . The house was empty.

. . . I turned & walked away. She had found asylum, found a place in the world in the leaving of it, & though I longed to see her face & hear her voice, or if that were denied me, to know simply that she did move & breathe inside these high stone walls, it would have been cruel & selfish to seek such crumbs for my own comfort when by so doing I might destroy hers. . . .

She was named Idoia. . . .

. . . as I went aboard at San Sebastian it was with no expectation of returning there, except in my dreams.

There was a blot of ink there, a small stain on the page where Stephen's racing pen had hesitated maybe just for a breath—a second—but that second had fallen on the page and marked it forever. The crease it lay across was dark too, as if the letter had been folded and unfolded often, read and read again, perhaps by Stephen, perhaps by Lucy, all those times showing even in the photocopy.

Lucy must have kept all the letters together for them still to be together now.

Or did she send them back to him because they'd stopped writing, as nearly happened before? Perhaps it was Stephen who kept them, because they were all he had. Suddenly I desperately wanted the letter to say—to show me—that it had all come out all right.

At last I was able to board the mail to Bury St. Edmunds, where my cousin's coachman met me, & drove me to Kersey Hall. . . .

I know I must not disturb Catalina. . . . I have no doubt that I may enquire closely enough into my daughter's well-being without—

And it stopped, halfway down the page, the sentence unfinished, the last word a bit smudged, as if Stephen had been startled and got up and left the blank grain of the unmarked paper empty, like the future. Had Lucy read this letter? There was no address that I could see, not even a shadow in a looking glass. How had it got to her? And what had she thought about, reading how he loved Catalina? Perhaps she loved Stephen, and hoped . . . Did she think the future might change—her future, and Stephen's future, which was Kersey's past?

Last night was Kersey's past too now, and mine, soaked into the stone forever. It was like when the camera shutter opened, and that moment—that scatter of light and dark—fell through the glass of the lens and onto the silver, and marked the film forever. Would my shadow be here, the way it almost felt as if Stephen's still was? Somewhere in the dark, in the golden shadows, in the light, in the plain, pale nothing between the times.

Penny found me sitting on the empty bed. "All done. Are you ready? I've spoken to Ray, so we can go."

I put all Stephen's letters together and slid them into my handbag. "I think so."

But Ray was standing on the landing. His face was gray and shadowy with stubble and he smelled.

"Anna—"

I couldn't help myself stopping. Behind me I could feel Penny's warmth.

"I'm sorry. I knew what she was, but I thought I could look after him all right . . . And then she . . . And I . . . But I never meant . . ."

"It's all right," I said.

"Nancy will explain. I hope. I've asked her to look after Cecil."

My brain felt stupid, clogged with everything. He was silent so I just said, "Okay. Good-bye, Ray," and went downstairs, with Penny close behind me.

Then we went out through the back way and put my cases in the car with Cecil's things. I wondered if the house would notice my going.

Penny opened the driver's door. "Have you got everything?"

"Yes," I said, and got in beside her. "That's it, isn't it? It's—it's done. Finished. Except for Cecil."

"He'll be all right," said Penny, starting the car. "We'll all look after him. It's not just your job. You've got enough to cope with." We turned out of the drive. "Look at all the swallows sitting on the telegraph wires. They must be talking about leaving."

When we got back to the stables Cecil was playing outside, throwing stones carefully into an old flowerpot and counting.

Eva was sitting on the tree trunk, smoking and reading a paper. When she saw us she got up and said, "Did you find everything?"

"I think so." Penny waved to Cecil. "Come on, Ciss, shall we go and find Susan?"

He dropped the stones and started to run towards us. He put his hand into mine. "Come on, Anna."

I was leaving. Now. This was the end. Penny was taking me away, away from Theo, away from everything. Another car full of suitcases, another place to live, because that was all that was left for me when everyone else's lives went wrong, when everyone else had to move on. No one trying to be unkind, no one specially wanting to hurt me. Just "Come on, Anna" because otherwise I'd be left behind. It was go with them, or have nowhere and nobody. It was go with them, or be lost.

"Anna, is that your F2 that's on the big desk upstairs?" Eva said suddenly.

"Well, it's yours, really," I said.

"No, it is yours," she said slowly, looking at me. "We gave it to you. If it's not there, it's in the darkroom. Don't forget it."

Penny said, "Perhaps you would be kind enough to send it on, and anything else that you find? I do need to be home by six."

Eva put a hand on Penny's arm. "Let her go."

I went in the front door and ran upstairs. The camera was on the desk, but I couldn't see Theo anywhere. Then I remembered the darkroom fan purring as I went past. Though it might just be that he'd left it on.

I knocked on the darkroom door.

"A moment, please," Theo's voice said, and then, "okay, come in."
I went in.

"Anna!" he said, as if he was surprised. I couldn't see his face well
in the safelight.

"I came to say good-bye."

And then I walked straight into his arms, because it was either that
or start crying alone, in the middle of the darkroom.

He held me and kissed my forehead. "Oh, sweet Anna," he said.

"When will I see you again?"

"I don't know," he said. "Perhaps at the gallery?"

And then I knew it wasn't just Eva, it was him too, and knowing it
hurt so much it was like my whole body was taken over with the
pain and I couldn't breathe or move. And he held me like he always
did so that I knew everything would be all right. Only now it wouldn't
be. I didn't have him: I wouldn't have his voice and the warmth of
his chest and the way he knew everything and could make me understand it. Without him I was lost.

"Don't cry so," he said. He took the camera gently out of my hand
and put it on the workbench. "You will make yourself ill."

"How can I help it, when I love you so much? And I won't even
see you. Not—not like we have been, not really. I know you don't love
me. You don't even want me. Not enough, anyway." The pain rolled
through me again, a great cramping misery so that I could hardly
stand, and Theo held me up and stroked my hair.

When the pain got less I could feel the cramps beginning to soften.
I straightened up a bit. He was staring down at me, looking sad.

"I always seem to cry at you," I said, sort of smiling.

He saw it, and half smiled too, and then suddenly, as if the smile
had opened some gate inside him, he bent his head as I put my face
up to his, so our mouths met, and I thought for a moment how sweet
tears could taste.

After a long time his mouth let go of mine, and he kissed my cold wet eyelids. "Oh, Anna, I shall miss you so much," he said, and his voice came out creaky and difficult. "I did not mean it to be like this. I knew it was wrong—ought not to happen. I never meant . . . but you were so sweet . . . and I came to care for you so much. I came to—" He stopped himself.

I felt like all my breath had been snatched away. His hands were hot on my back. For a moment we stood there, everything turned upside down, and I knew that we could make love there and then, on the darkroom floor, and he wouldn't—couldn't—have stopped himself, this time or more times, whenever we could, because what he'd nearly said was true. What he felt for me was something like love, a bit, only a little bit, but that was enough for me. If I was here, Theo wouldn't be able to stop himself. I could still have him, sort of.

It wasn't very much, but I learned long ago not to want more of things.

He was touching my cheek with a sort of half-drowned happiness in his face. His hands trembled against my throat. "What is it, *milácvku?*"

He called Eva that. Inside me something began to fizzle and spark.

But the spark was like a red flare, showing me everything that he knew, like strips of time rolling past, people laughing, people dying, the stare of a soldier gone mad with war, a great statue pushed crashing to the ground, the spilt remains of a refugee's life, sacks of grain dragged off an aeroplane, almonds and apricots in a garden in Seville.

I saw these things through his eyes now. I would see them like that forever, but they wouldn't be mine. They were Theo and Eva's. It was what they were made of, what had made them and damaged them and joined them. They went from one frame to the next, and I couldn't be part of it. There wasn't a place for me with him, however much I dreamed, however well we hid ourselves. I was the plain, pale nothing, pressed into a thin strip between their lives. And it wasn't enough for me. I knew that now.

I gripped him to me and gave him one long kiss. Then I let go.

"Good-bye, Theo. I don't suppose I'll see you around." I picked up my camera and went to the door. "Thank you for . . . for every-thing."

"Anna—" I thought he put a hand out to me, but I tried not to see it: I tried to think of Stephen, turning and walking away from Catalina because that was all he could do for either of them.

Then I pulled open the darkroom door, and went out, and it closed slowly behind me.

✦✦✦

I WALKED BACK towards the El Moro through the slackening noon-tide crowds, and it was as well that the streets were less full, for my thoughts were in disarray, and my feelings confused. Ahead of me was Lucy, true to her word, no doubt, in still being at the inn, but gone from me as surely as if she were already bound for England. Be-hind me was Idoia, Catalina's child, my child. Somewhere in that great, gray building she breathed, one white cap and apron among a hundred, not starving, not cold, not shut in a cupboard with the rats, but a child as alone and lost to love as I had ever been, flesh of my flesh, begotten in love and borne in grief.

I tapped on the door of Lucy's bedchamber and entered at her permission, all but stumbling on the packed and corded bags that stood at the door. She was sitting by the window, drawing.

She looked up quickly, then rose. "Did you see her? Is she well? Is she happy?"

"She is well. As to happy . . . The place is very well run. She said that she is happy."

"But you are not certain?"

Idoia had only nodded, I thought, her hands in her lap. I shook my head. "How can I tell? What do I know of little girls? And my own memories are . . . Well, I have nothing against which to measure what I saw of her life."

She came towards me. "I had not thought of that. You never speak of those times."

"There is nothing to tell." But even as I said these words I recognized their untruth. There was nothing I had told, it was true, for I had no wish to revisit such distant years by speaking of them, and few had enquired. But deep below so many griefs and loves, those years had stirred within me at the sight of Idoia. They were not strange, for they lay in my soul, so heavy that they were long since sunk, so much part of me that I might not call them a memory, but rather my familiars, who lived within me always. "I do not care to tell such old tales."

Lucy still regarded me steadily, but I knew that she was leaving me. I could not even be surprised, for I had learned long ago not to expect anything more. This was the pattern of my life, and I had been foolish, for these few days and hours, to dream that Lucy might see a place for herself in it.

She was fiddling with her pencil, twisting it round and round in her thin fingers. At last she said, with some difficulty, "I do realize that you . . . I have realized how . . ." She stopped, went to the open window, and looked out, although I could have sworn that her gaze was directed inwards as much as towards the world outside.

Then she turned her back on it, took a breath as deep as a sigh, and stood with her hands gripping the sill so that the light flared around her. "Stephen, I have done you an injustice. I ought to be grateful for your care, even when I do not need it, even when it chafes." She laughed, a little awkwardly. "I am not blind to how often you stop yourself, when most men would insist on helping me."

Her bags were closed and stood by the door, she wore her traveling gown, and her hat and gloves lay ready on the table. I had to find the words to make her understand, before she slipped away from me. If I stayed her for a moment, made her understand, and still she chose to leave, I would not prevent her.

I said, slowly, coaxing the thought from a tiny, wordless seed of relief, "I hope I have learned to accept your judgment, when it is a matter only of your well-being. But this morning . . . my fear was only . . . My love, I cannot change the world, or what it thinks, any more than a single soldier may request the enemy to change their ground to make his victory the easier. How I would wish you to do everything, to have every freedom, that you desire, and hang the whisperers! But . . ." I stopped, for how could I say that I would still sacrifice her freedom—that longed-for honesty—if to preserve it would endanger anything as dear to me as Catalina's child had become?

Lucy was looking at me, her frowning gaze seeming to grapple with my thoughts as much as with my words. To watch her was to feel a knife held to my throat. After a while she said, "I suppose . . . although it is my choice to do things that will earn me disapproval, it cannot be only my choice, when others' happiness is in question. Yours, Idoia's—"

Trembling, I said, "Can you forgive me for thinking that? For leaving you this morning? For insulting you—for injuring you—in wishing to protect you?"

A rather twisted smile flickered across her face. "I told you once that chivalry is not the point," she said. "I still think so. But when it joins with common sense, and love for others, how can I not accept it? Those are good things. How can I not try to find a place for myself in their pattern?"

"Then you do forgive me?" I said, but her expression, before she spoke, gave me enough hope to leave the doorway and cross the room towards her. Then suddenly she smiled, as if a great candle had been lit within her, and she had barely said yes before relief drove me to her, with passion close behind.

To embrace her again, after all my fear, was a joy that sought expression, but I dared not do so, for so great a matter, I felt, had Lucy's forgiveness been for her, that I feared to appear to press my advantage.

I did her an injustice, however, for Lucy did nothing except it was wholeheartedly, and she too, I realized wonderingly, was released from fears and doubts of her own that I had not perceived until now. So urgent was our desire to affirm what we had snatched back from such danger that we sought its fulfillment in the swiftest manner possible, and if it occurred to either of us that Lucy's gown would be sadly crushed by so doing, neither of us had any breath left with which to say so. When afterwards I briefly slept, I fell into a deeper and more peaceful oblivion than I could ever remember.

We dined at the inn, and it was the hour of the evening promenade before we set out to see Bilbao. The whole city, it seemed, was in the streets, greeting neighbors, displaying new gowns, advising friends and marrying off daughters. The lanes of the old town over the high-arched bridge were irresistible to Lucy, and time and again I leaned against a wall, and stood watching her as she laid down a few, swift lines, to show the crest of a Gothic window, an old man's hands, the iron filigree of a balcony, or a kerchief knotted like a flower about a girl's dark hair. When it was done, she would look up, laugh, and return to me. Thus we wandered through the town, Lucy's sketchbook catching and holding these things of ours, one after the other, line by line, page by page, the time between them pressed to insignificance as the pages turned.

We had reached the top of the calle del Perro. "There is Sant' Águeda," I said.

Lucy looked at the high gray walls, with their small windows far out of reach. "Are you going to see her again?"

"Yes. Did I forget to say so?"

"We were speaking of other matters," she said primly, but looking at me with a laugh in her eye.

"So we were. Are we doomed to such disagreements?"

"Yes," she said. "My impatience and your care are like oil and water. It is just as well that we seem likely to mix ourselves together frequently." Seeing me somewhat taken aback by so public an avowal, she laughed aloud. Then she said, "But what do you intend to do for Idoia?"

We were walking in the shadow of the orphanage walls, and to me came again the image of my daughter, standing alone, perhaps inside that same wall, and then suddenly, for no reason that I could discern, I saw in my mind's eye the lad that Nell and Titus had come across, shrinking against the hedge for fear, and with nowhere else to go. Then from further away, from longer ago, came a flicker of my own, childish memories—a door bolted against me; Pierce's face as he slipped into unconsciousness; the cry I had no use for, that the mails were come at last. Each one was as slightly drawn as the lines in Lucy's sketchbook, yet they followed one another and made a certainty: that Idoia must not stay at Sant' Águeda, that she was not truly found until she was housed and cared for in love, and not merely in Christian charity.

Lucy stopped under the yellow glow of a streetlamp. "Stephen?"

"I am sorry. I was pondering what it will be best to do. Beyond dowering her, that is."

"For Idoia? If you are pondering thus, then I take it that you are not content to leave her where she is."

"No," I said, and added, "she would not take the picture of her mother. She looked at it for a long time, but she said they would not allow her to keep it, so she gave it back to me."

"Oh, poor child!" she said. "Perhaps if you placed her in the town, with some respectable woman?"

"No!" I burst out. "Not that! Never that."

She looked up as if startled. Then she said, quite calmly, "No. Forgive me. I understand, I think." She said no more, but in her silence I felt my distress wash away, and with it some of my memories.

Then I saw the quick rise of her breast in the light as she took a breath and said slowly, "Would you . . . Are you thinking of having her with you at Kersey?"

"But she would not be with me. She would be with us, and that is not a decision that is mine to make alone."

She was silent for a long time, and although her eyes were narrowed, as they were when she observed a subject, I thought that it was not the scene before us at which she gazed. At last she said, "What is she like, Idoia?"

"Dark," I said. "And small, like . . . like her mother. Very quiet, I thought, but perhaps it would be difficult to be otherwise, in those surroundings." I recalled Estefanía. "She had a doll, a rag doll. She said that when she turns seven, she will have to give it to the poor box."

"Oh, the poor little thing!" she cried. "We cannot leave her to that!"

"Do you mean that?"

"Yes, we must rescue her, and give her a home where there are no rules to deny her what she loves."

I smiled, to conceal my relief, "My love, are you sure?"

"Yes," she said firmly, but then went on in a less certain tone, "Stephen, to have your love gives me such joy that to know that once it was given to another is not—will not always be—easy."

"I understand you," I said slowly, "but I wish I could make it so."

"You have lived with the image of that love for so long. And now we shall have an image of it before us both, every day."

To my mind's eye came the memory of Idoia, looking at her mother's picture, and I could not deny it.

She smiled suddenly. "But living with me in the flesh will not always be easy for you, either."

"On the contrary—" I felt bound to protest.

"Even your chivalry, Stephen, will find me wanting in the virtues men are said to look for in a wife." Before I could deny this, she went on. "And Idoia is not an image, but a little girl—a daughter—and I hope that she will be quite as naughty as any other child, and no less trouble to you, once she is in a place where her nature may find true expression."

I smiled at the notion and tucked my arm back into hers. "Then, tomorrow, will you come to the orphanage with me?" I said, "As my sister, or my betrothed, whichever you will? We will find Idoia to-gether, and take her home to Kersey."

❧❀❧

I CRIED ALMOST all the way to Penny's house, and the tears were running down my cheeks so fast that after a while I gave up trying to slide them away secretly, though I did manage not to make a noise. I was sitting in the back, to be with Cecil I said, and Penny didn't argue. Cecil squashed himself up close to me and I kept having to move so the tears dripping off my chin wouldn't fall on him. But it helped a bit to have him snuggling into my side, even with the lump of his plaster. It felt like here was something—someone—small and warm and real and rather grubby, who might stop me dissolving away to nothing while we ran quietly through the same deep green lanes as I had with Theo, with the swifts soaring and shrieking overhead, and the air cooler than it had been for weeks, and bitter with stubble smoke.

Susan was waiting in the doorway of Penny's house and almost before the car stopped, Cecil had scrambled out and run to her. Suddenly I felt so tired that everything ached.

We left Cecil laughing and proudly showing Susan his cast. I didn't know he could laugh, I thought, feeling even bigger tears in the back of my throat. Penny showed me upstairs and into the spare room. "Crispin's coming round later. Why don't you have a wash and a lie-down? You've had a very short night, and a terrible shock."

I nodded, and wondered again in a foggy sort of way whether she knew about me and Theo, but I was too tired to know if it mattered, and when she'd told me where the bathroom was and gone downstairs I shut the curtains against the yellow light and got undressed and into bed. It was one of those continental quilts instead of blankets, and it settled over me like a cloud while I sank down through endless sadness and into sleep.

I woke from a dream of Theo. It was late, I could tell, there was hardly any light coming in round the edges of the curtains. I uncurled, and then felt the pain still lying like hot lead in my gut. Already it felt familiar, like it had made a place for itself inside me. This was what it was going to be like, I thought. Always.

There was a quiet tap on the door, the sort that wouldn't have woken me if I'd still been asleep. It was Susan with a small pile of my clothes all neatly folded, and Cecil holding a tray very tightly with one and a half hands because of his plaster, with a teapot and a cup, and only a little bit spilled onto the plate of biscuits.

"Mum said Uncle Crispin's here for supper," said Susan, "and if you want to come down for a drink when you're ready that would be really nice. We're not eating till nine. And Mum's washed your clothes but there's only a few dry."

When they'd gone I went to the bathroom and had a quick shower and washed my hair, and came back and drank my tea. There were glossy magazines and books by the bed and cotton wool in a china jar on the dressing table and everything smelled of polish, and the tea was hot, running down inside me, scalding me awake, until I could even smell the potpourri on the windowsill where it was still warm from the day, and feel the heavy velvet of the towels against my nakedness, and the smooth cotton sweet with washing and ironing, as I got dressed. When I opened my bedroom door I could hear the radio news faintly from the kitchen, talking about Big Ben being started after it stopped. I wondered what they had to do to start a clock that size again.

Crispin was sitting on the patio where the blue evening mixed with the yellow light falling from the sitting room window. He saw me hesitating in the back doorway and uncoiled himself from his chair.

"Anna, my dear! How good to see you! I hope you slept well. I was so sorry to hear about your grandmother." He came to me and took my hands to kiss me on both cheeks. "Penny's doing something technical to the supper, and Susan's helping her, so do come and sit here on the terrace and let me get you a drink."

I really actually liked white wine now, I thought, while we sipped it and talked about the weather and the gallery. But I could feel Crispin tiptoeing round Theo's name. Suddenly he reached for a briefcase, which was standing by his chair.

"I thought you might like to have this," he said, taking something out. "I found it in a sale I went to, over towards Ipswich. It's not part of the Kersey Hall archive, so I'd like you to have it." It was a bit like one of those boxes you see posh necklaces in, but old and scuffed-looking. "Open it," he said.

The catch was a bit stiff. I lifted the lid, and inside was a photograph of the Hall. I knew it was very old because the Hall looked clean and new, but the picture wasn't blurry and pale like you'd expect. It was glass not paper for one thing, and every chimney and leaf and blade of grass was as sharp as if it had been cut into the surface with a needle. You had to tilt it to see it properly, and then the highlights glimmered against the black velvet; there was sun catching the windows and breaking up among the leaves. Half the front door was open, and it looked cool and shady inside, and in the dimness you could just see someone with dark hair in a dress with long, pale skirts.

"Whoever took it must have known exactly what they were doing. Daguerreotype wasn't an easy process to master." He leaned forward and touched my hand. "Look at the card."

Tucked against the satin inside the lid was a little card, thick and cream-colored. I didn't know the writing: the strokes were dark and quick and bigger than Stephen's.

IDOIA JOCELYN
NÉE IDOIA MAURA
KERSEY, JUNE '41

I sat and looked at it, trying to understand what I was holding.

He smiled at me. "To be honest, it was Theo who said I should give it to you. He said your middle name is Jocelyn."

"It is," I said, and blood started to drum in my ears. "And Idoia's in Stephen's letters. She must be my . . . I've never been bothered about relations and things. But Theo must have—"

Suddenly I found I couldn't speak or see or breathe for tears. I closed the lid of the box, and felt Crispin take it gently away. Everything was dark. After a bit he put a hankie into my hands. It was big and smelled of ironing and lavender and beeswax, and with all Penny's looking-after as well, it helped more than I'd thought anything could. Here were people who knew about us, who saw us, but they didn't judge us or try to change things. They were just friends.

"I wasn't sure if you knew," I said at last.

"It only took one look at Theo's face to see how he felt," he said. "Although for a while I had no idea it had gone so far—so deep. With either of you. And there was nothing any of us could do."

I nodded.

"He asked me to bring you your prints," he said, reaching for his briefcase again and taking out one of the big flat photo-paper boxes.

In it were the two sleeves of my negs, and the prints I'd done. The Hall, the portico with the shadow beyond the glass, Cecil's face, the saint on the Guildhall.

Theo's hands cradling his coffee cup.

When I saw that one, the lump of pain swelled up hot again inside me and I pushed the lid back on the box. Crispin was staring down at his fingertips. At last he said, without looking up, "Anna . . . Theo and Eva are leaving Kersey. He asked me to tell you. They're moving to Paris. He's flying out tonight to look for a flat, and Eva's packing up the stables in the next couple of days and following him. They hope to settle in Madrid, as soon as the political situation there makes it possible."

I must have made a noise, because he said, "Oh, my dear Anna, I'm so sorry."

"When did they decide?" I said croakily.

"Well, I think it's been in the air since Franco died, but of course no one knew what would happen. And they are—they are not people who ever stay in the same place for long. Besides, Eva wants to go home, that I do know. She still has family there."

"Theo can't go home. And he doesn't have any family left."

"No. But I suppose hers is the next best thing."

I thought about Theo, looking for the next best thing, always moving on, leaving Kersey, leaving the stables, being sucked back into that world, the aeroplanes and typewriters and cafés and hotel rooms. The world I knew only from photographs, films, strips of time flickering in the dark. I couldn't follow him there. I would have to find my . . . my own world. My next best thing.

At the bottom of the box of prints was a folder, the kind they kept single prints in.

It was the *miliciana* we had printed that first day, when he showed me that sunlight can be black, and shadows silver. *Who she was is not news, only what she was,* Theo'd said. But later he said, *This at least was something that I could do.*

On the back, in his small, black writing, he had written, *For Anna, from Theo, with memories of great happiness.*

I looked at it for a long time, hearing his voice, with my sadness murmuring in the background like the darkroom fan.

Cecil was standing beside me. He slipped his hand into mine. "Penny says it's suppertime. And then I want it to be you putting me to bed. Please, Anna?"

There is movement beyond the trees, but these days I do not start, or snatch for my pistol. The air is clean and sharp on the young leaves, and I see how they are yet to be sun-darkened, still only half unfurled, so that each vein and jagged edge appears engraved by the light. The spring sun is hot enough to draw the resin from the pines until the air is heady with the scent. My footsteps and my stick make no sound on the earth. It is as if I am not here.

Through the trees, across the soft new grass of the lawns about the Hall, I can see a child running. Sunlight catches glass and stone, and scatters about him where he squats down on the ground, playing with a handful of cowslips, and pinecones, and a pebble or two. He is not one of my sons, but I think perhaps I know his face, though not his name. He seems scarcely older, yet I think I have not seen him for many years. Is it he whom I have seen, crouching in the oak tree, flitting round a corner in the house, cowering from my dogs? He who was lost?

Now I see that he has been found, for he jumps up, laughs, runs with both arms out to where, along the path from the stables, come two women. The light dazzles my gaze, but as she looks about her, I can see that the older is not Lucy. The younger leads, showing the way, and it takes me longer to see that she is not Idoia, so like is she to my daughter, with her golden skin and black hair. It is as if I am, after all, watching my own wife and daughter, reflected in a glass: two women akin to each other and unconscious of my regard, at ease in their time and place, and yet present in mine. The older woman catches the boy's hand, ruffles his hair.

As I watch unseen, the younger stoops, embraces him, her hair unbound and curling about her shoulders. Then she takes his hand. For a long moment she stands, looking up at the house, though what she seeks from it, if anything, I cannot tell.

Then, together, they turn away, and take the path that leads to the village.

ACKNOWLEDGMENTS

The Mathematics of Love was written as part of the M.Phil. in Writing at the University of Glamorgan, and I would like to thank Christopher Meredith and all the tutors and students there for their help and support.

Insights,
Interviews
& More . . .

Meet Emma Darwin

© Roderick Field

I WAS BORN and brought up in London, the middle of three sisters. My mother is an English teacher, and my father was a lawyer in the Foreign Office, so we also spent three years in Manhattan and another three commuting between London and Brussels. Perhaps inevitably, in my memory, supper-table arguments were usually about words: their exact meaning, ambiguities, overtones, etymology, and changing use. Driving across the United States in a camper van, my father retold the stories of Homer's *Odyssey*, remembered from his days studying classics at university, and my mother read us Edward Lear, Noel Streatfeild, and George MacDonald's *The Princess and the Goblin*. She read us Laura Ingalls Wilder too: from that camper van I remember visiting the "Mary and Laura house" in De Smet, South Dakota, and driving through Quebec, hoping to see Susannah of the Mounties. Later, in airports and on cross-Channel ferries, my mother read us Shakespeare, Robert Louis Stevenson's *Kidnapped*, and Jane Austen.

We spent many holidays staying with my grandparents in the east of England, on the Essex-Suffolk border: I remember reading *Jane Eyre* from beginning to end in one long summer day, and hiding under the bed, still reading, when I heard my grandmother coming. She would never have dreamt of stopping me reading, but she was of the generation that believed in fresh air for children, even if you were dazzled by the sun on the page. Much of *The Mathematics of Love* is set in that Suffolk landscape, the landscape that Gainsborough and Constable painted so exquisitely. Other holidays we spent in Brussels—so often called the crossroads of Europe—having picnics in the great forests that still edge the city, walking the battlefield of Waterloo, and driving along the coast of northern Spain. We were even once caught by the Guardia Civil when we set up camp by mistake on General Franco's country estate.

I liked writing stories as a child, but history was my passion, and until I was sixteen, I was—without question—going to be an academic historian. The fiction I loved most was historical: Geoffrey Trease, Barbara Willard, Gillian Avery, the peerless Joan Aiken, and Antonia Forest's two novels about Shakespeare's theatre, *The Player's Boy* and *The Players and the Rebels*. Then as a teenager ▶

Meet Emma Darwin *(continued)*

I caught the theatre bug and went up to the University of Birmingham to study drama. I know that I still use what I learnt then of characterization, subtext, and stagecraft, and at any moment, when I'm writing a scene, I see exactly who is doing what and where they all are. But I also worked through my stage-struckness and out the other side. My finals dissertation was on play publishing, and realizing that the book industry was a place where I felt at home, I spent some years in academic publishing. It was only when I had two small children that I started writing as an adult. Then I was diverted: my first camera had been a tenth birthday present, I'd always taken photographs, and now I finally acquired a darkroom.

But I kept finding myself coming back to writing. I became more sure that writing is what I'm about, what I do best, and what makes sense of everything else in life. When I reached the end of what I could do on my own, I applied to study for an MPhil degree in Writing at the University of Glamorgan. By that time historical fiction for adults had become what it has always been for children: a unique space where serious writers can explore fundamental desires and fears, while reveling in the nearness and otherness of worlds that we know were here but can't quite see. The novel I wrote for the degree became *The Mathematics of Love*, and I also wrote a dissertation along the way in which

A. S. Byatt uses letters, diaries, poems, and stories in her novel *Possession*.

I graduated from Glamorgan just as *The Mathematics of Love* was being sold to Headline Review in the UK, as the first of a two-book deal, and then to William Morrow in the U.S. Since then it has been short-listed for the Commonwealth Writers' and Goss First Novel prizes. Obviously, I'd found the form of a research degree very fruitful for my own writing, but I'd also become deeply interested in writing as a discipline, so I applied to do a Ph.D. in Creative Writing at Goldsmiths College, University of London. It pleases me that a college founded by a medieval body like The Worshipful Company of Goldsmiths is now a hotbed of practice-based research in the creative and performing arts, as well as in more conventional humanities and social sciences. In the teeth of all the distractions waiting to pounce on a debut novelist who finds herself on prize shortlists at home and at literary festivals halfway round the world, I'm writing another historical novel for my Ph.D. All being well, that novel will be published in 2008. The Ph.D. is completed by a dissertation, which I hope will explore the ways that historical fiction emerges from the interaction between the time in which it's set and the time in which it's written.

I now live with my children in South East London, still surrounded by history: there was a Viking fort on ▶

66 The novel I wrote for the degree became *The Mathematics of Love*, and I also wrote a dissertation along the way in which A. S. Byatt uses letters, diaries, poems, and stories in her novel *Possession*. 99

Meet Emma Darwin *(continued)*

the hill behind my house, and down the road is Eltham Palace, where Richard II held his Christmas feasts, and the Courtaulds entertained film stars. I even take my own children to Suffolk for the summer holidays. ᵔ

Skyros, Suffolk, and San Sebastian
Origins of *The Mathematics of Love*

"I WANT YOU to spend twenty minutes writing a story entitled 'Watch,'" said the writing tutor, taking off her own watch and laying it on the table. We were on the Greek island of Skyros, looking out over the classic Mediterranean landscape: red earth and silvery olive trees punctuated by dark cypresses and outcrops of rock. As she spoke I saw a soldier on a watchtower, his coat scarlet against just such a Mediterranean landscape, but I knew he wasn't in Greece, but in Wellington's Peninsular Army, in central Spain. He was watching a woman bathing in a river. Years later, he cropped up again in another project, writing letters about some parts of his life and not writing about others. His body was damaged at Waterloo, just as his life had been damaged years earlier, on the rocky, pine-hung Atlantic coast of northern Spain that I remembered from a childhood holiday. I transferred him to the Rifle Brigade, so that I could borrow from my favorite contemporary memoir, and because his dark green coat would be invisible against the Pyrenean landscape where he sat, watching.

Years later still I was about to start a master's degree in writing, the bulk of which would be a novel. I was looking at earlier ideas that I'd never developed, and there were Stephen's letters. One of my ▶

> ❝ As the writing tutor spoke I saw a soldier on a watchtower, his coat scarlet against just such a Mediterranean landscape. ❞

Skyros, Suffolk, and San Sebastian
(continued)

ideas in writing them was to convey all the things he didn't say: now he could narrate his own story completely, or as completely as he ever would. But I couldn't let go of the idea of someone reading his letters and having her own life utterly changed by understanding his story of war, love, and the pain of loss. And for those things that Stephen would never speak of, but which must have soaked into the walls of the home he finally found, I wanted some kind of receptor. Anna Ware was born—young, cynical, cross, and lonely. She could be that receptor, though later Cecil became one even more clearly: an embodiment of my obsession with the way that layers of history can all exist in the same place. So I sent Anna to live in Stephen's house, in another landscape of my childhood: Suffolk in 1976.

I chose 1976 purely because Theo and Eva, no longer young in the novel, met in the Spanish Civil War. But friends I mentioned this to said instantly, "Oh, 1976, the hot summer," and when I incorporated this I found that the heat and drought became a powerful part of the atmosphere of Anna's story. I took a bargain-basement flight to Bilbao to drive the coast road that Stephen knew, and wandered round the museum in San Sebastian that really was once the Convent of San Telmo; I sat in Manchester Public Library to research the Peterloo Massacre; I read books about the Peninsular War and watched

> 66 I took a bargain-basement flight to Bilbao to drive the coast road that Stephen knew, and wandered round the museum in San Sebastian that really was once the Convent of San Telmo. 99

documentaries about Waterloo; I visited
Fox Talbot's house at Lacock Abbey
in Somerset to get a feeling for those
extraordinary, early days of what wasn't
yet called photography. Even 1976 turned
out to need historical research in a sense,
though I was twelve then myself: I had
to check what pictures of film stars Anna
would stick on her walls, and how much
things would cost. And I had to check
what I knew of the art, craft, and history
of photography. Every now and again,
just as with the hot summer, I would
stumble on something I hadn't known
I was looking for. It had been an easy
guess that San Sebastian would have
had a convent for Catalina, which I had
named appropriately, or ironically, Sacred
Heart, but not that San Telmo would fit
with my thread of buildings changing
their use and give me a thematically
perfect place to bring Theo and Eva
together. After that, I couldn't resist
adding a flash of St. Elmo's fire to the
storm that throws Stephen and Lucy
together. And in checking the news
for 1976, I picked up another little
serendipity: Anna's story begins when
she realizes the time on her clock has
been wiped by the journey, and as it ends,
the radio says that the great clock of Big
Ben—the one in all the movies—which
stopped, unprecedentedly, in the heat,
has been started again.

In other ways I made life easy for
myself by setting so much of the novel
in Suffolk. It's part of East Anglia, that ▶

9

Skyros, Suffolk, and San Sebastian
(continued)

great, prosperous, still rural rump on the map of England which sticks out eastward toward Holland and Belgium. The countryside looks much the same as it did in Anna's or even Stephen's time, though they no longer burn stubble in the fields after harvest, and the big old houses survive these days by becoming luxury hotels rather than boarding schools. The church towers that Constable painted still soar up from the fields and villages, and no one has restored the faces of the saints that Cromwell's puritan soldiers smashed. Theo was right to imagine Constable sitting and drinking in The Angel in Lavenham, for in 1820 it had already been a pub for 400 years, and you can still get an excellent lunch there today.

Other themes that I found emerging, as I worked on the first draft, included children lost and found, voyeurism, portraiture, windows and reflections, light imprinting the image of things, buildings that change their use, how people do or don't move on from pain and damage, and ideal love versus the other, realistic, messy kind.

One part of the research led to me introducing a member of my own family into the novel. Lucy is discovering the very beginnings of photography. I needed her to know of the "first photographer," Thomas Wedgwood, but he had died years earlier, in 1805. I also needed a doctor during the Peterloo Massacre, which opens the novel. So I introduced

> One part of the research led to me introducing a member of my own family into the novel.

Wedgwood's brother-in-law, Dr. Robert
Darwin, my own great-great-great-
grandfather. He's never named, but
he's there—complete with his vast
body, high-pitched voice, and stacks
of books in his carriage—to make
the link with photography that runs
like a seam through the rock of the
whole book. ∾

Author's Picks
Books Within the Book

NOVELS AREN'T HISTORIES and I don't think they should have bibliographies or notes or formal lists of further reading. But sometimes, I know, when you reach the end of a book you don't want it to end: you want to read on and round the story that's so recently (I hope) absorbed you. So, if you want to stay with *The Mathematics of Love*, or if your curiosity has been aroused by something in it, here are just a few of the books that have left their traces in its pages.

Possession, by A. S. Byatt

I hadn't read this when I originally wrote *The Mathematics of Love*, but I decided to study it for the dissertation element of my master's degree in writing because I'd got interested in how parallel narratives work by trying to write one myself. I loved the book as a reader, but as a writer I studied with increasing respect how sophisticatedly Byatt interweaves her narratives. From it I borrowed the way that letters and diaries have a real, physical presence in her novel: what state they're in and how they feel is part of the story they tell, which is part of the story Byatt tells us.

The Spanish Bride, by Georgette Heyer

One of Heyer's best, which introduced me to the Peninsular War and the memoirs of John Kincaid, of which more later. Thirty years after her death, Heyer is a still huge seller who is very—and very unfairly—underrated, though Byatt, among others, has written perceptively and enthusiastically about her. Powerful storytelling, stylish prose, and meticulous research lightly worn.

Charlotte Sometimes, by Penelope Farmer
The most perfect, and perfectly frightening, children's time-slip novel of all, to my mind, though Philippa Pearce's *Tom's Midnight Garden* comes a close second. It is at the same time one of the classic girls' school novels, with a strong atmosphere of the "ordinary" gone awry.

Hawksmoor, by Peter Ackroyd
Time-slip fiction for the seriously grown up, with an unreliable narrator, a powerful sense of evil, and brilliant writing: just describing it makes the hairs prickle on the back of my neck. This is the book which showed me in my teens what modern historical fiction could be. I was fascinated by a narrator who has a ferociously subjective view of events, and by how, if the story is told through his or her eyes and voice, the writer can still convey things the narrator doesn't understand or won't speak of. Ackroyd's *Chatterton* is equally compelling.

The Sidmouth Letters, by Jane Gardam
A wonderful short-story collection, which I encountered as a teenager. Reading Gardam was the first time I consciously realized that a writer was really using different voices and points of view in fiction. ▶

> " Just describing *Hawksmoor* makes the hairs prickle on the back of my neck. "

Author's Picks *(continued)*

Emma, **by Jane Austen**

I went back to Austen—not that I ever need much excuse—to get the rhythm and form of early nineteenth-century prose. Nothing is more horrible to read than pastiche Austen, so I put her and Kincaid's voices aside, to stew in that strange cauldron in one's head where fictional voices mature, until they're ready to be born as something authentic-seeming yet completely new on one's own page.

I Capture the Castle, **by Dodie Smith**

Cassandra is seventeen, "poised between childhood and adultery," marooned with her family in a crumbling house in 1930s Suffolk. It's very, very funny, as well as heartbreaking. It's such a beloved book that I didn't quite realize how many echoes there were in *The Mathematics of Love* until my editor pointed it out, though I'm not sure if Cassandra and Anna would like each other.

Adventures in the Rifle Brigade, **by John Kincaid**

Kincaid was a captain in Wellington's army and this is the first volume of his memoirs, published in 1819 and never since out of print. It was my source for some of Stephen's stories, the main inspiration for the tone of his letters, and an important flavor in his narrative too. Kincaid is wry and witty and warm, and I wish I'd known him, though I suspect he would have teased Stephen in the officers' mess.

The Armies of Wellington, by Philip J. Haythornthwaite

The kind of book all writers hope for when they start researching a new historical novel: a comprehensive and well-written account of all the different parts of Wellington's army, from cavalry to cannon to catering, and how they fitted together in theory and in practice, which was often a rather different matter. Much of what Stephen *doesn't* talk about—his nightmares—came from this book. At the end is a good, brief account of the Peninsular and Waterloo campaigns.

Slightly Out of Focus, by Robert Capa

Theo's origins and experience are very loosely those of this famous war photographer. Capa wrote his apparently unreliable, but certainly fascinating memoir some years before he was killed by a landmine in Indo-China in 1954. I hope he wouldn't mind that I borrowed one of his photographs of the Spanish Civil War and gave it to Theo, because it was so much better than anything I could have invented for him. Theo also quotes from Capa's account of the D-Day landings in Normandy.

On Photography, by Susan Sontag

A famous long essay or short book, which I discovered when I was studying photography. It was this that set me ▶

> **❝** Much of what Stephen *doesn't* talk about—his nightmares—came from *The Armies of Wellington.* **❞**

“ *Emma Darwin*, the biography of my great-great-grandmother, who was born Emma Wedgwood, supplied much of what I needed to know about Tom Wedgwood and Dr. Robert Darwin. ”

Don't miss the next book by your favorite author. Sign up now for AuthorTracker by visiting www.AuthorTracker.com.

thinking years ago about time, light, voyeurism, what's happening between two people when one takes the other's portrait, and the rights and wrongs of making and selling images of war. Lucy and Theo are particularly grateful for Sontag's insights, though they don't always agree with her.

Pioneers of Photography: An Album of Pictures and Words, by Aaron Scharf

Photographs and writings from the very beginnings of photography, including Wedgwood, Niépce (whom Lucy goes to see), and the wonderfully ebullient Nadar, who kindly supplied some of the epigraphs in *The Mathematics of Love.*

Emma Darwin, by Edna Healey

This biography of my great-great-grandmother, who was born Emma Wedgwood, supplied much of what I needed to know about Tom Wedgwood and Dr. Robert Darwin, who was married to Tom's sister. Emma's father was Tom's brother Josiah Wedgwood II; in *The Mathematics of Love*, when Lucy goes to see Tom Wedgwood's "sun pictures," Hetty is entertained by Mrs. Wedgwood's daughters, including Emma, who later married her first cousin, Robert Darwin's son Charles. ◡